THE ... AN
AN... IES

PAKISTAN WRITERS SERIES

SERIES EDITOR: MUHAMMAD UMAR MEMON

Pirzada Ahmad Shah, is known by his pen-name **Ahmad Nadeem Qasimi**. He is one of the most distinguished Urdu writers living today. Presently settled in Lahore, he is the director of Majlis-e-Taraqqi-e-Adab.

A prolific writer, he has produced more than a dozen collections of short stories, eight volumes of poetry and a number of essays on letters, besides editing three prestigious literary journals. He is admired for the courage of his convictions as much as for his gentlemanliness, compassion, and urbanity.

Faruq Hassan, poet, literary critic and translator, was born in Pakistan but now lives in Montreal, Canada, where he teaches at Dawson College and McGill University. He has published two volumes of poetry and has co-edited an anthology of Urdu stories in translation. His critical essays and translations have appeared in various journals and collections of short stories.

Muhammad Umar Memon, the Series Editor, is Professor at the University of Wisconsin. He is also a creative writer and critic, and has translated widely from Urdu fiction, of which six volumes appeared to date.

THE OLD BANYAN AND OTHER STORIES

Ahmad Nadeem Qasimi

Translated by
FARUQ HASSAN

Series Editor
MUHAMMAD UMAR MEMON

OXFORD
UNIVERSITY PRESS

Great Clarendon Street, Oxford OX2 6DP
Oxford University Press is a department of the University of Oxford.
It furthers the University's objective of excellence in research, scholarship,
and education by publishing worldwide in

Oxford New York

Athens Auckland Bangkok Bogotá Buenos Aires Calcutta
Cape Town Chennai Dar es Salaam Delhi Florence Hong Kong Istanbul
Karachi Kuala Lumpur Madrid Melbourne Mexico City Mumbai
Nairobi Paris São Paulo Singapore Taipei Tokyo Toronto Warsaw
with associated companies in Berlin Ibadan

Oxford is a registered trade mark of Oxford University Press
in the UK and in certain other countries

© Oxford University Press 2000

The moral rights of the author have been asserted

First published 2000

All rights reserved. No part of this publication may be reproduced,
translated, stored in a retrieval system, or transmitted, in any form or by any
means, without the prior permission in writing of Oxford University Press.
Enquiries concerning reproduction should be sent to
Oxford University Press at the address below.

This book is sold subject to the condition that it shall not, by way
of trade or otherwise, be lent, re-sold, hired out or otherwise circulated
without the publisher's prior consent in any form of binding or cover
other than that in which it is published and without a similar condition
including this condition being imposed on the subsequent purchaser.

ISBN 0 19 579328 5

Printed in Pakistan at
Mas Printers, Karachi.
Published by
Ameena Saiyid, Oxford University Press
5-Bangalore Town, Sharae Faisal
PO Box 13033, Karachi-75350, Pakistan.

CONTENTS

	page
Acknowledgements	vii
Introduction	ix
A Sample	1
The Burial	17
Lawrence of Thalabia	32
A Mother's Love	44
The Old Banyan	55
Old Man Noor	69
Parmeshar Singh	73
The Pond with the Bo Tree	94
Praise Be to Allah	99
Sultan, the Beggar Boy	126
The Thal Desert	134
Theft	147
The Unwanted	154
A Wild Woman	169
The Rest-house	177
Glossary	219
Bibliography	227

ACKNOWLEDGEMENTS

I owe thanks to many people who have helped me in one way or another during the time it took me to finish working on this translation. First and foremost, I am grateful to my dear friend M.U. Memon, general editor of the Pakistan Writers Series and Professor of Urdu, Persian and Islam at the University of Wisconsin, Madison. He assigned this translation project to me, and read through the whole manuscript patiently and thoroughly, offering invaluable suggestions for improving the idiom and expression. He was also kind enough to allow me to re-print in this volume his translation of Ahmad Nadeem Qasimi's story, *Parmeshar Singh*.

I am thankful to Dr. Siddique Javed, Professor of Urdu, of Government College, Lahore, for making all of Ahmad Nadeem Qasimi's works available to me. Without his help, I would not have been able even to undertake the project. I am also thankful to my colleague Professor Stanley Rajiva, in the English Department at Dawson College, for constant encouragement and for being ready with the *mot juste* whenever I was at a loss for one.

Thanks are also due to Mohammad Salim-ur-Rahman formerly for permitting me to include in this volume his translation of *Alhamd-o-Lillah* (Praise be to Allah). Finally, I would like to record my indebtedness to Daleara Jamasji-Hirjikaka of the Oxford University Press (Pakistan) for her patience with me for the inexcusable delays I know I caused in meeting her various deadlines.

Faruq Hassan

INTRODUCTION

Soft-spoken, genial, and extremely courtly,[1] Ahmad Nadeem Qasimi is probably the most admired of all living Pakistani writers. He is held in such reverence that not only the works dedicated to celebrating his various literary achievements and other milestones in his life, (such as his fiftieth or eightieth birthdays),[2] but even some of the professed critical analyses of his writing,[3] are nothing more than testimonials to his greatness—acts of homage rather than works seeking to offer any critical assessment or systematic evaluation of his output. More than his literary achievement, it is, perhaps, the exemplary life that he has lived, a life characterized by honesty, fairness and absence of hypocrisy, which has made him deserving of public esteem. An unwavering commitment to principles, and a consistent refusal to compromise his sense of moral right and wrong, resulting in want and deprivation, are qualities he has demonstrated time and again during his long life and various careers. They are among the reasons for the unqualified respect which he enjoys.

Born on 16 November 1916, in Anga, a small village in Punjab, in a religiously orthodox family, Ahmad Nadeem Qasimi's given name was Ahmad Shah. Until he became well-known by his pen-name, he carried the tag of Pirzada with his name because the family boasted a few learned theologians, mystics, and spiritual guides in its past. However, Qasimi himself has nothing but aversion for the whole institution of 'Pirhood', as some of his stories like *Bain* [A Lament] and *Chubhan* [Pricking (of Conscience)], dealing with the exploitative nature of the institution, amply testify. He received his early education, largely religious, at home. Later, he attended different schools and colleges in small towns, graduating from Sadiq Egerton College in Bahawalpur in 1935. After shuttling between his native village and Lahore during the four years preceding the Second World War, he found himself a job as a sub-inspector in the Excise Department. This proved to be a meretricious affair, and he did not last long in the job. In fact, all the jobs that he has taken up in his life, jobs in which writing was not the primary component of his responsibilities, have proved eminently unsuited to his temperament. All through his life, he has been content, whether gainfully employed or working voluntarily, only in professions involving writing: like journalism, editing, publishing and creative writing itself. During his life he has edited two weeklies, one *Tehzib-e-Niswan* for women and the other *Phool* for children, four literary journals *Adab-e-Latif*, *Savera*, *Nuqoosh* and *Funoon* and one daily newspaper, *Imroz*. Since 1974, he has been the director of Majlis-e-Tarraqi-e-Adab (Society for the Advancement of Literature), publishing books by classical writers and scholars.

Qasimi started writing at a fairly young age, composing his first poem—an elegy for Mohammad Ali Jauhar, the influential and charismatic leader of the Khilafat Movement—at the age of fifteen. It was published in 1931 in *Siyasat*, Lahore. He wrote his first short story at age 20. It was titled *Badnaseeb But Tarash* (The Unfortunate Sculptor), and was published in 1936 in *Rumaan*, Lahore. Retrospectively, Qasimi considers the story weak and excessively romantic and now ruefully wishes it had been ignored and forgotten by critics. Unlike many a young, beginning writer, who receives guidance from a mentor in the family or some other accomplished master, Qasimi was not kick-started into writing. Except for some encouragement from his friend and contemporary, Mohammad Khalid Akhtar, himself a short story writer and humourist, Qasimi is virtually a self-taught man. The creative urge was awakened in him by his exposure to the abundant literary material, books and journals, available in the house of his guardian uncle, his father having passed away when he was in the 3rd grade at school. That the urge remained active for almost half a century is evident from his output. Between 1940 and 1995, he published nine volumes of poetry and fifteen anthologies of short stories, besides editing four or five anthologies of representative writings by other writers and writing some books for children[4]—no mean achievement, by any standard.

Ahmad Nadeem Qasimi writes in a naturalistic vein. His short stories, from the earliest to the latest ones, whether short ones or novellas, as are two of the stories—'The Rest House' and 'Praise be to Allah' included in this volume—whether elaborately structured or mere vignettes, whether concerned with urban or rural settings, basically remain realistic stories, approaching reality in a linear and chronological fashion, as has traditionally been done in the fiction of the Indian subcontinent. Realism has been, for better or worse, the dominant mode of writing in the Indian subcontinent. Professor M.U. Memon's observation about Hasan Manzar's narrative technique, in his introduction to *A Requiem for the Earth*: '[His] mimetic strategy is pointed away from abstraction, allegorical meaning or any kind of creative equivocation; rather, it is oriented towards realism in the strict sense'[5] is as easily applicable to every other novelist and short story writer in India and Pakistan as it is to Hasan Manzar. With a few notable exceptions like Enver Sajjad and Balraj Meenra who have consistently produced experimental or, what is referred to as abstract stories, and a few others, who wanted to but perhaps could not write as candidly and forthrightly as they might have wished during the military dictatorship of General Ziaul Haq, every fiction writer in the Indian subcontinent casts 'his stories in the realistic mode, almost never deviating from the traditional geometry of plot and structure'.[6] This dependence upon observable phenomena may seem paradoxical since the indigenous forms of creative writing in India, the literary predecessors of the short story in Urdu literature, were *daastan* and *qissa*, neither of which was uniformly realistic. They were more a complex mix of allegory, fable, fantasy or non-naturalistic subject-matter.

The short story as an independent literary genre in undivided India grew from a study, and perhaps imitation, of the European models—Chekhov, Maupassant, Maugham—made available to Indians during the Colonial era. Prem Chand (pen-name of

Dhanpat Rai, 1880-1936), who is known to have written twelve novels and close to 300 short stories, was the pioneering and the most influential practitioner of the short story in India. Two anthologies of stories by Prem Chand in the library of Qasimi's elementary school were his first exposure to the genre and, indeed, to serious literature. On a number of occasions Qasimi has acknowledged having been influenced by this great master.[7]

A seminal figure in Urdu and Hindi literature, Prem Chand was clearly a product of his times, his imagination having been shaped by the contemporary religious, political and economic conditions. As M.U. Memon has observed, it was the self-same conditions which propelled 'Premchand inexorably towards defining literature as an instrument of protest, reform and redress'.[8] Born in a village near Benaras, the son of a village postmaster, he was exposed to the social problems facing villagers early in life. After being educated and becoming a school teacher and moving to the city, he was also exposed to the true nature of the politics of Colonization and Imperialism. When it was discovered that his first book *Soz-e-Watan*, a collection of patriotic stories, had been written by a teacher in the employ of the government, it was denounced as 'seditious' and quickly banned. That was when he is known to have changed his pen-name from Nawab Rai to Prem Chand.

Even though in the later stories he had become less limited in his choice of subject-matter, also bringing in the cities, the villages remained the richest source of inspiration and material for his narratives. The religious conception of the world order, promoting and despotically preserving conservatism, under which the villagers were clearly straining and suffering, and the feudal set-up that bound people to an exploitative economic system and shaped and circumscribed their relationships, became the first targets of his indignation. Religious obscurantism; belief in caste superiority which often displayed itself in merciless and supercilious disregard or dismissal of outsiders; a mortal fear of public disgrace; stigma of widowhood; an irrational hatred of daughters and a yearning for sons, are some of the recurrent themes in his stories. He deals with these subjects without sentimentality, but with compassion. At the same time, however, a sense of helplessness and moral indignation always seem to lurk behind the narrative which was what, perhaps, drove him to look for other, perhaps more radical, avenues to seek redress, avenues that may have been non-literary as taking part in Gandhi's Non-Cooperation Movement, or literary as joining the Progressive Writers Movement.

Prem Chand did a lot for literature in India. Firstly, he refined the genre of the short story and added it to the corpus of Indian letters, enlarging its canvas. He introduced a variety of subjects and a vast range of characters, dealing not only with their sociology but even their psychology, thus adding a new dimension to the study of character. He simplified the language of fiction, distancing it from the language of romance and bringing it closer to the language of the common man, loaded as it is with a stock of ordinary and humble, but dynamic, native expressions, metaphors and proverbs. Attributing a utilitarian motive to literature and employing his fiction for the crusading intent of reform and redress, he paved the way for a smooth reception of the Progressive Writers Movement.

We do not have Prem Chand's strident anti-Colonialism in Qasimi's work; nor do we have in him Prem Chand's undisguised moralizing which often took the form of editorializing by the narrator, introduced for the specific purpose of communicating some necessary social, economic or political element in the background of the story so that the reader would look for the right thematic strand in the story to appreciate, and for the right person to blame. In his youth, Qasimi may have understood little of Prem Chand's narrative technique. But surely, by reading Prem Chand's work, Qasimi would have gained critical awareness of his immediate surroundings, particularly the rural set-up in which he lived and with which, like Prem Chand, he has been deeply concerned, both personally and imaginatively, all through his life. Even though in his stories Prem Chand deals with life in the villages of Uttar Pradesh, while Qasimi limits himself to those of Punjab, the economic, social, and political problems such as those of economic disparity, injustice, ignorance and exploitation, problems spawned by religion, feudalism and Colonization, would have been the same. He would have learnt to regard writing as a useful literary implement, not for propaganda, but certainly for raising consciousness, creating awareness of the social problems.

Qasimi's view of the nature of realism, as it manifests itself in his short stories, is fairly straight-forward, unencumbered by empirical, epistemological or other philosophical theories of language, and is inextricably linked to his conception of the social function of a writer. He acknowledges the reality of the external world, the existence of a world outside of verifiable facts and objects, even though in the imaginative rendering this world may often be deeply coloured by the perceiver's or observer's intensely subjective viewpoint. There is no gainsaying the fact that the world out there is imperfect, beset as it is with various religious, social, political, and ethnic problems. Writing, like all arts, is a pointedly purposive activity. The writer, who of necessity has to be a socially responsible individual, even more so than others because he has been gifted with the ability to express feelings and ideas, has to take on the obligation of making others aware of those problems. The writer is not a physician dispensing mixtures, nor a preacher ready with prescriptions and/or proscriptions, nor even a political activist, carrying placards or shouting slogans, but he can certainly give voice to things that have been denied expression, and offer images of redress, of world-renewing possibilities which only the arts can furnish. As long as there is exploitation, obscurantism, hypocrisy, lack of fairness or harmony in the world, the writer is obliged to go on countering those by creating images of fairness, beauty, truth and harmony, so that the world may have a chance, by following the models invented by the writer and the dreams dreamed by the artist, to renew and remake itself, if it chooses to do so, and become a better place for posterity. One is reminded of two lines by Wallace Stevens which seem nicely to sum up Qasimi's view of the writer's role in society: 'Say this to Pravda, tell the damned rag / That the peaches are slowly ripening.'

When the Progressive Writers Movement started in India, in the mid-thirties, as a matter of course, 'it took over Prem Chand's assumptions about literature',[9] i.e., that literature was a utilitarian activity directed toward social and political change. The Manifesto adopted by the first meeting of the Progressive Writers Association on 10 April 1936, began with the regret that the spirit of reaction was still operative in India, and Indian literature still suffered from the tendency to escape from life's realities and to find refuge in baseless spiritualism. The duty of the writers in India, the Manifesto declared, was to 'assist the spirit of progress in the country', to criticize 'the spirit of reaction', to 'deal with the basic problems of our existence today—the problems of hunger and poverty, social backwardness and political subjugation', and 'to further the cause of Indian freedom and social regeneration'. In literary criticism the Progressive Writers opted for an attitude that will 'discourage the general reactionary and revivalist tendencies on questions like family, religion, sex, war and society, and...combat literary trends reflecting communalism, racial antagonism, sexual libertinism, and exploitation of man by man...'[10]

The ideological similarity between Prem Chand's views and the stance promoted by the Progressive Writers is evident. It was not surprising, then, that Prem Chand became the founding member, supporter and sponsor of the Movement. However, the Movement did not retain its original impetus and form for long. As pointed out by Ahmad Ali, by the end of the decade a difference of opinion among the Progressives had split the Movement down the middle, creating two distinct factions, 'the "ideological" (i.e., political) and "creative" (i.e., non-political, non-communist)', the former group being more vocal in forcing its agenda and seeking reform along socialist lines. In other words, Prem Chand's 'social realism' had quietly slipped into 'socialist realism'.[11] It was this unfortunate slippage which ultimately sealed the fate of the Movement. One belabours the obvious in stating that Pakistan, as soon as she was carved out of India, aligned herself with the Western, liberal, democratic bloc, making the pursuit of socialist ideology politically deleterious for those who were its sympathizers. In the late 40s and 50s, in true McCarthyite fashion, writers affiliated with the Movement were spied on, harried, and systematically hounded by the authorities. Some were thrown into prison, some forced to go underground. Some committed intellectual suicide by joining the film industry. Some stopped writing altogether. Qasimi too did not escape the official crackdown.

The Progressive Writers wrote freely and caused controversies, some of which excite passions even today. Their writings reflected their crusading zeal and to them no subject was taboo. They wrote poems and stories about prostitution, the degradation of the industrial poor, the abysmal poverty of the landless peasant or the share-cropper, and the inhumane and exploitative character of colonial rule. The subject of sex which in earlier writing had either been ignored or treated romantically, through suggestive evocation, was not shunned by the Progressive Writers who insisted upon dealing with it without any sentimental trappings. The first ten years of the Movement produced a formidable body of poetry and prose, some of which is as readable today as it was when it first appeared in print.

Keenly observant and aware, and desirous of social regeneration, Qasimi would have been the right candidate for joining the Movement. It was probably in the late 30s, during his early days in Lahore, days marked by poverty, hunger and joblessness, that Qasimi was first introduced to the Progressive Writers Movement. His conception of the social function of literature and of the writer's responsibilities in society, both perhaps inspired by his reading of Prem Chand's stories, coupled with his crusading spirit, brought him close to the literary mind-set of the Progressives. In 1949, he was made the secretary of the All Pakistan Progressive Writers Association in Lahore, despite his protest that there were far more 'committed' writers, like the poet Faiz Ahmad Faiz, the critic Mumtaz Hussain and the journalist Ibrahim Jalees, and far more outspoken ones like Zaheer Kashmiri, within the organization. Within two years, his conspicuous position and the Association's adoption of extreme socialist resolutions earned him, under the Safety Act of Pakistan, a stint in jail which lasted until late 1951.[12] Unable to save the organization from disintegration, Qasimi resigned from his secretaryship in 1954. However, he continued trying to revive the Progressive Writers Movement in Pakistan, even until 1976-77, but without success. Zia-ul-Haq's take-over and martial law in 1977 proved to be the proverbial last nail for its existence.

Nonetheless, Qasimi regards the Movement as having been enormously beneficial to the cause of letters in Pakistan Whenever he is questioned by interviewers about the ultimate contribution and value of the Movement, he responds that of all the literary movements launched in this century in the Indian subcontinent, only the Progressives have left an indelible mark on literature. They were, he argues, the first ones to attribute a utilitarian purpose to literature,[13] encouraging the writer to protest and rebel against soul-destroying conditions of life. They introduced an extensive range of subjects in fiction; they taught poets to devise a poetic use for a distinctly non-poetic language; they gave writers the courage to face life's realities, no matter how unsavoury and unappetizing; they instilled in the writers the courage of commitment, and love of humanity, and above all, they imparted an international dimension to their dreams and visions.

Qasimi's own indebtedness to the Progressives is no less inestimable. He is aware of the shortcomings of his early work—he has described one of his stories as weak and excessively emotional, and confesses that in the earlier stories, he had been writing 'prose poetry' rather than proper prose narratives.[14] There is considerable truth in this self-appraisal, for besides containing melodramatic resolutions, contrived endings or sudden unexpected twists in the plot, as, for instance, in *Bhoot* which stretches the limits of the reader's credulity, the early stories are also strewn with superfluous descriptions of nature, and over-extended poetic metaphors.[15] Note, for instance, the descriptions in the passage given below:

INTRODUCTION

> ...Faiz felt as if some sleeping fairy, tiny bells attached to her wrists, had indeed turned in bed beneath the water gathered in a pool in one corner of the graveyard. Sweat oozing from every pore of her body, sparks flickering in every bead of sweat, her body feverish and blazing, her soul dancing—Faiz lost his presence of mind, and in the cold loneliness of the dark scene felt as though he were flying in the air, traveling with Soni to some far-off country. Soni's head leaned on his shoulder, her tresses flying in the air like spell-bound serpents, the air humming with the tinkling of her anklet bells.[16]

The descriptions, in the form of images, similes, etc., do not seem to exist for any formal purpose, neither are they at the service of any viewpoint, but are there in the story for their own sake, unaligned to the setting in which they find themselves. If they were descriptions of nature, they would tend to remain unintegrated into the plot and unrelated to the character or situation, existing only for decorative purposes, much like a vase full of artificial flowers standing in the vestibule.

In contrast, take two examples from the story, 'The Rest-House'. These would indicate the change that has taken place in Qasimi's mature work.

> 1) Hot, searing winds swept over Khushab and Mianwali, the flatlands in the south and the west; and a coolness crept out of the rain-swept valley of Soon and Pakkhar in the north and east, but only a mysterious breeze—sometimes hot, sometimes cold and sometimes moist—fluttered the curtain of the bungalows in Sakesar, as the affluent sat looking through their binoculars at the clouds racing below in the valley.

> 2) The water from the foothills, glistening like sheets of silver, coursed down to the lake, and players at the tennis court interrupted their game to sit and smoke and yawn.

It is easy to see in the last two examples that the descriptions of nature are less poetic and verbose; they seem integral to the scene and are not being indulged in for their own sake. They are characterized by relevance, intimately linked as they are to human activity and character—the 'affluent' and the 'tennis players'.

In an interview Qasimi has described his later stories as characterized by 'compactness',—an accurate epithet indeed for his mature work. However, this quality could not have entered his writing suddenly or facilely or effortlessly. The contact with the Progressive Movement, along with some critical understanding of Prem Chand's work, and a resulting change in outlook, may have as much to do with it as Qasimi's own initial awareness of the lack of this quality in his writing. The Progressive outlook may have honed his realism and sharpened his sensibility, making him more receptive to life and more discerning in dealing with it, especially village life, which is the mainstay of his fiction. He considers his story *Hiroshima se Pehley; Hiroshima ke Ba'ad* (Before Hiroshima; After Hiroshim)[17] a watershed in his career. The story deals with the impact of the Second World War on village life in India, an issue Qasimi has been obsessively concerned with in many stories, two of which, 'Old Man Noor' and 'A Mother's Love', are included in this volume. Through the character of the half-crazed Patwari, who often raves like an unrestrained soothsayer or visionary, the Hiroshima story dissolves the world in the symbol of war, and transforms the explosion of the atomic bomb at Hiroshima into a very personal tragedy for the villagers, bringing to an end, as it does, the world as they know it, the world of loyalties, familial bonds and social relationships. It is a powerful story, deeply concerned with the nature of change ushered in by the war, observed with clinical realism, and it is easy to see why Qasimi regards it as signifying a crucial turning point in his story-writing career.

One of the more successful earlier stories, 'Theft'[18] has been chosen for inclusion here in order to indicate presence of protest in Qasimi's writing. There is protest at the very heart of Qasimi's fiction—against economic or religious exploitation, fate, loss, or forfeiting of opportunities, repressive social structures, poverty, injustice, helplessness and betrayal. In 'Theft', not only the headman of the village, but even the *imam* of the mosque, who knew the protagonist well, sides with the police in opposition to Mangu, who helplessly protests against unfairness and injustice; in 'The Burial' there is protest against poverty, against a society that has never bothered to establish a network of help for the needy, against selfishness under the guise of charity and generosity, and against moral values gone awry; in 'Lawrence of Thalabia', the first person narrator, a visitor from the city to the village, protests, though amicably and without rancour, against the helplessness of the serfs and the casually and callously destructive way of life of their masters; in 'A Wild Woman' the main character protests against loss of her identity and dignity.

In the earlier stories, consistent with Qasimi's own youthful, romantic character, the protest is expressed vehemently and tends to be loud and mutinous. Predictably, it leads to and culminates in some kind of common action by the community, a rebellion against the landowners for the privileges they and the other people in position of influence or authority, enjoy and is aimed at demonstrating some solidarity and a common way of feeling among the peasants or rural workers—in Communist parlance, among 'the proletariat'. In the later stories, such as the ones included in this anthology, the protest is less violent; it tends to get muted, as though the character were doing some loud thinking, stopping well short of an all-out revolt. Nonetheless, it is still expressed forcefully enough to make the reader feel the point of the protest. In his own life too, when Qasimi speaks in a public forum—at inaugurations, conferences, seminars, book launches and such, or when facing high-ranking officials or military dictators—particularly when discussing the situation of the writer and artist in Pakistan, and the total absence of any financial guarantees for him or her, he, like his own characters, remains undaunted. He does not shy way from verbalizing his protests, or telling the truth which cannot possibly ingratiate him with the authorities. In his newspaper columns, however, the protest assumes the form of satire or irony.

In the absence of any technical experimentation or 'newness' in Qasimi's stories, which is what becomes obvious immediately, one inexorably falls back on a discussion of the formal features of the narrative such as plot, character, setting, theme and language in dealing with the stories. Neither is there much variation in the modes of narration used in the stories. The stories are easily divided into those that employ a first person point of view and those that use an omniscient narrator. Occasionally, in the stories with omniscient narration, one notices the use of what approximates to the technique of interior monologue, a mode of narration in which the reader 'eavesdrops, as it were, on the actual thoughts and sensations of the character as he or she moves through time and space'.[19] Qasimi uses this technique sparingly, and only when the narrative itself is in hiatus, so to speak, and the character is going through some intense emotional turmoil or some deep self-introspection, as Fazloo does at one point in 'The Rest House', or Syed Amjad Hussain does in 'The Old Banyan'.

Of the fifteen stories being presented here, eight are squarely placed in the village setting, six play themselves out in some kind of cityscape, and one, 'A Mother's Love', though originating in and often referring nostalgically back to the village, takes place in Hong Kong and on an unnamed island nearby. The division here roughly parallels that in his fiction as a whole, with sixty per cent of all of his stories taking place in the village. Qasimi has often commented on his good fortune in having been born and raised in a village, and having had the opportunity in life to study the dramatic interplay of moral values, political interests and human character in the villages. One notices in him a belief in a definite correlation between the writer's personal experience and imaginative writing. If his stories about rural life make a lasting impact upon the readers, it is principally because of his own intimate and extended experience of village life which imparts genuineness, authenticity and a sense of certainty to his writing.

One of the stories, 'Parmeshar Singh', set in a village, takes place in 1947, during the partition of India. It cannot be gainsaid that Partition, a colossal convulsion in subcontinental history, involving the migration of six million people across the border between India and Pakistan and accompanied by frenzied and insane communal orgies of pillage, arson, abduction, rape, and murder on both sides of the border, in all claiming close to a million lives, left an indelible mark on the lives of the people trapped in it, and on the imaginations of creative writers such as Aziz Ahmad, Sa'adat Hasan Manto, Krishan Chandar, Rajinder Singh Bedi, Qudrat Ullah Shahab, Abdullah Hussein, Intezar Hussain, et al. The event provided them with extensive material for stories, novels and poetry, and they produced a sizeable body of literature based on it.

'Parmeshar Singh' is a story about a simple, somewhat sentimental, but a fair-minded and humane Sikh, who is more ecumenical in his outlook than most Indians and Pakistanis, and is basically a decent human being who loses his young son Kartar during the border-crossing into India. A month after being settled in a village, in a house abandoned by a Muslim, he once happens to come upon a group of grown-up Sikhs getting ready to slaughter a Muslim boy, who had been separated from his family, and is the same age as Parmeshar Singh's own son. Parmeshar persuades the Sikhs to let him take the boy home. He treats Akhtar as a surrogate son, and loves and indulges him as he would have his own Kartar. Because of pressure from his family and the villagers, Parmeshar lets Akhtar grow his hair long, wear a turban and a comb, making him look like any average Sikh boy, though, at heart, Parmeshar does not really care whether Akhtar remains a Muslim or converts to Sikhism. However, the hostility to a Muslim boy in a Sikh household and village does not let up and finally Parmeshar decides to let Akhtar go back to Pakistan. He accompanies him some distance towards the border, and then asks him to go on alone. Akhtar runs smack into two soldiers guarding the border who are astonished by the disparity between Akhtar's Muslim name and his Sikh appearance. They hear footsteps of Parmeshar who has followed the boy quietly at a distance and fire at him, wounding him in the thigh. Parmeshar's parting question to the soldiers is:

'Why did you have to shoot me?! I just forgot to clip Akhtar's *kes*. I only came to return Akhtar to his *dharam, yaaro!*'

The story is undoubtedly rich in acute observation of the life in the village. The characters of Parmeshar Singh, his wife, daughter, and the priest of the Sikh temple are memorable, drawn in precise detail. However, the question posed by Parmeshar at the end of the story may bother the readers as much as it bothers the character himself. Why, indeed, did he need to be shot at? What was to be gained by that, essentially gratuitous, act? The story does not attempt to engage in any deep philosophical discussion of the issue of faith and conversion. Like much of Qasimi's work, it is basically concerned with social amelioration. However, it seems that there may have been possibilities in the story that Qasimi did not choose to explore, implications which he did not wish to pursue. For instance, even though Akhtar never forgets that he is a Muslim, nor ceases to recite the few verses from the Quran that he has memorized, he does start pestering Parmeshar to get him a turban and tie it on his head, make his hair grow fast, and buy him a comb. His request may be nothing more than a representation of his wish to belong to a community. However, at the end of the story, as Akhtar moves towards the border, the narrator describes him as: '...the little boy Akhtar, like a strapping Sikh youth, ...walking briskly on the foggy foot trail'. There is, perhaps, the suggestion of the theme of the appearance subtly becoming or replacing the reality, or the mask becoming the face. An analogous situation, involving actions which are considered oppressive or constricting or hurtful and thus resented, sometimes becoming part of one's need, or making inroads into one's psychology, is examined in the story 'Sultan—the Beggar Boy', where Sultan may physically be free of the painful, crustacean grip of his blind grandfather's hand, yet, at the end of the story, he cries out emotionally for the same grip.

The four stories that capture the ethos of the village remarkably well are 'Praise be to Allah', 'The Unwanted', 'The Thal Desert' and 'The Rest-House'. The protagonist of 'Praise be to Allah' is Abul Barkaat, a village *maulvi*, the quality of whose life steadily deteriorates with his marriage, with the regular arrival of children, with the changes taking place in society and the consequent lessening of the hold of religion on people's lives. Religion, a characteristically backward-looking institution, which speaks in the name of fixed and eternal verities, is notoriously incapable of preparing one for what lies ahead in life. It is a story of the gradual deepening of the agony born of want and helplessness in the life of a person who has nothing else to sustain him and his family of nine children except his resolute and unshakable faith in God and the occasional material support of a fellow-villager, Chaudhari Fateh Dad, a local dignitary and the member of the District Board. His refusal to change his life-style to match the changing conditions of his life, and his insistence on seeking help from no one else but God, at best, seems perverse. His income from the votive offerings by people has become non-existent over the years as people no longer come to the mosque to say their prayers, nor do young children go to study the Quran from his wife's domestic school ever since a new government school has opened in the village. Inflation has driven the prices of all goods sky-high. On certain days the only food in his house is what is sent from Chaudhari Fateh Dad's house, and Maulvi Abul refuses to consider any other vocational options in his life besides serving God. In a world driven by industry, materialism and change, he has made himself into a dying breed. Like Don Quixote, Maulvi Abul ends up as a hero possessed by an *idee fixe*; only in his case the story of his life is more tragic than comic.

With Chaudhari Fateh Dad's help, and with whatever little money he has been able to save up, Maulvi Abul manages to marry off his oldest daughter Mehrun, but a year later, he is so destitute that he cannot even buy a gift for his newly-born grandson. There is mordant irony in the ending of the story when Maulvi Abul comes excitedly into the house and announces that his faith in God has paid off once again as Chaudhari Fateh Dad has died, and he hopes to receive enough money from conducting the funeral and the burial ceremonies to look after more than a gift for the newborn. It is after he has praised God for His grace and bounty that he suddenly realizes that in this case God's grace also means inescapable starvation for him and his family. 'Praise be to Allah' reminds one of a story by Prem Chand called 'Resignation' which ends equally ironically, though in the latter story the main character, the office clerk, is unaware of the starvation that awaits him after his resignation and his few moments of happiness and glory.

'The Unwanted', like 'The Old Banyan', is a story that deals with the problem of aging parents and their sons, and their inability to come to terms with each other when the new daughters-in-law come into their homes. In 'The Old Banyan' the conflict resolves itself quickly as Syed Amjad Hussain, the patriarch, avenges the destruction of his beloved banyan—almost his alter ego—by ravaging the flower-garden of his son and daughter-in-law. In 'The Unwanted', the conflict becomes more complex as the aging parents, Pir Bakhsh and his wife Nekan, leave their ancestral home to live in the mud-hut they had built on the farm. The source of the conflict is the power-struggle between the mother-in-law and the daughter-in-law, Habib's new bride Khatoon, the daughter of the richest landowner in the village. Despite Habib's entreaties and beseeching, his mother refuses to return home, takes ill while still at the mud-hut and dies. Pir Bakhsh returns home, but the tension between him and Khatoon, the daughter-in-law, continues unabated as Khatoon, unwilling to look after the needs of the old man and disrespectful in her attitude to him, once threatens to have both Habib and Pir Bakhsh publicly beaten by her father. Clearly, the young lady, unskilled in household chores and pampered in the rich household she comes from, has a lot of growing up to do and a number of skills to acquire before she can become indispensible in the household. Though Pir Bakhsh goes out of the house with the intention of telling on her to her husband, he changes his mind as he gets to his son's cloth store. On the surface, his transformation seems rather cowardly, something like having cold feet. But in reality it is anything but that. He rests comfortably in a relationship of trust with his son and does not see any need to destroy it. Telling on Habib's wife will create nothing but tension in the house for which both his son and daughter-in-law will inevitably blame him, making him 'the unwanted' in the house. He is wise enough not to want that. Someday, perhaps soon enough, Habib's eyes will open and he will learn the truth about his wife's upbringing and capabilities. It is better that he deals with her than Pir Bakhsh whom she resents anyway. The ending of 'The Unwanted', like those of 'The Old Banyan', 'Theft' and 'The Thal Desert' is distinctly Chekhovian, in that they all end, not on a high note, but on a later, almost anti-climactic, low note, as if saying that even though the stories come to an end, life goes on.

Even though every story by Qasimi is, in one way or another, a piece of social history, no story is more so than 'The Thal Desert', involving a whole swathe of history from the colonial days to the recent settling of the Thal region. The story celebrates honest and satisfying work and exults in the love of one's place of birth. It is a fascinating story in that it deals with much social, industrial and economic change and development, yet ironically admits at the end that it has all been futile as none of it has affected the minds and attitudes of whole generations of villagers. The benefits of change are visible to all and sundry, yet there is a resistance to it which defies all logic. And that resistance is built and re-enforced in the name of morality, social stability and security—values favoured by feudalism and religion, the latter of which operates more through superstition and the powerful institution of the shrine of Hazrat Pir than anything else. The warnings about people abandoning farming, leaving the villages, going to the cities, and becoming immoral because of the railways—represent a typically medieval, feudal attitude towards social mobility, change and development. Behind it clearly is the thought that it is easier to preserve the economic status quo, which obviously favours the moneyed and landed classes, if it is done in the name of religion and morality. No wonder, there is no attempt to help the people shed their ignorance and fear.

'The Thal Desert' is also one of the few stories by Qasimi involving non-Indian characters. An English engineer has been assigned to supervise the laying down of the railway tracks. The man orders the local labourers to start the work and himself just sits around, smoking cigars all day. Unlike some of the stories by Prem Chand, this story is not what George Orwell would have called a story of a grievance, a story voicing the bitterness of a subject people and aimed at giving their colonial masters a bad conscience about the injustice of their rule. In fact, the English engineer seems as much a victim of the circumstances in the Thal area, as much confused and troubled by the fight between two Pirs of the region as any resident of the area would be.

'The Rest-House' is a major story by Qasimi, almost a novella, elaborately structured, evoking a whole area in the mountains through visual details of variations in the weather and involving a vivid and extended portrayal of three characters. It is indeed one of his finest stories. Qasimi's social consciousness permeates the story and he observes humanity in its various contradictions. The linkage of greed, naivete and sexuality in a bizarre pattern of comic irony may remind one of Somerset Maugham's 'Rain' or Bernard Malamud's 'The Magic Barrel', although the story in itself clearly owes no debt to either.

The main players in the story are Fazloo, the caretaker of a rest-house, his wife Maryan, and the sahib, Yousuf, a visitor to the hilly resort of Sakesar, who is supposedly grieving for his dead wife Maryam, but in actuality lusting after the caretaker's wife. The clever manipulation of Fazloo by Yousuf, who puts on a spectacle of being without carnal desires, the succumbing to the temptation of easy money by Fazloo, and the reluctant, grudging and conditional agreement by Maryan to visit the sahib, are all part of the elaborate plot that brings Fazloo to his senses. Maryan agrees to go to Yousaf subject to the condition that he does not touch her; if he does, Maryan swears that that would be the end of her relationship with Fazloo. Fazloo agrees without hesitation, for he has been convinced of Yousuf's saintliness by the testimony of his own senses. But Yousuf has planned his stay at the rest-house only for one purpose—he has had his eye on Maryan; and he attacks her as soon as she enters his room. Maryan ought to have left Fazloo, but she does not. Perhaps, she gets scared of being left alone if Fazloo died on her, or, perhaps, in her view, she regards her break-up with Fazloo too severe a punishment for one error of judgment by him. In any case, she compromises her integrity and decides to resume her life with Fazloo and her son Sheroo.

The ending of the story, to say the least, is problematic. One may argue that, in the manner of Chekhov, Qasimi ends the story with two denouements—the first, a dramatically explosive one, a high note, when Maryan announces she is leaving Fazloo, accusing him of having sold her to Yousuf for money. That would seem to be the more authentic, appropriate and just end, though also more predictable. But then there is a second anti-climactic, and ironic end when after walking away from Fazloo, she returns to find him bloodied and unconscious and decides to stay with him. It is possible to rationalize issues of closure, but the fact remains that Maryan's reversal of her decision somehow rankles.

David Lodge points out that endings were 'apt to be particularly troublesome' to Victorian novelists, 'because they were always under pressure from readers and publishers to provide a happy one'.[20] Qasimi has not been under any such pressure from his readers or publishers, but it is likely that there was a compulsion from within him to design an agreeable, harmonizing and happy, indeed a sentimentally euphoric, ending for this story. Saadat Hasan Manto, in a letter to Qasimi had advised him to abjure sentimentality in his writing. He said he was afraid sentiment lay at the base of Qasimi's art and was becoming part of its wherewithal.[21] In retrospect, Manto's assessment seems fair and pertinent, for Qasimi has never written a nakedly realistic story, one completely devoid of sentimentality, like, for instance, Prem Chand's *Kafan* (The Shroud), a story that emerges from the habit of looking at life unflinchingly, with open, unclouded eyes, not balking at what it may divulge. As an extreme manifestation of sentimentality, Qasimi has confessed that he even winces at Allama Mohammad Iqbal's exploiting in his poetry of the symbol of *shaheen* [the royal white falcon] who pounces upon harmless, innocent birds like pigeons.[22] One suspects that the same sort of sentiment was part of the reason for the second ending of 'The Rest-House.' It is not possible to ascertain with any accuracy the source of this sentiment in Qasimi. It may be an aspect of his belief in basic human decency, civility and consideration, or it may be a consequence of the emotional empathy for the weak, the downtrodden, the oppressed, and the dispossessed, the sort of empathy the Progressives demanded from their fellow-travellers. If taken too far, such empathy can easily turn into mushy, lachrymose sentimentality and lead to contrived narrative contexts.

Qasimi's technique of characterization is fairly old-fashioned, i.e., based on observing what the characters say or do within their web of relationships, and recording the opinions, ironic or otherwise, which the others form of them. Whether the story is located in a village or a city, character is always its most important and memorable constituent. What Iris Murdoch once wrote about great novels: 'When we think of the works of Tolstoy or George Eliot, we are not remembering Tolstoy and George Eliot, we are remembering Dolly, Kitty, Stiva, Dorothea and Cauasabon'[23] applies equally to Qasimi. In thinking of his fiction, we are actually remembering the gallery of characters he has created. Besides Fazloo, Maryan, Yousuf, Parmeshar Singh, Maulvi Abul, mentioned above, there are remarkable characters like Sultan's blind grandfather who keeps his demonic fingers on the boy's head, practically stunting his emotional and psychological growth; the old woman in the bus who is so naturally aware of her dignity as a farmer and a working woman that she angrily and arrogantly spurns a passenger's attempt to pity her, and whose response to the situation, which would have been utterly normal in the village surroundings, turns her into a wild woman; Syed Amjad Hussain in 'The Old Banyan' who regards the 250 year-old banyan on the grounds of his house as not only symbolic of his history and past, but also an emblem of his own position in the family, so that when his son and his new bride have it cut while he is out of town, he begins to question his own identity and then clandestinely destroys his son and daughter-in-law's flower garden which had given them as much sense of self worth as the old banyan had given him; Miss Dorothy Skoda of 'A Sample' whose family is so obsessed with keeping up appearances that their whole life has turned into an extended enactment of dissimulation and lies; Mian Saiful Haq of 'The Burial', a pious, god-fearing man, who looks after all the burial-arrangements of Ghafoora's young wife without realizing that the decencies of burying the dead should have been linked as much to Ghafoora's sense of self-respect as they are to his own.

This is realism at its most competent. The human beings in the stories are well-characterized, placed in identifiably realistic and credible settings, and speak and act as authentically as people do in real life. Qasimi reveals not only his knowledge of human beings and his ability to describe them with skill and understanding, but also his compassion for people from every class, from the poorest to the most affluent. Even the most callous, the most cruel and overwhelming of individuals is observed with tolerance, thoughtfulness and consideration. There is no didacticism, no attempt to impose a point-of-view by the author, even though we know that Qasimi believes that writing is an activity with a tangible social purpose. The stories reveal themselves to be the work of a writer who has observed the lives of the people with the practiced eye of a shrewd observer and found them worth celebrating in his fiction.

Let me end with two short quotations from Margaret Atwood's essay, An End to Audience?' She observes:

> Writing, no matter what its subject, is an act of faith; the primary faith being that someone out there will read the results... The world exists; the writer bears witness; 'I believe that fiction writing is the guardian of the moral and ethical sense of the community. Especially now that organized religion is ...in disarray, and politicians have...lost their credibility, fiction is one of the few

forms left through which we may examine our society, ...through which we can see others and judge them and ourselves. [24]

Qasimi's output amply testifies to the validity of the above comments. His fundamental responsibility, like that of every writer, is surely to bear witness to the world around, but he also affords us an opportunity to examine and judge life. As a writer, he has unqualified faith in what he does, and is convinced of the nobility and necessity of his calling. His deep conviction, his confidence and optimism—rare and precious in the general gloom and discontent of the present-day world—may yet give others faith in writing as something worth living for.

Ahmad Nadeem Qasimi produced sixteen collections of short stories. The publication details of the stories included in the present selection are as follows: 'A Wild Woman' (Vehshi) from the collection *Barg-e-Hina* (Lahore: Naashereen, 1959. Reprinted in 1995 by Asatir); 'The Pond with the Bo Tree' (Pipal Wala Talaab) from the collection *Koh Paimaa* (Lahore: Asatir, 1995); 'Theft' (Chori) from the collection *Bagoolay* (Lahore: Maktaba-e-Urdu, 1941. Reprinted in 1995 by Asatir, Lahore); 'Praise Be to Allah' (Alhamd-o-Lillah), 'The Rest House' (Raees Khana), 'A Mother's Love' (Maamta) and 'A Sample' (Namoona) from the collection *Sannata* (Lahore: Naya Idara, 1952. Reprinted in 1995 by Asatir, Lahore); 'Parmeshar Singh' (Parmeshar Singh), 'The Burial' (Kafan Dafan) and 'Old Man Noor' (Baba Noor) from the collection *Baazaar-e-Hayaat* (Lahore: Idara-e-Farogh-e-Urdu, 1952. Reprinted in 1995 by Asatir, Lahore); 'The Unwanted' (Faaltoo) and 'Sultan, the Beggar Boy' (Sultan) from the collection *Ghar se Ghar Tak* (Rawalpindi: Rawal Kitab Ghar, 1963. Reprinted in 1995 by Asatir, Lahore); 'The Thal Desert' (Thal), 'The Old Banyan' (Aasaib) and 'Lawrence of Thalabia' (Lawrence of Thalabia) from the collection *Kapaas ka Phool* (Lahore: Maktaba-e-Funoon, 1973. Reprinted in 1995 by Asatir, Lahore).

Faruq Hassan

NOTES

1. He is known never to have used a swear-word in his life; in fact, in one of his letters to Saqi Farooqi, (*Naya Waraq* [The New Sheet], Bombay: 1998, pp. 181-2), he told Saqi, who is quite well-known for being rather unbridled in deriding those he considers his literary enemies, to forswear abusive language in criticism. He said he was appreciative of Saqi's frankness and forthrightness, but there was really no need for Saqi to indulge in obscenities in dealing with his literary rivals. 'Make use of harshness of tone, instead', he advised Saqi.
2. There are at least four such volumes—Nadeem Number of monthly *Afkaar*, Karachi, 1972; *Nadeem-Nama*, Lahore, 1976; Zia Sajed, ed., *Matti ka Samandar* (An Ocean of Clay), 1991; Nadeem Edition of *Ibarat* (A Passage) Hyderabad, 1997, besides a collection of laudatory poems in his honour, called *Gul Paashi* (Scattering Flowers), Lahore, 1996.
3. Such as the one by Fateh Mohammad Malik, *Ahmad Nadeem Qasimi: Shair aur Afsanah Nigar* (Poet and Short Story Writer), Lahore, 1991.
4. For information on Qasimi's life. I have depended heavily upon four interviews he has given at different times in his life. Two of these, 'Nadeem ke T'assuraat' (Nadeem's Impressions), with Asrar Zaidi, and 'Nadeem ke Jawabaat' (Nadeem's Responses) with Nadim Uppal, have been included in Zia Sajed's *Matti ke Samandar*, op. cit. pp. 515-41. The third one 'Mukaalima' (Dialogue) with Masrur Ahmad Zaee appeared in *Ibarat*, op. cit., pp. 50-68. The last one with Qurrat-ul-Ain Tahera appeared recently in 'Tasteer' (Composing Lines), Lahore (1999), pp. 33-47.
5. 'Editor's Introduction', *A Requiem for the Earth*, OUP: Karachi, 1998, p. vii.
6. Ibid.
7. See *Tasteer* and *Ibarat* interviews.
8. 'Introduction', *The Tale of the Old Fisherman*, Washington: Three Continents Press, 1991, p. 12.
9. M.U. Memon, 'Introduction', *The Seventh Door and Other Stories*. Colorado, London: Lynne Rienner, 1998, p. 9.
10. Ahmad Ali, 'The Progressive Writers' Movement in its Historical Perspective', *JSAL*, xiii (1977-78), pp. 94-5.
11. Memon, *Seventh Door*, p. 9.
12. Qasimi had been in jail earlier as editor of the journals *Naqoosh* and *Savera* for publishing Manto's sexually explicit stories. (*Tasteer* interview.)
13. See the Israr Zaidi interview, p. 22. This is an arguable issue, for as Memon states convincingly, Hali (1837-1914) too had attributed the same

purpose to literature ('Introduction', *Fisherman*, p. 9). Prem Chand too had the same view of the social function of literature. What Qasimi regards as having been given by PWM to literature, was in large part Prem Chand's legacy, and Qasimi could, perhaps have as easily learned what he did from Prem Chand, as from the Progressives, i.e., dealing with the life of the peasants and farmers with faithfulness, insight, understanding and compassion and voicing their protests.

14. *Tasteer* interview, p. 41.
15. Dr Salim Akhtar attributes this metaphor-making in Qasimi's stories—he hears their echo even in the later, more mature stories—to an innate impulse in Qasimi to beautify, aimed at lending grace and delicacy to his descriptions, but which often damages the realistic verisimilitude of the stories. Salim Akhtar adds that Qasimi engages in this beautifying impulse notwithstanding his clear perception that his art has a social and moral purpose. Salim Akhtar, *Ahmad Nadeem Qasimi ke Afsanay*, (Ahmad Nadeem Qasimi's Short Stories), *Afsanah: Haqeeqat se Ilamat Tak* (Short Story: From Reality to Symbol), Lahore: Maktaba Aalia, 1976, pp. 195-226.
16. *Talai Muhr* (Golden Seal), *Bagoolay* (Whirlwind), orig. pub. 1941; rep. Lahore: *Asateer*, 1995, p. 28.
17. Orig. pub. 1941.
18. Orig. pub. in *Bagoolay*, 1941.
19. David Lodge, *The Practice of Writing*, London: Seker & Warburg, 1996, p.185.
20. David Lodge, *The Art of Fiction*, Penguin, 1994, p. 224.
21. Salim Akhtar, p. 200.
22. See *Tasteer* interview, p. 39. A similar situation of a hawk hunting for a starling is used by Qasimi in the story 'Lawrence of Thalabia'. The narrator's view of the hunt is that it is an act of gratuitous violence. Even though the hunt is presented to him as a natural act for the hawk, he views it as an uncalled-for demonstration of sadistic tendencies and exploitative capabilities of the rich.
23. 'The Sublime and the Beautiful Revisited', *Yale Review*, 49 (1959), p. 226.
24. *Second Words*, Toronto: Anansi, 1982, pp. 349, 346.

A SAMPLE

No, no, I'm not sick. If I look pale, the reason for that is an incident that happened a few moments ago. Also, there's one other thing I'm thinking about.

Today is Miss Dorothy Skoda's birthday.

Twentieth or twenty-second, but that doesn't matter. I'm thinking of something different.

The sound that you heard just now, like the tinkling of bells, it wasn't that at all. It was the sound of Miss Dorothy Skoda's laughter. Miss Dorothy Skoda—all right, for your convenience I shall call her Dora—so, Dora always laughs like that. And her voice? You must have heard a nightingale. All right, then, if a nightingale starts talking in English, she will sound just like Dora. It seems as though some musical instrument is hidden in her chest, and her lips are just its frets, and she is not talking but pouring out melodies. Sometimes when she talks, her voice seems to come from afar, as though someone were playing a violin in some dark cave on a distant island. And the notes come coasting on the wings of breezes and rain down on this flat situated on Mayo Road.

I am sure you think I am using hyperbole because I'm also a poet, but believe me, if I had to dabble in poetry, I would have written an ode to Dora. But I am not composing verses at the moment; I'm telling you a story.

And the story begins with Dora's laughter.

A month ago when I came into this flat for the first time, it was around four in the afternoon. I had just stepped into the room when I heard a flourish of chimes. I was startled. Mrs Skoda was coming right behind me, or I would have stood entranced for long. You know how a flourish can startle one, eh?

Mrs Skoda had sub-let this room in her flat. As soon as we entered, she began informing me about the merits of the room, and even about its demerits which, as she described them, had now turned into merits. She rattled on and on, so incessantly that the chiming of the anklet-bells disappeared from my mind, and it was nearly five o'clock. Even though, by now, she had convinced me, turning the conviction into almost an article of faith for me, that no building in Lahore could match that flat of hers, and also that people in the bungalows around Jinnah Garden were not really living their lives but merely wasting their time. Her enthusiasm was such that if it were not checked then and there, it seemed to me she would go on talking for another hour, and all my plans for the evening would be ruined. I resolved to build a dike before the continuous flow and fluency of her rhetoric.

She said, 'Take this skylight, for instance.'

Immediately I responded, 'Yes, I noticed it as soon I entered. It's nice.'

She said, 'But you don't understand what I am trying to say. I am surprised why a skylight is given that moniker even after it is fitted with glass. Its purpose is to let in fresh air, but how can it serve that purpose when it's so blocked, damn it?'

'Yes, damn it,' I tried to build that dike.

But Mrs Skoda laughed heartily and said, 'It's so surprising and nice that you and I agree on everything. Anyway, as I was saying, one day it so happened that two pigeons came and perched on the other side of this skylight. Some street-boy shot at them with his catapult and broke both the panes into smithereens. Robert was so angry that he swore at the boy in Punjabi. Even Dora was infuriated. But to me it seemed that a secret door to some treasure trove had opened. Sometimes an accident solves some puzzle in life. A flood of fresh air inundated this room. If the houses of the cow-herders weren't located on the other side and the smell of dung weren't mixed in the fresh air, this room could match the Kashmir Point in Murree. Without fresh air a man begins to look like an owl.'

'Yes, and even an owl cannot do without fresh air,' I said.

Mrs Skoda laughed out loud again and said, 'Wonderful, wonderful. I see you've a sense of humour.'

I tried to take advantage of the pause. I was just planning to say something when Mrs Skoda blew up the dike by saying, 'Our conception of architecture is still the same old, moth-eaten one. One's flat may be on the Mall, but as you enter you feel you have walked into ancient Baghdad. I have a book on ancient Baghdad. You should read it. Dora is busy with it these days.' She paused in search of some new topic.

I tried, for the first time, to look into her eyes and say something, but our eyes couldn't meet, so it became hard to say anything. Age had lent her eyes a squint, and the one eye of hers that met mine was off-centre. I took my hand out of my pocket to rub my eyes but by that time she had found another topic to talk about.

'For sure, this wooden partition will at first seem awkward to you, but you'll soon get used to it. Man is a weird creature (i.e., you are a weird creature); you throw him in a raging fire, he'll twist and turn and writhe with agony, but then will begin to enjoy it ('i.e., he'll die,' I wanted to interject, but didn't for fear of upsetting the harmony of ideas between us). My daughter Dora practises dancing in the adjoining room; along with it she also hums the dance tune. This too might seem awkward to you at first, for I've heard you are a journalist, but soon you'll get used to it. You might even begin to wait for her humming. So far as Robert is concerned, he'll be leaving for Karachi soon. He has found a job there in an export-import firm. If he were to stay here, you'd have gotten used to him. You'd have found him to be an excellent friend. The gentleman who was staying in this room until recently, he was perhaps an opium-contractor, but was such a sweet man. Robert almost became a younger brother to him. He would eat his breakfast in this room, shave, sometimes even have his lunch here as well. They used to go to the movies together, sit in restaurants together. I wonder why he suddenly gave up the room and disappeared, and where to. It has been fifteen days and he hasn't bothered to inquire after his Robert ('Was Robert in need of a shave again,' I wanted to ask, but...). So, what was I saying? Yes, Robert is going to Karachi. That leaves poor me. I am here, but I'm as good as not being here. The most I do is cough a few times in the night, or scold Dora for being too excited about things. At our age one is no more valuable than a zero. Look at me now, just look.'

I tried to. I tried literally to see eye to eye with her, but it was impossible. In fact, I felt I too had begun squinting. Quickly, I rubbed my eyes. In that fraction of a second in which my eyes did meet hers, I noticed that she was tweaking the fold of loose skin under her chin. Then she said, 'There was a time when I used to carry as many as three chins under this bag. I used to be so fat and healthy that I wondered how long I would hold on to so much flesh and flab on my body. But then suddenly God called Johnson away. After that my body began developing all these loose bags all around.' She paused for a moment, took out a handkerchief, and blew her nose into it so noisily that the pigeons sitting in the skylight fluttered their wings in fright and took flight. I too looked at her in awe. She was crying. I didn't know what to say to her at that delicate moment. After some effort I uttered the words 'Mrs Skoda' in a manner that suggested comfort, sympathy, and wonder; all at once. 'I'm sorry,' she said and turned around to leave. At that very moment from across the partition I heard Dora's angry words, 'What's going on, Mommy?' This was the first time I had heard the nightingale in the flat.

After Mrs Skoda's departure, I surveyed the room for the first time. It was rectangular in shape. If the partition hadn't been there, it would perhaps have been square. Anyway, a square had been divided into two rectangles, and I had been given one. The skylight had been occupied by the pigeons whose dropping had streaked the wall. Underneath these streaks stood a cupboard whose doors displayed a number of pictures: of Ingrid Bergman as Joan of Arc, Bette Davis as Queen Elizabeth, Charles Boyer as Napoleon, and a nude of a youthful woman with an inscription in English underneath—Woman: thy name is nakedness. Below, there were the signatures of Robert Skoda. I suddenly recalled that that brilliant, modern-day philosopher was about to depart for Karachi; it would be such a loss to be deprived of his company. I thought of calling him out right then and asking him where he had culled those words of wisdom from. From what kind of seashell on the shores of which ocean had he got hold of that pearl? But I had been tired out, both mentally and physically. I had been standing in the same posture since I had entered this room. Mrs Skoda hadn't asked me to sit down or talk or even bang my head against the wall. If you stand leaning against a cupboard for an hour and a half, it becomes a part of your body. Often you wonder which part of you is you and which the cupboard. And the rest of the room? Well, it's all here before you. There's a door that faces the cupboard and that's all.

A day or so ago I had been told by my newspaper editor to visit Jehangir's tomb one evening and write an article after carefully observing the tomb on a moonlit night. I was expected to prove that if the Taj Mahal looked like a crown in the moonlight, Jehangir's tomb shone like a jewel in a finger-ring. I had tried my best to persuade the editor that the tomb was worth looking at only during the day. I had seen it many times at night; it was eerie; you felt as if non-human, other-worldly creatures were about to jump out of the hundreds of doors of its spread-out cells, and pounce upon you. If the stillness of the Taj Mahal was a lyric, the tomb's hush was a cry of pain. I didn't know if it was the fault of the architecture or of the viewers' intention, but that was the way it was. My editor did not agree. He insisted it had to do with the viewers' intention. If one went with the intention of enjoying its weightless towers and beautiful arches in the moonlight, one would obviously like the place. So, this evening I had to go to Shahdara with the best of intentions, but there was so much weight on my mind that I decided, instead, to go to bed.

One's observations are, indeed, affected by one's intentions, and believe me when I tell you that my intentions towards my neighbours were quite honourable. But some incidents took place that changed my view, not of my intentions, but of my neighbours. It so happened that after setting down my belongings in the room, when I sat down on the bed, I was feeling as though I would fall asleep as soon as my head would hit the pillow. But when I lay down, sleep somehow deserted me. I picked up the book *Masterpieces of Art* and began looking at the creations of the great painters. If there was anything wrong with my intentions then, the beauty of the pictures had set it right, and I began enjoying browsing through the book. Suddenly I heard a knock at the door.

Tonight I wanted only to sleep. I had even deferred my dinner till tomorrow morning and had lain on bed after bolting the door. The knock was annoying, but more than that, it was surprising. None of my friends yet knew of my new lodgings, so the knock seemed even more mysterious. When I got up from the bed to move towards the door, the pigeons in the skylight cooed in such a way as though they were consciously laughing at me. No, no, I told myself, there was nothing the matter with my intentions; the damned birds always cooed like that. I opened the door. Someone said, 'Hello neighbour! I'm Robert, Robert Skoda,' and without waiting for me to extend my hand for a shake, walked in. His hands in his pockets, he made a little pirouette on his heels and said, 'Amazing, my liking for this room never ceases to diminish. Whoever the tenant, I cannot stop treating this skylight, this cupboard, this partition and this crack in it as my property. It is wrong, but it's also true. Wrong but how true!' He moved towards my bed and my eyes started looking for the crack in the partition, but quickly I moved my eyes away, went to Robert and extended my hand saying, 'My name is Tariq.' He seemed a bit embarrassed. He shook hands with me and sat down on my bed. He picked up *Masterpieces of Art* and started turning the pages. 'Wonderful, awfully wonderful,' he said looking at a picture of Picasso. In this picture Picasso, in his shorts, stood haughtily, like a wrestler, by some of his own creations. Robert took Picasso's photograph to be his artistic creation; he moved his finger across the figure of Picasso and commented, 'He looks so life-like!' I didn't feel the need to correct him and sat in a chair facing the bed.

Robert was a fair-complexioned young man, of mercurial nature. His youthful blood seemed to leap and bound in his veins rather than just course through them. Only his eyes seemed lifeless. Time and again he would moisten his lips with his tongue.

I asked him, 'When are you leaving for Karachi?'
He answered surprised, 'Karachi? I'm not going to Karachi. Who told you that?'
'Your mother,' I said.
He thought something and said, 'Oh, I see. I'm not going now.'
I asked another question, 'So, what do you do these days?'
'What do I do?' he repeated my question and laughed out loud. 'I collect moths' wings, tooth paste boxes, and . . . and pictures of historical personalities.'
I pointed to the nude on the cupboard and asked, 'What historical personality is she?'
Robert again began laughing. He slapped his hand on mine and controlling his mirth said, 'She is the eternal woman. She's the one whom we call Eve, and she is also the one who lives around here in your neighbourhood. She is the woman incarnate.'
At that moment Robert Skoda seemed to me to be a fifty-year old. I was busy trying to figure out the philosophical import of his comments when he picked up my pen from the table and said, 'What a nice design!'
'It's an old design,' I said, 'It's an Eversharp. One can find it in any store.'
'But I have never seen this Eversharp design before,' he said.
'It's possible,' I agreed.
Then putting as much gentleness in his voice as he could, he asked, 'Do I have your permission to borrow it for a day or so to show it to the store-keeper as a sample? I would like to buy a pen like that for myself. May I?'
There was no way to say 'No,' so I said, 'By all means. It is a very common brand.'
'Thanks,' he said and got up from my bed. Near the door he turned around and said, 'Goodnight.'
'Goodnight,' I said and closed the door. From the crack in the partition I noticed that he stood looking at my pen, turning and turning it around in his hands. Then I heard the nightingale say, 'Let me see, Robbie,' and Dora came into focus through the crack. Her beauty, from head to toe, was eastern. We have a

different conception of beauty, and she seemed an embodiment of that. She almost snatched the pen away from Robert. Hiding it in her blouse, she pirouetted a couple of times and laughing, ran into the next room.

And the whole night I kept dreaming of the tinkling bells of her laughter. Needless to say, I had a good sleep. In the morning, if the pigeons in the skylight hadn't started cooing, I might have slept in until midday.

The next day I was in the office until evening and from there left for Shahdara. Unfortunately, the sky was overcast and the moon was nowhere to be seen. I stayed there until ten, staring at the clouds which occasionally seemed luminous. In the light darkness the tomb seemed suspended in air; the darkness in the doors of cells was assuming uncanny shapes, and the patches of grass looked like small lakes of dark water. Frustrated, I came back. When I entered the flat, Dora and Robert were humming a dance tune and dancing to it. Without turning on the light, I peeped through the crack. They were dressed in the same clothes as the night before, except that a number of curlers were stuck in Dora's hair. She was smiling as she danced. As she smiled, a dimple formed in one of her cheeks and an arc in the other, but both seemed artificial as though formed by mechanical means. Looking through the crack, as I extended my hand and turned on the light, they both stopped dancing and humming. 'So late?' Dora said quietly, and Robert answered with the poise of an intellectual, 'He's a journalist, a night-bird.' Suddenly Dora advanced towards the crack. I jumped up and moved away from it and began pacing about in the room. I felt as though her gaze, like something tangible, was following me through the crack. Perturbed, I put out the light and lay down on my bed. Then a little later when the light on the other side had been turned off, I turned on my light and began writing an article titled 'Jehangir's Tomb in Half-Light.' That was when I remembered my pen. I thought of knocking at the door and asking Robert for it, but it was late. They might be asleep, and it might be considered boorish on my part to disturb them. So I wrote the few pages that I did with a pencil.

On the third day, after getting ready, I came down the stairs of the building to go to my office. I was getting my bicycle from the watchman when a telegraph messenger came and began to ask me about my address. He had a telegram for me from my elder brother who had advised me that my niece was to be married a month later, so I should begin making the necessary purchases for the wedding. When I tried to sign the receipt, I noticed that the lead of the messenger's pencil was gone, and I had forgotten my pencil inside the flat. By chance, I saw Robert coming down the stairs. I asked him if he had a pencil. He took my pen out of his pocket, opened it, kept its cap with him and giving me the rest of it asked, 'Is everything all right?' I answered, 'Yes, it's about the wedding-date of a close-relation.' When I had finished signing, he took the pen back from me and was about to put it back in his pocket after closing the cap, when he suddenly turned pale, and in a voice somewhat shaky said, 'Forgive me. This is yours.' He thrust it into my hand, turned around and hurriedly climbed the stairs back into the house.

The incident had left me in shock. The pen had turned into an insult and stuck in my mind. Without putting it into my pocket, I went back in the house and knocked at Mrs Skoda's flat. A moment later the door was opened by Dora. She was wearing the same clothes she had worn last night. Her hair was so curly that it looked like a bird's nest, and her almond eyes had the misty look of the tomb of Jehangir. 'Hello,' she said and then moved aside. She invited me in and asked me to sit down. I sat down on the sofa. It was one of those heavy, thickly padded sofas which swallowed you in as you sat on them. Your knees rose up and the distance between the seat and the floor was reduced to just a few inches. After sinking in once, I lifted myself out and tried to sit more comfortably at the far end of it but sank in again and, at last, stayed contentedly where I was. I said, 'You too sit down.' She said, 'Thanks,' and sat down in front of me in a chair. I started twiddling the pen in my fingers. A little later I said, 'This pen probably belongs to Robert. I borrowed it from him to sign my name, but he left without taking it back.'

'No, it's yours,' she said and smiled, but this smile wasn't accompanied by a dimple and an arc in the cheeks. 'Robert has bought himself another one of the same design. The two are different only in colour. This is chocolate, and his is blue.'

I breathed a sigh of relief. I said, 'Good. This design will really look good in blue. May I have a look at it?'

Dora turned pale. She folded her hands between her knees and said, 'Sure, as soon as Robert is back.'

Newspapermen's merciless probing for truth has become my second nature. I said, 'But Robert came back in just a few moments ago!'

'No, no,' she said. Her voice was a little louder this time. 'He's not here. Perhaps he has gone to see some friend in the building. He has very many friends. His personality is such that he makes friends with whomever he is introduced to.'

To end the subject I asked, 'You have a book, . . . on ancient Baghdad. . . .'

'Ancient Baghdad?' she said surprised. 'No, I don't have any such book.'

'Mrs Skoda mentioned it,' I tried to prove that I wasn't making it up.

She again turned pale. Her red lips had a streak of blue in them. She pulled her hands out from between her knees and started cracking her knuckles. Startled by the noises she was making, she said, 'I'm sorry,' and without a break continued talking. 'Mommy might have it, I don't. I'll ask her, and if she hasn't lent it to anyone, I'll bring it to you by tomorrow or the day after. It should be a good book. Even its title is so full of romance—ancient Baghdad, Alf Lailah, Haroonur Rashid, the old magicians. . . . Yes, it will be nice to read it.'

She drew in a deep breath, smiled and said, 'I'm Dorothy, Dorothy Skoda.'

'I'm Tariq,' I said, 'And I am pleased to meet you.'

'Me too,' she smiled broadly and now there were the dimple and the arc in her cheeks again, her lips fully red. The mist in the eyes evaporated, the throbbing muscle under the ear became relaxed, and she began looking at me with the calm of a conqueror viewing the scattered bodies of his enemies in a battlefield. I got up, came back into my flat and glued my eyes to the crack. Robert came out of the back room, and brother and sister embraced each other warmly, as though they had met after years. Mrs Skoda also came into focus. She was smiling, but also had tears in her eyes. Then tears came to Dora's eyes as well. Robert disconsolately sank into the sofa.

I moved away from the crack. I felt as though I had come back after committing multiple murders. My heart began beating painfully, and I hurled the pen down on the table so hard that if it were a cheap one, it would have smashed into bits.

The next four or five days passed as if in a vacuum. I avoided my neighbours as much as they did me. As soon as I entered the flat, the whole house would turn into a soundless desert. Even the sound of Mrs Skoda's cough indicated that she was trying to suppress it so that I wouldn't hear it. Dora and Robert had just about disappeared from the world. I didn't try to look for them either. I was feeling guilty, and every time I came up the stairs of the building, I would, for no apparent reason, feel a tingling run down my spine.

About ten days after I had rented the flat, one evening I returned from the office at about nine o'clock. I hadn't turned on the light yet when I heard Dora and Robert whispering on the other side of the partition. Dora was saying, 'You go,' and Robert replying, 'No, no, you!' Back and forth they kept asking each other until Mrs Skoda interjected, 'It's better if you go, Dora. After the incident of the pen, Robert hesitates to go before him. And you know that men are polite towards women, even if for appearance's sake.' Since I was the subject of their conversation, I turned on the light and the whisperings stopped. I was undoing my shoe-laces when there was a knock on the door. I leapt up to open the door, and Dora walked in. She was dressed in the same old clothes. The curls in her hair had smoothed down now, and the polish on the nails was peeling off like plaster on ruins. She said, 'Forgive me, I've knocked at an awkward time. You see, what I was afraid of did actually happen. Mommy had lent her *Ancient Baghdad* to a friend.

Robert brought it back only today. I thought since you had shown much interest, so I should give it to you today. Here it is.' She handed over a voluminous tome in my hands and turned around to leave.

'Thank you very much,' I said, 'but why are you in such a hurry? Please stay for a minute.'

She sat down in a chair near where she had been standing. 'Thanks,' she said, and I began leafing through the book.

The first page had the signature of Johnson Skoda and the date, November 1943. The book was full of pictures and had been set in elegant type. But I was surprised to note that the book seemed quite new. An eight or nine year old book, even if it remains untouched, fades in colour, but this one carried a fresh smell.

For a few moments, we sat quietly. Noticing the silence becoming ugly, I said, 'I haven't seen Robert lately!'

Dora said, 'He is unwell. Has been down with flu for three or four days.'

'And Mrs Skoda?' I asked.

'She too hasn't been well. Didn't go out,' she said. 'The weather has been like that, you know.'

After a moment's silence, I asked, 'And you?'

'Me?' she was surprised as though she wasn't expecting that question. Then she bent her head down and smiled. The dimple and the arc appeared in her cheeks. 'I was all right. Just didn't get out. There was no reason.'

The subject had exhausted itself. Perhaps Dora too was waiting for that. She asked my leave and got up. Near the door, she turned around and said, 'Goodnight.'

'Goodnight,' I answered, bowing a little, chivalrously.

After her departure, I picked up the book, not because I wanted to read it, but because it had recently been in Dora's long, slender fingers. It sounds silly, but I was beginning to be interested in Dora upon seeing her gentle and normal manner. I have used the word 'interested' carefully and advisedly, so that you do not mistake me for having fallen in love. I have been in love a couple of times before, and it's basing upon my experience that I say I was beginning to be interested in Dora, for one can have an interest in a singing mynah in a cage as much as in a slip of a girl begging for alms.

So, it was because of my interest in Dora that I picked up the book. But my eyes became wide open with astonishment. The book was published in the year 1951. Did that mean then that Johnson Skoda had signed his name in the book eight years before it was published? I was astounded and sat up in bed. I understood the whole story. To keep their self-esteem, today Mrs Skoda, Dora, and Robert had somehow gathered thirteen rupees and purchased the book, and then without looking at its publication date, themselves signed and dated it 1943.

After the pen, the book became another insult that wouldn't let go of me. I can't describe to you the states of mind and feelings I underwent because of the presence of that book in my room. I didn't read a word of it, neither looked at any of its pictures. I just kept watching it lie there and thinking how the integrity and honour of a whole family lay with that book. Opening and reading it would be like opening up old tombs and tossing the bones out.

A week later I knocked at Mrs Skoda's door. Robert opened it. He greeted me cordially. 'I'm very sorry,' he said, 'I haven't been able to see you the past few days. I was unwell for a few days, and then became busy with a personal matter. How have you been?'

Sinking in the sofa I said, 'Thank you. I've been quite well, except for the harrowing work at the office. Well, I came to return the book.'

'Oh, *Ancient Baghdad*,' he said and called his mother.

Mrs Skoda came in. Out of respect, I stood up and was about to sit down when Dora too walked in. Once again I stood up, and then again sank back in the sofa and said, 'I haven't read a more interesting book in my life. And it's so informative that I can now call myself a native of Baghdad. The book has just about taken over my mind.'

Mrs Skoda smiled and accepted my praise gracefully, as though she herself was the author of the book. Then with great poise she began talking: 'You know, Johnson loved this book dearly. He used to say it reminded him of the land which gave birth to so many of God's messengers. I had wrapped it in a cover, in memory of Johnson. Dora dear, you must read this book. Have you read it, Robert?'

'Yes,' he said and offered me a Capstan cigarette. After asking Dora's and Mrs Skoda's permission I lit it. After I had drawn on it a couple of times, I felt that it tasted different from a Capstan. I didn't want to let on that I was trying to find out its brand. Casually, while talking, I discovered that it was a King Stork cigarette which had been placed in a Capstan packet. Something seemed to break in my heart.

Despite being their neighbour, I could easily have lived my life apart from them, but the charm of their very weaknesses had tempted me at least to hover about their world, if I couldn't actually enter it. And for the next two weeks I did just that, listening to the tinkling of bells and the song of the nightingale from across the partition. I heard so much of Mrs Skoda's talk that I could have written her biography. And Robert, indeed, became very intimate with me. He would shave in my room, have his breakfast there, at times he would even have his lunch with me. We would go to the movies and restaurants together. In those fifteen or so days we traversed fifteen years. The interest in Dora began transforming into friendship. Once she brought a bouquet of flowers for me and was so happy and laughed so much having set it on my table that there was a veritable avalanche of dimples and arcs in her cheeks. Then one day when she noticed that a buckle of my trousers had been broken, she took off a safety-pin from her blouse and put it in its place. And then yesterday evening this incident took place. I went to the market to look for some gifts for my niece and purchased a five-yard piece of georgette. When I came back to my flat, I called Robert. Hurriedly he came in and was stunned to see the cloth. Then he touched it and said, 'Have you lost your mind? This cloth is not for men.'

I said, 'Yes, I know. It's for ladies.'

He stayed quiet for a moment. Then a smile appeared on his face and he asked, 'Who is it for?'

I said, 'A niece of mine is getting married. I've bought it for her.'

'I'll be back soon,' he said and went out.

A few minutes later Mrs Skoda came to my door and asked, 'May I come in?'

'Please do,' I said and stood up. 'Come, have a seat.'

She said, 'I hear you have bought a piece of georgette from the market.'

I said, 'Yes, here it is.'

She said, 'What a beautiful colour. You have excellent taste. Bravo!' She opened the piece and held it in front of her. 'How many yards is it?' she asked.

'Five,' I answered.

She said, 'Excellent.' While folding it back she asked, 'I too have to buy a piece for Dora. If you allow me, can I take it to show as a sample. I shall return it tomorrow.'

'By all means,' I said, 'You didn't need to ask.'

She picked up the cloth and left, and I went to sleep.

This morning when I woke up I heard a lot of activity going on in Mrs Skoda's flat. Furniture was being dragged here and there. Pots and pans were clinking. Dora was chirping and Robert was chiding her about the setting of the furniture. After a long while I looked through the crack. Dora was clad in her customary clothes, a lot of curlers glistening in her hair. Robert had just a shorts on and was trying to place the sofa at a different angle. Mrs Skoda was either absent or out of range of the crack.

I couldn't understand the reason for all that hullabaloo. I changed my clothes and came out of the room to go to a restaurant and then my office. I had just locked my room when Robert came out from the other side. He said, 'Today is Dora's twenty-second birthday. My mother wants to apologize to you that she cannot invite you. Some of the elders of our family who are coming over are rather intolerant of people of other religions, especially at such family gatherings. It's stupid, but we cannot do much about it. We hope you won't mind.'

I appreciated Robert's honesty. Quite pleased, I said, 'I know. Every religion is blessed with such elders who consider those outside their religion as simply asses. If I cannot participate in Dora's party in person, I shall be there spiritually. Tell your mother that no elder shall be able to stop me from giving her my gift. OK?'

We both laughed heartily. Dora didn't come out, perhaps because of shyness. And Mrs Skoda was, of course, absent.

Until late in the evening, I kept looking in the market for an appropriate gift for Dora. The value of whatever I chose seemed to be diminished by what stood beside it. Finally, I came back empty-handed, hoping to ask Dora or Mrs Skoda to go with me the next day and choose the gift.

I returned home quite late. Mrs Skoda's door was shut but I could hear the laughter, the screams of joy, and the clinking of forks, knives, and plates—a flood of noises—pouring out. Quietly I opened the door to my room and the noises became very loud. Without turning on the light, I went to the crack. I wanted to see Dora in glory on her birthday. The first person I saw was a man from another flat in our building. He was a head-clerk in a firm and sat there wearing a loose suit of clothes. And, he was a Muslim.

I moved away from the crack. I suddenly felt disgusted by Robert, Mrs Skoda, and even Dora. For a moment I thought I should scream out what I thought of them, but before that I wanted to have a look at Dora.

I went back to the crack. Dora stood at one end of the table smiling. But I had a reeling sensation. You know why?

Dora was wearing the same piece of georgette as sari that Mrs Skoda had borrowed from me as a sample yesterday, and she looked amazingly beautiful. But let that pass.

So, if you find me looking a little pale today, it's not because I am sick. It's because I have just sent a little note to Mrs Skoda that that piece of georgette should be accepted as my gift to Dora.

And what I am still busy trying to figure out is whether I should love Dora or feel sorry for her.

THE BURIAL

The Burial...the only time of the day when no armies of angels interfered between man and his Lord.

He took out a four-anna piece from his pocket and tossed it from afar to the beggar. He had never before given charity in this manner; like throwing a bone at a dog, but Sharif's stall was close by, and even though it was closed, Mian Saiful Haq could still imagine marijuana smoke bellowing out of the cracks in the shutters.

The four-anna piece fell on the stomach of the person who lay stretched on the pavement. However, the other person stood up agitatedly, as though he had suddenely been awakened from his sleep. Mian Saiful Haq attributed the man's confusion to his feeling of awe at the scale of generosity shown. He smiled contentedly, and rolling the beads of his *tasbih* one by one, thus scattering their fragrance, he moved along.

Suddenly he heard the sound of hurried footsteps following him and turned around to look. The beggar was walking towards him, while also looking behind himself time and again. As he came near him, he placed the four-anna piece in Mianji's hand which held the *tasbih*.

Mianji noticed that the beggar's face was the colour of mud. Tears on a sallow face would produce that impression. He looked squeezed and crushed like the sugarcane husk hanging out of the press. Mianji felt pity for the man. Looking through his pockets, he asked the beggar, 'The four annas weren't enough, were they?'

The beggar answered him in a choked voice, as though he was barely managing to hold back a falling roof on his raised hands. He said, 'Sir, I am not a beggar. But the four-anna piece was too little. I need fifteen to twenty rupees and also a number of people.'

Mian Saiful Haq's hand froze in his pocket. The beggar breathed in a lot of air as though swallowing a big swig of water and said through his tears, 'If I could buy a shroud for one anna, I would return the change to you, but cotton has become very dear these days. What would I do with a four-anna bit?'

Mian Saiful Haq stood where he was, stunned.

'That is my wife's body,' the man said. 'She passed away.'

'From God we come and unto Him shall we return,' Mian Saiful Haq uttered the customary formula in a shivering voice. He pressed his lower lip hard between his teeth; his nostrils fluttered vigorously and soon tears drenched his cheeks and beard. His face looked forlorn as though he too had gone through the sugarcane press.

A crowd of screaming paperboys passed them by on the street. Smoke, laden with the smell of marijuana, along with Sharif's hacking cough, started to pour out from the closed doors of Sharif's stall. A frisky pack of pariah dogs came out of one street and ran into another. Flocks of birds descended on the trees, and the morning began to settle in.

Mian Saiful Haq walked back to the corpse and stopped in front of it. His lower lip was still pressed between his teeth and his face was unusually flushed. Tears flowed into his beard continually, the older ones dropping onto his chest to make room for fresh ones. 'So, you don't even have enough money to bury your wife?' he asked in a strange voice. 'So, even such things can happen in my God's world?' And after a pause he added in a choking voice, 'So, did my Hamid's dead-body also...' and he began to weep like a child. He didn't even bother to notice that he was leaning against the board that jutted out of Sharif's stall, and that the air was heavy with marijuana fumes.

Suddenly he picked the facecloth from his shoulder and wiped his face down to the neck as though he had just finished his ablutions. Then he walked up to the corpse, cleared his throat and said to the man, 'Do you have no one here?'

'No, I don't,' the man said and sat down near the corpse. Tears streamed from his eyes ceaselessly. It seemed as though he would die if he tried stopping them.

'Then why did you come here?' Mianji asked.

He began to explain, but in a manner as though he was lifting a heavy load off his head with Mianji's help: 'When Kalli started having the pains,...' he paused for a moment, and resumed, 'Kalli is my wife's name...' He paused again, and, suddenly, a lot of tears flowed from his eyes, 'was my wife's name,' he corrected himself. 'At that time she said to me, listen Ghafooray, these sparks that I see dancing before my eyes, as my mother said, they mean the arrival of Hazrat Izrael sometime soon.'

'Wait. There'll be time to listen to all that later,' Mianji said. Once again mopping his face with his facecloth, he walked towards a passing ox-cart. 'Listen brother,' he said to the driver, 'will you do something for us?'

The cart-driver stopped his oxen. Mian Saiful Haq told him he wanted him to carry a woman's body at a furlong's distance.

In confusion the cart-driver jumped down from his perch.

'How much would you charge for this service?' Mianji asked.

'Sir, you must be one of the innocents. Does anyone ever charge for carrying a dead-body?' the cart-driver asked in a tone that showed both his astonishment and reproach. 'But how did the woman die here, on the roadside?'

'Sometimes such things do happen in my God's world,' Mian Saiful Haq said. 'May God reward you. Bring your cart over on this side.'

When Saiful Haq went back to the corpse, Ghafoora stood up out of a sense of respect and in wonder. Mianji said, as though handing out a verdict, 'The corpse will be taken to my house.'

'Your house?' Ghafoora stammered.

'She is my daughter,' he said. 'I take the responsibility for her burial. After all, someone must have done as much for my Hamid.'

By that time the cart had drawn near. Before touching the woman's body to lift her, Mian Saiful Haq asked Ghafoora, 'Do I have your permission?'

And Ghafoora, crying bitterly and loudly, clung to Mianji's legs. A few passers-by stopped to look in alarm and then started moving towards them. The door of Sharif's stall opened with a screech and he asked from inside, 'What happened, folks?'

Loudly reciting the *Kalima*, 'I declare that there is no god but Allah,' as Ghafoora and Mianji heaved the body up, the dead woman's glass-bangles clinked, and Ghafoora wept so bitterly and helplessly that if Mianji hadn't held the body aloft, it would have fallen down on the pavement. People moved ahead in panic to help out, but Mianji held everyone back, saying, 'It's a woman.'

'A woman?' one person said, 'And she died on the roadside?'

'Someone should inform the police,' another said.

'Are you a near relative of hers, like perhaps an uncle?' the first one asked him.

Meanwhile Mian Saiful Haq's voice was heard instructing the cart-driver. 'All right, my good man, go straight and keep on reciting the *Kalima-e Shahadat*,' and he himself recited loudly, 'I declare there is no god but Allah.'

The minute the cart started moving, Ghafoora called out loudly, 'Stop, driver. Wait a moment. Kalli's head is moving.' Mian Saiful Haq took the facecloth off his shoulder and put it on one side of Kalli's head, and Ghafoora placed his turban on the other. The cart moved on again.

The three men kept reciting the *Kalima* under their breath and the wheels of the cart kept wailing and screeching as though mourning the deceased. When the cart stopped in front of Mian Saiful Haq's house, the whole neighbourhood gathered around it. Mianji, without saying anything to anybody, hurried into the house.

A little while later, loud lamentation began to emerge from the house. Neighbourhood women leaned out of their windows to look. People standing outside could hear Mianji's wife and her maid-servant crying inside. Mianji came out with his three sons, carrying a cot. He took one of the elders of the neighbourhood aside and briefly explained the whole matter to him. Within seconds the whole neighbourhood knew what had happened. People from adjoining neighbourhoods also learnt the story, They came in droves and started gathering.

Mianji and Ghafoora lifted the corpse from the cart and put it on the cot. This time Ghafoora didn't let her bangles clink. Earlier when that had happened, Ghafoora had felt as though someone had pulled off the sheet from over Kalli's body. Mianji said to Ghafoora, 'These are my sons. Consider them the brothers of the deceased.'

Ghafoora was feeling a lump in his throat and was barely able to mutter a 'Yes.' He sat down in the street, throwing his head between his knees to hide his tears from the crowd. People surrounded him as though he were some kind of curious object.

Mian Saiful Haq and his sons took Kalli's body inside the house. By the time the cot was lowered down, dozens of women from the neighbourhood, who had been earlier jumping over their rooftops, had now gathered inside Mainji's house. The lamentation was so loud, it seemed the whole city of Lahore was grieving the hapless woman's death.

One of Mianji's sons left for the graveyard. The second one went to bring the woman who bathed the dead. The third one was sent to bring camphor and essence of vetiver. Mianji gave him instructions, 'The shroud must be of the best cotton. Don't worry about the cost. Just think you're bringing it for Hamid.'

Mian Saiful Haq invited all the sympathetic elders of the neighbourhood into his sitting room. The young stayed out in the street, hanging about in small groups. Then he accompanied Ghafoora into the room where he used to keep his copy of the Koran on a folding stand, *Du'a-e Ganju ul-Arsh*, and *Qasidah Burdah*. Under the window with the broken glass lay the day's newspaper.

There, Ghafoora unburdened himself and laid bare before Mian Saiful Haq each and everyone of his sufferings and miseries. 'Kalli was with child, you know,' he began his story but felt a lump in his throat and stopped. He started again, 'Forgive me, Mianji, it is not right for men to cry, but to tell you the truth, Kalli has taken away all my pride.'

Mian Saiful Haq's eyes also became tearful, as though he were in agreement with what Ghafoora was saying.

Now Ghafoora talked without stopping. His voice would sometimes become husky, sometimes low, sometimes drowned out in tears, but he went on talking, and Mian Saiful Haq, his eyes damp, kept watching and listening with rapt attention.

'Kalli was with child. She said, "Listen Ghafooray, these sparks that are dancing before my eyes, these are a sign that I am bound for the next world." She went through so much pain during the past ten days, Mianji, that if she were not young, just sixteen or seventeen, or if she were like me, thirty-five or forty, she would have died of it long ago. I am employed in the post office in Chuniyan. There I talked to a knowledgeable woman. She told me that Kalli would have to have a c-section. If she didn't, the child would die, and if the child died inside her, she would die too. Kalli said, "Listen Ghafooray, get me a section, I don't want to die yet. I haven't even begun to love you yet." That was what she said. So I asked the woman to give her a section. She said, "Take her to Lahore; it would be done better there." I carried Kalli like a child in my lap in the bus and brought her here. Here the Miss said no beds were vacant. I said, we were not that kind of people. If we couldn't get cots, we would lie on the floor. I said, "Let her lie on the floor in some corner of the hospital, but do something about her." But the Miss didn't listen to me. I said to Kalli, "Let's go and find a tree to sit under." Then the Miss felt some pity for us and let Kalli have a bed and told me to leave because everything was going to be all right. When Kalli heard that, she started crying loudly and saying that if I left her, she would die. But the Miss forced me out of there and asked me what my address was. I gave her my address in Chuniyan. She asked for an address in Lahore also. I said I would always be at the hospital gates. I had nowhere to go. What would I be doing anywhere else? And then I didn't have much money, and Kalli wouldn't let me ever borrow any. She would say if I borrowed once, I would be borrowing for the rest of my life. The day before yesterday when I went back to the hospital, another nurse was on duty. She told me that Kalli had delivered the child even before they could operate on her. But, she said, I wouldn't be able to see her, as she was bleeding and unconscious. She told me to go and think of a name for my child. When I went back yesterday, the nurse said, now Kalli was having a nosebleed. I went in to see her. She was lying with her eyes shut. When I called her, she opened her eyes and started to smile. I swear to you, Mianji, she smiled. Then she started crying and said, "Listen Ghafooray, why didn't you tell me that all this can happen when one has a child?" Mianji, I saw death dancing on her forehead. She had already become pale, but the paleness was never so shining as it was that night. I told her not to cry; she was going to be all right. She said, "Listen Ghafooray, when my nosebleed started, the woman in the next bed called the Miss and said to her that I was dying. Since then I have been really frightened. Ghafooray, once the Miss brought my child to me. He looks like another Ghafoora, only he is small. I had him with me, but I didn't know how to breast-feed. So I asked the nurse how one did that. All these women around me started laughing. They don't know that he is my first-born, and that I am from a small place like Chuniyan." Kalli held my hand and said, "Don't leave me tonight." When I said it was time and all the visitors had to leave, she said, "Daata Ganj Baksh is in Lahore, isn't he, Ghafooray? Go to him and beg for my life. Tell him Kalli must not die. Tell him, Kalli had found Ghafoora because she had made a votive offering at Daata Sahib's shrine, and so far Kalli had loved Ghafoora only as much as the nail of her little finger." Mianji, her hand was very cold. Ice is cold, I know, but that's a different kind of cold. The cold of Kalli's hand was really strange; it went straight through my bones. I started shivering. Then I went to Daata Sahib. When I came back to the hospital, I saw the same Miss whom we had met the first day standing by the half-open hospital gate. She called me to her and said, "Kalli has sent her *salaam* to you." I said cheerfully, Kalli must have become a *mem sahib* since she had come to Lahore. She was sending salaams. The Miss held my hand firmly and said, "Listen, she has sent her last *salaam*." I ran from there like a lunatic. The watchman ran after me and so did the Miss. When I got to Kalli's ward, I saw they were preparing to take her somewhere. The women-sweepers had arrived, and all the occupants of the neighbouring beds had turned their faces away from her. The women-sweepers tried to stop me and then the watchman grabbed me. Just then the Miss arrived and told them that I was Kalli's husband. When I took the sheet off her face, I could see, Mianji, that she was dead. There was dried blood at places on her upper lip. The nurses had stuffed cotton in her nostrils. No one had shut her eyes or tied a band of cloth around her face to close her mouth. It looked like she was about to say to me, "Listen, Ghafooray..." But, Mianji, she had died. The Miss showed me my child. He looked like a miniature Kalli. The Miss said, "You go and bury her, and then come back and take away your child." I brought her corpse out of the hospital. I carried it as if it were a child. At every step her bangles clinked. First I thought I should break them, but when I made her lie down on the ground and looked at her wrists, the bangles looked very nice. I sat down by the roadside and stayed there the whole night. The policemen questioned me once, but I told them the truth. They said, "May God never make one poor." Once or twice, Mianji, I thought of digging a hole right there by the roadside and burying her. But the final prayer for the dead had to be said. Then, in the morning, God sent you there. If you hadn't come, I would have carried her around as a mother-monkey carries her dead baby. This was what happened, Mianji.'

He drew a deep breath, shook his head and wiped his eyes with the loose end of his turban. Then, as if he had forgotten to tell an important detail, he said, 'Mianji, Kalli loved me very much. I am so much older than her, but she had fought her whole family and married me. I too had to fight everyone to be with her. We had fought against the whole world to love each other, Mianji.'

After a brief pause and some thinking, he clasped Mian Saiful Haq's feet and said, 'I shouldn't have been talking about such personal matters. Mianji, please don't mind my telling you all these things.'

Mian Saiful Haq patted him on the shoulder and after wiping his face with the facecloth, went out of the room. He returned a little later to tell him the woman who bathed the dead was there. The shroud too had arrived, and Shafqat, Mianji's son, had arranged for the grave as well.

Ghafoora came and stood by him. With the innocence of a child, he said, 'After she is bathed, Mianji, I would like to take a last look at her.'

And Mian Saiful Haq went out with the facecloth stuffed between his teeth.

When he came back again, his hands smelled of camphor and the essence of vetiver. The bath had been given. He didn't say anything to Ghafoora who sat holding a corner of a table-cover over his hand, looking at an embroidered flower. As soon as he saw Mian Saiful Haq, he stood up, walked over to him and said, 'Mianji, I forgot to tell you that Kalli was very clever with embroidering.' Mianji started walking towards the door without saying anything. Ghafoora followed him. At the door he stopped and asked, 'May I come in, Mianji?'

'Yes, yes,' Mian Saiful Haq said, 'No one will observe purdah from you,' and moved on. Ghafoora was behind him.

A number of women had gathered in the courtyard, most of them shedding tears. Some sat to a side reading the Holy Book. When Ghafoora came in, no one bothered covering herself up, but the crying became more intense. Mian Saiful Haq took out a five-rupee note and extended it towards the woman who had bathed Kalli. But she rubbed her red eyes and said, 'No, Mianji, I too have to die one day. Who knows I too may die by the roadside. No, sir, I won't take the money.'

'By the roadside!' Mianji's wife screamed, 'Like my Hamid.'

Unmindful of the women around, Mian Saiful Haq cried openly. Then he stuffed his facecloth between his teeth, and stood with his hand on Ghafoora's shoulder. A while later he took the facecloth out and said, 'Strange things happen in my God's world. Some die by the roadside and yet get a decent burial. You say Hamid died years ago, but I say he died today and his dead-body is lying right here before our eyes.'

The women resumed crying.

Ghafoora stood quietly, looking at the pink silk sheet covering Kalli's body and gently moving in the light breeze. After crying her fill, Mianji's wife lifted a corner of the sheet, and reciting the *Kalima-e Shahadat*, opened the folds of the shroud over Kalli's face. She looked at Ghafoora.

All the women were looking at Ghafoora.

In agitation Mian Saiful Haq looked at Ghafoora and said, 'Why man? Don't you recognize her? It is my Hamid. It is your Kalli.'

Ghafoora's eyes suddenly turned dry. Without batting his eye-lids he kept staring at Kalli's face. The women were absolutely silent.

Then Ghafoora's hand moved. As he extended it to touch Kalli, Mianji's wife said, 'No, no, you cannot do that. After her death she has become a stranger to you. It would be sinful of you even to touch her bed.'

Ghafoora was stunned. For a while he stood frozen, leaning a little, his hand extended. Then he straightened up but didn't take his eyes off Kalli's face.

Suddenly, Mian Saiful Haq shook him hard by his shoulders and said, 'Come on man, cry; cry openly, unashamedly. You'll die if you don't. Your heartbeat will stop. You'll be paralyzed. When my Hamid died, I felt the same way. The last six years I have spent in a daze. Today that I have cried, I feel relieved.'

'I'm all right, Mianji,' Ghafoora said slowly. He walked up to the corner of the courtyard where Kalli had been given the ritual funeral bath. Like a guilty man, he stole a glance at Mian Saiful Haq, bent down, picked up the pieces of broken bangles and put them in his pocket.

The women cried so bitterly that, for once, even the men sitting in the guest room and standing outside in the street were shaken up.

And just as Ghafoora moved to return, Mian Saiful Haq said, 'Let all the women move to one side. I decree that Ghafoora can touch his wife's body.'

'If he isn't allowed to do that, he is going to lose his mind,' he whispered in the ears of his daughter who stood nearby.

In his dazed state, Ghafoora moved forward, lowered himself on Kalli's face, and lifted a lock of her hair that had fallen on her forehead and joined it with the rest of her wet hair. Instead of saying something to Kalli, he said, 'Listen, Ghafooray . . .'

Then dry-eyed and pale-faced, he walked out of the house.

'I am more worried about that unfortunate man now,' Mian Saiful Haq said.

When Kalli's body was carried out for burial, a large number of people went along. It was a well-attended funeral prayer. When the grave was ready, Ghafoora took out a piece of the broken bangle and stuck it in the dirt on the grave.

Mian Saiful Haq was telling people, 'If I had had a chance to bury Hamid, I couldn't have done better than this. I have just done my duty.'

When he returned from the graveyard, a huge crowd of dedicated men were with him. Everyone was talking about his piety and goodness, and everybody agreed that man's humanity hadn't died out in the fourteenth century. It was very much alive, especially in people like Mian Saiful Haq.

Whenever Mian Saiful Haq heard those words of praise, he protested, 'No, no, I'm not capable of anything. No man is capable of much. It's all God's favour. Only my God enabled me to do what I did. It's His favour.'

Then tears would glint in his eyes. He would take a deep breath and say, 'I did not bury a poor indigent woman. I have come back from burying my Hamid after six long years. I swear I'll go to her grave to sprinkle water over it and pray for her soul every Muharram.' People listening to him felt they had noticed a halo around his head.

He said goodbye to people once he was in his street. He brought some of the elders with him into his sitting room. All of a sudden he asked, 'Where is Ghafoora?'

After looking around for him in the sitting room, he came out in the street and in a loud voice, as it were, asked himself, 'Where did Ghafoora go to?'

Almost at a run, he went through the street as far as the main road. Seeing him in that state, people who were going back home suddenly turned and gathered around him. 'I don't know where that Ghafoora vanished,' he said.

'And neither do we,' the people said looking at each other. 'We didn't see him anywhere along the way.'

When he returned, he went straight inside his house and said to his wife, 'I don't know where that Ghafoora went.'

His wife, in answer, fired a question at him, 'When will you take me to visit the grave?'

'Soon,' he answered.

The next day he took his wife, and all his sons and daughters to see the grave.

The soyem for the dead was held. Until the fortieth day, the imam of the mosque was called every Thursday to say a prayer for the dead and to partake of the food. Then the fortieth day ceremony was held. That day Hamid's sisters put a string of flowers around his picture.

After this enormous bump, Mian Saiful Haq's life again became the same paved road, shining and straight, shaded by trees on either side, over which he glided smoothly with the ease of a casual stroller. He again became like a man who may be talking about Jallianwala Bagh massacre while eating, but not letting even a single morsel of food to miss the opening of his mouth. Even the wall which earlier on would suddenly appear on his way and block it, no longer did so. Now, it was all bright and clear ahead.

It happened about a year later. Mian Saiful Haq again woke up with the call for the morning prayer—'Salaat is better than sleep,' and went to the mosque with the blue facecloth slunk over his shoulder. He returned telling his sandal-wood beads, as usual carefully avoiding to walk near the marijuana addict Sharif's stall. He read some passages from the Holy Book, *Du'a-e Ganj ul-Arsh*, and *Qasidah Burdah*. The paperboy rolled up the newspaper and slid it through the broken glass in the window and said, 'Greetings, Mianji.'

Blowing on his chest, Mian Saiful Haq said, 'So, you are here. Greetings to you too.'

Suddenly he heard again, 'Greetings, Mianji.'

'So you are here,' he said out of habit and was about to respond to the greetings when his mouth fell open and stayed open for some time. He narrowed his eyes to peer behind the broken glass. It seemed as if his eyes had been glued to some object there.

'Mianji,' he heard again.

Mian Saiful Haq blinked his eyes for the first time during all this. He jumped up to open the door, and said, 'Come in, come on in. Where have you been? Where had you suddenly disappeared to? I kept looking for you everywhere in the streets. And what an unusual shape you are in! Come on in. Wonder of wonders. I thought you had . . .'

Ghafoora came in. He had wrapped himself in a discoloured old sheet and was wearing a soiled, oily cap. His eyes had receded into his sockets, and the cheekbones and eyebrows seemed unnaturally prominent. His nose had become more hooked. He hadn't shaved for days, and his beard looked like salt and pepper now. His lips were so tightly stuck to each other that it seemed they would begin to bleed if they were separated. He followed Mian Saiful Haq into the room and stopped exactly where a year ago he had sat down to tell him his whole story.

Mian Saiful Haq seemed to be staring in space as he looked at Ghafoora. He too went and stood where he had earlier been sitting down to listen to Ghafoora's story. Then when Mianji sat down, Ghafoora did too. The day's newspaper lay under the window, and in front, on the table, stood the Koran on a folding stand, *Du'a-e Ganj ul-Arsh* and *Qasidah Burdah*. It seemed as if the story that Ghafoora had begun a year ago was still continuing and with the same intensity, so that both the teller and the listener had been frozen in their positions.

'We thought,' Mian Saiful Haq said, 'you had forgotten us completely.'

'How can that be, Mianji?' Ghafoora said. 'Only when I forget Kalli, will I forget you. And I shall never forget her as long as I live.'

After a pause he continued: 'Mianji you are a very pious person, and I am such a selfish wretch. The first selfishness I did was that after Kalli was buried, I left without saying goodbye to you. And my second selfishness was that... it seems to me that...'

He paused, rubbed his eyes and said, 'It seems to me as if my Kalli is still lying where she was, by the roadside.'

'You must be going crazy,' Mian Saiful Haq remonstrated him mildly. 'Man, didn't I tell you that day to let go of yourself and have a good cry, or you'll lose your mind?'

'No, Mianji,' Ghafoora said, 'I haven't lost my mind. If I had to lose it, I would have lost it at the time when I heard dead Kalli's bangles clinking. I swear to you Mianji, there hasn't been a day in my life when Kalli's memory hasn't cursed me, hasn't told me that she was still lying on the side of the road wrapped in that sheet.'

'Something has surely gone wrong with you, my good man,' Mianji said, troubled.

'Mianji,' Ghafoora began. Tears began to flow from his eyes as generously as they did a year ago, and his voice started becoming alternately hoarse and low. 'Kalli loved me very much, Mianji. I am so much older than her, but she had fought everyone in her family to be with me. We had fought the whole world to love each other. But I am such a miserable creature that I couldn't even spend a pice on her burial. I was sorely remiss. I didn't pay her what was her due after death, did I? But I have worked very hard in the past year. I fell ill too, even had to stay in the hospital. But I have done what I could. I don't know how much you spent on her burial. It must have been a lot, for you had just made her your own. But if I could myself have spent on her burial, . . .' He put his hand in his pocket and brought out a few crumpled notes. He put them on the floor and said, 'If I could have, I wouldn't have spent more than this; perhaps may even have spent less.'

He kept quiet for a moment.

Mianji too didn't say anything.

After some time, Ghafoora said, 'Mianji, please take this money. If you do that, my heart will be content. I will believe that I myself had arranged for Kalli's funeral. Kalli wouldn't curse me either. Her soul would be happy. Please take it, Mianji.'

By now, Mianji had begun panting. He thundered, 'So, you think I had made some kind of deal with you? Take away this money. I am not hungry for your measly rupees. You think like you I too...' He picked up the notes and threw them at Ghafoora, scattering them all over the floor. Ghafoora just stood there dumbfounded.

But when he noticed that Mian Saiful Haq had begun shaking as well, he said quietly, 'Listen, Mianji, please don't get angry at me. You have done me the greatest favour that anyone could do. I am not a low wretch to forget that. But the thing is, Mianji, that you had buried Hamid that day in place of Kalli. My Kalli was still left lying by the roadside unburied. You may throw these rupees into the gutter if you wish, but it's only today that I have lowered my Kalli into the grave.'

LAWRENCE OF THALABIA

The bed was so wide that the sheet covering it was bigger than four single sheets. In its middle, resting against a large bolster cushion, was the senior Malik Sahib, a huge heap of flesh. A troop of menials—a *mirasi*, a barber, a cook, a washer-man, a cobbler, a potter, a farmer—were busy massaging his fingers, toes, calves, thighs, back, and shoulders. I sat at a little distance from them. From my vantage point they looked like a bevy of children holding down a big helium-filled balloon, keeping it from flying away. Then when Khuda Bakhsh stepped into the *chaupal*, the senior Malik said, 'Junior Malik is very happy today. He has his friend visiting him from Lahore.' He tried to side-glance at me and, perhaps, even smile, but the smile never reached me. It was lost somewhere within his bulging cheeks and thick walrus moustache.

I was sitting at a distance because I was soon to be served tea. Bashkoo, placing two chairs and a teapoy at the other end of the *chaupal*, and making me sit in a chair had gone in to call Khuda Bakhsh and bring tea. Bashkoo was Khuda Bakhsh's favourite servant. His name too was Khuda Bakhsh, but Khuda Bakhsh had begun calling him Bashkoo, and now everybody called him Bashkoo.

Khuda Bakhsh's mother had come down with the flu, so he had been going in and out of the *haveli* to inquire after her. This time when he came out, he sat down in a chair facing me and told me that his mother's fever had gone down, and that she was resting. 'If her fever had stayed up, I wouldn't have been able to take you to the falcon-hunt,' he said. 'I call my falcon Lawrence of Thalabia, after Lawrence of Arabia. Doesn't sound too odd, eh?' He laughed and continued, 'After tea, you, I, and Bashkoo will go out of the village. Bashkoo is my falcon's attendant. Consider him his orderly.' He laughed again and said, 'He'll make Lawrence perch on his fist and…'

We were startled by some thwacking sounds. We turned to look towards the group of men. Two men were holding one man down, and the senior Malik was thrashing him and cursing him, using swear-words that only someone in his position could have used. At the same time he was panting and saying, 'Look at the bastard. Some cheek he's got. Telling me in front of all the people to watch my loin-cloth. My privates are showing. Why should it trouble him? After all, it wasn't his mother whose privates were showing.'

Khuda Bakhsh looked at me, smiled, and said, 'The poor fellow has come in for some real thrashing. Until he drops down, father isn't about to stop pounding him.'

Arrogance of his position was noticeable in Khuda Bakhsh's tone. I said, 'But Khuda Bakhsh, you are an educated man. How can you allow this?'

He became apologetic and said, 'What can we do, friend? You can get straight work out of these people only with such treatment.'

Meanwhile, in walked Bashkoo with the tea. Placing the tea on the teapoy, he whispered in Khuda Bakhsh's ear, 'This Skeen is not that kind of a boy, junior Malik; why is he getting such a rough deal?'

'Oh, so this is Skeen!' Even Khuda Bakhsh was surprised. He said, 'This boy hardly ever says a word. Prays five times a day. He chants the *azan* so sweetly that even sparrows alight on the minarets of the mosque to listen. I wonder what nonsense he uttered before father.'

The senior Malik had let up on his pounding. Skeen was hanging listless in the hands of the two men grabbing him.

'Let go of the wretch,' senior Malik thundered, and like a stone, Skeen was let drop on the ground, face down. 'Remove this consort of your mothers from here,' Malik Sahib thundered again, and a whole crowd of people rushed eagerly to pick Skeen up, so eagerly, in fact, that one would have thought they were instead going to lift Malik Sahib himself and throw him out. From among those who rushed to help the boy get up, one straightened himself and in consternation said, 'Skeen is chanting the *azan*!'

Then Skeen himself sat up, looked around, and, as though seeking Malik Sahib's permission to leave, asked, 'Time for the Asr prayer must be over by now?'

Nobody dared answer him. He stood up. I noticed that he was a six-foot tall, straight-backed, good-looking young man. And as he went down the steps of the *chaupal*, he looked like the minaret of a mosque.

The senior Malik was telling those around him, 'Such mother's consorts dare come to the *chaupal* to make small-talk, but don't have the manners to conduct themselves in a *chaupal*. Says, "Malikji, you are showing your privates." If that was indeed the case, he could have looked elsewhere. If a person closes his eyes at midday, even the sun is lost from sight. Why the hell did he have to go on staring at me?' After a pause, he made an attempt to turn around, and asked, 'Why, junior Malik? Have you offered tea to your friend yet?' And without waiting for the answer, asked one of his menials to massage his right arm. He said, 'It's hurting from the thrashing I've had to give to the bastard.'

'Who was that bastard?' I asked Khuda Bakhsh quietly.

'His name is Skeen,' Khuda Bakhsh said. 'A weaver by profession. See that sheet covering father's bed? He wove that himself. Quite a skilful artisan. Very pious too, but also a bit of a simpleton. I don't know how the hapless fellow dared to question my father. He looks such a humble, self-effacing person.'

Bashkoo said, 'Sir, his real name is Miskeen, meaning humble. Muhammad Miskeen. People have given him the nickname Skeen, as they have given me Bashkoo.'

I said, 'I had to come here to find out that even a simple word like Miskeen can be twisted out of shape.'

'Speak softly, friend,' Khuda Bakhsh said and looked fearfully at the senior Malik. 'If he hears you, you may well be spared, but I will be in hot soup.'

'Not much fear of that. His hand is already hurting.'

Khuda Bakhsh didn't appreciate my comment. He gave me a disparaging look and said to Bashkoo, 'Go to the stable. See if

Beg has got the horses ready. If he has saddled them, then go and wake up Lawrence. He's been hungry since morning.'

When Bashkoo was gone, he turned to me and said, 'Look here, man. You haven't been here more than a day and already you have started finding fault with my father. There's a saying here that the size of one's head determines the size of one's headache. My father is obliged to give such beatings. If he doesn't do that, he can't run this big estate.' He paused, then added, 'What are you thinking about?'

I said, 'Just wondering about the posts of Malik Sahib's bed. They're huge. Yet when I looked closely, they seemed to be made of wood.'

'What do you mean? What did you expect them to be made of?' Khuda Bakhsh asked surprised.

I said, 'When I looked at them the first time, I thought each corner of the bed was being propped up by a Miskeen.'

'The open air of the village has definitely affected your mind, Khuda Bakhsh said. 'You're flipping.'

I continued, 'And I also thought, Khuda Bakhsh, that if all the four Miskeens decided to let go of their posts, the bed will collapse.'

'The horses are ready, junior Malik,' Bashkoo came and announced.

His left fist was encased in a leather gauntlet upon which sat Lawrence of Thalabia. A light chain, one end of which was attached to the gauntlet, dangled from one of the bird's claws. Its eyes were hooded by leather covers. When Khuda Bakhsh removed them, I noticed a terrible ferocity in the bird's eyes.

'So, what do you think of my falcon?' Khuda Bakhsh asked. I whispered in his ears, 'He seems to be the senior Malik of the falcons.'

Khuda Bakhsh chortled, as though by necessity. He put the covers back on the falcon's eyes, and we moved on to the stable.

******

Khuda Bakhsh swore that the horse given to me for the ride was the gentlest of all the steeds in his father's stable. I had my doubts and said, 'A well-fed, sturdy horse like this cannot be too gentle.' But he said, 'Believe me, all its obstinacy has been purged out. Now it's the humblest and tamest of the beasts. It is necessary to keep it well-fed. The district officials who come to visit here are not adept riders, being more used to leisurely rides in cars. But one has to be sharp and alert while horse-riding. So, for visiting officials, father always chooses this horse. One looks dignified riding it, and it isn't quick to gallop and dislodge the rider if its reins are loosened. That's why this horse has been ridden either by deputy commissioners, or, today, by you.'

'No wonder,' I said, 'You look like a junior court functionary to me.'

Khuda Bakhsh's own horse was a head-strong animal. Its ears were raised, nostrils dilated, and it was ready to chew off the bit and the reins as it trod. But Khuda Bakhsh was a good rider. He always kept his horse ahead of mine. My horse too had its ears raised high but walked like a bashful bride stepping into her in-laws' for the first time.

Bashkoo followed us with the falcon on his fist, moving at a pace between a run and a walk.

As soon as we turned, after passing the clutch of acacias, there was a vast stretch of barren land ahead with solitary acacias growing here and there. These trees didn't look too healthy; they were stunted, and their branches were twisted and bare, but they were the favourite perch of the starlings before evening, Khuda Bakhsh told me, 'And a starling is a falcon's favourite food. My Lawrence becomes frantic as soon as it spots a starling. Its meat is as potent for Lawrence as a shot of Scotch is for me.'

'But Khuda Bakhsh,' I said, 'a starling is a gentle bird, even gentler than a sparrow. The pale and raw skin at the edges of its beak make it look so innocent. And it is perhaps the mildest, the most harmless of all the birds. Why do you people crave for the blood of such creatures?'

Khuda Bakhsh said, 'If you are so intent on making a speech, wait till we get to a mound on the way. Then you can climb it and deliver your sermon. Bashkoo and I swear to give you all our attention. Just hold your reins a while; watch my Lawrence. See, it's already fluttering its wings; it must have smelled the desert air.'

'A starling!' hissed Bashkoo, like a snake, and Khuda Bakhsh reined in his horse. My horse that was just behind his, stopped too. Before taking the covers off the falcon's eyes, Khuda Bakhsh asked me to watch attentively. 'This will be a memorable experience in your life,' he said. 'The sound of the falcon swooping down on the starling is like that of a sword cutting through the air. Watch!'

Khuda Bakhsh removed the covers from the bird's eyes, and turned it towards the crooked acacia far away, on which fate had brought a starling. The falcon suddenly became wild. 'He has seen the starling,' Khuda Bakhsh told me, exulting. Taking the chain off, Bashkoo freed the falcon from the gauntlet, and the sword of death went cutting through the air. The starling flew off, but the falcon swooped down and fell upon it. The starling's quick, sharp scream echoed through the vastness, but soon the falcon returned to Bashkoo's hand, with the starling caught in its claws. It began tearing at the starling's body immediately, and its curved beak became drenched in blood. Khuda Bakhsh kept enlightening me: 'Watch the way he eats. See how skilfully he removes the meat from the bones; even human beings cannot demonstrate such neatness. And then this is raw meat, fresh and loaded with nutrition.'

'Damn you,' I said. 'You are as bad as a cannibal.'

But Khuda Bakhsh kept laughing and looking at me as though I were handicapped, and he didn't want to hurt my feelings.

After the falcon had devoured its prey, it looked as though it were inebriated. It shut its eyes, and Khuda Bakhsh said, 'Lawrence is sloshed.' Then he laughed and got on his horse. He drew in the reins to turn around, but stopped. After some thinking, he asked Bashkoo, 'Now that we've come so far, why not visit Baba Yaru as well?'

Bashkoo said, 'Baba Yaru's eyes are as sharp as a falcon's. It's possible he may have seen us. He'll protest if we go back without saying hello to him.'

'Yes, that's right,' Khuda Bakhsh agreed and turned towards me. 'Let's go have a cup of some authentic Thal tea. Baba Yaru's *dera* is not very far from here. He is one of our old tenant-farmers. You'll like him.'

The beastly manner in which the falcon had devoured the starling still lay heavy on my heart. I said, 'It doesn't matter. Take me wherever you wish.'

After travelling about three miles, we came to a farm-house, neatly plastered with reddish clay. Khuda Bakhsh proposed dismounting quietly and approaching the house stealthily. He said, 'It'll be great fun. Once Bashkoo and I arrived here very quietly and sat down on the cot besides Baba Yaru. He kept twining his rope, his old lady Began was busy blowing into the hearth to get the fire going, and their daughter Rangi kept on chopping fodder with the chaff-cutter. Nobody noticed us. And when they did, he was so embarrassed, he couldn't utter a word, and Began started cursing their old age. And Rangi laughed so much that she didn't stop in spite of Baba Yaru's scolding, and ran inside the store-room.'

We dismounted behind the house and moved forward slowly. There were some large acacias in the courtyard. A cow and some sheep and goats sat under one tree, perhaps out of habit, for the tree wasn't casting any shade over them. Nearby, on a cot, sat Baba Yaru twining wool. The fire was burning in the hearth next to the wall, and Began sat next to it vigorously stirring a pot, as though she were cooking stones. They were so busy in their work that neither of them noticed our arrival. At last Began said, 'I'm getting worried. Rangi should have been back by now.'

'She'll be here,' Baba Yaru said. 'If she has gone to our Maliks, then it's like going to her own home. Don't you know how friendly Malik's daughter and Rangi are? Remember the head-cover she gave Rangi last year? It was such fine silk. Rangi kept folding and folding it, and finally it became so small that it went through the eyelet of your pair of tongs. It must have cost at least a hundred rupees. If she has gone to visit her dear friend, then there's nothing to worry about. Staying there for the night will be like being a guest of angels.'

'I think we should go back,' Khuda Bakhsh said quietly. 'If they see us, they will go overboard in showing us their hospitality.'

And Bashkoo whispered, 'The old lady has no sense of how to make tea. It tastes like cough medicine. If Rangi were here, it would have been a different matter. Her tea gives you a high.'

Khuda Bakhsh burst out laughing. The old man and his wife were startled. They turned to look and were flustered. They immediately began importuning Khuda Bakhsh to sit down and have tea, as if their humble abode would turn into a golden palace and their goats into horses by his gracious stay.

Khuda Bakhsh explained that it was dusk and they weren't without enemies. He reminded Baba Yaru that there was a guard of armed men on the ramparts of their *haveli* everyday after sunset. If he were not back before nightfall, the senior Malik Sahib was sure to raise a huge fuss. He said he had come out for the falcon's hunt, and just thought of inquiring after Baba Yaru. Was he well? Was there any problem? No? All right, they'd better be on their way now. Lifting his foot into the stirrup, Khuda Bakhsh said, 'Don't worry about Rangi. If it gets late, my sister will make her sleep over. And now, it does seem late.'

Baba Yaru said, 'This morning she came upon some chongan vegetable growing in a bush. She knows her friend likes it, so she insisted she would take it to the haveli. She washed her clothes, dried them by afternoon, put them on and tying the chongan in a pouch left for the *haveli*. She's a sensible adult, but I worry if it gets dark on the way. There's vast barrenness out there—that scares me.'

Khuda Bakhsh tried to assure him, 'Rangi has nothing to fear; even the sparrows are safe on our estate. Everyone knows she is your daughter, and everyone knows you are our man. Don't worry. All right, we'll be leaving now.'

******

On the way back, Khuda Bakhsh kept talking about birds of prey—falcons, hawks, etc. Knowing my literary taste, he mentioned Khushhal Khan Khattak's and Allama Iqbal's hawks. He talked of the royal raiments, sword-hilts, and coins of ancient emperors embossed with images of birds of prey and tried to prove that the falcon was a species of regal birds. Finally, he came up with an argument to quell all doubt; he said, 'Have you ever seen any poor man own a falcon?'

'No,' I said, 'the poor usually go for starlings.'

Khuda Bakhsh was about to give a suitable rejoinder to my sarcasm when he suddenly reined in his horse. A young girl stood at the edge of the clutch of acacias. She was Rangi. Whatever her real name was, she could have been called a creature of colours. Of the seven hues of the rainbow, none was missing from her person. Whatever was spared from her eyes, hair, face, and lips, had merged into her clothes—her lungi, kurta, and the head-cover. At that moment the sun, at the far end of the flatland, lay hugging the horizon, reclining as it were, and taking a parting look at the earth. A few patches of cloud in the middle of the sky had already turned pink, and a dazzling pink was lending one edge of that clutch of acacias a radiant glow. If Rangi's toes with their broken nails weren't sticking out of her plain sandals, I would have had to struggle hard to convince myself that she wasn't simply out of this world. One look at her was enough to convince even the staunchest of atheists of the existence of God, the creator of such exquisite beauty.

All that passed through my mind in that one moment when Khuda Bakhsh reined in his horse. Rangi halted. Bashkoo came running up from behind and said: 'Look, junior Malik, how stupid this girl is.' Then he asked the girl, 'Is this any time for setting out on such a long journey? Didn't the lady of the house stop you?'

'Come with us,' Khuda Bakhsh ordered her indulgently. 'Those who are our enemies are also the enemies of our tenants. And our enemies are legion. The sun is setting, and it will be a moonless night. It is a long and deserted way back to your house, and you have started out at this time. That won't do. You must come with us. And I'm going to go and ask my sister if this is any way to treat one's friends. You may be poor but still you are human. Come Rangi.'

'My poor father...' Rangi uttered just three words, but set a ripple going through her beauty.

'We just explained to your father,' Khuda Bakhsh said. 'We told him if we found you near the village, we'll take you back to the *haveli*. You silly girl, you don't go out into the wilderness at this hour. These are not good times, you know. Come.'

Rangi accompanied us. When we returned to the village, she went towards the *haveli* with Bashkoo, and we to the *chaupal*. After supper, the senior Malik Sahib questioned me about the falcon-hunt and then, for a long while, kept taking about hawks, falcons, dogs, and horses. I whispered into Khuda Bakhsh's ears, 'Do people here talk only about hawks and dogs, never about human beings?'

'Watch it, man,' Khuda Bakhsh warned me, 'or father will turn you into another Skeen.'

After the senior Malik had retired, it was now time for the junior Malik to shoot the breeze. He held forth in praise of his Lawrence of Thalabia for a long time. Only when Bashkoo came with some message and interrupted him, did his listeners get a chance to put in a word edgewise. One said, 'Baba Rehman is about a hundred. He says in all his years he hasn't come across another falcon as sharp as Lawrence. He says the junior Malik's falcon is a lion among falcons.'

******

After Khuda Bakhsh had gone inside the *haveli*, and Bashkoo had made my bed ready and had departed after placing a jug of water on the teapoy, I lay down on the bed. The sky was dark and clear; stars so numerous that one reeled just looking at them. Utter silence ruled over the village. Since it was early in the night, even the dogs were quiet yet. One heard only the crickets chirping, but that sound is very much part of the stillness.

It was then that Rangi's image came and stood before me, the image of a confident, assertive young woman asking me, if I dared, to find any flaw in her. I viewed that image, which I had preserved in my mind since that colourful moment in the evening, from every possible angle, and said to her, 'Yes Rangi, I can spot one. Your flaw is that you are human, and human beings can be very weak and vulnerable creatures.'

When the sparrows in the acacia in the lower yard of the *chaupal* began their colloquy, I woke up. The early morning prayer was about to be said in the neighbouring mosque, and someone was loudly urging the faithful to form rows. The minarets of the mosque seemed to quiver against the sky in the first light. A kite swooped down and tried to perch on the spire of the dome, but after fluttering a few times and being unable to keep its balance, flew back up. I asked myself where that kite had come from so early in the morning, and answered myself, 'From the same place as the sparrows had.'

The sun wasn't up yet when Bashkoo brought me a glass of milk, full to the brim with thick cream. Hurriedly I splashed some water on my face. As I was coming out of the washroom, I saw Khuda Bakhsh coming up the steps of the *chaupal*. 'Let's go for a walk to the clutch of acacias,' he said, 'I promise to talk to you only about human beings today.'

'All right,' I said. Then I stopped at the steps and asked him, 'Listen, is Rangi gone?' Suddenly he burst out laughing, doubled over and fell on my cot. 'So, the stone has bled at last,' he spluttered. He slapped his thighs amid the bursts of laughter and said, 'The layer of ice was thick, but it began to melt at last, eh?' Then he clasped me in his embrace and said, 'You've suddenly become very dear to me. For a long time I thought you were made of stone.' With difficulty he brought his laughter under control and said, 'How can Rangi go away just like that? She'll have some butter-milk, eat some parathas. Her friend wouldn't let her go back just like that. If my mother hadn't been unwell, Rangi would have slept in the same room as my sister. She may not even be up yet.' Then after a pause he added, 'I'll take you to see her before she leaves. In fact, why don't we have our afternoon tea at Baba Yaru's place?'

Just then Bashkoo came running and screaming, 'Junior Malik! junior Malik!' He was running so fast the sparrows flew off the acacia.

'What is it?' Khuda Bakhsh asked anxiously. 'Is mother all right?'

'Mother is well, but... but... ,' Bashkoo's eyes were bulging out of their sockets, his nostrils were swelled and his mouth agape.

'But what? Spill it out, man?' Khuda Bakhsh snapped at him.

And Bashkoo gave him, as it were, the news of the greatest disaster in the universe: 'Someone has wrung Lawrence's neck. He's dead.'

Khuda Bakhsh was stunned, unable to move. After a long pause, he said, 'Bring Rangi over here.'

Bashkoo ran back inside. I asked Khuda Bakhsh, 'What has Rangi to do with it?'

'Everything. Just wait,' Khuda Bakhsh said. The incident was so grave that I couldn't utter a word.

Bashkoo soon returned with the news that Rangi had left before dawn.

Khuda Bakhsh trained his murderous eyes on me and said, 'See? Didn't I tell you that that wretch murdered my falcon? The whole night she kept threatening to kill me, and I told her not to be silly; starlings could not kill falcons. She's the one who has done it. That ill-bred, miserable wretch. I'll flay her. Just let me get my hands on her!'

A MOTHER'S LOVE

An English officer recruited me from Punjab and sent me to Hong Kong, a Chinese island inhabited by the Chinese and ruled by the English. For a long time, men for the Hong Kong police had been imported from Punjab, but ever since Hitler had begun the war in Europe, the English had got very busy over there, so the demand for Punjabi young men to serve in the Hong Kong police had doubled. I'm a young man, though not of a very solid build—have been rejected by the army recruiting office many times—but this time the doctor, overlooking my flesh-less ribs, complimented me on my height and said that the miniature Chinese would just be scared to death seeing a tall young policeman like me. It was a common belief that sending any young man who was shorter than six feet into the Hong Kong police would be a strategic mistake; the desire to verify the truth of that belief had brought me to Hong Kong.

I had heard from the veterans of the Hong Kong police force that Hong Kong was a fun place to be. All the countries which were ruled by foreigners were fun places to be in, and Hong Kong was a veritable paradise for policemen. To get a commendation from the police headquarters, the public service you needed to perform was to drive the dwarfy Chinese begging-women away from the city streets and pavements, and to pick their children with your thumb and forefinger like dirty rags and toss them back to their mothers when they slipped out of their laps like shoes from feet. You could search every Chinese traveller entering Hong Kong at the China-Kowloon border and, after lightening some of his load, push him back into China. You could choose any young Chinese girl walking the streets along the sea-front and, after handing out some small change to her closely chaperoning mother, take her to your barracks and make everybody there happy and grateful. And if some sergeant happened to come by for a surprise inspection, hand the girl over to him and go have a restful sleep. In short, it was fun to be there. But as soon as our ship docked at Singapore, a Madrasi seaman started the rumour that war was about to start in the Eastern seas as well. The English captain of the ship, incensed by the rumour, fired the Madrasi seaman from his job for wilfully spreading rumours and handed him over to the Singapore police—so the rumour didn't spread far.

When we reached Hong Kong, the air was rife with whispers about the impending war. It could begin any day, we heard. Wide, staring eyes of the multitudes told volumes, and people staggered about as if they had already been shot at. The Chinese refugees, squatting on the Hong Kong pavements or on the winding Kowloon roads, would sit staring at the horizon as if waiting for the bombers, only one inquiry squirming on their lacerated lips and scabs: Whatever is to happen, why doesn't it happen quickly? Terror-stricken refugee women were giving birth prematurely. Mobs of famished Chinese children roamed the streets in search of food. An English administrator had gone even so far as to declare in an official meeting that it could not be the government's responsibility to look after the needs of each and every child. Children whose parents were alive should wear collars around their necks, as dogs do, and any such child found without a collar should be taken to the Kowloon border and driven back into China. It was becoming impossible for the police to keep the pavements clear for the promenading sahibs. Trenches were being dug; shelters built; the beauty of the buildings getting buried behind sandbags. It looked as though the whole city was under construction. Utter silence reigned over Hong Kong and Kowloon after dark. It was said that in the days gone by, the Hong Kong lights, after diving into the sea and bouncing back, would stir desire even in old, decrepit bodies. But now the sea between Hong Kong and Kowloon seemed the repository of the world's darkness. In the dark, after being exhausted by the day's training parade, I would lay myself down on the cot and try to think pleasant thoughts, but the terror of stillness and darkness would echo in my ears like the rumble of bomber planes. I would think of my mother and weep.

Even during the day, people's stony stares and fear-stricken faces made me feel as though they had lost their mothers and were looking for them. They had the bewildered look of babies who had been pulled away from their mother's breast before having had their fill of milk. Time and again I would think of my mother. I could still succeed in eluding her image during the day; but at night it would haunt me and cling to my eyes. I used to hide my face in the pillow and cry like a child.

Mother had tried to dissuade me from going to Hong Kong. She had said, 'I hear, Hong Kong lies where the earth ends. Son, if you were going to Delhi or Calcutta, I could still dream about you. But you are going so far, to Hong Kong. There will be oceans and mountains between us. And then, my son, if the war starts over there as well, and you, God forbid, are wounded, whose hand in this accursed village, tell me, will I hold to raise myself from my cot? Don't go, my son. I am used to living in want. It worries me to think who will wash your clothes over there. Who will massage oil in your hair? Who will pull out the hair of your eye-lash from your eye if it lodges there? Who will sew the buttons on your shirts? And what will happen if, God forbid, you come down with pneumonia, as you did last year? Who will rub almond oil on your temples if you suffer from headache in half your head, as you did the year before last? No, son, don't go. Come, sit here, next to me. If we starve, we'll starve together. And, son, suppose you are over there in Hong Kong, and I die here, who is going to take your place to throw in my grave the handful of dirt which Maulviji says glitters like a cluster of stars in the grave's darkness. Tell me that.' Despite all that, I went. And when on parting I looked at her face, not one of its wrinkles was dry. The image of the tear-drenched face was engraved on my eye-balls, and at night, lying down in my barracks, I would see nothing besides that pallid, woe-begone face. I would question her, 'Mother, why don't you blink your eyes? Why don't your eyeballs move? Who are you staring at, mother?' And I asked those questions because she looked to me like the Chinese refugees staring at the horizon from where the bombers were to appear, bombers which were going to drop a thousand bombs per minute.

But one day those staring eyes stayed glued to the horizon, for the bombers arrived from an altogether different direction. Hong Kong, the city awash in the sounds of pianos and organ music, racked with the bomb blasts. The anti-aircraft guns fired a few volleys and then became silent and lay down, their necks lowered, like exhausted boas. The uprooted lamp-posts, tumbling down from the heights and smashing the brains of the refugees scattered on the streets, rolled down to the sea-front. The city buildings changed places. Debris of the outer walls flew into the back-gardens, and the uprooted garden bushes came to rest in drawing rooms. A splinter from a bomb pierced through the belly of a Punjabi policeman on duty. His guts spilled out. In the agony of death he squirmed a few times and his neck got entangled in his gut. An English officer, not caring for the horror of the bombs, photographed the scene. We, the trainees, were driven into shelters where English children and even their mothers were crying, 'Mother, mother.' An old Englishwoman passed by the shelter door, scanning each face. Her eyes brimful of tears, as she moved forward, she kept rubbing with her hands the flabby skin under her chin. After she had studied the face of the last one of us, saying the words, 'My son,' she fell down on the ground with a thud. We were all filled with enormous pity. It didn't take long for the Japanese to arrive. They came and took over. And I, who had come from Punjab to become a policeman, became a prisoner of war. That day I cried bitter tears. I felt as though I had lost what was most precious to me in life—my mother, as though it was the war that had snatched her away from my arms, as though until now I had been sitting next to her, but now I had just buried her and had been left empty-handed. Despite effort, I couldn't recall my mother's pallid face any longer; its familiar features had dimmed, lost in the haze in front of my eyes.

In the same state of mind, I stayed locked up in the pen for the prisoners of war. Every limb in my body ached, and my whole body felt hollow. If even by mistake I happened to shake my head, I felt a heavy stone rolling from one of my ears to the other. At times when I breathed in, the air would stay stuck in my lungs. I would have to hit my chest to exhale. But soon I got used to life in imprisonment. And it took me even less time to get to know the Japanese. Some buttons on my shirt had come off. I begged a Japanese for a button. With a jerk, he pulled off a bunch of hair from my chest and handing it to me said, 'Tie your button-holes with this.' The blood oozing from where the hair had been pulled out helped me overcome the first stage of acquaintanceship with the Japanese. One day a Japanese officer ordered us to line up. As he was stepping back, his foot fell into a pothole and he staggered. His cap fell off his head and one arm of his eye-glasses was dislodged. Sarbuland, who was standing next to me, smiled. 'You find it funny, eh?' the officer asked him and shot him. The bullet tore through his ribs. For a moment I felt as though I was the one who had been shot at. I fainted. Then when I heard the Japanese laughing uproariously, I came to and looked. I also understood the reason for their laughter. The bullet going through Sarbuland's chest had lodged itself into the entrails of Waris who was standing right behind him. And while Sarbuland had fallen backwards, Waris had fallen forward, face down. And in the agony of death the two of them had torn each other's limbs. Waris' death was a hilarious joke for the Japanese. That day, we knew in an instant all there was to know about the Japanese. Smile or raise your eyes if you were ordered to; swallow your spit to wet your dry throats if you were ordered to, otherwise, just stand stock-still, in whatever position you were, facing whichever direction, like clay figurines. And then I had become a little too greedy for life. I wanted to live at all costs. Someday, I knew, the war would end, and some ship carrying me on board and passing through the Hoogly, would take me to Calcutta. And then some train would deliver me from there to Punjab, where I would go and sit down, next to my mother, holding her knees, and not abandon that posture till doomsday. That greed for life had kept me from showing any cheek to the Japanese.

For a number of days we stayed in Hong Kong, serving our new masters. Our shorts were torn but we covered our nakedness by stuffing newspapers in them; our chests, sticking out of our buttonless shirts, were bare; we shielded them with folded arms. We had been tamed so well that we could have beaten circus elephants at obedience. One day a Japanese officer told us that on a small island nearby some fishermen, between a hundred and hundred-fifty in all, had set up a front against the Japanese government and were intending to raid Hong Kong. To teach them a lesson, a contingent of Japanese soldiers was to be dispatched from Hong Kong, which would also include some loyal and obedient prisoners of war. My name, for obvious reasons, was at the top of the list. We boarded a steamboat at about 2:00 a.m. An unusually cold breeze was blowing that morning. The open front of my shirt became packed, as it were, with ice-pellets. Snuggling together and huddling close to each other we reached the island before dawn. We landed cautiously and crawling through the bushes inched forward. Suddenly I felt as if a fireworks display was in progress in the east. Even in Punjab I hadn't witnessed a brighter morning. It was like seeing a woman, alone and naked in the privacy of her bedroom. The chirping of the birds was like laughter, and herons, their long legs hanging down, had begun flying over our heads and taking dips in the water.

A small valley, shaped like a Chinese tea-bowl, suddenly appeared before our eyes. Smack in its middle were some huts, and tracks from various directions came and ended near them. There were grass plots around the huts; fringing these was a circle of trees, then there was a circle of bushes and beyond that the golden sand of the shore and the circle of the heaving sea. The whole scene seemed somehow manufactured, almost like a toy, and when I observed the billowing waves in the sea, the Chinese tea-bowl below seemed to be rolling and pitching. We were all baffled by the fact that despite our long wait, we had seen nobody moving about in the huts, not even any children. No smoke had arisen from any of the huts; there wasn't even the sound of any old man's cough. A dog, the only living creature, was rolling on a grassy patch. Getting tired of the wait, the commander shot a bullet into the air. We all cringed and lay down on the ground. But even the shot was unable to stir any movement around the huts. Only the dog stopped its play, lifted its ears for a moment, and then dashed towards the huts, and flocks of sparrows flew up towards the east in such alarm as though they would stop only when they reached the rising sun.

Just then we launched our attack. When we got near the huts we shot a few volleys, and the Japanese commander bellowed the warning in Chinese: 'Anyone hiding in there better come out now. If we come into the huts, no one will be spared.'

Then I witnessed a scene which one may come across only in books about genies and fairies. From one end to the other of that compound, women, in large numbers, old and middle-aged, clad in old and torn rags, emerged from the huts, as though they had just been waiting for that command from the Japanese officer. In an instant we were facing columns of wrinkled faces, sagging skins, and stony eyes. I felt as though some disaster was at hand. The stillness of that moment was awesome. Our shadows, frightfully lengthened by the rising sun, lay, as it were, sprawling on the grassy plots; the women were muttering some *mantras* under their breaths; the whole scene had suddenly become eerie. I felt as if the Chinese tea-bowl was about to be overturned, and all of us to be dumped into the sea.

By the orders of the officer, we surrounded the women. The officer moved up and blared: 'Where are all the men?'

For a moment there was utter silence, like the silence when the canon is being re-loaded to be fired.

Then an old woman, her hair completely grey, took one step forward and said, 'They're at their daily work.'

'Daily work?' the officer roared, 'You mean, to sabotage the Japanese government, to build support for saboteurs on Chinese soil?'

'No,' the old woman said, 'to catch fish.'

'And where are the children and old men? And the girls?'

'Today is the annual celebration of us fishermen,' the old woman kept talking in the same tone, 'They are on the waters to make ready for ...'

'Come here,' the officer pulled her by her hand with a jerk. She fell on the ground, face down. Another officer fired a shot in her back. She uttered a scream; her body convulsed as if she were trying to heave herself up. She turned around. The next moment she fell down again and after a couple of spasms, became motionless, her glazed eyes staring at us. The other women covered their eyes with their hands, and I bit my lip so hard that a tooth went through my flesh.

The flocks of sparrows which had probably returned, took flight once again, squalling, towards Hong Kong.

The long-legged herons dispersed and began flying skittishly as though they were the ones fired at.

Two dogs started barking in the distant huts.

Leaving us Punjabis to watch over the women, the Japanese went into the huts. They kicked things about and did a lot of cursing in there. I was watching the faces of the Chinese women. The sagging skins under their chins were trembling, because of fear of death or perhaps some other sensation, and their misty, meditative eyes were trained on something far off. Finished with the huts, the Japanese shuffled towards the distant seashore, firing at the bushes.

Suddenly one of the women squatted down. When I looked at her, she started and quickly stood up and began to mutter under the breath once again. I was reminded of my mother. I averted my eyes, pretending I couldn't care less what they did. From the corner of my eye, I saw the woman squat down again and begin inching forward, hiding behind the legs of the other women. Reaching the dead body, she looked at me with sheer terror in her eyes. Quickly she spread a piece of cloth over the dead woman's face, turned around and walked back to her place. I tried hard to keep my emotions under wraps, clenching my quivering lips between my teeth; tears welled up in my eyes, nonetheless. The one who had covered the face of the dead woman leaned forward and began observing me closely. When I looked at her, her eyelids blinked and a torrent of tears ran down her eyes into the wrinkles of her face. The cold moist breeze from the sea was piercing through my ribs because of my shirt which was open at the neck, and I was crying. I looked at the other women. No eye was dry. I looked at the old woman's dead body. The breeze had lifted the cloth off her face. Bending down I lifted her head and wrapped the cloth around it. A Japanese soldier charged at me yelling and gave me a hard kick in the back. All the women, except the one who had covered the face of the dead body, hid their faces behind their hands, and I stood up rubbing my back. The Japanese soldier ripped the cloth off the dead woman's face. The knot that had held her hair in a tiny bun came undone and her hair spread over her gaping mouth and stony eyes. The soldiers returned from their search. The officer commanding the contingent gave the women a piece of his mind: 'It seems you people have underground groups working for you in Hong Kong. That is how you had knowledge of our raid. Otherwise, how could the young girls, children, and young and old men disappear from the island like that. But mark my words: we are not leaving empty-handed. We'll wait all day long and when they return, we'll kill your sons, daughters, brothers, fathers, husbands right in front of your eyes, and then you too will be driven into the sea.' He thundered on for long. Finally, after leaving us to guard the women, the Japanese went far into the round of trees where they took out bottles of liquor from their bags and began drinking, dancing, and laughing.

Cordoned off by us, the women sat down. The sky had become overcast now, and the sun had disappeared. Even though it had been morning for so long, it was still dark. Cold, moist draught was piercing my chest like a gimlet. When I held together the two flaps of my shirt, my hands would become numb from cold. When I let go of the flaps, my whole body would begin to shiver. The presence of the old woman's dead body was making my shivers worse. The women's muttering went on. The woman who had covered the corpse was not crying any longer, but now her face looked pallid, and she was staring at me uninterruptedly.

This went on for some time. Then a Japanese soldier came back and told us that the decision had been made to head towards another island nearby. They would be leaving in a short while. In the meantime the women were to prepare the food for them. He ordered them to get started and told us to hold our posts. Then he went back.

The women withdrew into their huts. Clouds thundered. Snow started to fall and the flakes, like pointed shards, began to pierce my chest. My thoughts sailed back to the corner of our house in the village where my mother and I used to spend much of the winter huddled together. The smoke from the dung-cakes would envelope us and my mother would, time and again, cover my chest with her shawl and tell me, 'Son, protect you chest from cold. Pneumonia enters your ribs through the chest.' It was after a long time that the tear-drenched face of my mother had appeared in all its clarity before my eyes. The tears trapped in the wrinkles of her face glittered in the lightning. The skin sagging under her chin was trembling, and her face was coming closer and closer to me.

It was not my mother I saw coming towards me; instead, it was the woman who had wrapped the face of the dead body. She was holding something in her hand. With each step she would turn around to see if the Japanese, carousing in the distance, were watching her.

This woman's face was remarkably like my mother's. In old age people do begin to look alike. Her wrinkles were also drenched with tears. She stopped in front of me and asked me in Chinese, 'A prisoner, are you?'

I did not speak but nodded my head in assent.

She said, 'My son was in a hurry to leave. I kept calling after him, but he didn't heed me. Like you, he too had a button missing from his shirt.'

I was startled.

She kept talking, 'Is your mother alive?'

Once again I didn't say anything but nodded my head. I tried very hard to keep my feelings in check but couldn't and broke into tears.

She came near me and started sewing a button on my shirt. When she had finished, she smiled through her tears. Looking at the Japanese through the corners of her eyes, she furtively planted a kiss on my cheek, and, wiping her tears with my shirt, went back into her hut.

For a moment I felt as though the Chinese tea-bowl had lifted itself in the air and overturned, and I had fallen into my mother's arms in Punjab.

THE OLD BANYAN

The room hadn't changed; the window still looked the same; only the banyan, Syed Amjad Hussain's old companion and friendly elder, had been cut. Even though the old banyan had been connected to every nook and cranny of this house, it had a special relationship with the window of this room. Amjad Hussain used to wonder how the window would feel without the banyan outside it. Now the banyan was gone, and even though the window was still there, it wasn't showing any signs of astonishment or dismay. Even the strongest gust of wind passing through the leaves and branches of the banyan used to become a whisper as it reached the window. The heart-shaped leaves of the creeper inching up to the roof of the second floor of the house would just peep into the room through the window, like naughty children, but then turn their faces in another direction. Now they came barging into the room, stopping for a long time at one spot, all the while shaking, as though having difficulty suppressing their mirth. But the window just stood there in its cavernous indifference. It should have burst into bits, like Syed Amjad Hussain's heart and brain, after the cutting of the banyan.

Last night as he was shutting the window, he noticed the moon looking so sad it had turned blue. This morning on opening the window, he spied a flock of sparrows swooping down, looking for the safety of the banyan, but finding none and flying back up again. They seemed to be asking each other what tragedy had befallen them. For years, they had been perching in the banyan, making their plans for the toil of the day, but now with the tree gone, it seemed as though the earth had been pulled from under their feet.

He stood in front of the brilliantly shining window, watching all of that. He was going to build a wall in front of this window. He was going to build walls in front of all the doors, windows and skylights of the house. Syed Amjad Hussain felt as though the cut banyan had started growing inside him, its branches stretching and piercing through his bones. As he snapped the window shut, a leaf, severed off the creeper, fell between his feet. Then the creeper began banging its head against the panes. A ray of light came into the room and cutting cleanly through it, like a sword, got embedded in the facing wall. If the banyan were there, nothing from outside would have dared to disturb the peace of his secluded life. The banyan had been guarding his whole being. It was like a canopy, or the sky over his head. In those days, he used to think that if the banyan were ever cut, the entire bungalow would collapse, burying him under the debris. But now the banyan had disappeared, yet the bungalow was still there, so was the room with the window, and, wonder of wonders, so was he himself.

'Am I all there?' he wondered as he looked at himself in the mirror.

And then he felt his features melting, pouring across from his face into another face standing over his shoulder. The other face spoke to him, 'Come on, Father, the only distinction the banyan has is that it's old. If it has any other quality besides that, please tell me, and if not, then allow me to have it . . .'

'No,' he screamed back, and the mirror returned him his face. It looked horrible. He had never before thought about the ugliness of his features. He noticed, as he rubbed his hands over his face, that he had been crying.

That day Syed Amjad Hussain cried the whole day, involuntarily, unselfconsciously, and lay in the room wondering what to do—whether to put a bullet through his head or wreak destruction on the world outside.

It was out of affection for his son that he had named him Syed Socrat Shah and helped him get his master's degree in philosophy. Then one day, the same Socrat had come to him with a cup full of poison and told him, 'Father, face it. You are too old now. You don't seem to fit in this palatial bungalow. You scare the leaves off the trees and sadden the golden rays of the sun when, stretching in the reclining chair, your legs resting on a foot-stool, you begin to snooze with the newspaper spread over your face. Even the servants walk about stealthily as though a dead body were lying in the lawn. It's totally unacceptable. So, please make a final gesture of parental affection: drink this cup of poison and die. You educated me, you made me civilized; now do me this last favour.'

What had actually taken place was not much different. One day, after the preparations for Socrat's wedding had been completed, as Amjad Hussain lay in his reclining chair in the lawn reading the newspaper, Socrat came and sat in front of him on a rattan stool. Amjad Hussain waited for sometime for Socrat to initiate a conversation, but when he said nothing, he asked, 'Want the newspaper, son?'

'No,' he answered. 'I came to ask a favour.'

He was surprised by Socrat's unusual seriousness and putting the paper aside asked, 'What's the matter?'

'First promise that you won't get angry,' Socrat said in the manner of someone fifteen years his junior.

Socrat's posture of dutifulness delighted him. 'Son,' he replied, 'Why would I be angry with you? What will I do in the world after doing that, except commit suicide? And I don't want to die yet. I have yet to see you grow and prosper in the world like this banyan. You understand?'

'Yes.' Despite that assurance, Socrat was hesitant.

'Then tell me what it is.'

'Father, the thing is that...,' Socrat paused as though collecting his dispersed thoughts. 'The thing is that this banyan...'

'Yes, yes,' Syed Amjad Hussain felt somewhat apprehensive.

'Get rid of it,' Socrat blurted out those words, taking only as much time to utter them as it takes to utter just one word.

Syed Amjad Hussain stood up suddenly, as though he were a mechanical toy and someone had pushed his button.

Socrat also stood up. He went on talking: 'The tree is hiding the entire bungalow from view. People passing by it don't even know they're passing by a house. Only an arch of the veranda balustrade is visible from the road, making the place look like a servant's quarters. The car seems to enter into a cave as it comes into the porch. My friends make fun of me; the world, they say, has entered the atomic age, while our family still hasn't come down from the tree. After all, what great beauty do you see in it? Once when a gardener cut off, at my behest, some of the leaves from a branch in front of the window, you not only beat him up but also fired him for good. Such ugly trees look suitable only in forests. In urban areas one grows flowers, or trees which always look pretty and young. Please get rid of it and free this big patch of land, so that we may put flower-beds there and grow some really nice flowers. I'll get saplings from the nurseries around the country, even from Europe and America, and we will have such exotic flowers that you'll be astonished to look at them. The wedding reception is only a week away, and here you insist that we hold it under the tree, with all those hundreds of creatures hanging down from its branches.'

Socrat paused for breath. Amjad Hussain asked, 'Are you finished?'

'Yes, just about. That was all I had to say.'

'Then listen,' Amjad Hussain said, 'this banyan will be cut over my dead body. After my dead body has been taken out of its shade to be buried, you can do anything you like with it.'

Socrat could only go on staring into his father's eyes. And the father went on talking, 'You know it and I have told you many times that this banyan has witnessed four generations of our family. It's even older than the English rule in Punjab. When my grandfather built this bungalow in 1880, the elders alive at the time said the banyan was then already more than half a century old. In those days, it was still young and beautiful. My grandfather used to say that if it were not there, this house would not have been built, at least, not at this spot. At that time, there was nothing but wilderness all around it. My grandfather transformed the area into a scenic spot, and this banyan presided over it. It was under this banyan that my grandfather had arranged a tea-party for the then lieutenant-governor. A swing, made of silken rope, was hung from one of its branches and the English ladies had swung on it. Her ladyship, the lieutenant-governor's wife, herself had swung on it and had said that if it were possible, she would have taken this tree to England and transplanted it in the lawn of her bungalow.'

They both continued to stand facing each other, the father telling the son all the things that the latter had been hearing since childhood, but now with some new revelations also thrown in. 'If a strong wind drives the leaves of this tree onto the road, I run after them, pick them up and bring them back. I burn them but do not allow anyone to step over them. Son, this banyan is sacred to me; its leaves are like the pages of a holy book. Your grandfather spent his childhood under it; his English governess would take him out for a round in the baby-carriage under it. My father himself told me that when negotiations were going on for his marriage to my mother, which her father was dead set against, it was under this banyan that my father had opened and read the letter my mother had written him, which said that she would commit suicide if she couldn't marry him. My own wedding reception was held under this tree in 1938. The Governor Sahib himself had attended it and looking at this banyan had pronounced it to be a veritable fort, not just a tree. Ever since, I've done everything within my power to make it just that—a veritable fort. Wherever one of its aerial roots hangs down from a branch, I plant a creeper there, so that now the roof of this fort seems from afar to stand on dozens of green columns. You yourself have grown up in this fort. Since 1943 you have been growing in its shadow. Every branch and root of this tree considers you its friend and protector, and here you are, bent on getting rid of it. You want to show off your bungalow at the cost of destroying your fort. Your bungalow will be naked under the sun; it will be washed away by the rains. The weather these days can be merciless. If this banyan goes, I feel that the stature and dignity of our family will vanish with it. I wonder why you have begun having such thoughts. Who or what makes such ideas enter your head?'

Then taking his son by the hand, Syed Amjad Hussain sank into the shadow of the tree. Above them, in the branches, all kinds of birds were singing their different songs. Below, on the green columns of the fort, purple flowers, which looked black in the heavy shade, were growing. Reaching the trunk the father said, 'Look son, how many trunks have intertwined into this one trunk. Doesn't it seem to you as if the sky has lowered itself and is shielding us and the bungalow? Doesn't it?'

'Yes,' Socrat said; he had spoken after a long time. 'It does seem like the sky has lowered itself.'

******

The reception was held the day after Socrat's wedding, and Syed Amjad Hussain literally made the banyan look like the night sky. Bulbs lit each of its long, incredibly spread-out branches. The guests had nothing but praise for the host's arrangements. However, an accident happened. There was a power failure as the dinner was in progress. All the stars went out, and it seemed as if the sky had lowered itself further and begun to hum and echo. The women broke into screaming and the clatter of falling glasses and plates made the panic more frightening. Quickly, the servants brought in gas lamps which had been arranged for just such an emergency, as well as the news that a dust storm was blowing outside.

'See, there is a dust storm outside, but nothing seems to have happened in here,' Syed Amjad Hussain said, laughing with pride. No one responded to his laughter, not even out of courtesy, because everybody was listening to Socrat's announcement: 'Ladies and gentlemen, now that we have the gas lights working, I have an important announcement to make. When the lights went out, a lady came and embraced me, thinking I was her husband. But I told her who I was and requested her to let go of me. I said if my bride saw this, she would never forgive me for the rest of her life. The lady moved away, but I forgot to apologize to her. I would like to express my apologies to her. So the lady who had embraced me, please raise your hand. I didn't see her face, but I remember she was wearing a perfume, a silk sari, and had pins in her hair.'

All the women looked at each other in surprise. They were all wearing perfumes, silk saris, and had pins in their hair. Then, in embarrassment they all laughed. And later there was an explosion of laughter when an elderly woman came from one side in a huff and said to Syed Amjad Hussain, 'Ay Syed, does this forest of yours have any way of getting out of it?'

******

Three or four days later, as Amjad Hussain lay in his chair in the lawn, reading the newspaper, his feet on a teapoy, Socrat and his bride Nagina came and sat near him on rattan stools.

'Hello, daughter, how are you?' He asked Nagina and was astonished to notice how so many edges and furrows had suddenly surfaced on her face so soon after the marriage.

'I have a request, Uncle,' Nagina said, looking askance at Socrat and smiling. 'The day I stepped into this bungalow, remember you promised to give me the gift I asked for?'

'Yes, of course, I did.' He was so happy that he slid to the very edge of the reclining chair. And then, leaning forward, he said, 'Go ahead, ask. Socrat was saying that a six month trip to America would be fine, but your wish comes first. Yes, say it.'

'Then I would like to ask you to . . .' Nagina hesitated. 'Are you sure you'll really give me what I ask?'

Syed Amjad Hussain laughed recklessly and said, 'Come on, girl, ask it.'

And Nagina said, 'Then, have this banyan chopped. I cannot stand it.'

He was struck dumb. His eyes became dilated, and his neck stuck out, like that of a turtle. He jerked it and looked at Socrat. But Socrat stood up; so did Nagina, and the two walked into the bungalow through the arch in the veranda.

'Akbar!' Syed Amjad Hussain screamed to his servant, so loudly that the birds perching in the banyan fluttered their wings in fright. The scream was like that of someone being murdered.

A little later, when Socrat and Nagina looked out of the window of their room, Akbar was putting two suitcases in the trunk of the car. Presently Amjad Hussain came out of his room, went downstairs, and, as it were, walked straight out of the sprawl of the banyan into his car. Dilawar started the car, and Socrat rushed out of the house and walking fast to keep pace with the moving car, asked his father, 'Are you going somewhere, Father?' In the meanwhile, Nagina too came out.

After some careful thinking, Amjad Hussain announced, 'I'm going to inspect all the sub-offices of my firm. Will be back in a year or two.'

'In a year or two?' Socrat and Nagina said, surprised.

'But Uncle,' Nagina leaned forward and said, 'If you're going for so long, why not fulfill your promise to me and give me my gift...'

Socrat quickly pulled her away by her arm. The car moved on, and Nagina had a fit of laughter.

'Stop it, Nagi,' Socrat said, 'You've just had your breakfast. If you laugh too hard, your gut will get all twisted up. Father says so.'

Socrat's last three words induced another fit of laughter. A strong gust of wind blew all over the lawn the pages of the newspaper that lay on the teapoy.

******

Six or seven months later, when Syed Amjad Hussain's car entered the main gate of the bungalow, he just about jumped out of the rear seat. 'Stop, Dilawar, where are you going? This isn't our bungalow.'

'This is it, Sahib,' Dilawar stopped the car and turned back to look at Syed Amjad Hussain, observing him with the anxiety of a physician.

From inside the bungalow, Akbar came running. The other servants also came out of their living quarters, but all stopped short, forming an uneven line. They stood dumbfounded, as though waiting for an explosion to occur. Seeing Akbar, Syed Amjad Hussain stepped out of the car, slamming the door behind him so violently that the whole car shook with the impact. He didn't even respond to Akbar's perturbed greetings. With the full force of his lungs he blared, 'Socrat!'

Socrat emerged from the bungalow, putting on his tie. Before he could say anything, Amjad Hussain screamed, 'Where's the banyan?'

'Ah, you're back, Father!' Socrat said as he came out of the veranda.

'I am asking you, where's my banyan?' Amjad Hussain screamed. A high-pitched whine was noticeable in his scream.

Socrat turned around to look. Nagina had also come out. 'Ask your daughter-in-law,' he said, as though he was finished answering his father's question.

With perfect ease and calm, Nagina came closer and said, 'That was my gift, Uncle, wasn't it?'

For a few moments everyone except Nagina stood stock-still. Then Syed Amjad Hussain pulled out a handkerchief from his pocket, stuffed it between his teeth and doddered into the house.

Dilawar drove the car into the garage. Akbar began walking back to the house, his head bowed. Nagina said to Socrat, 'Precisely what you said would happen!'

'What do you think? I didn't study philosophy for nothing. Haven't been shovelling dirt all these years, you know,' Socrat said. 'He'll get over the loss in a couple of days, I'm sure.'

Akbar walked by them in a hurry. 'The Sahib has rung the bell,' he said, as though giving them an important piece of news.

Instantly he came back. 'The Sahib wants to see you, both of you, in his room upstairs,' he told them.

Socrat looked gravely at Nagina and the two of them went inside the house.

When they parted the curtains of his room to enter, Syed Amjad Hussain was standing nearby. Immediately he said, 'I have asked you here to tell you never to enter this room again. After a dead body is lowered into the grave, a veil falls between it and the world. A veil has fallen between you and me. Go now.'

The patriarch noticed that it was the first time in his memory that the moon had shone in his room. He recalled having read somewhere that there were people who lost their heads beholding the moon. He had laughed at the idea and remarked that only those who were already crazy could lose their heads looking at something so pretty as the moon. And how scared he was of the moon today! He shut the window. The moon outside the panes became so sad that it turned almost blue. And he thought: it was the same room, the same window, and yet how utterly different everything looked in the absence of the ancient banyan. He felt he was not in his home, but in some hotel. Meanwhile a strong gust of wind threw open the window, and the curtains began to flutter. He felt as if, along with the wind, the moon would also rush into the room and smash itself against the facing wall, making the nights pitch dark until doomsday. He bolted the window shut and plopped down on his bed.

The next morning he couldn't recall whether he had slept the night before or was awake the whole time. He felt feverish; his eyeballs hurt, and his ears rang without a break. He got up from the bed and opened the window; a flock of birds swished past the window and flew back up in the air. Had the birds come to offer him their sympathy? A ray of the rising sun spilled through the window and pierced the facing wall like the point of a sword. The banyan, in departing, seemed also to have taken his sense of security along. Now everything came barging into the room—the wind, the sun, even the creeper as it thrust itself upward to the roof. He shut the window and a leaf, severed from the creeper, fell between his feet. The patriach picked it up and stood holding it as though he were holding the entire banyan in his fist. It seemed to him that he was unable to bear so much weight, and felt crushed under it.

He didn't know whether he had been crying or had slept or lost consciousness. Anyway, when he woke up again at Akbar's knock, the sun, which had been shining earlier on the facing wall, had travelled across the room and receded to the base of the window. 'What is it?' he asked. From outside the door came Akbar's humble, pleading voice: 'Sir, the younger Sahib says you didn't have your breakfast. Will you have your lunch now?'

'Tell the younger Sahib to mind his own bloody business,' he said, grinding his teeth behind the closed door.

The same thing happened in the evening. Akbar begged him from behind the door to have a cup of tea at least, but he declined rudely.

Once again he didn't know whether he had been crying or had slept or had lost consciousness. When he woke up, the moon was shining through the window, looking as blue as it did yesterday. A sudden noise startled him. He got up and turned the light on. He went to the adjoining room, which served as both library and study, and came back with the step-ladder that he had kept for bringing down books from the top shelves of his ebony book-cases. He placed it against the wall under the skylight whose panes, sometime ago, were brushed by the leaves of the banyan. When the leaves rustled in the wind, they gave the impression as though they were scratching the bungalow's back. He turned off the light and stealthily went up the ladder to look at the part of his front yard where the murdered banyan had once stood.

He saw a row of milky-white lights with shades on, running along a large expanse of the lawn densely carpeted by grass. Bordering the lawn on all sides were flower-beds. In the electric lights the beds looked as brightly lit as they must have looked during the day. Every bed had flowers different from those in the adjoining bed. Some had red, some yellow, some blue. In the centre of the vast lawn where the trunk of the banyan used to stand, there was a large round of roses. In the middle of the round was a raised dais of transparent glass. There was light somewhere behind or beneath the glass which was making the stripes on its surface shimmer. Socrat and Nagina, sitting in delicate canvas chairs on the dais, seemed to be swimming in a glittering pool of water. They were drinking coffee and laughing with abandon. Then they got up. Nagina cupped a rose fondly in her hands and smelled and kissed it. Socrat plucked it from the bush and tucked it in Nagina's hair. But the flower was too large for her hair and fell over. He plucked all its petals and showered Nagina with them. Nagina hugged him. Then they began taking a stroll along the flower-beds. At every few steps Socrat would hug Nagina and kiss her. Walking around as they passed under Syed Amjad Hussain's room, he heard them talk. They were talking about flowers, some of which had come from England, others from Holland. They had even asked some friend to get them some flowers from Japan and America. Socrat thanked Nagina for showing the courage to rid the house of the haunted monster. 'What haunted monster?' she protested. 'It was my gift that I snatched from Uncle's hands.' They both laughed. Then they suddenly became quiet and raised their eyes to look at the skylight above them in his room. Syed Amjad Hussain felt as though they had caught him spying on them. He stepped down the ladder quickly, took it back into the library and came and lay down on his bed. For a few moments he lay there almost senseless. Then he jumped up with the same suddenness that he had exhibited the day Socrat had first sought his permission to get rid of the banyan. He turned on the light, stepped out of his room barefooted, and stood hiding in a turning in the staircase for a long while. Then he felt as if someone was coming up the stairs. With the swiftness of a child he ran back to his room and, closing the door gently, lay down on his bed. He recognized the knock at the door. 'What is it, Akbar?' he asked, without bitterness.

'Sahibji, please have your meal now.'

'I'll ask for it, if I need it,' Amjad Hussain said.

Akbar said, 'Sir, the younger Sahib says go ask again.'

Amjad Hussain thought for a bit and then said, 'All right, bring it in.'

Akbar opened the door and placed a large tray on the table. 'Shall I serve it to you, sir?'

'No, I'll help myself,' he said. 'And tell the younger Sahib to go to sleep peacefully. So long as one is alive and breathing, one has to eat. You can take the dishes down in the morning. I'm planning to go to bed right after my meal.'

Akbar seemed happy to notice this pleasant change in Syed Amjad Hussain's mood. As he was about to depart, Amjad Hussain asked, 'Has Socrat gone to his room yet?'

'No, sir,' Akbar answered. 'He came to the kitchen, asked us to deliver the food to you and went back.'

'Tell him,' Amjad Hussain said, 'that I have had my meal and have gone to sleep.'

'Yes, sir,' Akbar said and left.

As soon as he was gone, Amjad Hussain got up, walked on tip-toes to the landing in the stairs and stood there, hiding. He heard Akbar giving Socrat and Nagina the good news about his having eaten and gone to bed. Then Nagina said, 'Amazing, Saki. It's all unfolding exactly as you predicted.' And Socrat answered, 'Hey, I told you so. I studied philosophy, didn't spend my time digging dirt for years.'

******

The next morning when Socrat and Nagina emerged from the bungalow, in their dressing gowns, they were amazed to see Syed Amjad Hussain ensconced in a chair in the lawn. He was still in his robe. His hands were in his pockets, and he was leaning forward and reading the newspaper that lay in front of him on the teapoy.

'Greetings, father,' Socrat said.

'Greetings,' Amjad Hussain lifted his eyes and responded. 'May you live long.'

'Greetings, Uncle,' Nagina said.

'May you live long,' he said lovingly and leant forward to read the paper.

Socrat and Nagina's faces lit up. Then Socrat gestured to Nagina to leave and sat down in the chair close by.

Suddenly Nagina's frightful scream was heard. 'Saki, Saki,' she was screaming hysterically.

In a flash, Socrat leapt up and dashed, but Syed Amjad Hussain just sat there, calmly reading the newspaper.

A panic broke out everywhere. Nagina's persistent, childlike crying continued, and Socrat was scolding the servants. Nagina's screams became steadily louder, and Amjad Hussain, his eyes still glued to the paper, wondered how a beautiful girl could cry in such a graceless, ugly manner.

Socrat took a crying, writhing Nagina into their room and shut the door. When he came out a little later, Syed Amjad Hussain asked, 'What happened, son?'

Socrat said, 'Some miscreant devastated our garden last night, Father. He plucked all the flowers and uprooted all the plants. The whole thing was done so mercilessly, it couldn't have been done by an animal. It's surely some man's job. Nagina had herself tilled and raked each one of the flower-beds. With my own hands I had...'

Interrupting his son's words, Syed Amjad Hussain said, 'That's all fine, but that's no reason to scream and cry, is it?'

As if defeated, Socrat went back inside. Syed Amjad Hussain took his hands out of his gown-pockets, and after stretching himself, put them on the newspaper. Blood was beginning to dry on them; his finger-tips had been pierced by thorns. But there was a smile on his lips such as one saw only on a conqueror's face. He began laughing out loud, without worrying what Socrat and Nagina might think.

OLD MAN NOOR

'Where are you headed, Baba Noor?' one of the children asked.
'Oh, not far. Just to the post office,' Baba Noor replied with measured seriousness and moved on. And all the children laughed.
Only Maulvi Qudratullah watched the old man speechlessly. Then he said to the children, 'Don't laugh. You should not be laughing at such matters. The Lord alone is all-knowing.'
The children became quiet, but laughed out loud again after Maulvi Qudratullah had left.
Baba Noor stopped by the entrance arch of the mosque. He took his shoes off, leaned forward and put both his hands on the arch. He kissed it and rubbed each of his eyes on it. Then he turned back, put his shoes back on and made to leave.
The children started slinking away into the alleys, as if shy of each other.
Baba Noor had on a suit of washed homespun cotton. On his head he had a white cap which, blending with his white hair, seemed to hang all the way down to the neck. His white beard had recently been combed and was spread out on his chest in an orderly fashion. His fair colour was almost pallid, and the pupils in his small eyes were so dark that they did not look natural. The jet-black pupils seemed alien to the whiteness of his clothes, skin and hair, but nonetheless gave his face the innocent look of a child. On his shoulder rested a big facecloth, again white and homespun, which had changed shoulders three or four times between his meeting with the crowd of people and his arrival at the mosque.
'Heading to the post office, Baba Noor?' a young man standing in the door of a shop asked.
'Yes, son. May you live long,' Baba Noor replied.
A child stood nearby. He clapped his hands and said out loud, 'Aha! Baba Noor is going to the post office!'

'Get lost, you,' the young man scowled at him.

And Baba Noor who hadn't gone far, came back and said, 'Why are you scolding the child? He's right; I am going to the post office.'

Children from all around had begun laughing and gathering together. A crowd began to form behind Baba Noor. Some young men lunged at them and drove them away.

By now Baba Noor had reached the farms. When the raised dirt track suddenly descended into lush green fields, Baba Noor's pace slowed down, and he waded his way cautiously away from the tender wheat stalks. If, because of some traveller's carelessness, a stalk had fallen on the track, he would lift it carefully and make it lean against the upstanding stalks. If a stalk had been bent, he would pick it up and straighten it as gently as one handles an injured limb. Reaching the mound at the other end of the farm, he started walking fast again.

Four farmers sat on the mound smoking hookah, while the daughter of one of them went around with her sickle removing grass from between the wheat plants so deftly that not one plant got injured. Baba Noor paused to watch her. She would cut a swathe of grass, stuff it into the bag hanging from her back and begin working the sickle again.

'Amazing,' Baba Noor addressed the farmers from afar. 'This young lady is a veritable magician. She's cutting in such long swathes; at every inch there's a wheat plant; her sickle cuts the grass but doesn't even touch the wheat. Whose daughter is she?' And then he asked the girl directly, 'Whose daughter are you, child?'

As the girl turned around to look, a farmer answered, 'She's mine, Baba.'

'She's yours?' he asked. 'What a clever girl she is! A good farmer. May God give her long life.'

'Where are you off to today, Baba?' the girl's father asked.

'To the post office?' another farmer inquired.

'Yes,' Baba Noor said, stopping by them. 'I thought I'd go and ask. Maybe there was some letter.'

The farmers became quiet. They moved aside from the mound to make way for Baba Noor, and he moved ahead. He had barely reached the other end of the field when the girl asked, 'Will you have some buttermilk, Baba Noor?' Baba Noor turned around, looked and smiled for the first time since leaving the village that morning. He said, 'Yes, daughter, I'd like to.' Then, after a short pause, he added, 'But, please hurry up, daughter, the clerk at the post office is always in a rush. I fear he might leave soon.'

The girl put aside the bag hanging from her back and ran to the berry tree near the mound. She picked up a pot lying in the shade of the tree, shook it hard, filled an aluminum bowl with buttermilk, and hurried back with it.

The old man downed the whole thing in one gulp, without pausing for breath. He wiped his lips clean with his facecloth and saying, 'May your lot in life be as smooth as this buttermilk,' he moved on.

The postal clerk sat in the school veranda filling his daily supply of forms as well as conversing with the villagers, doling out all kinds of information to them. 'My brother-in-law used to work as peon in Karachi,' he was saying. 'When he passed away, I had to go to Karachi for condolence. The fact is, friends, you must visit Karachi at least once, even though you may be yoked to a donkey-cart there. There are more motorcars in Karachi than there are sparrows in our village, and each motorcar carrying such wonderful women, I can't even begin to tell you about them. They are other-worldly creatures, fairies. And what man can handle fairies? One is so overwhelmed by their beauty that one immediately wants to prostrate oneself and praise the Lord for His handiwork. I heard a *seth* say that if there were another big war, Karachi will become like Europe. They say people die in the war. Don't they die anyway? In the war they die from bombs; if there's no war, they die from hunger. Isn't that right?'

'Absolutely,' one villager said. 'But, Munshiji, when is the postage for an envelope going back down to an anna?'

Just as the clerk looked in front of him to explain something to the villager, his eyes became glued to a spot in the distance. His face blanched and he said in a sinking voice, 'Baba Noor's coming.'

Everybody turned around to look. Everybody's face fell. Children gathered in the doors and windows of the school and began whispering 'Baba Noor, Baba Noor.' The postal clerk admonished them to return to their seats.

Dressed in pure white, Baba Noor was heading straight towards the school veranda, sending, as it were, a wave of terror through the people.

Stepping into the veranda, he asked, 'Is the mail in, Munshiji?'

'Yes, Baba,' he replied.

'Was there a letter from my son?' the old man asked. 'No, Baba,' the clerk said.

Baba Noor went back quietly. A white spot moved along the road for quite sometime, and people, holding their breath, kept watching it. The clerk explained, 'For the past ten years Baba Noor has been coming here just like this. He asks the same question and gets the same answer. The poor fellow has forgotten that I myself read him the letter from the army bearing the news that his son had been killed in a bomb blast in Burma. Since then he has just lost his marbles. But, I swear to you, by God, my friends, if he ever comes again to ask me the same question, he will drive me crazy too.'

PARMESHAR SINGH

Akhtar was suddenly separated from his mother, like a coin falling from the pocket of someone in a great hurry—there one moment, gone the next. A search was made of course, but it amounted to little more than a commotion at the tail end of the ragged train of refugees—stirred up like soapsuds, only to die down and disappear. 'He's got to be coming along somewhere,' someone said. 'There are thousands of people in the caravan.'

Bracing herself with just such hope, Akhtar's mother trudged on toward Pakistan, thinking again and again, 'He must be coming along. He probably wandered off chasing after a butterfly. Surely he must have missed me at some point, cried some, and—he must be coming along. He's a smart boy. More than five years old. He'll show up. After we've arrived in Pakistan, I can search for him more carefully there.'

But Akhtar had lost touch with the big caravan some fifteen miles from the border—whether chasing after a butterfly as his mother had speculated, or losing track of time as he forayed into a sugarcane field to pick himself a stalk. Anyway, as he ran screaming and crying inconsolably in one direction, a party of Sikhs closed in on him. The boy yelled at them angrily, 'Keep away, or I'll shout *Allahu Akbar*!' The words were barely out of his mouth when he blanched with fright.

The Sikhs, all of them, burst out laughing. But one of them, Parmeshar Singh, didn't find it at all funny. His tousled *kes* poked out of his loosely wrapped turban, which left his topknot at the back completely exposed. 'Don't laugh, *yaaro*,' he said. 'After all, the same Vahguruji made this child as made you and your children.'

A Sikh youth, who had meanwhile bared his *kirpan*, retorted, 'Wait a minute, Parmeshar, let my dagger pay its dues to its religion, then we'll worry about paying ours to our religion.'

'Don't kill him, *yaaro*,' Parmeshar Singh pleaded. 'He's so small! Just look at him. The same Vahguruji has made him ...'

'Well then, let's ask him,' another Sikh said. He came over to the frightened boy and asked, 'Tell us, who's made you— Khuda or Vahguruji?'

Akhtar made a valiant attempt to swallow the terrible dryness that had spread from the tip of his tongue down to the pit of his stomach, and he blinked the tears from his eyelashes, which had accumulated there like grit. He looked at Parmeshar Singh as though he were looking at his own mother. He spat out a tear which had run into his mouth and said, 'I don't know.' 'Listen to this!' one of the Sikhs said. He swore at Akhtar and started to laugh.

The boy, who hadn't finished, resumed, 'Amma says that she found me lying on a pile of hay inside a little barn.'

The Sikhs exploded with laughter. But Parmeshar Singh, beside himself with anguish, broke down in tears, leaving his companions absolutely stunned. He started to wail, 'All children are alike, *yaaro*. Exactly the words of my darling Kartar. Wasn't he too found by his mother lying on a pile of hay inside a barn?'

The bared kirpan was put back into its sheath. The group withdrew to one side. After whispering among themselves for a bit, one of the men stepped forward, grabbed the boy's arm and led him over to Parmeshar Singh, who was sobbing quietly. 'Here, Parmeshar, take him. Let him grow his *kes*, make him your Kartar. Here, take him!'

Parmeshar dashed forward and picked the boy up with such impatience that his turban came completely undone, allowing his hair to hang down loosely. He kissed the boy like someone possessed. He hugged him tightly and gazed into his eyes, thinking of things that lit his face up with joy. He then turned around and looked at the other Sikhs. He quickly put the boy down and rushed past them, toward the bushes up ahead, where he started to caper about like a monkey, his free-floating *kes* matching the wild movements of his body. The rest of the party just gawked at him. Finally, he ran back to them, his hands joined together in a hollow ball. There was a smile on his lips, deep inside the thick mop of his sweaty beard, and his red eyes were shining with unusual brilliance. He was out of breath.

He came over to the boy and squatted down on folded knees and asked, 'What's your name?'

'Akhtar,' the boy answered, his voice no longer ragged with fear.

'Akhtar, my son,' Parmeshar Singh said with great tenderness. 'Come, have a look.'

Akhtar leaned forward a little. Parmeshar Singh opened his balled hands a crack, just long enough for the boy to get a peek.

'Aa-haa!' Akhtar clapped jubilantly and joined his hands into a hollow ball, just like Parmeshar Singh, and smiled through his tears. 'A butterfly!'

'Would you like to have it?'

'Yes,' Akhtar rubbed his hands in excitement.

'Here,' Parmeshar Singh opened his hands. Akhtar tried to catch the butterfly, but it swiftly flew away, leaving fine flecks of colour on the boy's fingertips.

Disappointment was evident on the boy's face.

Parmeshar Singh looked at the other Sikhs and said, 'Why are all children alike, *yaaro*? Kartar too would draw a long face whenever his butterfly flew away.'

'Parmeshar Singh's gone half-mad,' the Sikh youth said with disgust. And the entire group started to head back.

Parmeshar Singh picked Akhtar up and sat him on his shoulders, and then started out behind the party. But the boy began to cry uncontrollably, 'I want my mother! I want my mother!'

Parmeshar Singh lifted his hand to pat the boy, but he pushed it away. When he told him, 'Yes, yes, son, I'm taking you to your mother,' the boy stopped sobbing, though now and then he still cried some, barely tolerating all the patting and caressing.

Parmeshar Singh brought the boy to his house, which formerly had belonged to a Muslim. After he'd lost all his possessions in his native Lahore and come over to Amritsar, the villagers had allotted him this house. The moment he'd stepped into the house with his wife and daughter, he froze and his eyes glazed over. He whispered in a mysterious voice, 'Something's reciting the Koran in this place. I hear it,' which had made the Granthiji and other village folk just laugh. His wife had already told them that ever since Kartar Singh's disappearance, her husband was no longer his usual self. 'God knows what's happened to him,' she'd said. 'Back there, and may Vahguruji not make me lie, he used to beat Kartar up and down like a donkey ten times a day. But while I've come to accept the disappearance of our son, after much crying and screaming, to be sure, he can't accept it, even after crying himself silly. There, I wouldn't dare give our daughter Amar Kaur even an angry side-glance. It was enough to send him flying into a rage. He'd always say, "Don't be harsh with her. Daughters are meek, vulnerable creatures. They are like travellers who have stopped a while to catch a little breath at one's house, and will move on when the time comes." But now, look what he does. She makes the slightest mistake and he hits the roof. He doesn't even think twice before screaming, "Abduction of daughters and wives—yes, *yaaro*, that's nothing new. But when did you ever hear of five and six-year-old boys disappearing?"'

Parmeshar Singh had been living in this new house for about a month now. Every night he would go on tossing and turning, then mumble something and sit up with a start. 'You hear it, don't you?' he'd whisper to his wife, as if he'd seen a ghost. 'Something is reciting the Koran in the house!'

His wife would say something vague and dismissive, then roll over and go back to sleep.

But Amar Kaur would be unable to go back to sleep after that. She would see shapes everywhere in the darkness, intoning the verses of the Koran. In the wee hours of the morning she would involuntarily stuff her fingers in her ears.

Back in Lahore district their house was located near a mosque. It was a delight to hear the *muezzin* call out the *azan* early in the morning. One had the feeling that the light filtering in from the east had itself suddenly started to sing. But all this changed after her neighbour Pritam Kaur had been gang-raped by some young men who later dumped her dead body on the garbage heap like an old discarded rag. Now, whenever the *muezzin* issued the call to prayer, all Amar Kaur heard were the pathetic screams of Pritam Kaur. Indeed, quite forgetting that she was no longer living next to a mosque, the very thought of *azan* made her tremble with fear.

With her fingers stuffed in her ears, she'd eventually fall asleep. Having stayed awake the whole night, she usually got up late in the morning, which was as good a reason as any for Parmeshar Singh to get mad at her. 'Yes, that's all she can do—sleep, sleep, sleep! Girls—useless layabouts! That's what they are! Had she been a boy, *yaaro*, who knows how much work she'd already have finished!'

But when Parmeshar Singh entered the courtyard of the house today, he was uncharacteristically all smiles. His untucked hair was hanging loose and dishevelled over his shoulders and back, the comb still stuck in it, and he was lovingly patting Akhtar's back. His wife sat to one side diligently working the winnowing fan. Her hands froze in mid-air and she just gawked at Parmeshar Singh. Then she leapt over the winnowing fan, ran to him and asked, 'Who is he?'

Still smiling, Parmeshar Singh said, 'Don't be afraid, silly woman! He's so much like Kartar. Do you know, he too was found by his mother on a pile of hay in a barn? And he too loves butterflies. His name is Akhtar.'

'Akhtar!' Her expression changed completely.

'Well, OK, Akhtar Singh, if it bothers you.' After a pause he explained, 'Don't worry about the *kes*. It'll grow long before you even know it. But you must slip a *kara* and a *kachhera* on him right away. We'll give him a comb to wear in his *kes* after it's grown long enough.'

'Fine, fine. But whose child is he?' she pressed him.

'Whose child?' Parmeshar Singh repeated his wife's words as he gently took Akhtar down from his shoulder. He ran his hand tenderly through the boy's hair and replied, 'Why, he's Vahguruji's son. Our own. Darn it, *yaaro*, this woman can't even see that this tiny mole on Akhtar's forehead is exactly like the one Kartar had on his, exactly in the same spot. Well, I know, Kartar's was a little bit bigger. We used to kiss him on that very spot, didn't we? Akhtar's earlobes are pink like a rose blossom, and Kartar's were the same. A bit thicker perhaps. Can't she see that, *yaaro*? And...'

Akhtar, who had sat still so far totally befuddled, suddenly screamed, 'I don't want to stay here! I want to go to my mother! My mother!'

Parmeshar Singh took the boy's hand and gently nudged him towards his wife. 'There, take him into your arms,' he said. 'He wants to go to his mother.'

'Well then, let him go.' She appeared possessed by the same apparition that had taken hold of Parmeshar Singh when his gang had come upon Akhtar in the field—an apparition he'd had the hardest time shaking off.

'Look at the big hero!' the woman yelled. 'He went out to rob. And what does he bring back? This brat, barely a handful! Why couldn't you kidnap a girl? At least she'd have fetched a couple of hundred rupees. We could have bought a few things for this decrepit house. Oh, you've gone off your rocker! Didn't you see this is a Musalla boy? Go, dump him where you picked him up. And make sure he doesn't set foot in my kitchen.'

Parmeshar Singh pleaded, 'Kartar and Akhtar were brought into the world by the same Vahguruji. Surely you understand that.'

'No!' she screamed, 'I don't understand that! Nor do I want to! I'll slash his throat at night and hack him to pieces and throw the pieces out! Why did you have to bring him here? Take him away! Throw him out!'

'Better yet, why not throw you out?' Parmeshar Singh said hotly. 'Maybe I should slash your throat instead.' He took a step towards his wife, who promptly ran off, screaming and beating her chest. Amar Kaur came running from the house next door, followed by some of the women who lived in the same lane. A group of men also rushed to the scene, thereby saving Parmeshar Singh's wife from a thrashing.

The people reasoned with her: Parmeshar Singh was doing a good thing. Making a Musalman into a Sikh was not an everyday occurrence. If it were the olden days, Parmeshar Singh would already have become famous as a 'Guru'.

That gave her some comfort, but she still cried on, huddled in a corner, her head bent over her knees.

All of a sudden Parmeshar Singh let out a thunderous scream that shook the entire crowd. 'Where's Akhtar? My Akhtar, where did he go? You butchers better not have taken him, *yaaro*.'

Then screaming 'Akhtar! Akhtar!' at the top of his lungs, he searched every conceivable place in the house, and then dashed out.

The neighbourhood kids trailed behind him out of sheer curiosity. Women climbed up to the rooftops to watch. By then Parmeshar Singh had already crossed over into the fields, babbling, 'I was going to take him to his mother, wasn't I, *yaaro*? Where has he run off to?'

'Akhtar! Akhtar!' he yelled.

'I'm not going with you!' taunted Akhtar, who stood crying at a bend in the raised mud path along Gyan Singh's sugarcane field. 'You're a Sikh.'

'Yes, that's right, son,' the helpless Parmeshar Singh confessed. 'I am a Sikh.'

'So I'm not coming along with you,' Akhtar wiped his drying tears, clearing the way for the new ones forming in his eyes.

'You're not coming, then?' Suddenly Parmeshar Singh's tone changed.

'No!'

'You're sure?'

'No, no, no!'

'We'll see about that!' Biting his lips Parmeshar Singh grabbed Akhtar's ear and slapped the boy hard on the face. 'Now let's go!' he snapped.

Akhtar turned pale with fear, as though all his blood had been wrung out of him. Suddenly he threw himself down on the bare earth and started to thrash and scream, kicking up a cloud of dust. 'No, I won't! I won't! I won't! You're a Sikh! I'm not going anywhere near a Sikh! I want to go back to my mother! I'll kill you!'

This time it was Parmeshar Singh's turn to cringe. He too blanched, as if all his blood had been drained. He dug his teeth into his hand. His nostrils flared. He broke down in tears, screaming so loud that it froze some of the neighbours and children coming up behind them.

Parmeshar Singh folded his knees and squatted down in front of Akhtar. He started to sob like a child, hard and long, his lower lip out-thrust. In a voice overcome with emotion, he begged the boy, 'Please forgive me, Akhtar. I swear by your God, I am your friend. If you try to go back alone, somebody will kill you on the way. And then your mother will come after me from Pakistan and kill me too. Listen, I myself will take you back to Pakistan. OK? If you run into a boy there named Kartar, promise that you will bring him back here. You will, won't you?'

'All right,' Akhtar made the deal as he wiped his tears with the back of his hand.

Parmeshar Singh hoisted him to his shoulder and started to walk, but stopped suddenly. Up ahead a group of village children and some neighbours had been watching him closely. A middle-aged man among them said, 'Don't cry, Parmeshar, don't cry. A month isn't such a long time after all. His *kes* will grow long and he will look exactly like Kartar.'

He said nothing and walked away with quick strides. At a point along the way he stopped and looked back at the crowd and said, '*Yaaro*, you couldn't be more cruel. You want to make Akhtar into Kartar. What if somebody over there made Kartar into Akhtar? Wouldn't you call such a person heartless?'

Suddenly his voice boomed, 'This boy, I'm telling you, will remain Muslim. I swear by Darbar Sahib. I'll take him to Amritsar first thing tomorrow and get him the English haircut he wears. What the hell do you think I am? I am a Khalsa, in case you didn't know. I have a lion's heart in my chest, not a chicken's.'

Parmeshar Singh had just entered his house and was ordering his wife and daughter to treat Akhtar with the utmost deference and hospitality when the village Granthi, Sardar Santookh Singh, stepped in and barked, 'Parmeshar Singh!'

'Yes,' Parmeshar Singh looked over his shoulder. Granthiji had brought the entire neighbourhood along with him.

'Look,' the Granthiji said very gravely. 'Starting tomorrow, the boy will wear a turban, in the proper manner of Khalsas. As well as a *kara*. Also, he will come to the *dharmshala* and partake in the *parshad*. And yes, his hair will not come in contact with a scissors, ever. If it does, you will have to vacate this house at once. You understand?'

'Yes,' Parmeshar Singh said quietly.

'Very well then,' the Granthiji drove in the last nail.

'As you say, Granthiji, as you say,' Parmeshar Singh's wife answered instead. 'As it is, he keeps hearing the Koran recited at night all through the house. Looks like he was a Musalla in his previous incarnation. Our daughter Amar Kaur is quite beside herself. Ever since she heard that a Musalla boy has come into the house, she's been huddled in a corner, crying. She fears something terrible is going to happen to us. If Parmeshar fails to carry out your command, I as well as Amar Kaur will both come to stay in the *dharmshala*. Let him just stay with his darling boy if he wants. Good for nothing! He has no regard for Vahguruji.'

'You stupid ass, what do you mean? Who has no regard for Vahguruji?' Parmeshar Singh yelled at his wife, taking the sting of the Granthiji's words out on her. He mumbled obscenities under his breath for some time, and then got up and came directly before Granthiji. 'All right, I hear your words,' he said in such a way that Granthiji promptly departed with the rest of the neighbours trailing behind him.

In just a few days one could scarcely tell Akhtar apart from the other Sikh boys—the same turban tied tightly around his head to the earlobes, the same bracelet worn on his forearm, and the same *kachhera*. Only at home, after he had removed the turban, could one see that he was not a Sikh. But his hair was growing fast. Whenever Parmeshar Singh's wife touched it, she felt a sense of satisfaction and happiness take hold of her. 'Hey, Amar Kaur, come over here!' she would call her daughter. 'See how well it's growing! Before long it'll grow long enough to roll into a bun and put a comb in it. And he will be called Kartar Singh.'

'No, Mother,' Amar Kaur replied from where she sat. 'Just as there is only one Vahguruji, and one Granth Sahib, and one moon, so was there only one Kartar, one and only one, my sweet little brother.' Amar Kaur would then break down in tears. 'No, Mother,' she'd pout, 'you can't distract me with this toy. You just can't! I know he's a Musalla. And Kartar just can't ever be a Musalla!'

'When did I say that he's the real Kartar? My darling son, my moon!' Parmeshar Singh's wife too would break down in tears.

Then leaving Akhtar alone, the two women would sit in a corner and cry their hearts out, commiserating with each other all the while.

Akhtar cried for his mother for a few days; but now he cried for something else. Whenever Parmeshar Singh brought home a little grain or a piece of cloth from the *panchayat* that had been set up for the relief of the refugees, Akhtar would run over to him, wrap himself around his legs and say between sobs, 'Tie me a turban! Make my hair grow fast! Buy me a comb!'

Parmeshar Singh would draw him to his chest and hug him tightly. In a voice choked with emotion he'd say, 'Yes, yes. In due time, child. All in due time. Everything'll happen as you say, hair and all the rest. But one thing will not happen. Never. I shall never do that. You understand, don't you?'

Akhtar recalled his mother only rarely now. He would stick to Parmeshar Singh the entire time he remained at home, and when he had to go out, the boy looked at Parmeshar Singh's wife and Amar Kaur, as though begging them for a little love. Parmeshar Singh's wife bathed him, washed his clothes, and broke into tears as she combed his hair. She would go on crying for a long time. Amar Kaur, on the other hand, never looked at the boy without thumbing her nose at him. In the first days after his arrival, she had even whacked him once or twice. But when Akhtar complained about it to Parmeshar Singh, he became furious. Mouthing obscenities, he pounced at his daughter in such a fury that, had his wife not thrown herself at his feet, he surely would have physically picked the girl up and thrown her over the wall into the alley. '*Ulloo ki patthi*!' he roared at her. 'Who said only girls were being kidnapped? How come this slut is still hanging around here then? And who gets kidnapped instead?—a five-year old boy who doesn't even know how to wipe his nose! For heaven's sake, *yaaro*, what an outrage!'

From that moment onward Amar Kaur never dared hit the boy again, but she started hating him twice as much.

One day Akhtar started running a high fever. Parmeshar went out to consult the village *ved*. Shortly thereafter his wife too went out, to borrow a little bit of fennel seed from one of the neighbours. Meanwhile, Akhtar, feeling terribly thirsty, asked for a drink of water. After a while, having received none, he opened his swollen red eyes and looked around. 'Water!' he moaned loudly. When nobody responded, he threw off the quilt and sat up. Amar Kaur was sitting in the doorway straight in front of him, weaving a basket of palm leaves.

'Give me some water!' he ordered hotly.

Amar Kaur knit her brows and stared at him. Altogether ignoring his request, she went on with her work.

'Give me water,' he screamed, 'or I'll beat you up!'

This time Amar Kaur didn't even bother to look at him. She screamed back, 'Just try it! You're no Kartar that I'd take your beating lying down. I'll hack you to pieces!'

Akhtar started to weep bitterly. For the first time in a long time he suddenly remembered his mother. After Parmeshar Singh and his wife had returned, he with medicine, she with fennel seed, Akhtar was crying his heart out. 'That's enough,' he began, sobbing. 'I want to go back to my mother. This Amar Kaur, the bitch, doesn't even give me water! I want to go back to my mother!'

Parmeshar Singh glowered at Amar Kaur. She had started to cry and was telling her mother, "Why should I? Somewhere Kartar must be begging someone for water. If nobody takes pity on my brother, why should I take pity on him? Why should I?'

Parmeshar took a step toward Akhtar and said, pointing at his wife, 'Son, she too is your mother.' 'No, she's not!' Akhtar screamed angrily. 'She is a Sikh. My mother offers *namaz* five times a day, and when she gives me water to drink, she never forgets to say *"Bismillah."*

Parmeshar Singh's wife quickly filled a cup with water and brought it over. When she offered it to the boy, he smashed it against the wall and shrieked, 'No, not from your hand! You're the mother of this bitch, Amar Kaur! I'll drink only from Parmun's hand!'

'But this man is the father of a bitch like me,' Amar Kaur snapped, burnt up. 'So what? Let him be!' Akhtar screamed. 'It's none of your business!'

Parmeshar Singh's face was beset by strange, conflicting emotions. Akhtar's demand to drink water only from his hands made him smile and cry at the same time. He gave the boy his drink of water, kissed him on the forehead, patted his back, and having eased him into bed, he went on gently massaging his head. Only towards evening did the boy stir. By then his fever had subsided and he was sleeping peacefully.

That night, for the first time in a long time, Parmeshar Singh once again started in his sleep. He woke his wife up and whispered to her, 'Hey, you hear it, don't you? Something's reciting the Koran in the house.'

First she dismissed it as one of his old hallucinations, then she quickly got up mumbling something, reached out for the cot on which Amar Kaur was sleeping, shook her gently and said, 'Daughter!'

'Yes, Mother, what is it?' Amar Kaur sat up.

The mother whispered, 'Listen—something really is reciting the Koran!'

The ensuing moment of silence was frightening; and even more dreadful was the scream from Amar Kaur's throat that followed. Akhtar's scream after that was more terrible still.

'What's the matter, son?' Parmeshar Singh jumped out of his bed and rushed over to Akhtar's bed. Hugging him he asked, 'Has something frightened you?'

'Yes,' Akhtar poked his head from the quilt and said, 'I heard a scream.'

'It was Amar Kaur,' Parmeshar Singh explained. 'We all thought we heard something reciting the Koran.'

'That was me,' Akhtar said. 'I was reciting it.'

A muffled scream escaped from Amar Kaur's lips once again.

Parmeshar Singh's wife quickly lit an oil lamp and sat down on Amar Kaur's cot. Both mother and daughter now gawked at the boy as if he would turn into a wisp of smoke any moment and escape from the cracks in the door, calling back at them in a dreadful voice, 'I'm a *jinn*! Tomorrow I'll return and again recite the Koran!'

'Won't you tell us what you were reciting?' Parmeshar Singh asked.

'You want me to recite it for you?'

'Yes, yes,' Parmeshar Singh said, eagerly.

Akhtar started to recite: 'Qul Huwa 'l-Lahu Ahad!' Finishing with 'Kufuwan Ahad,' he quickly poked his face into his collar and blew on his chest. Then he smiled at Parmeshar Singh and asked, 'Want me to blow on you too?'

'Yes, yes,' Parmeshar Singh quickly flung open his collar, and Akhtar blew on his chest too.

This time around Amar Kaur had the hardest time suppressing her scream.

'You couldn't fall asleep—is that it?'

'Yes. I missed Mother. She said that any time you couldn't sleep, just recite the *Qul Huwa 'l-Lah* three times, and sleep will come. I was just getting drowsy when Amar Kaur shrieked and frightened me.'

'Well, recite it once again and try to sleep,' Parmeshar Singh told the boy. 'You should recite it every day. Loudly. Never forget it. Or your mother will spank you. OK, now go to sleep.'

He laid the boy back down and tucked him into the quilt. Just as he made to put out the lamp, Amar Kaur shouted, 'No, Baba, no! Don't put it out! I'm scared!'

'Scared?' Parmeshar Singh asked, surprised. 'What's there to be scared of?'

'Oh, it won't hurt to let it burn,' his wife said.

But Parmeshar Singh did put it out. 'Crazy women!' he laughed in the darkness. 'Absolute asses!'

Akhtar softly went on reciting the *Qul Huwa 'l-Lah* in the darkness. After a while he began to snore. Parmeshar Singh also went back to sleep, as did his wife, but all night long, in her incomplete sleep, Amar Kaur remained afraid, imagining that she heard the *azan* coming from the 'neighbourhood' mosque.

Akhtar's *kes* had by now grown quite long, long enough to be rolled into a tiny topknot and hold a comb. Like everyone else in the village, Parmeshar Singh's wife too had began to call him Kartar and treated him with considerable affection. But Amar Kaur always looked at him as though he were an imposter, who at any minute would discard his turban and comb, and disappear reciting *Qul Huwa 'l-Lah*.

One day Parmeshar Singh barged into the house, huffing and puffing, and asked his wife, 'Where is the child?'

'Who? Amar Kaur?'

'No, no. Not she.'

'Kartar?'

'No.' But after a moment's thought he said, 'Yes, yes, Kartar.'

'He's gone out to play. Must be out in the alley.'

Parmeshar Singh darted back out. Once in the alley, he started to run. When he came to the fields, he ran faster. Far in the distance he spotted a few boys playing *kabaddi* near Gyan Singh's sugarcane field. As he approached, he peered around the cane stalks and saw that Akhtar had pinned one of the boys to the ground with his knees. Blood was oozing from the boy's lips but he diligently kept up the litany of *kabaddi, kabaddi, kabaddi.*

The boy, finally admitting defeat, stopped the repetitions. After Akhtar had let go of him, he asked, 'Hey Kartar, why did you hit me in the mouth with your knee?'

'I'm glad I did,' Akhtar shot back, haughtily, meanwhile tying his loose hair into a knot and sticking the comb into it.

'Is that what your Prophet has taught you to do?' the boy mocked him.

For a moment Akhtar was totally confused. Then, after some thought, he replied with a question of his own. 'And what has your Guru taught you?'

'Musla!' the boy cursed Akhtar.

'Sikhra!' Akhtar cursed back.

All the other boys then ganged up on Akhtar, but a single roar from Parmeshar Singh sent them running every which way. Parmeshar Singh tied Akhtar's turban back on, took him to one side and said, 'Tell me, son. Do you want to stay with me or do you want to go back to your mother?'

Akhtar was flustered, unable to decide. He stood staring into Parmeshar Singh's eyes for a while, and then smiled and said, 'To my mother.'

'You don't want to stay here with me?' Parmeshar Singh's face turned so red that he seemed about to cry.

'I'll stay with you too,' Akhtar replied, offering what looked like a good solution.

Parmeshar Singh picked him up and hugged him. Tears, which had been born of disappointment, now streamed down his face as tears of joy. He said, 'Listen, Akhtar, my son. The army is coming here today. They're coming to take you away from me. You understand? You go hide yourself somewhere. When they leave, I'll come and get you.'

Just then Parmeshar Singh spotted a spiralling cloud of dust far in the distance. He climbed up the raised mud trail around the field and looked closely at the spiral, which was getting bigger by the second. He said with a shiver, 'The army truck is here.'

He stepped down from the raised trail and ran around the sugarcane field shouting, 'Gyan, O Gyan Singh!'

Gyan Singh emerged from the field. He had a sickle in one hand and some grass in the other. Parmeshar Singh took him aside, explained something to him, and then both men returned to Akhtar. Gyan Singh snapped a cane stalk from the field, shaved the leaves off with his sickle, and gave it to Akhtar. 'All right, Kartar, come. You sit with me and enjoy the sugarcane until the army men have gone back. Look at them! What audacity! They've come to grab such a fine Khalsa boy. Huh!'

'Is it all right with you if I leave now?' Parmeshar Singh asked Akhtar for permission.

Akhtar, holding a long piece of the sugarcane peel in his teeth, tried to smile. Parmeshar Singh ran back to the village, as the cloud of dust drew progressively nearer.

At home, he explained the situation to his wife and daughter, then took off for Granthiji. Having explained the matter to him too, he tried to do the same with some of the other people.

The army vehicle stopped in a field beyond the *dharmshala*. The soldiers, accompanied by the village *nambardar*, came straight over to Granthiji. They asked if the village folks were keeping any Muslim girls. Granthiji gave them his word that there wasn't a single Muslim girl in the entire village, and backed it up by swearing on the Granth Sahib.

'Boys are something else again,' someone whispered into Parmeshar Singh's ear, which made him and some of the other Sikhs around him smile to themselves.

One of the army men then treated the villagers to a speech, stressing how the maternal affection of those mothers whose daughters had been stolen away from them had now turned into a torrent of pain. He also drew a touching picture of the plight of those brothers and husbands whose sisters and wives had been forcibly taken away from them. 'And what is religion, my friends?' he concluded. 'Doesn't every religion teach man to be truly a human being after all? Now look at your conduct. In the name of religion you take away from man his humanity. You trample on his dignity. You call yourselves Sikhs, you call yourselves Muslims. You say we are followers of Vahguruji, we are slaves of the Prophet.'

After the speech the crowd began to disperse. The army officer thanked Granthiji, shook his hands, and the vehicle moved along.

Promptly thereafter Granthiji congratulated Parmeshar Singh. The rest of the people crowded around him and started to offer their congratulations. But Parmeshar Singh, scared out of his wits before the arrival of the army vehicle, seemed utterly lost after its departure.

He walked outside the village and came to Gyan Singh's field. He hoisted Akhtar onto his shoulder and brought him home. After feeding him he put him to bed and caressed him with such affection that the boy fell asleep right away. Parmeshar Singh sat on the boy's cot for a long while. He would scratch his beard now and then, look around, and drift off into his thoughts. A boy playing on the rooftop of the house next door suddenly grabbed his heel and doubled over with pain, screaming bitterly, 'Oh, I've got such a big thorn in my foot! It's sunk all the way in!' The boy's mother ran up the stairs without even bothering to cover her head. She picked him up and took him in her lap. Then she called out to her daughter, telling her to bring a needle. She deftly removed the thorn, kissed him madly, and then leaning down from the edge of the roof she shouted, 'Hey, throw me my dupatta. I can't believe I did it—so shamelessly running up the stairs without a head-cover.'

Parmeshar Singh, after a while, started and asked his wife, 'Listen, do you still miss Kartar?' 'Listen to this!' she blurted out, and then suddenly broke into tears. 'Parmeshar! Kartar is the wound in my heart which will never heal.'

Hearing her brother's name mentioned, Amar Kaur came over and sat at her mother's knee, crying herself.

Parmeshar Singh jumped up, as though he had dropped a tray full of glass dishes on the floor.

In the evening after supper, holding the boy's finger he led him into the open courtyard and said, 'Today you've slept plenty, son. Let's go out for a walk. It's a beautiful moonlit night.'

Akhtar agreed right away. Parmeshar Singh wrapped a blanket carefully around the boy and put him on his shoulder. When he reached the fields, he said, 'This moon you see rising in the east, son, it will be morning by the time it's directly overhead.'

Akhtar looked at the moon.

'The moon which is shining here, must be shinning back in your mother's country too.'

This time Akhtar leaned over to look at Parmeshar Singh.

'When it reaches straight above our heads, it will also be straight above your mother's head.'

Akhtar asked, 'Would my mother also be watching the moon just as we are watching it here?'

'Absolutely.' There was a loud resonance in Parmeshar Singh's voice. 'Would you like to go to your mother?'

'Yes, very much,' Akhtar said. 'But you never take me to her. You're bad. Very bad. You are a Sikh.'

'No, son,' Parmeshar Singh said, 'I will. Today. You can be sure of that. A letter came from your mother. She says "I miss my Akhtar very much." '

'I miss her a lot, too,' Akhtar said, as if remembering something suddenly.

'Actually, I'm taking you to your mother right now.'

'Really?' Akhtar began to jump up and down on Parmeshar Singh's shoulder. 'I'm going to my mother! Parmun'll take me to her! When I'm there, I'll write Parmun a letter!'

Down below, Parmeshar Singh wept silently. He wiped his tears, cleared his throat, and asked, 'Would you like me to sing you a song?'

'Yes.'

'But first you should recite the Koran for me.'

'OK.' Akhtar intoned the verses beginning with *Qul Huwa 'l-Lah*. When he concluded the recitation with *Kufuwan Ahad*, he blew on his chest and said, 'Come, let me blow on your chest too.'

Parmeshar Singh stopped walking, unbuttoned the front of his shirt, and looked up. The boy hung down and blew into the open collar. 'Your turn now.'

Parmeshar Singh shifted the boy onto his other shoulder. Since he didn't remember any children's songs, he started singing all kinds of other songs, picking up his pace as he went along. Akhtar listened to him quietly.

Banto—her hair is like a dense forest.
Banto—her face is like the moon.
Banto—her broad hips flow sweetly.

O hey, O hear, people,
Banto—her broad hips flow sweetly.

'Who is Banto?' Akhtar interrupted.

Parmeshar Singh laughed. After a pause he said, 'You know, my wife, Amar Kaur's mother, she is Banto, and so is Amar Kaur, and so must be your mother too.'

'Why my mother?' Akhtar was angered. 'She's not a Sikh.'

Parmeshar Singh fell silent.

The moon had risen well into the sky. The night was perfectly calm. A few jackals howled near the cane fields now and then, followed by the same absolute silence. At first the howls frightened Akhtar, but Parmeshar Singh's assurances calmed him. After a long silence, he asked, 'Why aren't the jackals howling now?'

Parmeshar Singh laughed. He recalled a story. The story of Guru Gobind. As he told it, he deftly changed the Sikh names to Muslim names. Akhtar kept asking, 'And then what happened?... And then what happened?...'

The story wasn't yet finished when Akhtar suddenly shouted, 'Arey, the moon—it's right above our heads!'

Parmeshar Singh broke his stride and he too looked up. He then climbed up a small hill and peered into the distance. 'Who knows where your mother's country is,' he said.

He stood on the hill for a while. Suddenly the sound of *azan* came floating in from afar. Akhtar, beside himself with a rush of excitement, jumped so awkwardly that Parmeshar Singh had the hardest time holding on to him. He put him down and himself sat on the ground. Then, putting his hand on Akhtar's shoulder, who was standing beside him, he said, 'Go, son. Your mother's calling you. Just follow the sound.'

'Sh-shshsh!' Akhtar put his finger to his lips and whispered, 'One doesn't talk during the *azan*.'

'But I am a Sikh, son.'

'Sh-shshsh!' This time Akhtar, feeling piqued, glowered at him.

Parmeshar Singh drew the boy closer and sat him in his lap. He gave him a long kiss on the forehead. After the *azan* was over, he wiped his eyes with his sleeve and said in a voice crumbling with emotion, 'This is as far as I can come. You go on ahead.'

'Why? Why can't you?'

'Your mother's orders. She writes that you should come alone.' Parmeshar Singh wheedled. 'Now, keep walking straight, until you come to the village up ahead. There, tell them your name. Remember, not Kartar, but Akhtar. Then tell them your mother's name, and the name of your village. And don't you forget to write me a letter.'

'I won't,' Akhtar promised.

'And, yes, if you find a boy there called Kartar, send him back over to us. You will—won't you?'

'All right, I will.'

Parmeshar Singh kissed the boy on the forehead once again and, swallowing the lump in his throat, said, 'Now go!'

Akhtar took a few steps, turned around, and walked back to the older man. 'Why don't you come too?'

'No, I can't,' Parmeshar Singh explained. 'Your mother didn't say that I should come too.'

'But I'm scared,' Akhtar said.

'Recite the Koran and you'll be okay,' Parmeshar Singh suggested.

'All right,' the boy agreed. He broke into a litany of *Qul Huwa 'l-Lah* as he walked away from the older man.

The soft, faint light of the dawn was struggling with the darkness on the horizon. And the little boy Akhtar, like a strapping Sikh youth, was walking briskly away on the foggy foot trail. Parmeshar Singh, his eyes trained on the receding figure, sat on the hilltop, coming down from it only after the receding dot had become indistinct in the space up ahead.

Akhtar had barely reached the outskirts of the village when two soldiers rushed towards him. They stopped and asked him, 'Who are you?'

'Akhtar!' he said, as if the entire world knew who he was.

'Akhtar!' The soldiers looked, now at his face, now at his Sikh turban. Then one of them stepped forward and jerked the turban from the boy's head. Akhtar's *kes* came undone and cascaded down.

The boy became furious and snatched the turban back from the soldier. He felt his head with his hand, lay down on the ground, and wept bitterly. 'Give me back my comb!' he shouted. 'You've stolen my comb! Give it back, or I'll kill you!'

Instantly the two soldiers dropped to the ground with a thud, their rifle butts against their shoulders, as if to take aim.

'Halt!' one of the soldiers shouted and waited for a reply.

In the breaking daylight they both looked at each other, and one of them fired.

The report made the boy jump. Seeing the soldiers run off, he too followed them, shouting and crying.

Coming to the spot the soldiers stopped. By then Parmeshar Singh had wrapped his turban tightly round his thigh. But the blood was gushing out even through the innumerable folds. He was saying: 'Why did you have to shoot me?! I just forgot to clip Akhtar's *kes*! I only came to return Akhtar to his *dharm*, *yaaro*!'

In the distance, Akhtar was running over to them, his *kes* flowing in the air.

Translated by Muhammad Umar Memon

THE POND WITH THE BO TREE

Some months before independance of the subcontinent in 1947, I left for England to look for work. Near my mountain village just off the dirt road, there was a pond with the bo tree surrounded by high cliffs. A Hindu *sadhu* used to live there. The pond wasn't big, nor the area around it very large. Smack in the middle of the pond was a small mound which remained over-shadowed by the huge bo growing on the edge of the pond. There was a small hut on the mound and the *sadhu*, displaying a long, thick vermilion tilak on his forehead, used to sit at its doorstep, shouting '*Alakh Niranjan, Alakh Niranjan.*' Two armed watchmen also stayed there all the time, one of whom was a Hindu, the other a Sikh. Hindu young ladies would come to the pond and stand in front of the *sadhu*, hands folded, eyes closed, muttering some phrases under their breath. They came and went constantly and in droves. They came there to ask God through the *sadhu's* agency for children. If the *sadhu*, sitting on the mound, plucked up a flower from any of the bushes growing around and tossed it to a woman, she would be certain of becoming a mother soon.

The majority of people in the village were Muslims, but the pond with the bo had been occupied by the Hindus. It was known that centuries ago the pond was an ordinary rural water-reservoir, until Chandergupt Maurya had ordered solid brick steps to be built on all its sides. A crooked warping viaduct connected the last step to the mound. This was the *sadhu's* means to travel to and from the mound. No one dared touch the lush green bushes and the deep-red flowers growing in the cracks between the steps. The *sadhu maharaj* alone was privileged to do that. Once, a passerby, who was a Muslim, got entranced by the beauty of the flowers and, unawares, plucked one. The Hindu watchman assailed him with a drawn dagger, and the Sikh ran with his axe to help his companion. Then some elder pilgrim pointed out that that man didn't seem to be a native of the area. He couldn't have known that it was a dreadful sin to pluck a flower from those celestial bushes. He should be forgiven and let go, but also given the warning to throw the flower into the pond on his way out or demons would wring his neck well before he made it to the bend in the road.

A well-read man had done research and proved that ages ago a king named Chandergupt Maurya ruled that area. One day he, like other kings before him, while on a hunt, passed by the place pursuing a deer. At the edge of the pond, stood some young girls, taking clay-pots off their hips and heads. As they bent down to fill their pots, one of them slipped and fell down so hard that her bangles broke and pierced her wrists. The pot also slipped from her hands and began drifting towards the farther bank. Chandergupt was affected by all this. He patted the hurt and crying girl on her head and asked her how many bangles she had lost. She replied sobbing, 'Five.' The king forthwith called the headman of the village and ordered him to have five steps, of brick or stone, built all around the pond in five days; if he didn't do that, the king warned, he and four other members of his family would be ground in an oil-press at the end of five days. Then the king gave each of the girls five *ashrafis* and went on his way. The headman used the entire population of the village as forced labour and had them build the required number of brick steps within a day and a half; he didn't wait for the five days to be over. But the king didn't return to check; perhaps the deer had gone too far.

The pond was surrounded by tall, steep cliffs. The dirt road leading to the village passed by them. It was said that sometimes at night a sound was heard, such as could only be heard in the stillness of the night, coming from inside the pond, of some stone being ground somewhere far below in the depth, or of sand continually falling and piling up on a tin-roof. According to folk belief, the pool was a resting place of the demons. People with knowledge and intelligence would say that the ripples seen on the water's surface, ripples which at sunrise seemed to have acquired the colours of the rainbow, were proof that there were deposits of oil under the pool. The common folk, when they heard such stories, laughed out loud at the so-called wisdom of the intelligent, and countered by saying that ripples with the oily sheen were in fact the toys of the demons' children. Once an educated man had tried to hold one of the ripples on a wooden stick and lift it out but had fallen headlong into the water, as though someone had shoved him from behind. Since then no one had dared touch the ripples. If some ignorant person as much as extended his hand towards the ripples, the *sadhu* would jump up in a panic, shivering all over. He would glare at the offender and yell, 'No, no, no, no. Let the sleeping demons lie. Don't wake them up. *Alakh Niranjan. Alakh Niranjan.*'

I had a Hindu friend by the name of Makund Lal who lived in a village near this area. He was my college-mate, a graduate, and his conversations were always full of logic and reason. But one day when I went to visit him at his house, he brought out his baby boy and left me dumbfounded by saying, 'The *sadhu maharaj* of the pond with the bo of your village had one day plucked a flower and tossed it towards my wife. That was when this nephew of yours was born.'

I said, 'Makund, if it were that easy to have children, the whole institution of marriage would have crumbled. The *sadhu maharaj* doesn't have any children of his own, does he? Or they would have been roaming around the mound, but he is tossing babies towards others. Come on, man, talk sense. How could you ever start believing that this child started growing in your wife's womb when a flower came her way from the *sadhu*?'

Having said that, I laughed heartily. I was hoping he would join in my mirth, but he spoke earnestly, unable to hide his annoyance as though I had somehow assailed his faith, 'My advice to you is that after you are married and are without a child for four or five years, then come to the pond with the bo in your village and see how the *sadhu maharaj* fulfils your wish. This soil on which you stand, try raising yourself a little above it, and you'll witness an entirely different world. *Sadhu maharaj* hails from there.'

In England, with a friend's help, I found work. I wrote to Makund that if he ever went to my village, he should visit the *sadhu maharaj* at the pond, give him my regards and ask him how he was doing. He replied: 'First marry and then bother sending your regards to the *sadhu maharaj.*'

I was in England when Pakistan came into being. A few friends of mine and I danced about the streets of London. Then I found a job delivering hosiery products to different stores all over town, and I started earning good money. I also got married into an educated Pakistani family settled there.

Makund Lal became a refugee and going through Ambala, Delhi, and Lucknow, finally got to Allahabad, where he found a teaching job in a school and settled down. We kept writing to each other. When I gave him news of my marriage, he sent his congratulations and added that if I didn't have children in the next three or four years, I should remember the pond with the bo in my village in Pakistan. If the *sadhu maharaj* hadn't gone to India as a refugee, he would certainly toss a flower towards my wife.

In response, I made fun of his superstitions, but when, for four years, my wife remained unable to conceive, I did begin to think of Makund Lal, of the pond with the bo, and of the *sadhu maharaj*. When I mentioned this to my wife, she bent over with laughter. Barely controlling herself, she said, 'If that's the way things happen, then what are you doing sitting here? Go back to Pakistan. Advertise the *sadhu's* miracles in the major newspapers here and in Europe and America, and then see how the childless of the world rush to you. You'll become a millionaire in no time at all.' And she burst out laughing again.

The next year when God gave me a son, I wrote to Makund Lal, telling him not to be angry with me, but that my wife had become a mother without having to visit any *sadhu*. Two years later we had another son. I had been having a full and rich life in England when in 1972 I heard the news that my mother was seriously ill and wanted to see me and my children. My older son was in Cambridge and the younger one a student in London. I left them there and went to Pakistan with my wife.

It was already evening when the bus entered the area of my village. Passing by the pond the only thing I saw was a lot of lamps lit on a certain spot. I thought it might be *divali*—the festival of lights—tonight; otherwise so many lighted lamps didn't make much sense.

My younger aunt and her young granddaughter were in our house looking after my ailing mother. By now my mother's condition had stabilized. She said, 'Whatever little illness is left in me will disappear when I hug my son and daughter-in-law.'

In the morning my aunt took me aside and told me that her granddaughter had been childless five years after her marriage. My aunt said, 'Take her to Saint Jamalay Shah. I've heard that he tosses a flower and a leaf which have to be ground and drunk with milk, and that mixture cures infertility.'

I saw Makund Lal sitting on the far side of the wall in front and laughing. I asked, 'But Aunt, where is this Saint Jamalay Shah?' She said, 'He is the custodian of the holy shrine of Saint Kamalay Shah. Your bus must have passed by the shrine last evening. You belong to this village and yet don't know the pond with the bo tree?'

'The pond with the bo?' I said surprised. 'But Aunt, a Hindu *sadhu* used to live there.'

My aunt began smiling, and said, 'You are still a simpleton, son. Saint Kamalay Shah was Emperor Aurangzeb's *pir*, and Aurengzeb was the one who built his shrine. When the Mughal rule ended, the Hindus occupied the shrine. The shrine was situated on top of the mound in the middle of the pond. That ruthless *sadhu* built his hut right above it and took up living there. By God's grace, when Pakistan came into being, the *sadhu* fled, and one of the descendants of the older saint, Saint Jamalay Shah, repossessed the place. He now sits at the edge of the pond in front of the shrine and bestows children on the childless. Didn't you even see from the bus the many lamps lit on the holy shrine?'

I felt like running out of my house, climbing the highest hill in the area, looking eastward and shouting with all the power of my lungs: 'Makund Lal! O' brother Makund Lal! Come over here. Look. I have a wonderful spectacle to show you!'

PRAISE BE TO ALLAH

Maulvi Abul was quite a dashing figure before his marriage. Always dressed up, sporting a rose-coloured, green-striped waistwrap of handmade silk, no waistcloth made of homespun or long cloth for him, a shirt of fine quality silk, its sleeves crimped into hundreds of folds, a waistcoat of mauve velvet with a compass in one of its pockets and a silver snuff-case in the other, a headgear of light brown silk with a contrasting border and the gilded skull-cap partly visible through its folds, a walking-stick in his hand, studded with hoops of silver-gilt and brass tacks, some very bewitching oil dabbed on his hair, whose perfume lingered in the lanes as he walked by, the lids of his eyes, in which the pupils were placed a little higher than usual, almost deep-dyed in kohl, his fingers loaded with silver rings tricked out with large stones which had been brought back by pilgrims from the Holy land. He took these rings off at least four to five times every day while he performed his ablutions before the prayers and then put them back on his fingers in exactly the same order. And to top it all, his voice! Thank God he used his wonderful talent only to recite the Holy Koran; indeed, if he had thought it fit to croon some popular ditty it would have been difficult to keep the village girls in check. At every Eid, after he had preached the sermon, he was presented with a bag, heavy and jingling with something like a hundred and fifty to two hundred and fifty rupees, a collection to which every family in the village contributed. What is more, he gave away forty to fifty rupees out of it to the poor and the needy then and there, right in front of his congregation, saying all the while to those who received the alms: 'There is no need to call down blessings upon me. Remember Allah alone, exalted be His grandeur, who can not only bring a worm to life plumb in the heart of a stone but also provide it even there with sustenance. Don't bless me. Look! What's there He hasn't bestowed upon me? Health and contentment and a life without care. I desire nothing else from His gracious bounty.'

But following his marriage the blessings of Allah, exalted be His grandeur, underwent a transformation. His wife displayed such a clockwork consistency in presenting him with children that one year, when she failed to live up to her promise, Maulvi Abul, convinced that her failure to give birth to a baby meant there was something amiss with her creative mechanism, dashed off to see a physician. Indeed, as far as she was concerned, her departure from her routine of a child a year was as though the sun itself had failed to appear at the close of night. And so, when next year the sun duly appeared, right on time, Maulvi Abul heaved a sigh of relief. Of course, to have many children was one of Allah's blessings. But the trouble was that in the process his silken waistwrap became a kitchen-rag. His shirt of fine silk, changing piecemeal into diapers, disappeared before long, and was replaced by a loose shirt of coarse cloth which no amount of washing could make look clean. It always seemed a shade soiled as if while shaping it the weaver had used not only cotton yarn but also a bit of rubbish. The gilded skull-cap looked as if it had sprouted a moustache and a beard—so ragged did it now appear. His silver rings and the silver-gilt of his walking-stick had been used up to make earrings for the girls. Underneath his eyelids his eyeballs had moved further up, so much so that one got the impression that he was in his death throes. While his children kept tumbling in without let-up, the times in which he lived were also changing at a rattling pace. The kind of shoes which he had once purchased for just one rupee for his eldest daughter, Mehrunnisa, were now priced at six. He found this out when he ordered the cobbler to make a pair of shoes for his youngest daughter, Umdatunnisa; and as he complained about the price the cobbler said: 'It was because of you, sir, that I didn't ask for more. From anyone else I would have wangled ten rupees, not six. There is a hell of a demand for leather. Its price has increased so alarmingly you would think all the cattle on earth has been rustled away to some cloud-cuckoo-land. This pair of shoes has cost me a quarter less than six rupees. All I am going to make out of it is twenty-five paisas. Okay, let us forget these twenty-five paisas. May I drown, may there be no burial service for me, if I haven't told you the truth and nothing but the truth.'

If it were within the realm of possibility to get all you need merely by praying to heaven, Maulvi Abul would have begged God to send down a pair of shoes that very day for his little daughter. That night he spoke about it to his wife and when, instead of saying something, she turned up a corner of the quilt to show the state Umda's feet were in, he suddenly started crying like a child. And the very next day, after saying his morning prayers and attending to his other duties, he went and handed over the money, a quarter less than six rupees, to the cobbler. As he left his shop and stepped out into the street he called upon Allah, exalted be His grandeur, to be his witness and swore never to take snuff again.

The number of those who turned up at the mosque to offer their prayers was falling off, while the prices of consumer goods were going up instead of coming down; and then his children too were growing up and like some reflex action more and more of his hair was taking on a silver hue. No sooner did Mehrunnisa turn fourteen than Maulvi Abul began to have fits of absent-mindedness. If he bowed down while leading the prayer, he clean forgot to straighten up; if he prostrated himself, it seemed he would never get up again. Then some of the more vigilant of his followers would start coughing on purpose to prevent his staying in that position from the prayer of *Zuhr* to the prayer of *Asr*. During the blessed month of *Ramzan* he, as usual, had the honour of leading the *Taravih* prayers but whereas in former days Maulvi Abul Barkaat, far from misreading a word or a holy verse, didn't even mispronounce a single short vowel, he now mixed up *surah* 'Nisa' with *surah* 'Baqra' and what's more, recited *surah* 'Ar-Rahman' twice during the same *rakat*. When Chaudhari Fateh Dad, officially regarded as a local dignitary and a member of the district board, rebuked him for his lapse of memory, Maulvi Abul felt like blurting out: 'You have sons by the houseful, sir, that's why! If you too had a daughter, a big girl in her prime, then and then alone I could have explained to you how one can say the same *surah* twice over.' But the Chaudhari's censure was in the main of a religious nature, otherwise he was the same man who sent each evening, as was his wont for many years, a flat griddle bread smeared with clarified butter and an earthen bowl full of lentil soup to Maulvi Abul's house and was, in fact, so particular about the whole thing as if a single day's omission on his part would bring the heavens down; and as if it wasn't enough, even the slightest delay in the dispatch of his bread and soup sufficed to bring the Chaudhari to Maulvi Abul's house in person to beg his pardon: 'The commons must have come to hand a trifle late tonight, your reverence. I beg you to forgive this oversight. My wife was a little indisposed and the cooking was done by an attendant. The bitch of a cook forgot that if the commons were not sent you in time I would have to observe a day's fast by way of repentence.'

These commons of provisions were of various kinds; and on Thursdays nothing at all was cooked or baked in Maulvi Abul's house. About a dozen large and nourishing flat breads were sent in by those who held him in regard. Besides, his wife, barely three months after her marriage, had opened up a sort of school at their place where she taught the girls to read the Holy Koran. On Thursdays every pupil brought with her a humble commons with a thimbleful of sugar on top, and Zebunnisa had to lay out two more bread-baskets expressly to hold it all. On such occasions they all enjoyed a hearty meal morning and evening. The leftovers were put out in the sun to dry, later to be boiled in molasses and turned into a kind of candy. But human beings don't live by bread alone; they need clothes also to cover their nakedness and this was yet another problem. Every time a harvest was gathered in, the Chaudhari presented Maulvi Abul with a brand-new outfit. However, as soon as he came home with his new set of clothes, the entire household took on the appearance of a tailoring shop. With the help of her daughters, Mehrun, Zubda, and Shamsun, Zebunnisa soon made short work of the waist-wrap of long-cloth and in this manner many shirts for the infants were made out of it. A similar treatment was meted out to his muslin turban to enable his sons and daughters to fend off nakedness for a few months more. Meanwhile, the few rupees which were earned by him now and then as fee for formalizing a marriage contract or for leading a funeral prayer were put aside in a tin-box to help defray the cost of Mehrunnisa's trousseau. His children's bellies became bigger and bigger while the rest of their bodies kept shrinking. The bracelets which once filled Zebunnisa's forearms like a clamp now went sliding down to her wrists at the slightest motion. And behind her long eyelashes the glow of her youth had long turned to ashes; and when she blinked her eyes these ashes seemed to drift across her face. Even Maulvi Abul himself had been completely crushed by life's trivial harassments. These were the days when people stopped calling him Maulvi Abul Barkaat and slashed his name down to Maulvi Abul. His temples were completely grey by now and his gums no longer firm. When he recited the Holy Koran one could sometimes note a wheezing sound as his breath whistled through the chinks which had appeared between his teeth. But his voice had lost none of its magnificence. The words, as he properly articulated them, made a ringing sound, like playing marbles clinking down on a salver of brass. However, a trembling note had crept into his voice which seemed a bit odd to those who regularly prayed at the mosque and had known him for long. But the Chaudhari knew what it was that made Maulvi Abul's voice tremble, because he had already spoken to him to help find a suitable young man for his daughter. With this in mind the Chaudhari had a close look at the village night after night. As he lay awake in his bed, he literally went over into each and every house, weighing the possibilities. And some of the young men in the village did appeal to him but the trouble was that Maulvi Abul was too familiar a figure. Everyone knew that Mehrunnisa had been brought up on scraps of dry bread and leavings, and a girl fed on such humble fare is lachrymose rather than full-blooded. Moreover, the fact that Maulvi Abul received no more than twenty to twenty-five rupees now on both the Eids was not unknown to them. And this paltry sum, which in all probability was insufficient to fit out his nine children, could be of no help in improvising a dowry for Mehrunnisa. The Chaudhari did broach the subject with a couple of parties but his listeners staggered back as if they had suddenly spotted a wasp within a flower.

But the prayers of Maulvi Abul and his wife didn't go unanswered. Right then a young man, who was formerly known as Khuda Yar but now called himself Shamim Ahmad, returned from the city and set up a small cloth-shop in the village. He was the only son of a man who had committed the entire Holy Koran to memory. After his father's death he tried for a while, with the help of Maulvi Abul, to memorize the Holy Koran himself. The down had hardly appeared on his face when, leaving his aged mother behind him, he ran away to the city. It was found out later that he had taken up a job in some head clerk's house. After a while the head clerk got hold of a bit of a spot in front of a shop and installed him there. He began to deal in cut-pieces and sent for his mother to come and live with him. When he had mastered his trade, he changed his name from Khuda Yar to Shamim Ahmad and returned to his village. It needed a great deal of coaxing and wheedling on the part of Shamim Ahmad before Maulvi Abul declared himself willing to inaugurate his shop and be his first customer and by doing so bring him the best of luck and plenty of ready money.

On that day, to please his former pupil and his aged mother, Maulvi Abul made what was probably the most momentous decision of his life. He went and said to his wife: 'Arif's mother, Shamim Ahmad wants me, and no one else, to handsel his shop. Don't you think we might as well buy a suit's length for Mehrunnisa? We do need it after all for her trousseau. Besides, this ceremonial opening of his shop will take place with the whole village looking on and every one will be a little impressed. In any case, I feel morally bound to encourage Shamim Ahmad. In the first place he is an old pupil of mine. Secondly, he is the beloved son of Hafiz Abdur Rahim, may Allah bless his soul. Thirdly,' here Maulvi Abul paused, looked around him and added in a whisper, 'Arif's mother, I swear by Allah, exalted be His grandeur, it seems to me as if he had been sent here by providence specially for Mehrunnisa's sake.'

When she heard this the ashen look departed from her eyes and they sparkled again as if the warmth of a gone out fire was showing up for a moment. 'May your words come true,' she said, put her hand inside her shirt to take out the key which hung round her neck, opened the trunk and placed the tin-box in front of Maulvi Abul. 'May Allah bless what you said. Every time I look at Mehrunnisa I think of a bread that has been left too long on the griddle and is getting burnt.' She began to weep and smile all at the same time, and when Mehrunnisa came in to see to something, she at once said, 'Daughter, aren't the scraps of bread drying in the sun out there? Place a cooking pot over them, or else the crows will make off with the lot. Do go, my dear.' And the flush which appeared on Mehrunnisa's cheeks seemed to say, 'I can see through it all, Mother. Father is off to Shamim Ahmad's shop to try and handsel me.'

When Mehrunnisa left the room Maulvi Abul took out all that was in the tin-box, forty-three rupees all told, put them away in his pocket and said, as he stood up, 'Now pray that she gets married and if it comes to pass I would feel, for the next five or six years at least, light as a feather.'

Zebunissa kept on smiling and wiping her tears and Maulvi Abul set out for Shamim Ahmad's shop. There was quite a crowd in front of it, mostly women, who stood there with their fingers on their lips and noses and stared at the colourful fabrics as if in a trance. Shamim Ahmad became a picture of obsequiousness as Maulvi Abul stepped into his shop; and when he recited a few verses from the Holy Koran the whole crowd was charmed. The recitation over, he chose a pink fabric with blue flowers which had golden specks on them. 'Give me a piece from it for a woman's suit,' he said in a louder than usual voice and cast a glance at the crowd. Shamim Ahmad said 'Bismillah' as he reached for the yardstick and measured out seven yards. Then he took up the scissors, said 'Bismillah' again, cut the cloth, folded it and with a final 'Bismillah' laid it in front of Maulvi Abul in a manner which suggested as if he were giving it away for nothing, like a gift.

'How much?' Maulvi Abul didn't look towards the crowd as he said it but merely put his hand in his pocket.

Shamim Ahmad respectfully tried to make himself as unobtrusive as possible, rubbed his hands together for a moment, cleared his throat and said, 'At six rupees a yard it comes to forty-two rupees, your reverence.'

Maulvi Abul felt as if all the bolts in the shop had suddenly fallen down upon him. Completely disconcerted, he took his hand out of his pocket, replaced a rupee back in it and handed over the rest to Shamim Ahmad. The fingers of the onlooker women jumped from their lips to their noses and those already on the noses moved away and came to rest in the air. As Maulvi Abul put his purchase under his arm, Shamim Ahmad said, 'As your reverence was my first customer, I did not allow you any discount. I am, as I was in the past, loyal to you. Allah willing, I will repay you someday for all this inconvenience you have put up with for my sake.'

Maulvi Abul got up with the suit's length under his arm and felt like saying to Shamim Ahmad, 'Allah alone, exalted be His grandeur, will make amends for it, my dear; and the reason is that while you have sold a few yard's length of cloth to me, I too have tried to make a deal for my daughter.' But this was merely because he felt a bit incensed at having been cleaned out like this, and he managed to subdue his feelings as he got to his feet and said instead, 'You were within your rights, Shamim Ahmad. You need not mention it at all. May Allah, exalted be His grandeur, make you and your business prosper!'

'Amen!' exclaimed Zebunnisa when, while she looked at the cloth's softness, slipperiness and stylish appearance, she heard her husband say, 'May Allah will it so that our Mehruunisa wear a suit made out of it on her wedding day.'

Only a few days later one evening a knock was heard at Maulvi Abul's door. Those who came to see him so late in the day usually brought with them an offering of rice or halva or pudding and his children, as soon as they heard their door-chain jingle, scampered towards the door. But for some reason known to him alone, Maulvi Abul said in a threatening tone, which he rarely used, 'Wait!' The children checked themselves and pulled long faces and Umdatunnisa in fact began to whimper but Maulvi Abul, quite unmoved, said nothing to clear them up, strode onward and as he flung the door open, a gush of aroma invaded the ante-room connecting the house with the doorway and heard a voice say, 'Peace be with you, your reverence!'

It was Shamim Ahmad. As he held out his hand to be shaken, his waistwrap of new long cloth snapped like a sheet of tin and when he said, pausing every now and then, 'I have come here with a petition, your reverence. That's why I made bold to disturb you at this odd time,' Maulvi Abul felt as if the perfume emanating from Shamim Ahmad's person was almost humming. He could have heard the petition right there in the ante-room but called out, looking over his shoulder, 'I'll be back in a minute, Arif's mother!' and then holding Shamim Ahmad by his hand, set off for the mosque at such a clipping pace that the young man was compelled to lift his waistwrap right up to his knees with his other hand to keep it from setting up a commotion.

When they arrived at the mosque, they found one of its cells occupied by a few worshippers who squatted round a fire, listening to the tales of Caliph Haroon ar-Rashid and his acts of justice. The other cell lay dark, as it had been set aside for those who liked to pray in seclusion for forty days on end to attain some supernatural power. Leaving Shamim Ahmad in the gloomy cell, Maulvi Abul went out, brought back a burning stick from the blaze next door, and walked up to a recess. An earthen lamp tilled with mustard oil was soon alight. This done, Maulvi Abul left the cell a second time, tossed the brand back in the fire and hurried in again. Shamim Ahmad hadn't shaved himself for some days and the black down on his face, very tastefully trimmed along his cheeks and chin and rubbed over gently with attar of henna, glistened in the light thrown out by the lamp.

'Speak,' said Maulvi Abul, and the manner in which he prompted Shamim Ahmad suggested as if he had just completed giving final touches to a hall festooned and bedecked in honour of his guest.

Shamim Ahmad lowered his eyes and his lips, parting slightly, trembled. Then raising his head he looked at the lamp smoking like a chimney. He went up to it and lowered its wick with the help of a straw and said, 'Do I have your permission to express myself?'

'Yes, yes! Do!' Maulvi Abul began by patting his shoulder and then somewhat abruptly placed both his hands on his shoulders. The muscles over his shoulder-bones felt like big balls of flesh to his touch, 'Speak out, my dear.'

Shamim Ahmad started rubbing his hands. After a moment's silence, swallowing something with great difficulty, he said, 'As a matter of fact it is something which should have been handled by my mother. She should have approached your reverence, as is right and proper. However, for some years now she has become so soft of heart that she can't control her feelings, starts weeping and cursing over the most trivial of matters. In these circumstances I thought that the right course of action would be to come and see you all by myself.'

'You did very well,' Maulvi Abul said very affectionately.

'I am an old servant of yours,' said Shamim Ahmad, trying to shrink to half his normal size, surged out once and shrank back again. 'I beseech you, sir, to regard me forever...,' he stared once more at the lamp and lowering his gaze blew at some imaginary spot on his sleeve. 'Sir, regard me forever as your slave.' The way he said this suggested he was about to pass away.

Maulvi Abul felt like cutting a caper and laughed a little for formality's sake before he remarked, 'I couldn't divine your meaning, Shamim Ahmad.'

Amazed and hurt Shamim Ahmad looked him straight in the eye. How could it be possible that the man who could, and did, at a moment's notice render intelligible many difficult portions of the Holy Koran in lucid and simple language and solve innumerable knotty issues relating to Islamic canonical law, did not know the meaning of words 'Regard me as your slave?' In a voice which sounded hoarse, he said, as if in the midst of some fatal spasm, 'Sir, I mean, that is, sir... sir, regard me as your slave.'

It looked as if this utterance which left no room for doubt satisfied Maulvi Abul. He did not think it necessary to press for any further explanations. For a while Shamim Ahmad stood there, looking at his feet, rubbing and wringing his hands but when Maulvi Abul kept quiet, he hesitantly dared to look up, and it cost him such an effort, as if he had to throw his full weight against his eyes. A few tears hung in Maulvi Abul's beard. While the attar of henna lent a wet sheen to the young man's down, tears glimmered and trembled in the old man's beard. The lamp was again sending up a dense cloud of smoke but now it didn't occur to Shamim Ahmad to go and mend its flame. He was anxious to say something but couldn't speak, although his lips had parted. All at once, just as if he had realized something, Maulvi Abul wiped his eyes with the hem of his turban and said in a voice trembling with emotion, 'How meek a creature of Yours is a daughter, Allah, exalted be Your grandeur! How meek!' Tears ran down his cheek and hung like drops in his beard. 'She is a thing to be given away, Shamim Ahmad. I will give her away. Why shouldn't I! I have to do it. And then you are like someone related to me. The son of my brother Hafiz Abdur Rahim, may Allah bless his soul, is like my own son. Come on, come closer.' And Maulvi Abul drew Shamim Ahmad in his embrace.

When he returned to his house, Zebunnisa almost at once remarked, although he was still at some distance from her: 'Where have you been? What a lovely perfume!'

Mehrunnisa, who was busy baking a bread, the last of the lot, on the griddle, also chimed in, 'Really, Father, the whole house is smelling like a rose.'

Maulvi Abul looked at the huddle of his children with complete equanimity. However, as he had come home empty-handed they all stared at him in a miserable way. It was hard to pacify them at one go, so he said, 'Tonight, my children, you shall not only get your share of the bread but also a lump of jaggery.' The unhappy faces brightened up while Mehrunnisa found it impossible to look away from the griddle.

'Let me tell you, Arif's mother,' Maulvi Abul said as he moved towards the door.

She heard him out and said, 'Now lay your hand on my head and swear.'

Maulvi Abul twittered happily: 'I would swear by Allah, exalted be His grandeur. And you want me to swear by your head. Are you, Allah forbid, of more account than Allah Himself, exalted be His grandeur? If only the mind of women were somewhere around here, closer to their skull,' and with a smile he playfully slapped Zebunnisa on her crown.

Zebunnisa began to weep like a child. She knew what all this was about. Hadn't he himself, a little while ago, shed similar tears? In a moment he went up to her and laid down his sodden beard on her wet cheek.

'This is how one's prayers are granted,' Maulvi Abul told her, summoning to his face a grandeur which bespoke of years of worship and pious meditation. 'To Allah belongs all praise. This is how He, Who hears all, heeds our pleas; this is how He showers whom He will with good fortune. Do you hear me, Zebun?' It was perhaps the first time since their first night together as husband and wife that he had called his wife 'Zebun' instead of 'Arif's mother.'

Wiping her eyes she said, 'When Shamim Ahmad was Khuda Yar, when he was only a boy and used to come here to take his lessons from you, he always looked at Mehrun with eyes wide with wonder just as you stare at me sometimes, I swear by Allah.'

And the husband and wife had not been able to wipe away their tears properly yet when someone rattled their door-chain; it sent the children scurrying towards the door once more.

'Wait!' This time Maulvi Abul's voice had no harshness in it. 'I'll go myself.' Then he went up to his children, stroked their heads and said in a low voice, 'Don't be such a glutton for food. It isn't nice, you see? Not everyone who comes to see me brings halva and rice with him. See, what I mean? Now go in.' And raising his voice a little he said: 'Don't let them come out in the cold, Mehrun, my daughter. All I have are those children.'

He crossed the ante-room and as he opened the door, Chaudhari Fateh Dad, muffled in a warm blanket, caught hold of him, pulled him out into the lane, and embracing him, said, 'Congratulations, your reverence! A thousand congratulations! My efforts were not in vain, after all.'

At the moment the only reason why Maulvi Abul could not take the Chaudhari for an angel was that he lacked a pair of wings. 'Allah, exalted be His grandeur, be thanked for this stroke of luck and you for your magnanimity,' he said to his visitor glibly, as if the very words were melting in his mouth.

'God helped me to acquit myself honourably of my obligation towards you,' said the Chaudhari and added, 'Now you must not waste any time in fixing a date for the marriage. Shamim Ahmad is a nice chap. But, nonetheless, he is a young man and shopkeeper as well. Every day scores of women visit his shop and you are, of course, well aware of the times we live in, no shame left in it. The boys and girls seem to be loaded with gunpowder. You never know when they are going to blow up. It was I who told Shamim Ahmad to go and see you. It was, as custom demands, his mother's duty to approach you and make an offer but the old hag no longer has her wits about her. Do something against her wishes and the wretch gets her dander up, cursing and abusing you and your family right back to your seventh generation. Shamim Ahmad just now told me that you have agreed to his proposal. When I insisted that he should get married as quickly as possible, he requested me to speak about it to your reverence and decide upon a date. That's why I am here. Think it over and let me know in the morning and give this ... this...' and he brought forth a small bundle from within his blanket, 'Give this to my daughter.'

As Maulvi Abul took the bundle from him in silence, Chaudhari said in a low voice, 'May Allah approve of it.'

'Amen,' said Maulvi Abul without thinking, out of sheer force of habit.

Once inside, he undid the bundle and found a big silken kerchief on which lay a hundred rupee note topped by a pair of golden earrings with pendants. The collets, big as bubbles, were inlaid with what were either precious stones or a job of enameling.

Having shaken up the kerchief in the hope of finding something else, Zebunnisa cheerfully said, 'Did Shamim Ahmad send these?'

And before Maulvi Abul could say a word, Mehrunnisa got up and ran out of the room.

'Oh!' He looked at his wife in astonishment and both of them burst out laughing.

'She guessed it!' Zebunnisa announced looking towards the door with her index finger on her nose-pin.

'What about you, putting it so bluntly, "Did Shamim Ahmad send these?"' Perhaps for the first time in his life Maulvi Abul mimicked a woman's voice and accent and the children, till now lost in amazement, gave a roar of laughter, thoroughly enjoying it. Umda timidly tried to touch the earring.

'Chaudhari Fateh Dad gave these for Mehrun,' he divulged the secret in a very casual way as though it was of no consequence at all.

'May Allah approve of it,' Zebunnisa said as if from within her tomb on which a fresh covering had been placed.

A few days later Mehrunnisa was made to sit in bridal seclusion with some girl-friends of her age for company, and her soles were dyed in henna. Although a marriage was about to be celebrated in the house, no one dared to bring in a drum and play a tune on it because it belonged to Maulvi Abul and while he knew, having read about it, that when the Holy Prophet arrived at the city of Medina he was greeted by girls who played at tambourines and sang, he could find no injunction concerning the playing of drums and in Punjab, unfortunately, tambourine was yet a thing unknown. 'If you can find a tambourine you are welcome to play on it and sing but just you dare to bring a drum here and I will throw it on the rooftop,' he warned the professional singing and dancing women in a menacing tone. In the end the village girls sat down in a ring, with Mehrun in their middle, and all night long, without the accompaniment of drums, weaved around her, with their sweet voices, a glamorous wonderland made up of songs about love and friendship, flowers and spring showers, and the meetings and partings of lovers.

But what on earth could have prevented Shamim Ahmad from bustling in with drums and clarinets and from letting off firecrackers. The nuptial procession turned out to be a spectacular affair and there was such a furor, at Maulvi Abul's door that, at every roll of the drums, his house of mud-walls and un-baked bricks seemed to shake down to its very foundations.

At the sight of so great a festivity Maulvi Abul and his wife withdrew into a corner of their house and whispering to each other soon came to a decision. During the night one could hear, while the girls sang on and on, in the background a scratchy sound of trunks being dragged about and opened and shut. And next morning when the paraphernalia of Mehrunnisa's dowry was laid out in the courtyard and on the rooftop for public viewing, the villagers, one and all, almost reeled back at the sight. Well, one can somehow or the other provide a number of clothes but where did those large earrings of gold come from?

'The Maulvi has an amulet which enables him to draw upon invisible riches,' suggested an onlooker.

An old woman, thrusting her finger in her dewlap, pronounced, 'My sinful eyes have already recognized a number of suits. Some of these Zebunnisa received as part of her own dowry. She is a thrifty one, so she kept them safe for her daughter. The bracelets and the nose-pin also belong to the mother. But the earrings?' and withdrawing her finger from the folds of her dewlap she raised it towards the sky.

As Mehrunnisa took her seat in the palanquin, nickels and dried dates were strewn around as a propitiatory gesture. The village urchins made a rush for them. Maulvi Abul's children, who had been snivelling simply because they had seen their father weep, suddenly looked alive, bobbing up and down as if springs were pushing up against their soles. 'Don't move!' Maulvi Abul thundered and the springs shrank back into the earth. The children stayed put where they were. Arif alone managed to cover a nickel with his toes while he stood there and only after the bridal procession had moved off did his fortune transfer itself from his foot to his hand.

Maulvi Abul accompanied the palanquin for some distance. The reddened appearance of his eyes and nose matched the pallor of his face and looked like a pied rose. It seemed as if both sorrow and contentment had divided the spread of his face equally between themselves for their manifestations. He checked himself when they came to a turning and kept staring at the silken curtain of the receding palanquin. Then he drew a deep breath, interlocked his fingers, snapped them and turned back to go home.

In the lane the village kids were still looking for nickels and dried dates. As soon as Arif and his siblings, who were standing at the door, spied their father, they vanished, like so many will o' the wisps. The tingling pain and itch Maulvi Abul's lips had been conscious of for quite some time now resolved themselves into a smile and brightened his eyes. As he was about to step into the ante-room, he noticed the gleam of a nickel lying against the wall but moved on as if it didn't mean a thing to him. As he went in, Zebunnisa, who was probably standing just behind the door, caught hold of his hand, wept bitterly like a child and when they stepped into the courtyard, walking side by side, she waved her hands, describing two large circles and added, 'Now that our Mehrun has left, the house seems as silent as a graveyard.'

'You have taken leave of your senses,' Maulvi Abul said and his smile became more noticeable. 'If she is gone did she also take away Zubda with her? And has Shamsun also left the house like her?' Then pausing a little he asked, 'Arif, my boy, what is Zubda doing?'

'She is weeping, sir,' replied Arif, stepping out from the children lined against the wall.

'Where is she?' Maulvi Abul asked.

'At the same place where our elder sister, Mehrunnisa, was made to sit all by herself before her marriage,' Arif told him.

'Zubda!' Maulvi Abul called her. Zebunnisa was still weeping.

Zubda appeared at the door. Her new pink scarf had turned purplish at places because of her tears; and her palms dyed red in henna, to which she had imparted a sheen by rubbing up some clarified butter early in the morning, were now coated with dirt at places; and her coiffure was becoming undone.

But as soon as Maulvi Abul saw her he was thunderstruck. His smile crept back to his lips, became smaller, as if dying out and a pallor spread over his face. Zubda came to a stop a few paces away and sobbed.

And Maulvi Abul firmly gripping his wife's hand literally dragged her clumsily to a corner of the courtyard and the way he spoke, it seemed he was telling her the house was on fire! 'Listen, Arif's mother, this Zubda of ours, why she is already a big girl!'

Zebunnisa stared at Zubda as if, while her parents knew nothing about it, she had been coming of age furtively, using Mehrun as a front.

After a while he cleared his throat without any call and put his hand on the shoulder of his dumbfounded wife and said, 'Don't you worry, woman. To despair of Allah's mercy, exalted be His grandeur, is an act of sacrilege.'

Zebunnisa pushed away his hand from her shoulder somewhat brusquely, 'Aren't you ashamed of yourself? First you took me by the hand and tugged me here. Now you caress my shoulder. What would our grown-up daughters think! With the children looking on, you...' and instead of finishing her sentence, Zebunnisa merely shrugged the very shoulder her husband had touched.

Suddenly a thought flashed through Maulvi Abul's mind. He shouted, 'Shamsun!'

Shamsun had hardly left her place in the row when Maulvi Abul, trying to lean against something, groped for the wall behind him and finding nothing close at hand, swayed like a branch that had been snapped off. As she moved, her soles didn't all at the same time touch the ground but her body and feet alike suggested a rocking motion. First her heel touched the ground, then her arch and finally her curled up toes, one by one, came down as supple as could be and only then did she lift her other foot.

'Nothing, daughter, It's nothing. You may go,' Maulvi Abul told her and walked briskly towards the door.

Shamsunnisa stared at her mother in astonishment.

And Zebunnisa, weeping as bitterly as before, collapsed then and there in a heap and Zubda and Shamsun ran up to her.

Once outside, Maulvi Abul looked around stealthily and picking up the nickel lying against the wall dropped it in his pocket.

There were but two trunks in the house. One of them was being used to store scraps of bread and the other housed Qamrun and Umda's dolls and the marbles the kids played with. There was also a primary school in the village now and the number of girls who came to Maulvi Abul's house to have a lesson of the Holy Koran had steeply declined, one reason why the dried scraps of bread were now boiled not once a week but once a fortnight. Those who used to come to the mosque to offer their prayers also seemed to have been spoiled by the times. Sometimes, after having summoned the people to prayer, Maulvi Abul sat back, expecting them to turn up, but when he realized that if he waited any longer the ordained time for the prayer would lapse, he got to his feet and went inside the mosque all by himself, completely distraught, as if going in to discharge some unpleasant duty. During the Friday prayer, when a few peasants did show up, he preached the sermon in a poignant manner, spoke about the importance of prayers in Islam and the blessed nature of the services rendered by the theologians, and said, 'Don't you remember there was an earthquake in Quetta? Why was there an earthquake? When an earthquake hit Turkey many villages were simply swallowed up by the earth. What made the earth do it? Everywhere the Muslims are being slaughtered like sheep. Why are they being killed? Why? Have you ever given it a thought? Oh! why should you bother about such things? The good food you fatten upon has gone to your head and you turn a cold shoulder to your religion. The earthquakes and the killings are taking place because you don't say your prayers and care not a rap for the theologians. It is the wrath of Allah. These are the portents of doomsday. Don't you see? And would you let your own village also disappear within the maw of the earth? Speak out! Say something!'

These sermons, which played upon the sentiments of the people helped bring up somewhat the number of those who came to say their prayers and for a day or two Maulvi Abul's house did not lack bread spread over with clarified butter, but very soon the same old emptiness returned to it through which Zubda's eyes gleamed and Shamsun's body swayed, the dried scraps of bread and marbles rattled in the tin-trunk, and Qamrun's dolls divesting themselves of their rags barged into each other.

There were a couple of sustaining factors in Maulvi Abul's life which had never let him down. One was Allah, exalted be His grandeur, and the other, Chaudhari Fateh Dad. Wasn't it enough of mercy on Allah's part that he and his wife and all their children were still alive and the marriage of Mehrunnisa had been such a dazzling affair that ever since that day a steady stream of importunate suitors had been seeking the hands of Zubda and Shamsun. But Maulvi Abul was as apathetic to these requests as he had once been keen to find a husband for Mehrunnisa. 'Well, the girls are just out of their childhood,' he would say. 'They still play with their dolls. Shamsun hasn't even read the Holy Koran through yet. How can I bring myself to part from my dear little fledglings and shove them into some stranger's home. I am not going to commit myself. We shall see about it next year.'

Every time Zebunnisa let him know that Zubda and Shamsun were simply bursting with youth, he said, 'We shall see to it. Allah, exalted be His grandeur, will take pity on us. It is a great thing to trust in Him, Arif's mother. When the peasant sows the seed he trusts in Allah, exalted be His grandeur. Were he not to trust in Him, the seed would go to waste. It is this very trust which helps the seed to germinate and push out, which ripens the corn within the green womb of leaves. Do you follow me, Arif's mother?'

'But the peasant does sow the seed,' Zebunnisa argued with him. 'What have you done?'

'Praise be to Allah,' Maulvi Abul replied. 'I have done a great deal. Every time I say my prayers I entreat Allah to come to help.'

And this silenced Zebunnisa.

Chaudhari Fateh Dad was never far from his mind each time he prayed for deliverance. What a kind-hearted man he was, sending him bread and soup in the evening, day after day, for so many years and fitting him out in new clothes every time the harvest was gathered in, and unlike others he never boasted of it, which made his charity all the more pleasant. But the Chaudhari had been unwell for some time now. A boil had appeared on his spine. An old barber was called in, an amateurish but seasoned surgeon, and he used his lancet to such effect that it took the boil less than a day to swell and burst. At the same time the Chaudhari was seized by a fit of ague and all the physicians in the neighbourhood flocked to his bedside. Meanwhile Maulvi Abul's house presented a dismal appearance. Not only did the ill-treatment meted out to Mehrunnisa by her mother-in-law weigh on their souls but the Chaudhari's illness tended to make matters worse.

If the children set up a rumpus at times, Maulvi Abul shouted, 'Keep quiet, you wretches. The Chaudhari is seriously ill and you are making merry, you ungrateful ones. If the Chaudhari were not here to look after us, half of us would have starved to death by now. Pray to Allah, exalted be His grandeur, that he gets well again, you miserable ones.'

At that time Maulvi Abul went every morning and evening to the Chaudhari's place to inquire after his health, but as there were always a large number of people present to wish the ailing man well, he didn't get a chance to talk about his family affairs. All that happened was that as soon as the Chaudhari noticed the presence of Maulvi Abul, he tried to sit up to show him respect only to fall back, face downwards, with a groan. 'Pray for me, your reverence,' he would say in a low voice and Maulvi Abul, with tears in his eyes, would raise a finger towards the sky and reply, 'The Absolute Healer will make you well again.' However, one day, when Maulvi Abul arrived at the Chaudhari's place, there was no one with him except one of his sons. The Chaudhari also, for once, felt a little better. He made a show of getting up respectfully but did not groan. He made a sign to his son to leave them alone and asked, 'How are your daughters, your reverence?'

'Praise be to Allah. They are well and remember you in their prayers.'

'I have heard that there are many who wish to marry them.'

Maulvi Abul was under the impression that the negotiations which had taken place between him and the various suitors were a closely-guarded secret. He had no idea that girls, once in their prime, cannot be hidden away and every secret is but an open one. Taken aback he said, 'Yes, indeed, there are many who seek their hand.'

'Well? Have you made up your mind?' the Chaudhari looked at him rather pointedly.

Maulvi Abul became a little panicky. He moved his lips to say something but felt as if all at once his mouth and throat had gone completely dry. Swallowing a bit he said, 'Well, how can I make up my mind? Allah, exalted be His grandeur, alone can decide what is to be done. If someone lives in an empty rambling house where you would be hard put to find even a toothpick, you can't expect him to sort out the details of his daughters' betrothals, can you?'

'Must you reckon without me, your reverence, as if I am no more!' the Chaudhari's trembling voice sounded a shade piqued.

'May your enemies die,' Maulvi Abul hastily said, 'May Allah, exalted be His grandeur, through His grace restore you back to health and then we will sit down together and come to a decision.'

'Yes, sir,' the Chaudhari said in a sympathetic tone. 'It must be decided forthwith. When you have a fully grown-up daughter in your house, each passing day seems as long as a century. Allah, be He exalted, will let us have the wherewithal and we shall see the whole thing through. Are you receiving the commons regularly?'

'Yes, sir,' replied Maulvi Abul, 'Regularly.'

'May Allah approve of it,' the Chaudhari suggested in a low voice.

'Amen!' Maulvi Abul responded unthinkingly, out of habit.

They remained silent for a while. Chaudhari groaned a little before he said, 'They say that Mehrunnisa and Shamim Ahmad have taken to each other but her mother-in-law is bent upon running her down.'

'Yes, sir,' Maulvi Abul said in a sorrowful voice. 'But I have never interfered in these matters. Once you marry your daughter to someone, she ceases to belong to you.'

'But why can't she get along with her mother-in-law?'

'Because she always taunts her for being so poor and down and out. Keeps railing at her like this, "You are penniless, you were brought up on scraps of bread, your clothes smell of winding-sheets, you came to us empty-handed"—the way women are wont to talk.'

'Hmm,' the Chaudhari thought about it for a while. 'It is not true to say that your daughter no longer belongs to you, your reverence. In fact, she has the right to expect more from you following her marriage. Her mother-in-law being what she is, you must see to it that all these insults and jeers come to a stop. She calls Mehrunnisa penniless, does she? Now when your daughter has a baby, you must send her a present of silken clothes, gilded caps, and golden bracelets bedecked with tiny bells and see if your daughter's prestige does not go up. That's the way to cut the harridan's cackle. Am I right, your reverence?'

Indeed you are. What you have just said makes a great deal of sense but at the same time it is also somewhat impracticable. How on earth am I going to get hold of the things you have mentioned, said Maulvi Abul to himself, So, the guess Arif's mother had made about Mehrunnisa eight months ago was a correct one! All at once Maulvi Abul, made fidgety by his curiosity, found it impossible to stay by the Chaudhari's bedside any longer. Was it true that Mehrunnisa was about to have a child? He had never asked Zebunnisa about it and she too had told him nothing out of modesty. She knew her husband was dead set against poking about in order to find out if one's daughter were pregnant or not.

As soon as he set his foot in the ante-room he called out, 'Arif's mother!'

Zebunnisa ran up to him, saying, 'Good God! I hope everything is all right. What's the matter? How is the Chaudhari?'

'Allah, exalted be His grandeur, will take pity on him,' he said, 'Tell me, Arif's mother, how is our dear Mehrun?'

Zebunnisa was startled, 'Who told you that?'

'When is she going to have it?' He seemed to have lost, for once, all control over himself.

'Well, should Allah but wish it, in a couple of days,' she told him, looking abashed, 'but who told you that?'

He said as if he was delivering a sermon, 'Now is our chance to help our dear daughter by bringing her bad-tempered lousy mother-in-law to her senses. We shall see to it that our grandson or granddaughter gets a lot of...'

'May God make it a grandson,' she exclaimed, chipping in.

'Whatever it is,' said he, resuming his harangue, 'we will send a lot of gifts for the child, gifts like gilded caps and golden bracelets, so that our daughter can hold her head high again and also muzzle that mealy-mouthed harridan of a mother-in-law of hers for good. Isn't it right?'

'Easier said than done. How will you manage it?' she asked him.

'Trust in Him, Arif's mother, trust in Him,' he said, while his mind savoured the honeyed and sympathetic tone in which the Chaudhari had spoken to him a little while ago. 'Trust in Allah, exalted be His grandeur,' although at the moment he was banking rather on the Chaudhari.

As soon as twilight deepened, Zebunnisa put on her *burqa*, took Arif along with her, and went to see Mehrunnisa. She came back late at night. Taking off her *burqa* she said in a whisper, 'Are you awake, Arif's father?'

'Yes, Arif's mother. What is it?' He put his head out from the quilt.

'Mehrun is in terrible pain. Poor Shamim Ahmad was weeping. Maybe she will have it by tomorrow,' she whispered to him in a tinkling voice.

'Really, Ma!' Zubda was up on her bed like a flash. 'Oh!' cried out Maulvi Abul and Zebunnisa, taken by surprise, and without saying anything more on the subject, they quietly went to sleep.

It was the same thing all over the following day, a daughter crying out in pain and her parents feeling jubilant.

And then at midnight an errand-woman knocked at their door. Maulvi Abul had the door open in a trice. Mehrun had given birth to a son. Everyone in the house woke up and much later when, putting away the smiles which had been playing on their faces, they began to doze, Maulvi Abul approached his wife and said, 'What now?'

'How is the Chaudhari?' Zebunnisa asked.

'Allah, exalted be His grandeur, alone can take pity on him,' he told her.

Zebunnisa sat down by his side, their bodies touching, and said, 'To hell with gilded caps and golden bracelets. I say, if we can manage somehow just a silk shirt for the baby we would be able to save our face. Is there any way?'

'A way?' He mused upon it and when he spoke again, he fairly raged, 'Your wits seem to be in your heels and God knows if they are to be found even there or not. You have seven daughters and when you married the first one you gave away everything, all the clothes and trinkets in the house and even the rings on your fingers. After all she was merely the daughter of a starving, miserable-looking caretaker of a mosque and no princess, and there was no likelihood of anyone finding fault with her dowry. Now that she has given birth to a little one-footer we are hard put to hatch out an arm's length of cloth for her baby. And you have the cheek to ask, "Is there any way?" There is no way out, none! I don't even have a winding-sheet to drape my grandson in.'

'Don't talk rot,' Zebunnisa too had her hackles up. 'May his enemies be wrapped in winding-sheets. Allah willing, he will be wreathed in marriage garlands one day. Look here, I certainly can't go there to see Mehrun like this, swinging my arms about, with nothing on me, put up with that lousy mother-in-law of hers, mouth a lot of sweet nothings, and march back home, bent double under a load of curses and reproaches. I can't do it. It would make life so miserable for my daughter. Her mother-in-law won't let her have a moment of peace. We would lose face before everyone. No one will care a hoot for Zubda and Shamsun. They will come to learn we spilled all we had at one go and have nothing left and are back to the same old dry scraps. Our daughters will end up as old-maids.'

'Let them be old-maids,' he flared up. 'Do you want me to go and beat my head against the wall? Haven't I made it perfectly plain to you that I don't even have a winding-sheet and you want me to give you some silken cloth. I have nothing on me, do you hear? I have nothing at all.' And he stormed out of the room.

For a while Zebunnisa kept quiet, thinking that he would walk up and down the courtyard and come back, but when she heard the rattle of the chain as the door was opened, she broke down and wept. And Zubda and Shamsun jumped down from their beds and clasped their mother, blubbering.

Maulvi Abul went straight to the mosque. He performed his ablutions and began to say a prayer which belongs to the small hours. It kept him occupied a long time. Then he summoned the people to the morning prayer and studied the Holy Koran. Meanwhile a few persons showed up at the mosque and he led the prayer. The sun had already risen by the time he reached home and found Zebunnisa sitting exactly where he had left her, her eyes swollen and fixed on the wall. Zubda and Shamsun slept nearby, doubled up. He went towards his cot like a criminal and sat down on it, rigid and bolt upright, as if posing for a photograph.

Zebunnisa's stare slid down the wall and fixed itself on the floor. Maulvi Abul tried to meet her eyes but could not succeed. So, for some reason or the other, he heaved a deep sigh. Zebunnisa could not control herself. She at once looked up at him. A wan smile appeared on his lips and his look said, 'Come here.'

She got up and went to him. By now he had completely cooled down.

'Where did you go?' She complained lovingly.

'To the mosque,' he answered like a child.
'Why did you go?'
'Why do people go there?'
'Did you think it over?'
'Yes.'
'What did you come up with?'
'Only this much that it is morning now. Being her mother, you should have gone straight away to Mehrun's place last night. But since you could not make it then, you absolutely must go there now.'
'Empty-handed?'
'No.'
'Well?'
'That's what I am thinking about. Did you think up something?'
'Same as you.'
They remained silent for some time.
'Listen,' she said, 'can you make someone lend you ten rupees?'
Raising his eyebrows he looked at her a long time. Then he pursed his lips, stared at the floor, got up very slowly, resting his hands on his knees, as if his back had buckled in, and said in a tired voice, 'Let me know if you can find anyone silly enough, Arif's mother, who would risk lending some money to Abul Barkaat. They all know me through and through. If dry scraps are all you have to live by, your misery shows up in your eyes. I can see no way out of the gloom. It seems to me that if I am not able this very day to find just two yards of cloth to give to my grandson, I would have no good reason to stay on in the village.'
She held back her tears very deftly and said: 'How is the Chaudhari?'
'That's what I mean to do, go and see him,' he yawned as he said this, 'He would certainly ask me about Mehrun if he is feeling any better. Who knows, maybe Allah, exalted be His grandeur, will show us some way out of this predicament.'
Maulvi Abul was away for quite some time. Zebunnisa shook her *burqa* and threw it on the clothes-line. She told Arif to wash

his hands and get ready. Zubda and Shamsun too insisted on going with her to have a look at their nephew. 'Wait a little, daughters,' she said so faintly as though something would break into pieces were she to raise her voice somewhat.

They waited and waited.

The children, seeing the mood their mother was in, the way she was startled by the slightest noise and kept glancing towards the door, too appeared out of heart.

And then the door was flung open and Maulvi Abul, perhaps for the first time in his life, came running in, puffed out, and shouted, 'Arif's mother! Hey, Arif's mother!'

Zebunissa rushed out of the room followed by Zubda, Shamsun, Arif, Qamrun, Umda, and the rest of the children, and it looked as if they had been snatched up by a whirlwind and thrown out pell-mell.

And Maulvi Abul called out in his sonorous voice, 'Congratulations, Arif's mother! You were so grieved because it seemed quite beyond our means to present a shirt to our grandson. Thank Allah, exalted be Whose grandeur, we can now not only give him a shirt but a scarf and a cap as well. I am sure to get twenty rupees, if not more, for the burial-service. It won't be long before the funeral gets under way. Chaudhari Fateh Dad has died, you know.'

Zebunnisa struck her breast with both her hands so violently that even the children, completely terrified, began to weep.

And then suddenly it seemed as if someone had grabbed Maulvi Abul by his scruff and his pupils already high up in his eyes, rolled still higher. After a moment's painful silence, Maulvi Abul, who always used to say that it was unlawful and blasphemous for a man to lament in a loud voice, began to wail, and stamping his feet like a child, moved towards the door and ran out into the lane.

Translated by M. Salim-ur-Rahman

SULTAN, THE BEGGAR BOY

As the two of them walked, his grandfather had Sultan's head in the claw of his left hand, while in his right hand he held a staff that rang on the cement pavement whenever he tapped it.

When Sultan stopped for a moment, his grandfather immediately called out: 'Babuji, alms for the blind,...'

'No, no, Grandfather,' Sultan said, 'It's just a juggler's show.'

'Oh, damn the jug...' Before he could complete the curse, he had a fit of coughing. He took his hand off Sultan's head and sank down, coughing and holding his chest with both hands.

By the time his grandfather's breathing steadied, Sultan had watched the juggler transform the rags under the basket into two sparkling white pigeons.

The old man waved his left hand in front of him and asked, 'Where are you?'

Sultan immediately placed his head in the crustacean grip of his grandfather's hand, and they moved along.

At one place, the old man's staff hit a lamp-post. It rang. Sultan said, 'Did you hear, Grandfather? What a wonderful sound!'

'Yes,' the grandfather said and tried to hit the lamp-post again but missed. 'Lamp-posts do ring. Here, take the staff and hit it.'

Sultan took the staff and hit on the lamp-post. The grandfather said, 'See? When I was small like you, I used to listen to the lamp-post, my ears glued to them. They used to sound like English ladies.' Then he mimicked the voices of English ladies: 'You good; you bad.'

'English ladies?' Sultan was astonished. 'Who do they sound like nowadays?'

Suddenly Sultan's tone changed. He whispered, 'Grandfather, two men are coming this way.'

The old man started shouting quickly, 'Alms for the blind; give in God's name for some food. May you prosper. May God give you sons and grandsons.'

One of the men laughed out loud and said to the other, 'This old man seems to be carrying on a propaganda against family planning.' They both moved ahead.

'They're gone,' Sultan whispered. After a brief pause he swore at them.

The grandfather pressed his claw into Sultan's skull, and said, 'Stop this nonsense. What did I tell you yesterday? If anyone hears you, you'll be flayed.'

Sultan walked quietly with his grandfather. After a while he said, 'Grandfather, scratch my scalp a little where you have your thumb.'

The grandfather rubbed his thumb on Sultan's temple.

'Sultan?' the grandfather asked after a long pause, 'You're not stopping anywhere. Where are all the people today?'

'They're dead,' Sultan replied. Then he stopped and suddenly asked, 'What day is it today, Grandfather?'

'How would I know, son?' the old man answered. 'To me the days and nights are the same.' He paused, thought for a while and said, 'The day before yesterday you took me to the Mosque of the Blue Dome, didn't you? So, two days ago it was Friday. That means today is Sunday. Oh, damn. All the folks must be home today, enjoying themselves with their wives and children.'

Sultan stood stock-still as though he had witnessed some serious accident.

Suddenly they heard the sound of a coin dropping. Some passer-by had thrown a pice in their begging-bowl.

'What did you get?' grandfather asked.

'A pice,' Sultan answered. 'It's the new pice, the small one.'

The grandfather rotated his claw over Sultan's head and said, 'Go buy yourself something to eat. I'll wait for you here.'

'Can't buy anything with a pice,' Sultan said. 'If I had two or three, I could buy sugarcane bits.'

The old man removed his hand from Sultan's head and thrust it in his pocket. 'Here, these two pice were left over from yesterday. Take these and buy something. You haven't eaten anything since morning. Children can get mighty hungry, I know. Go.'

Sultan took the pice, while his grandfather said, 'Come back quickly. All right? I'll wait for you here. Where am I standing?'

'Move a little to the left,' Sultan said, took his hand and moved him. 'There, now lean against the lamp-post.'

The grandfather stood leaning against the lamp-post for some time. Then he placed his ear against the lamp-post as if trying to listen to something and smiled. Suddenly, fear gripped him and he started to shout, 'Sultan? Sultan?' Then he started to hurl curses at him, 'You bastard Sultan. Where are you? Are you dead?' When no answer was forthcoming, he turned on his heels and said, 'Good folks, please look for my grandson. He is a small boy. He went to buy himself something for a pice or two. His name is Sultan. Please see that he hasn't been run over by a motor car or tonga, the poor ill-fated boy.' Once again he screamed, 'O, Sultan!'

'Coming, Grandfather,' Sultan answered from afar. But because of screaming, his grandfather had had a fit of coughing.

As soon as his breathing became normal again, he turned towards the lamp-post and asked, 'Where the hell were you?'

Sultan put his grandfather's hand over his head and said, 'The juggler was showing a trick; he was pulling balls out of his mouth.'

Grandfather pressed his claw hard into Sultan's head, as though he was going to lift him up. 'Wait till you get home. I'll show you more juggler's tricks than you will ever want to see in your life. You bastard, it didn't occur to you that I, a helpless blind man, was standing on the roadside,' the old man remonstrated him.

Sultan walked on quietly. A little later, his grandfather asked gently, 'What did you buy to eat?'

'Sugarcane bits,' Sultan said.

'You ill-fated brat! Sugarcane bits are nothing but water,' he again became angry. 'Why didn't buy some gram? It would have sustained you until afternoon.'

Sultan didn't say anything.

'The bowl is not hanging down in your hand, is it?' grandfather asked.

'No, Grandfather,' Sultan said.

'Yes,' the grandfather gave him a piece of advice gently, 'Always keep the bowl straight, otherwise people think you are not a beggar but are going shopping.'

Sultan said cheerfully, 'Grandfather, once I was going, holding a cup in hand, to buy oil and someone dropped a two-anna piece into it. Remember?'

'Yes,' the grandfather said, 'But such things happen rarely. There aren't too many people like that.'

'Grandfather,' Sultan asked, 'Please scratch me again in the same place.'

The old man rubbed his thumb hard on the boy's temple and said, 'When we get home today, I am going to ask daughter Zebo to pick lice out of your hair. You do something for her, too. Fetch her a bucket of water from the tap. All right?'

'Yes,' Sultan responded.

Usually when they returned home, Sultan would lead his grandfather to the post of his cot and tell him to sit. The old man would take his hand off Sultan's head and sit down. As soon as the hand was off his head, Sultan would feel light as air, as if he were wearing canvas shoes, instead of heavy lead-boots. Without making any noise, he would come out of the hut and stand under the curtained awning, and then when his aunt Zebo wasn't looking, slip away to the playground surrounded by bungalows where the children of the rich played cricket, while the poor boys fielded the ball and brought it back to them. When they were finished with their game, the children of their cooks, gardeners, peons, and sweepers took over the playground and played marbles. Once Sultan tried to join in the game, and even managed to play for a few days, but then a sweeper's son pointed out that Sultan was a blind beggar's son. After that, no one would allow him to participate. However, whenever a child threw his marble far, Sultan would dash to pick it up and bring it back. But before handing it back to the owner, he would roll it in his fingers for a few seconds. Once, because of crying bitterly and wailing before his grandfather, he was able to get some money, and bought himself some marbles, but as soon as he reached the playground and the other children saw marbles in his hand, they pounced upon him and snatched them away, saying they were theirs, and when did anyone hear of beggars' children owning any marbles? That day he stamped his feet and cried, but the next day he was back in the playground.

Once he got to the playground, he was afraid to go back home, lest his grandfather again clutch his head in his bony hand and drag him through the town. He knew that as soon as he woke up the next morning, he would have to go begging with his grandfather. Getting up from his cot, he knew he had to put on his steel-cap, and his grandfather's fingers would grip his scalp so tightly that it would hurt. So, after saying his morning prayers, when his grandfather got hold of his staff, called Sultan to him, and fixed his hand on his head, Sultan would go half-dead. The old coot's demonic hand scared him whether he was awake or asleep. This hand shackled him; he walked under its thrust on the pavements as handcuffed prisoners walked with policemen, and peered through the main gate of the prison-house at the happy faces of the people walking about the roads freely. But they could do no more than look, with the prison-bars stuck to their eyes like crosses.

With his grandfather's hand on his head, when he was thus walking, he would sometimes wish he could stop to pick up and eat a sugarcane bit that might have fallen off a barrow and rolled down to the edge of a gutter, or lift a banana peel thrown by a passer-by and lick it, but whenever, and for whatever reason, he asked his grandfather to stop for a moment, the old man merely sank his fingers into his scalp and inquired: 'Have you come out to help me beg, or have I come out to take you for a walk? You hapless child, if we don't even get four or five annas by the end of the day, where is Zebo going to get food for us? As it is, isn't she already showing us enough kindness in letting us stay under her roof?'

A while back, as the blind beggar had emerged from the area of a bungalow where he had gone for alms, and was now passing in front of Begoo the tonga-driver's hut, by the sweepers' quarters, Begoo's mother had scurried out of the hut and said, 'Old man, will you pray for my son's health? He is suffering from pain in the ribs. If God cures him, I'll give you a whole rupee.'

And he had prayed, standing right there. A few days later, he had asked Sultan to go by the same bungalow. They hadn't yet reached it, when Zebo had got hold of him, and giving him the promised rupee had asked, 'Where do you live, old man? I would like to come every Thursday to pay my respects to you.' When she found out that the two of them, grandfather and grandson, slept under whatever shop awning they could find on the street, she had her son clear the curtained awning in front of her hut. Since then, the two of them had been living there. They would hand over the day's earnings to her, and depending on their take, she would buy and cook their food for them. These days she was asking the old man to pray to God to give her son children.

Sultan disliked this aunt Zebo as much as he disliked his grandfather. Whenever he went out of the hut, after the two had returned from begging, he did so stealthily. If she saw him go out, she would raise a fuss and say, 'Look at him! He is leaving his old, handicapped grandfather alone to go and play.'

On days when the grandfather came back home before evening, Sultan wouldn't get a chance to slip out. The old man would take a little rest and then ask the boy to take him on another round of the town square. 'If we get more today, tomorrow you can have a day off.' But Sultan never got that day off, for they never got much.

However, what had been happening more frequently now was that the grandfather would have his asthma attacks in the middle of the night. By morning, after a prolonged fit of coughing and panting, he would feel half-dead and stayed home. But Sultan didn't get a break even then, for he would have to massage his grandfather's ribs and shoulders the whole day long. If he as much as even paused for a second, his grandfather would question him in his subdued, asthmatic whisper, 'Why, Sultan, what are you up to? Are you dead?'

Sultan would immediately start kneading the old man's shoulders. Somewhere inside him, he earnestly prayed for his grandfather to die. By God, he mused, what a tremendous relief it would be. If his grandfather died right there and then, he, Sultan, would go to the mistress of the bungalow and beg her to give him her child's cap, so that he might cover his head with it.

Then one day, his grandfather did actually die. He had been coughing and panting almost the whole night, with an excruciating pain in his ribs. Sultan kept massaging his shoulders and pressing the edges of his ribs with his finger-tips. Finally, the boy fell asleep. When he woke up in the morning, Zebo told him that his grandfather had passed away.

Suddenly Sultan felt as if fireworks were going all around him. He asked Zebo, 'Really?' as if he couldn't believe that grandfathers could die. Shortly thereafter, Begoo gathered some people from the neighbourhood. They gave the dead-body its ritual wash and took it away for burial.

At intervals, Aunt Zebo kept crying. Her daughter-in-law lovingly kept Sultan close to her the whole of that day. When Begoo came back from the graveyard, he brought sugarcane bits for Sultan. As he ate them, the boy thought that it sure was a lot of fun when grandfathers passed away.

Even at night, Aunt Zebo didn't let him sleep under the awning. After all, he was just a child and might take fright. In the morning she gave him a chapati and a bowl of buttermilk. After he had had his fill, he stood up. Zebo asked him, 'Where are you off to, son?'

Sultan found the question quite inappropriate. What did she mean? He could go anywhere now that his grandfather was dead.

Finding him speechless, she said, 'Listen, son. Beggars' children do not go out to play.' Then she held him by his hand and brought him under the awning. She picked up his begging-bowl and handing it to him said, 'Beggars can't eat if they do not beg. Go bring eight or ten annas from somewhere, and I'll cook you some rice tonight. Go, son. Go make a round of some busy street. May God be with you.'

Sultan took the bowl from her but stopped short as soon as he came out from under the awning. He went back inside as though he had forgotten something. Then he began to cry bitter tears but ran out again before Aunt Zebo could envelop him in her out-stretched arms.

His face was drenched in tears when he pushed his bowl in front of someone on the street. 'Babuji, please give some charity to a blind beggar,' he repeated his grandfather's phrase, still shedding tears.

'Are you blind?' the man asked him sternly.

Sultan suddenly realized his mistake and in confusion shook his head. Then he again burst out crying.

'You're a liar and you are crying at the same time,' the man admonished him. 'Will you like to do some work?' he asked. But since Sultan wouldn't stop crying, he decided to move along.

Sultan begged in his hoarse, tear-drenched voice, 'Babuji, please give me a pice or two in God's name.'

The man moved ahead without looking back. When he had gone quite far, Sultan began to run after him, calling him, 'Babuji, hey Babuji?'

The man stopped. Some passers-by also stopped to watch.

'Want to work?' the man asked again.

Panting, Sultan stopped near the man. His lower lip was hanging down. He said, 'Babuji, I don't ask for work. I don't want charity either.' He threw the begging-bowl down on the ground.

'Then why did you call me?' the man asked angrily while surveying the crowd gathering around them.

A spate of tears suddenly flowed from Sultan's eyes. His lips trembled. With effort he muttered, 'Babuji, may God bless you. May He give you plenty. Please walk a little distance with me with your hand on my head.'

Looking foolishly at the crowd, the man said, 'Hey, folks, listen to this kid's crazy request!'

THE THAL DESERT

It is said that when the railways were being built in the Thal Desert, as always, the dust storms would rage there everyday, and sand-dunes form over the laid-down tracks everywhere. An old Munshiji used to tell very interesting stories about that whole period of the building of the railways. He would say that the tracks were at one time laid down in the area around Hazrat Pir's shrine. The trustee of the shrine was an old faithful of the British, hence his title of Khan Bahadur, and was afraid of them, but there was no reason for Hazrat Pir to fear them. So, during the night it so happened that an army of ghosts and goblins came down and chewed up the tracks. In the morning, when the British engineer came to work, chewed-up husks of the tracks were flying about everywhere. Then, as a propitiatory gesture, seven cauldrons of sweetened rice were cooked at the place and distributed among the poor. Also, the tracks were re-routed. That was why the train reached the next station in such a roundabout way.

About that British engineer, Munshiji used to say that he was perturbed by the eternal dust-storms of the Thal. He used to write to his bosses in England that he was unable to do much with the area whose geography assumed a different shape after each dust-storm, its sand-dunes shifting all the time. He asked his government for some help. They got in touch with the government in Delhi, which obtained an amulet from some accomplished pir in Delhi. That amulet was hung on an acacia tree near the tracks, so that when the storms came raging in, they somehow bypassed the tracks. Apparently the pir in question was far more accomplished than the local Hazrat Pir. However, it is said that once when the storm blew, a dune, not minding the amulet hanging in the acacia, settled itself on the tracks. Then another amulet was ordered from Delhi. As soon as the new amulet was hung in place of the old one, with a sudden hiss the offending dune caught fire and simply vanished. In short, while the railways were being built in the Thal, the local pir and the pir in Delhi stayed locked in a deadly combat. Actually, Hazrat Pir's ghosts and goblins were active even now. Only a few days ago, Allah Jawaya and his water-buffalo were run over by a train, for the simple reason that he would ride a train on the flimsiest of excuses. The elders had warned him not to travel by train so much; he was provoking Hazrat Pir, but he wouldn't listen. So, of course, as he was trying to drag one of his buffaloes off the tracks he was run over along with the buffalo. People scraped his hide off the wheels with shovels.

In fact, when the railways were advancing from Khushab to Kundian, the elders had sounded a clear warning that people's morals would deteriorate; people would abandon farming and go to the cities looking for work; villages would become empty; and no one would show care or consideration to others any longer. This was exactly what happened. But something else also happened. About a hundred labourers were taken from Misri Khan's village to help lay down the tracks. In a short while these people had earned so much money that one of them had had a well dug on his land; another had felled his mud-house and in its place raised a pukka brick-house, and another one had bought some farmland. Misri's father too had bought some land in those days. Where earlier, at harvest time, he'd have to travel to far-off villages and work for daily wages on other people's farms, harvesting crops and thrashing and lugging grain, he had now become a small landowner himself, one who pulled a lot of weight in his family-at-large.

Misri Khan was a teenager when his father passed away. That was why he still remembered many things his father had told him about the railways. For example, his father had said that there would have been no trace of the trains that trundled past their village at a distance of about two miles if he, along with the others, hadn't laid down the tracks. The British engineer would measure the land and order them to get started, after which he'd just smoke cigars or whistle his day away. The entire stretch of the track, between here and there, had been laid down by the local labourers. Their sweat, and sometimes even their blood, had dripped over every inch of the track, the reason why the track was considered ill-omened. His father prayed to God to keep everyone, by His grace and that of Hazrat Pir's, safe from the menace of that iron-demon.

Misri had been watching the trains since he was a child. The train would still be far away, but the people in the village would begin hearing the rumble, as though some giant was working a gargantuan mill. Then the village boys would run up to their rooftops and when the train passed them at a distance of two miles, they would tell each other that the train had started where the earth ended. The women in the village believed that whoever once travelled in the train would end up being a wanderer for the rest of his life. The railways had the evil shadow of the ghosts and goblins over it, who had once chewed up the tracks upon Hazrat Pir's instructions. Those from the Thal who still ventured to take the train, first got themselves amulets from the trustee of Hazrat Pir's shrine. A man named Khan Beg from the village once got on the train without first visiting the shrine. Well, he spent the rest of his life knocking about from place to place. At last, he found a brick-layer's job in a town called Chiniot, on the far side of the river Chenab. One day he was working in a seth's house. He got on the ladder, carrying a load of bricks on his head, but slipped. He fell on the ground, the bricks falling on top of him, smashing his head. When the news of his death reached the village, the ire of the shrine's trustee rose. He thundered, 'Yes, you ill-fated morons, go ahead and travel in the train without an amulet from me. This is how Hazrat Pir deals with his detractors.'

Misri had watched the train from far as well as near. He had thrown rocks at it as well as put stones on the tracks of the approaching train and seen them turn into powder. He had seen strange faces in its windows; men wearing turbans with tall, upstanding crests, or those with long tresses; women with heavy bunches of gold-rings in their ears; children who would throw peanut shells on him or bits of sugarcane. Once when a child had thrown an untasted sugarcane bit on him, he had caught it, eaten half of it and brought the other half home to his mother. That was all he knew about the trains, nothing more. For instance, he didn't know how one boarded the train, how one sat in it, and what it looked like inside. How did the passengers feel when it started moving? How did it stop and start up again? Why did it spew out so much smoke? Once he had even pestered his father to take him for a train ride; so many other children, he insisted, travelled by train and nothing happened to them. His father explained to him that all those children were not from Hazrat Pir's area. The children here had to get an amulet before travelling, otherwise they'd fall out of the windows of the train and end up in a jackal's belly.

Even after he had grown up, Misri didn't have any need or occasion to go out of his area. His village was his world; the places outside were inhabited by ghosts, goblins, and witches; by giants and magicians. And big cities like Mianwali and Khushab were populated by cannibalistic savages who roasted and devoured simple-minded peasants.

Only once did Misri have to go out of his village. His father, when he fell ill, decided to get himself treated by a man in a village in the north, at a place called Chitta, near Soon Sakesar. He took Misri along. But the train didn't go that way. Misri walked the whole day with his father. Then there in Chitta, the son of an old friend of his father's, a young man named Khuda Bakhsh, had told him that the village maulvi had said that the Dajjal was going to make his appearance in the world before doomsday, and that it was the Dajjal who pulled those trains that went up and down in the Thal area.

Misri had been quite content in his land of dust-storms and grit, of sparse crops of gram, of whey-coloured houses with black-stemmed, thorny acacias in their courtyards. But it was in Chitta that he realized for the first time that the world outside was so beautiful. For many miles, in front of Chitta, at the foot of Sakesar, lay the glittering lake. In the north stood the undulating crops. The air was crisp and dry, filled with the fragrance of the tall, flexing grass which grew along the mountain slopes. Early in the morning, soon after the prayer, sounds of yogurt being churned would float out of the houses, and people had flushed, healthy faces and a glitter in their eyes. He wished his own village were somewhere near, along the mountain slope. After sowing time, he would visit his crops occasionally, but more often, sit in the *chaupal* for long hours shooting the breeze and singing. Like Khuda Bakhsh's hair, his too would be drenched in oil; he too would visit the village barber every third or fourth day for a shave and go to watch kabaddi competitions, animal fairs and the shows put on by professional entertainers and slapstick comedians on wedding days. The whitewashed walls and the multi-levelled, staircased houses of Chitta had charmed his heart away. He thought, he wanted his father to stay alive, but if he died, he, Misri, would sell his land in the Thal and move up here, never again to look back at the desert where the sun kept an oven-fire going, where the hot wind hit your face like a slap, and where the only green things to be seen were the gram plants and the leaves of the acacias.

For days after returning to his village, Misri's mind was beset with the same perplexity. But then his father passed away, and he fell in love once again with his native sand-swept plain where his father had battled with cliffs and dunes. So what, he argued, if in the Thal the mirages glared at you during the day, the winds howled at night, and the dust rained from the sky all day long? So what if the clay plastered on the walls had been baked red with the heat? So what if the raging sand had etched its fury on the village walls, leaving them as disfigured as the faces of small-pox victims? After all, three generations of his family lay in the graveyards here, and his great-grandfather too, like his father, had looked up in the sky searching for clouds and instead found only dust-storms.

And did Soon Sakesar have anything to match the acacias which stood on their solid stems in the courtyards here, and echoed in the strong winds? How pretty they looked when they were laden with fragrant yellow blossoms! When people woke up in the mornings they'd find beds covered with those blossoms; whenever anyone tilted an earthen-pot to pour out a bowlful of water for himself, a yellow flower would tumble down into the bowl. At such times, some girl or other of the village would be abducted. The elders said that acacia-blossoms housed genies, which only the unmarried young men and women could see. And whoever saw them would fall in love. One would abduct the other, the other willingly submitting to the offence.

It was the very season of the flowering of acacias when Misri kidnapped a girl from his village and ran to the mountains of Soon Sakesar. The girl wanted to leave by train, but Misri knew that if he boarded the train, Hazrat Pir would get him arrested. He went to his friend Khuda Bakhsh in Chitta and hid in his mud-hut which was located two miles away from the village, returning to his village only after the girl's father had agreed with Khuda Bakhsh to tell everyone in his village that he had, in fact, married his daughter off to Misri. He did that and, thus, saved himself from disgrace. And he hadn't lied to his people; for, upon getting to Chitta, the first thing Misri had done was ask a maulvi to marry him and Nisho in the presence of two witnesses Khuda Bakhsh had brought along. So when he returned to his native village, Nisho was with child, a legitimate one, of course.

They named their son Shakoor Khan, but the people around called him Shakkar Khan, because of his connection with Misri. Nisho and Misri themselves used to call him Sweetoo.

When Sweetoo became a little bigger, one day he went with his playmates to see the train from up close. That day he had a pice-coin on him which he showed to all the other children. A boy told him that if he put it on the track, and if the whole train went over it, it would stretch and turn into a knife-blade. For Sweetoo this was an amazing piece of information. So when the tracks began humming and the children knew that the train was making the big round of Hazrat Pir, Sweetoo put the pice on the tracks. But when the train came near, the tracks began to ring and shake, causing the pice to fall off the edge. Sweetoo's gaze was fixed on his pice. As soon as he saw it fall, he said, 'Oh!' and ran to put it back on the tracks. An older boy, sensing the danger, lunged at Sweetoo and pulled him away. It was very thoughtful of that boy, as the engine trundled past them at a yard's distance on its arrogant, rattling wheels.

If the boy hadn't pulled Sweetoo away in time, he would have turned into mincemeat. As the word passed from the children to the farmers working in the nearby fields, to the women in the alleys, and then to Nisho, it underwent a complete transformation. What Nisho heard was that her son had been cut in two by the train, and that one half still lay on the tracks while the other had been dragged away by the train.

Seeing Nisho crying, beating her breast, and running wildly, people rushed to her from their fields and houses. Just then Nisho, along with all the others, saw the children returning, Sweetoo among them, riding a stick like a toy-horse, jumping, kicking his legs and neighing. Even the sight of her son didn't stop Nisho from running at the same pace. She picked him up and folded him in her embrace. She hurried back with him, as though she was the one who had just saved him from the train, as though if she relaxed her grip just a little bit, the train would snatch him away again.

That day some of the men in the village decided to visit the animal fair in Mianwali. Misri also got ready to go along, for he had never been to Mianwali; indeed, he had never had any need to. Then when somebody pointed out that they would take the train both ways, Misri refused to accompany them. They said they were not fools; they would first obtain an amulet from Hazrat Pir's shrine. Someone commented that everything had gone up in price due to the war; even the trustee of the shrine had hiked the price for an amulet, to which Misri said, 'I am not going to ride the monster that was going to devour my own child today. A hundred people from this village had taken part in laying down the tracks. That's why Hazrat Pir is unhappy with this village. I don't want to die a messy death at the hands of the train; I want to die a clean death after saying the kalima.'

Sweetoo was in the first grade at the village school when the rumour went around that a canal as wide as a river was going to be dug from the river Indus. With its waters, the Thal desert would bloom like the cities of Lyallpur and Sargodha. Orchards would be planted and factories set up. There would be cinema houses and wide roads on which the English would go out for walks. And whoever among the Thal residents received most education, would be made the local deputy commissioner.

The next day Misri and Nisho went to their farmland to look at their crop. The sparse plants stood like sulking children, their faces rubbed in dirt. It seemed that they would begin crying if anyone as much as touched them. Misri and Nisho decided that when the canal came to this area, they would plant orchards of oranges and tangerine. They also decided that they would get Sweetoo so highly educated that the government itself would approach them and beg them to let it have their child in return for a thousand rupees a month so that it might make him the deputy commissioner. Thinking such sweet thoughts, Nisho began crying. She pulled Sweetoo close to her bosom and sat holding him thus for long. When Misri took Sweetoo away from her, the boy said in amazement, 'Father, here, put your ear to mother's chest and listen. It sounds like the train.'

Both Misri and Nisho laughed at that. Soon Misri became serious. He said, 'Nisho, deputy commissioners must travel by train, mustn't they?' And Nisho, taking her closed fists to her lips, kissed both her thumb-nails and then touched her eyes with them. She said, 'I'll get an amulet from Hazrat Pir's shrine, even though it may cost a hundred rupees.' Thus they planned their whole life.

Just as Misri's father had worked hard to build the railways in the Thal, so did Misri on the network of canals. And after getting an amulet from the shrine and tying it to Sweetoo's arm, he sent the boy off to town and then on to the big city. He himself escaped having to travel by train, and always managed to find some grown-up headed for town to take Sweetoo along.

In due course, the sand dunes disappeared from the Thal, its mirages replaced by swaying crops. Where once only sparsely growing gram plants could be seen, now one saw rich and glistening fields of paddy. Where before children ate only half of sugarcane bits and brought the other half home to their mothers, they now had whole crops to pick from. Roads were built throughout the area, and wind-storms held sway in other far-off places. Misri couldn't grow orchards on his land but had no difficulty raising full lush crops. Brimming with joy, he would tease Nisho, saying, 'I feel so young I want to abduct you all over again and take you to Soon Sakesar.' And Nisho would answer, 'No thanks, I wouldn't go back there even for a day. Don't you remember lending grain and husk to your friend Khuda Bakhsh from Chitta only the other day? Now people from that paradise have begun coming down to this hell to work for wages.'

The village elementary school had now become a middle school. It was a teacher from that school who had advised Misri to send his son into civil engineering. When the teacher discovered that Misri had been dreaming of making his son a deputy commissioner, he explained to him that every person in his place was a deputy commissioner. He, the teacher, was a deputy commissioner in his school; if his son became an overseer, he would be the deputy commissioner of roads and canals. Misri understood the teacher's argument, and did as he was advised. So, when after graduating from Rasool Engineering School, Malik Abdul Shakoor Khan, alias Sweetoo, got a job somewhere near Bhakkar, he began sending his parents fifty rupees every month and parcels of clothes and English tonics. He never failed to send something or another through someone returning to their village—suitcases, tables, chairs, a large mirror in which Nisho and Misri would see their reflections together.

Once when Sweetoo came on leave, he brought his father a blanket from Chitral and his mother a suit made from Lady Hamilton cloth. That day Misri applied henna to Nisho's temples with his own hands, and when she donned the suit, he took her inside the room on some excuse and hugged her. When Nisho pushed him away, she laughed to see him crying. 'Don't be a child,' she said, 'We have entered the age when we should begin saying our prayers.'

After supper one evening, the day before Sweetoo's holidays ended, Nisho and Misri told him that they had found an excellent match for him. 'It's the daughter of the headman's brother. You know Halima, don't you?' But the son sat there speechless. And when Misri and Nisho were finished talking, he just said, 'Marriage is my own affair. I'll marry when and wherever I want to. Please stop worrying about it.'

'What an impertinent boy!' Misri said angrily as he watched him go out of the courtyard. 'If we don't worry about his marriage, who will?'

This was the first setback Nisho had suffered at her son's hands. She said, 'It's these rail-cars and tracks and roads and motorcars—they have hardened everybody's heart. Don't you see young men walking about without covering their heads and laughing in front of their elders, like dogs, with their mouths wide open?'

And Misri thought, indeed, that was true. People had become quite inconsiderate and selfish. Those who borrowed money never returned it, and if they did return it, it was as if they were doing you a favour. Children went to Joharabad to watch the cinema without their parents' permission. People travelled around in the trains freely, without bothering about getting amulets from the shrine. The Thal had been populated but people had become desolate, just as he himself had. Hadn't his son told him to his face that he would himself decide when and where to marry?

The next day they went after Sweetoo with a vengeance. The bitterness became so acute that the son even tried to tell them that they themselves had married without getting anybody's permission, which made Nisho shed tears and Misri throw a few curses at him. But something did come of that confrontation: before leaving, Sweetoo promised to think about the matter and let them know within the month. Seeing him off at the station, Misri groped around his arm for the amulet. 'Where do you carry the amulet from Hazrat Pir's shrine?' he asked him. Sweetoo smiled and said, 'I gave it away to a friend who was afraid of travelling by train.' Then Sweetoo left, and the whole night Misri kept having nightmares about the train cleaving his son into two and departing with a guffaw.

'What a shameless lad he has turned out to be!' Misri said to his wife in the morning. 'Forget about us; we are his parents; that hapless boy didn't even show consideration for Hazrat Pir, didn't bother to think that the trains had been cursed by Hazrat Pir.'

Then one day Misri received a letter from Sweetoo, informing him that he was going to Warsak Dam for a two-month training course. He asked his father to meet him at the train station at Kundian, because, firstly, he was now ready to let him and his mother know his decision regarding that particular issue, and secondly, he had purchased a radio for him which did not require electricity to work. All one did was put the same material in it that was used in flashlights. And the amazing thing was it could be carried anywhere—to the *chaupal*, to the fields, on the road, in the village square— and played. When Misri went to work on the farm, he could take it with him, or leave it behind to entertain mother. When he saw him in Kundian, he would present it to him.

At first the two of them, soaked in joy, kept gazing at each other. Then Misri suddenly realized something and blurted out, 'But today is the seventh of the English month!'

Saying that, he stood up but sat down again. He said, 'If I leave for Kundian on foot now, I won't be able to reach there on time. I shall have to go by train.'

'So what?' Nisho said, 'I'll go to the shrine right now and get you an amulet. Fifteen or twenty rupees is no big expense.'

'Fifteen or twenty?' Misri was astounded. 'When the tracks were laid down, the amulet used to cost one anna.' Then after a bit of musing he said, 'How inconsiderate the world has become!' Nisho immediately reproached him, 'Do you realize whom you're calling inconsiderate?'

A shudder ran through Misri. Contrite, he at once touched his ears in apology and began muttering something under his breath. Worry about money had made him utter those profane words. He too had quietly changed like the rest of the world. He actually began crying after Nisho had left, and kept on asking for Hazrat Pir's forgiveness until she returned.

Nisho got the amulet for ten rupees. She helped him put on clean clothes. She brought down from a basket his shoes, inlaid with gold-thread, and took his starched turban out of the box. But he was very nervous and kept fidgeting with the amulet under his sleeve, afraid that Hazrat Pir's ghosts and goblins would remove it in punishment for his audacity. Many times Nisho tried to calm him down and at last agreed to go with him to the railway station and be with him until he boarded the train.

The station was about seven or eight miles away. When they reached there, the train had not yet arrived. They sat down in the shade of a tree and decided that if Sweetoo agreed, the wedding should take place in the month of Kattak. And what if he said no—the world, after all, had become so lacking in consideration? 'No,' Nisho said, 'if he had to say no, why would he ask you to come to Kundian? And why would he buy a radio for you? He is our lawfully begotten son. He will not say no.' They also wondered how they would deal with all the children who might gather in their house to listen to the radio, and how respond to someone who might ask to borrow the radio.

Suddenly they heard the whistle of the train in the distance. In panic Misri stood up and began checking his arm to make sure the amulet was there. The train got in and stopped. A passenger from Misri's village got down. He asked Misri how he had whipped up enough courage to travel by train. Nisho replied, 'He is going with Hazrat Pir's permission. Sweetoo has asked to see him in Kundian. He's going to bring the radio.'

The passenger began talking of Sweetoo in glowing words. The train started moving in the meanwhile. Agitated, Misri ran. He was able to catch hold of the bar but couldn't set his foot on the running-board. He began to swing and suddenly fell on the ground, the toes of one foot going over the track. The wheels went over it, all seven of them, one by one.

The train stopped. Screaming, Nisho ran to him and dragged him into her embrace like a child. A number of people gathered. Misri Khan was sitting holding in his hand the toes that were smashed and bleeding.

Then a railway employee came there and said, 'Are you blind or something? Why didn't you see where you were going?'

Hearing that Nisho squirmed and started screaming at the employee, 'May you go blind and your elders and all your offspring . . .'

Grumbling, the employee left. Nisho squatted down near Misri. The passenger from Misri's village tore a piece from his turban and tried to bandage Misri's foot. The train started moving again.

'It has started again,' Misri said as he looked in surprise at Nisho.

'Let it go, the bastard,' Nisho said and caught him by his arm.

But Misri shot up with a jerk. He dragged his foot, leaving a line of blood behind him, and started running along the tracks, shouting, 'Aye, stop it; I'm going to Kundian; I have the ticket.'

The last cars rushed by him with a swish. He just stood there, his mouth open, like a beaten man. Nisho and others also came and joined him. He looked at the train and said, 'How inconsiderate this stupid blockhead has been. What would it have lost if it had stopped for me a little longer? Everything in this century is like that, callous and uncaring.'

Then he sat down holding his injured foot in his hands, but Nisho moved his hands aside and took his foot in her hands. She burst into tears and asked, 'Why did you have to utter that nonsense about Hazrat Pir?'

The expression on Misri's face said that it would yet take the Thal centuries to be settled.

THEFT

Poor Mangu, after chopping wood in the forest all day long for the *thanedar*, finally sat down leaning against a wall at a street-corner, to catch his breath awhile. His eyes were fixed on his feet. His heels were cracked and blood, oozing from the toes, had started to congeal along the edges of the nails. He got up after a little rest. He had to go home to knead some dough. His mother had died, and he was still a bachelor. Through one of the village elders he had tried to initiate negotiations for marriage, but the girl's family had asked for five hundred rupees. Mangu, on the other hand, was having a hard time earning five pice a day for his keep. So, he just bore it all patiently. He thought, his days will pass anyway. He will regard himself as a widower, one whose wife had died soon after marriage. And yet, whenever a woman passed him by coquettishly, carrying clay-pots on her head, her breasts jutting out, espying him through the corners of her eyes, or when a young lady, sunning herself on her rooftop, locked eyes with him, he would become aware of something sorely missing in his life. Soon, however, the worries of earning a living would help him overcome the painful deprivation.

He had walked only a few steps when he heard fireworks go off with a blast at the edge of the village. He pricked his ears. Now, he could also distinguish the sounds of drums and *shehnai*. 'A wedding procession,' he told himself and started walking towards it eagerly. Then again, bachelors and widowers are particularly fond of watching weddings, aren't they?

A man asked him, 'Where are you off to, Mangu? Everything all right?'

'Yes, brother, everything is fine. I just heard the drums playing. Thought I'll go and watch the fanfare. Whose wedding is it?'

'Better not ask. These are all counterfeit weddings!'
'Counterfeit?' Mangu said surprised.
'Yes, indeed. The only true wedding will be when you become the bridegroom, riding a horse, a *sehra* hanging from your forehead.'

Mangu blushed, and the man walked away laughing.

From a distance Mangu saw a number of torches, being fed again and again by black hands with oil from flasks. Ahead of everybody were two famous local entertainers. There were two drums with silken bead-strings hanging from each; two *shehnais* with gilt rings, a bagpipes with glittering golden tassels hanging from each of its various pipes. Behind the entertainers were horse-riders whose turbans sported crests higher than a peacock's fanned feathers, and whose twirled moustache-ends were pointing skyward. Some riders, astride their half-dead mares, who hung their heads down abjectly and disgustingly, were spurring them on vigorously to make them dance, or at least trot, with their heads held high. Some others mounted on their handsome and fully decked out steeds, were constantly losing their balance in an effort to dance their animals and were screaming for help from those around. Behind the horses were four camels whose knees, chests, necks, and foreheads were decked with thick bells, and whose saddles carried shy young girls with blushing cheeks, drawing into themselves with modesty, their earrings shimmering in the light. In their effort to pull back their fluttering head-covers, they looked like winged fairies, flying back to their luminous abodes in the stars after a tryst with their earthly lovers. Some of the women, past their prime, sat as self-consciously as though the crowd were looking only at them, even though they were objects of attention only for aged widowers. Their lips were painted bright red and their heads were heavy with the weight of their jewellery. In the rear of the train came those who walked on foot. Their rustling clothes gave off the fragrance of vetiver, which was what the soldiers usually wore to impress young girls with.

Mangu hurried over and after ogling a few shy girls and mopping the perspiration off his brow, got in with the pedestrians. Whenever a firecracker went off, and the horses reared up in fright, a new wave of life and activity stirred the crowd. When the *shehnai*-players, throwing their heads back, lifted their instruments and sounded an elongated note, and the firecrackers flew like arrows into the sky, leaving lines of blue, yellow, red, and green sparks in their wake, it seemed as though enthralled by the music, the stars were rushing down to be gathered into the *shehnais*.

The night was flush with happiness.

The wedding procession entered the village. People ran up to their roofs to watch the well-dressed, pretty young girls. Mangu thought he should at least take a look at the bridegroom. Who was the lucky man to take away a young lady with long tresses and rosy cheeks from his village? He was nowhere to be seen. Mangu was about to tear through the crowd and lunge forward when someone screamed, 'My wallet! Somebody stole my wallet!' And suddenly many hands fell upon Mangu's shoulders. Someone shouted, 'Where are you trying to run off to? You miscreant, you scoundrel.'

Mangu turned around to look. Blood-shot eyes were bulging out in faces which were shining from a generous coat of oil and ghee. The procession came to a stop, and Mangu stood surrounded by the whole crowd.

For a moment everybody was quiet. Then there was a murmur of whispers around, and somebody moved up to grab Mangu by his hair. Mangu wondered for a split second how this man ever dared to grab a young man from another village, how he ever found out that Mangu was a poor man whom nobody would sympathize with. He looked down at his torn shirt, its exposed collar showing his hair, and all mysteries were solved for him.

The person barked at Mangu, 'Where's the wallet? Where's my wallet, you son of a bitch?'

Mangu's blood rushed to his eyes. He forgot that a poor man couldn't fight a whole wedding procession. His biceps began to itch. He was about to clench his fist and land a blow on the man's jaw when he saw the headman of his village astride a horse in front of him. Thoughts began hurriedly circling in his brain: 'I should appeal to the headman of my village. So many times I have massaged his feet at the *chaupal*, haven't I? I have chopped wood for his household. I have walked fifty miles to do his errands. These people from another village are humiliating me. Doesn't this mean disgrace for the entire village? If I have stolen the wallet, I should have it on me.' He started screaming, 'Malikji, may God enhance your honour. These scoundrels have ganged up on me.' The hand grabbing his hair had now slipped away. 'Malikji, these people are accusing me wrongly. You know me well, Malikji. I've never stolen anything in my life. I am poor but earn my living honestly. You know it. The whole village knows it. God knows it.'

With eyes full of hopeful expectation he stared at the headman's face. He was expecting a spate of abuse to erupt from the headman's mouth and confound the bridal group, so that, strutting with pride, he would return home and get busy with kneading the dough.

Instead, the headman's shouts hit him like a shaft of lightning, 'You scoundrel! You pick-pocket! You bastard! Don't you have any sense of shame? Is this how one honours one's guests? You've put the whole village to shame. Where's the wallet? Out with it. Now!' and the headman's whip came cracking down on his back. The headman roared, 'Out with it or I'll have you tied up, and hang you upside-down and smoke chillies under your nose. Chillies.'

'Huzoor, I swear by God, I swear by the Holy Book, I don't...'

Mangu heard questions shouted at him: 'Take out the wallet. Where did you hide it? In which bush? Who did you give it to? Where's the wallet? Where is it?' And every question came with a lash that shook him from head to toe like the plucked strings of a guitar. But he stayed silent. He knew now that no one was going to listen to him. God and the Holy Book were toys in the eyes of such people. No amount of oath-taking would have any effect on them. The old man who had lost his wallet was screaming like a maniac, 'Seven notes of ten rupees each. Seventy rupees. Ten less than four-score. Folks, I've been ruined. This is the man I saw running away. He's the thief.'

Words spluttered out of his mouth, and so did the froth gathering at the edges of his lips, and fell into his dense beard.

The bridal procession moved ahead by the headman's orders and Mangu was handed over to two village watchmen to be taken to the *chaupal*. A little later the whole village, as well all the visitors, gathered there. It was a dark night, the only light coming from a torch held by a barber. A *havaldar* and a policeman were also called in from the police station who gave Mangu a body-search. They found a four-anna piece in his pocket and confiscated it.

Mangu sat on the ground tracing lines in dirt with a straw and thinking: 'Why doesn't the hapless man who stole the wallet show some compassion for me and throw it in the *chaupal*? Why don't people take any pity on the poor? Why is everyone smirking at my misery and misfortune? What a strange custom!.'

He got up, walked up to the *havaldar* and said, '*Havaldarji*, I'm going to tell you the truth. I beg you to believe me. If you don't, there's nothing I can do. You have all the power. The whole village knows me well. By some stroke of ill-luck I went to look at the wedding procession. I thought I should have a look at the bridegroom. Just as I made to do so, the trouble started, and these guys pounced upon me. They were misled by my quick pace. The thief must be one of their own.'

But the *havaldar's* pocket had already been lined. He smiled and blowing the cigarette smoke out of his wide nostrils said, 'If all culprits confessed their crimes straight away, the government wouldn't need the police department, would they? When we place live coals on your palms, grind stone on your chest and keep you without food in a cell for a week, you will spit it all out, of your own accord. You'll come and tell us where you've hid the wallet. Young man, we are the police; you should know that.' And the *havaldar* flexed his neck as though trying to show that it was well within his power to incarcerate both heaven and earth.

Mangu looked once again towards the headman, but his manner bespoke total lack of care and concern. He was busy discussing the rates of wheat with a land-holder.

The *havaldar* glared at Mangu, his eyes ready to pop out of their sockets. The whole crowd stood holding its breath.

'Go,' he said and placed his fat baton on Mangu's neck. 'What are you standing waiting for?'

'But Huzoor, I don't know anything about the wallet. Where am I going to get it from? I have heard about wallets, but I don't even know what they look like. I am a poor man.'

'Bring it back, wherever you put it, from whomever you gave it to. Otherwise...,' the *havaldar* said and dropped the baton on his chest.

Mangu spotted the Maulvi Sahib, the imam of the local mosque, in the crowd and called to him, 'Maulviji, please, see what...'

'But child, it's wrong to steal things.'

Mangu considered all the prayers he had said behind this man as having been wasted. He got another shove from the *havaldar*, 'Go, get the wallet.'

Feeling utterly helpless, Mangu started to go down the *chaupal* steps, his head bowed, followed by a policeman and the two village watchmen. Suddenly someone passing him by hurriedly asked, 'Are the members of the wedding party here?'

'Yes,' Mangu told him. Perhaps he too was part of the group, for the crest of his turban was also starched and standing high.

The man climbed the stairs up to the *chaupal* and asked, 'Sher Baaz? Baba Sher Baaz, are you here?'

'Yes, yes,' Sher Baaz stood up. He was the same man who had lost his wallet.

'I heard, as I was coming this way, that you were accusing some innocent man of stealing your wallet even though you had given it to me for safe-keeping, fearing you will lose it in the crowd,' he said.

'Oh, my God. I completely forgot that. You have my wallet?' The old man was joyful and smiling from ear to ear.

Mangu was burning up with anger. The watchmen and the policeman turned around to leave, but Mangu asked them from where he stood, 'Can I go now?'

The thought of the lost four-anna piece began to bother him as he got home. 'My whole day's wage in the *havaldar's* pocket. What kind of a law is it? I've got to get it back, I must,' he thought and turned back.

When he got to the *chaupal*, there was nobody there. He ran towards the police station. The window was open. Inside, a lamp was lit. He walked towards the window. When he peeped inside, he saw the same *havaldar* and the policeman sitting on cots, drinking some pink liquid out of glasses.

'Huzoor,' he said softly.

The two men simultaneously moved the glasses away from their lips and placed them under the cots.

'Who is it?' the *havaldar* inquired.

'Huzoor, it's me, Mangu.'

'What is it?'

'Huzoor, that man got his wallet, didn't he?'

'Yes.'

'Then, huzoor, . . .'

'What?'

'I should get my four-anna piece back.'

The *havaldar* and the policeman burst out laughing. They laughed so loudly that the bars of the prison began to ring with the echo. Mangu was just trying to understand the reason for their senseless laughter when the window was banged shut in his face. All he could do was wince with pain and pinch his chin and nose between his fingers.

THE UNWANTED

One afternoon, barely ten days after Habib's wedding, people saw his father Pir Bakhsh walking out of his house. He was carrying two cots on his head and a box under his arm whose handle clanked at every step. He walked looking straight ahead of him through the long alley. Suddenly he turned around and called, 'Pick up the pace, Nekan, walk fast.'

People turned around to see his wife, Nek Bakht, trudging slowly behind, at the far end of the alley, carrying a bundle on her head.

'Where are these two going?' people asked each other. An elderly man mustered enough courage to walk up to Pir Bakhsh and ask, 'Why, brother, where are you off to?'

'To the farms,' was the answer Pir Bakhsh gave, but so curtly that the other man had to pause before asking another question:

'With bag and baggage?'

'Right.'

'You mean you are going to live there now?'

'Right.'

'Why?'

'Well.'

The old man's stock of questions was exhausted.

By this time, Nekan had caught up with her husband. Her knees, hands and lips were shaking and tears flowed into the wrinkles on her face. When she noticed that every eye was trained on her, she became perturbed and looked at her husband, and then burst into tears. Pulling and twisting the loose end of the cloth wrapping of the bundle on her head, she said in a hoarse voice choking with emotion, 'Don't ask us. Go ask Habib who…'

Pir Bakhsh cut her short: 'Why didn't you shout it from the rooftop before leaving? Then you wouldn't have to stop at every step to explain.'

'Oh, go away, you,' she said, thrusting her hand at Pir Bakhsh like a dagger and walking away.

People kept watching them until they had reached the end of the long alley. In a little while the news went round the village that merely four days after Habib's wedding there had been a falling out between his new bride and his mother. What had happened was that Nekan, as her son looked on, was placing in dovecotes and cornices the pieces of china that her daughter-in-law had brought as dowry when a glass fell out of her hand. It fell on a saucer and both pieces were smashed. The bride who sat surrounded by her friends in another room of the house sprang up when she heard the clatter, and taking a few long strides and jangling her jewellery, was at the scene of the mishap in a second. For a moment she stared at the damaged pieces, and then raising her voice—it was the first time she had done so since coming to her new home—said, 'Auntie, these were the pieces I brought from my parents' home!'

'Yes, daughter, they were, but they also belonged to my son,' Nek Bakht retorted, looking at Habib Ahmad.

Habib said, 'Even so, one does feels sorry for the loss of new dishes.'

And Nek Bakht felt as though she too had broken with the glass and the saucer. In the evening she complained about the incident to her husband who spoke to his son. The son rushed in to see his bride. No one knew what they said to each other, but when he came back, he just stood quietly by his father.

Pir Bakhsh waited for him to say something. When he didn't, Pir Bakhsh asked, 'What does she say?'

'What can she say, the poor thing,' Habib said, without looking at his parents.

'No, son, the poor thing must have said something!' Nek Bakht said with cutting irony.

'Poor thing!' Pir Bakhsh said, as though reflecting on the phrase.

'Well, what do you want me to do? Divorce her?' Habib shouted, glowering at them.

'Don't bully me, son,' Nek Bakht said and started crying. 'First go and wash my milk off your lips.'

Pir Bakhsh said, 'Some money is still left from the wedding expenses. I'll go to town tomorrow and get your wife a new glass and saucer. That should settle matters.'

Habib stared at his father sullenly. Then he rushed out of the room.

Five days passed without incident. The son didn't speak to his parents. They too were subdued and somewhat scared. They didn't talk much to each other either, and when they did, it was in whispers, as though loud words would break something. At night they would have their beds laid out in one corner of the courtyard, on the other side of the kitchen wall. After hours of tossing and turning in their beds, unable to fall asleep, they would lie flat on their backs and stare at the sky. From the other side of the dividing wall, from the colourful beds laid out there, whispers would come floating their way.

'They are talking,' Nek Bakht would whisper spitefully.

When Pir Bakhsh didn't respond, she would ask, 'Are you alive or dead?'

'What is it?' he would ask sullenly.

'I said they're talking.'

'Well, why not? They're husband and wife.'

'I mean they talk to each other; why don't they talk to us?'

'Let them first tire of talking to each other.'

'Listen,' Nek Bakht said one night, five days after the incident, 'Why don't you go buy the glass and saucer and throw them in your daughter-in-law's face? What are you waiting for?'

'Well,' Pir Bakhsh said, 'That would be such a petty thing to do. You know Khatoon does not come from a poor home. If I did what you ask, I am afraid the girl would consider us ill-bred for the rest of her life. After all, we have to spend the rest of our days in this house.'

'Oh, you men don't understand these matters. Just go and get those things.'

'All right, I will.'

'No, do it tomorrow; otherwise, my own son will go on looking like a stranger to me.'

The next day, the tenth after the wedding, soon after his morning prayers, Pir Bakhsh went to town, returning before midday with the replacements. He placed the two pieces in front of Nek Bakht, who picked them up, walked up to her son sitting behind the kitchen wall, smoking his hookah and watching his bride smiling and rubbing ghee on her palms to lend sparkle to the henna-dye.

'Here are the glass and saucer, daughter. This squares up matters between us,' Nek Bakht addressed her daughter-in-law, but instead of her, it was the son who stood up, snatched the two pieces from his mother's hands and smashed them against the wall.

As if dazed, Nek Bakht sat down. Pir Bakhsh came up to the kitchen wall, but then turned back. Later, Nek Bakht, crying hysterically, joined him. The two of them, without uttering a word to each other, as if by an unstated agreement, started packing their stuff. They noisily dragged their cots off the wall to the middle of the courtyard, and then lugging them, walked out of the house as the son and daughter-in-law looked on.

The son did once say, 'You're not doing the right thing,' but made no attempt to run after them to stop them, and they went far, after crossing the long alley and leaving the crowd of on-lookers behind.

Pir Bakhsh used to till his land himself, so he had built a small mud-hut on a ridge in the north of the fields. When the crops ripened, he would go with Nek Bakht to live there. They would look after the crop and harvest it, staying there until the grain was carried away from the field. Habib Ahmad was at school, in the village. They would leave him there for about three months, with Pir Bakhsh's sister. He would come to the farm every Saturday evening, to spend his Sundays with his parents. When he went to the millet crop and made a lot of noise to scare the sparrows away, Pir Bakhsh would tell him he didn't look nice doing that. And Nek Bakht would chime in, 'Don't shout at the birds, son. This work is not for you. You are going to become a clerk when you grow up.'

Habib didn't become a clerk; however, he did become a store-owner, first a grocer, then a cloth-merchant. One day he returned to the village with bolts of cloth and a sign which he had got painted in the city: it read, MALIK HABIB AHMAD, CLOTH MERCHANT. Within three or four years he had earned enough to be considered among the well-to-do in the village. To make his entry into gentlemanly class stick, he persuaded his father to sell his plough and the pair of oxen and lease his land to tenant-farmers. He bought tables and chairs for his house and a transistor radio whose aerial, attached to the bamboos on his roof, looked no less impressive than a royal pennant.

The shift from the cot to the chair automatically resulted in excellent marriage proposals for Habib, some so impressive that Nek Bakht was dazed by the mere mention of the name of the head of the family. But when she looked at her tables and chairs, at the china dishes and copper platters lined on shelves, and as she heard the radio announce, 'This is Lahore,' she would shake her head and tell the match-makers, 'Are you crazy? You should have known better than to have come barging into my house like that. Even Caucasian fairies are not good enough for my Habib.'

Then one day she received the proposal she had been waiting for all along. The richest man in the village, one on whose fields Pir Bakhsh himself had once, in his lean days, been a cultivator, came to their house to make the offer. When Pir Bakhsh told this to Nek Bakht, she was delirious with joy. The marriage was performed with much fanfare. And then the fourth day after the wedding Nek Bakht broke the bride's china pieces.

At the mud-hut, Nek Bakht kept sweeping the floor and crying and coughing. Pir Bakhsh sat outside the hut, viewing the fields lying at his feet, fields whose soil had been overturned by his plough scores of times. But now he felt as if he had come to an alien land and was looking at it for the first time.

Peasants' mud-huts were scattered far and wide, but by the end of the day everybody had come to know about Pir Bakhsh and his wife's exile from the village. By the next morning there was a crowd of peasant men and women at their door. It was true, they said, that a son was split in two after marriage, and the mother was left longing for his return, but why had they come out only ten days after their son's wedding? The henna-dye on the bride's palms would still be there, wouldn't it?

Pir Bakhsh would counter, 'No, no, it isn't anything of the sort. The Hakim Sahib has advised Nekan to spend a few days in the open. We aren't going to stay here long.'

As instructed by Pir Bakhsh, even Nek Bakht kept using the same excuse for some time, but one day when two of their own tenant-farmers came and asked if they could do anything for them, she couldn't contain herself and burst out crying. And in a wailing tone told them: 'Why are you asking us? Go ask Habib who has sold off his parents for a wife.'

And when she lifted her eyes after uttering those words, she saw Habib standing in front. 'Have some regard for my good name in the village,' he remonstrated with his mother.

Nek Bakht who had been stunned to see her son there, turned upon him, 'Your good name? And what about ours? Or did you think we didn't have any? Or did you think we squandered it at your wedding, as we did our life's savings? Don't you forget, I carried you in my belly for nine months,' she drummed her stomach hard with both hands. 'I gave birth to you, boy, and you have come to tell me about your good name!'

Pir Bakhsh came face to face with her and said, 'Again the same taunts and recriminations?'

'Oh, go away, you,' Nek Bakht said.

Thrusting her hand at Pir Bakhsh like a dagger and crying, she went inside the hut.

'I had come to take you home, both of you,' Habib said to Nek Bakht as she was going in, 'but you have gathered a crowd here to disgrace me and put me to shame in public.'

'We aren't dead yet, son,' Nek Bakht retorted from the doorway. 'When that happens, and if your wife permits you, come and take our bodies away. While we are alive, we will not enter that house. Go.'

'You are out of your mind!' Pir Bakhsh shouted at his wife, but as he turned, he saw Habib walk away, taking quick, long strides.

A few days later, Nek Bakht fell ill. Habib came to inquire after her many times. He came with the village elders and once even with his father-in-law to persuade Nek Bakht to return home, but she refused to yield. Then one day she died, and when Habib Ahmad and the other relatives came to take her body back to the village, Pir Bakhsh tagged along without saying a word.

When the dead-body was carried into the house, Pir Bakhsh was reminded of one of his own remarks. In her younger days, Nek Bakht used to burst into tears at every trifle. He would say to her, 'Men too want to cry at times, but in this matter of shedding tears at every little thing, women are clearly one up on them.' Hearing him, she would begin to smile through her tears. Now she was gone, and even if he were to cry, no one would smile at him. Then again, no husband ever cried in public over his wife's death. And Pir Bakhsh wasn't about to change that. But it gave him consolation to notice that Habib was crying. Nek Bakht was a wife, of course, but a mother as well. The son's tears were going to keep at least half of her grave cool.

After the burial, Habib Ahmad and Pir Bakhsh spread a mat in one corner of the courtyard, where after Habib's wedding Pir Bakhsh and Nek Bakht used to set their cots, and sat down to talk to those who had gathered for condolence. When the evening meal, sent by a relative, was about to be served, Pir Bakhsh noticed that Habib, holding a clay pot, was ready to help him wash his hands. At that moment, for a little while, Pir Bakhsh even forgot his wife's death.

After the call for the Isha prayer, when the mourning women had retired and Pir Bakhsh was left alone in the house with his son and daughter-in-law, Habib came to him. He stood near him silently for some time; then he started crying. He sat down placing his hands on his father's knees, and said, 'Please forgive me, father. Mother didn't forgive me the milk she had fed me, but I'll ask for her forgiveness on the Judgement Day. If you forgive me, she will too.'

The whole day's sadness and pain that Pir Bakhsh had been trying to hold back, suddenly burst like a storm. Habib too shed tears, keeping his hand on his father's knee. Pir Bakhsh cried so much that his hands and feet grew cold. Habib noticed that and called his wife, 'Come here, Khatoon. Massage father's feet.'

This was the first time Khatoon had appeared before Pir Bakhsh since Nek Bakht's death. Pir Bakhsh looked at her and noticed that she too had been crying. She took off the sheet with which she had covered her head, rolled it into a ball and started rubbing the soles of Pir Bakhsh's feet, with such force that her untied hair fell on her face and hid half of it. On the other side, Habib too was rubbing Pir Bakhsh's palms with equal vigour. At that moment Pir Bakhsh felt himself to be the luckiest father in the whole world. He took a deep breath and shut his eyes. Even though this was his wife's first night in the grave, this was the first night that Pir Bakhsh had had a sound and peaceful sleep since his son's wedding.

Until the Thursday following his mother's death, Habib kept the store closed in mourning. He would stay home the whole day reciting the Koran and wouldn't let his father get up even for a glass of water. He would help him wash his hands sitting on the cot, and Khatoon would bring him his food and sit there while he ate. Once, to ward off flies, she started fanning the food with the loose end of her head-cover. The sight of the nooks and crannies of the yard where Nek Bakht used to sit and work the spinning wheel, or where she patted dung-cakes on the walls would bring a lump to his throat, but the kindness and love he was receiving from his son and daughter-in-law had dried his tears. Recalling his past, he would just heave a sigh and begin to talk to his son or daughter-in-law. 'Don't sit so close to the fire, daughter, or it'll burn your complexion,' he would tell Khatoon; or, say to Habib, 'Son, do open the shop on Friday; you are suffering a loss.'

On the following Thursday, Habib arranged a lavish feast. Half the village attended. The professional reciters read the Koran eighteen times to bless the soul of the departed. Habib himself read the Holy Book two times and Khatoon read a third of it. Beggars from far and wide came and after having had their fill, were given abundant food to take with them. Pir Bakhsh sat in a corner of the yard, supervising the event with visible pride. He was thinking, 'If Nek Bakht were here, the poor woman would have been so happy to see all that.'

In the morning when Habib left for the shop, Pir Bakhsh had his first fit of depression. He heard Nek Bakht whispering in his ears and saw her walking about in the courtyard. Frantic, he came out in the street, and sitting at a bend in the street, watched passers-by come and go. Older women, as they walked past him, seeing him sitting there alone, sat down with him and wept and talked about Nek Bakht's good qualities. Then he went back inside the house. The daughter-in-law was sitting in the kitchen, cooking food. Dragging a pirhi, he sat near her and said, 'Poor Nek Bakht also used to sit exactly where you are sitting now and did her cooking.'

The daughter-in-law looked at him anxiously. Fear lurked in her eyes, but Pir Bakhsh was lost in memories. He continued, 'Before Nek Bakht it was my mother who sat here for forty years and did the cooking. And sitting where I am now, I would insist that she pour a lot of ghee on my *paratha*, or I would throw it before the dog.' Pir Bakhsh laughed out loud, like a child. His laughter sounded foreign to him, for he had heard himself laugh for the first time since his son's wedding. 'I used to love ghee,' he said, attempting to give an excuse for laughing.

'But father, ghee is very expensive these days. One cannot use more than a spoonful on a *paratha* now,' Khatoon said.

'No, no, daughter, I didn't mean that,' Pir Bakhsh said, noting the pointed tone of her remark. 'I couldn't even digest it now. I'd fall sick if I ate it. I was just thinking of how quickly time passes. The day before yesterday, it was my mother in front of the hearth; yesterday, it was Nek Bakht, and today it is you.'

Khatoon looked at Pir Bakhsh with eyes full of fear and said, 'Then why don't you say, father, that you are awaiting my death?'

Pir Bakhsh felt as if Khatoon had given him a kick in the stomach. He could only mutter a 'Ha!' and then like a whipped boy, he got up quietly and walked up to the kitchen wall. Standing in its shadow, he stared at the wall in front as if he was looking at something far away. He pressed his trembling lower lip between his teeth; the veins of his neck swelled up, but despite all this effort, tears welled up in his eyes. For fear of letting it all hang out before Khatoon, he went out into the street. When Habib came home for lunch, he saw his father sitting down at the bend in the street, drawing lines in the dirt with a straw.

He came inside the house with his son. As usual, he was helped with the washing of hands, and when Khatoon brought him food, all his tension suddenly disappeared. After the meal, he sat on the cot smoking hookah. Habib left for the shop after the meal, and Khatoon got busy in the kitchen with dishwashing. He called out to Khatoon, 'Daughter, the hookah is getting cold. Get me some fire.'

'I'm doing the dishes,' Khatoon replied.

'Pick some cinders up with a pair of tongs,' Pir Bakhsh said.

The dishes clanged as though they had been banged down. Shortly thereafter Khatoon emerged carrying a few cinders in a pair of tongs; she looked so incensed that Pir Bakhsh kept staring at her face. She just threw the cinders and the pair of tongs at Pir Bakhsh's feet and went back into the kitchen. The dishes clanged again.

Pir Bakhsh forgot to smoke. The cinders went cold lying where they had fallen.

In the evening when Habib returned from the shop, Pir Bakhsh was waiting for him at the turning in the street. 'Listen, son,' he said and holding his hand narrated the day's incident. Habib kept listening quietly; then pulling his hand free, hurried into the house.

Pir Bakhsh stood where he was for a long while. He thought of his sister. If she were alive today, he would have gone straight to her house. He wondered if his son had forgotten about him. Once, he even thought of putting his son to the test: he'd stay out in the street the whole night if Habib didn't come out to fetch him. He sat down next to the wall. When he looked in front, he saw the two bamboo poles of the aerial on his roof. In the backdrop of the darkening sky they looked to him like two people, maybe Habib and Khatoon, watching him. Like a sulking child he wanted to crawl inside the wall. But then he heard voices at the end of the alley. Two people, talking, were approaching him. It agitated him, and he got up and ran inside the house. In the courtyard, Habib stood hugging the wall like a shadow, and Khatoon sat staring at the burning fire in the hearth.

Pir Bakhsh felt as if he had plucked all the flowers in his garden and now the plants sported nothing but unsheathed daggers. To break the silence, he dragged his cot noisily into the corner where he and Nek Bakht used to sleep after Habib's wedding, and where the mat had been spread for the mourners.

Nobody ate that night. Pir Bakhsh lay awake the whole night. Even when he dozed off for a while, his ears stayed alert. Time and again, he would raise his head from the pillow to listen to what he thought was the sound of laughter coming from the other side of the kitchen wall. Early on in the night, he did hear Khatoon sob a few times, but after that the silence was so dense that Pir Bakhsh was frightened of it and longed to hear some sound—any sound. He coughed to assure himself that it wasn't the end of the world yet. Once, he even thought of picking up his cot on his head and leaving his house forever to live in the open, on his land, but he recalled that even his land now belonged to Habib. And then, before leaving, he wanted to hear Habib and Khatoon talk lovingly to each other. It was true that Habib hadn't done anything about his complaint—he hadn't even asked him if he wanted his dinner—but after all, Habib and Khatoon were husband and wife, and when husband and wife quarrelled with each other, they didn't look beyond themselves. His uneasiness grew worse when he realized that he himself was responsible for causing that maddening stillness.

Once, he recalled, when Nek Bakht had had a quarrel with him, he had begun to detest life. He hadn't even said his prayers that day, roaming aimlessly in the streets until midday. Then, in the afternoon, as he was clipping branches of the berry tree in the yard to feed them to his goats, a thorn had got lodged in his palm. He didn't know how Nek Bakht had found out about it—she wasn't even looking at him. She had been sitting leaning against the wall, busily husking grain. Anyway, she had got up, gone inside and come back with a needle. Pir Bakhsh had also climbed down from the tree. She had held his hand in hers and prised out the broken thorn. She had also said, 'Next time, when a thorn gets stuck in your hand, shout for me, for we are fated, aren't we, to share each other's joys and pain.' They had then vowed never to quarrel with each other again. As Pir Bakhsh recalled that incident, he felt as if he himself was the brambly berry tree whose thorns he had driven into his son's and daughter-in-law's palms.

Agitated, he rubbed his arms with his hands and raised his head hoping to hear some sound from behind the kitchen wall. Roosters had begun crowing and the darkness of the star-studded sky had begun to dissipate.

He heard the muezzin's call from the mosque. Reciting the *kalima*, he rose from the bed. Suddenly he felt his eyes burning, his head in a whirl, and his heart pounding in his temples, stomach and even ankles. An earthen goblet stood on the wall at the end of the kitchen. He tip-toed towards it, and as he lifted it to fill himself a glass of water, Habib asked, 'Are you up, Father? Is there enough water in the goblet, or should I fill it up?'

Pir Bakhsh shook it and said, 'There is some.'

When Pir Bakhsh turned to go back to his cot, he heard Habib say to Khatoon, 'It's morning, do you see?'

'I have been awake for a long time,' Khatoon replied.

'You think I wasn't?' Habib said.

Then something happened between them. Perhaps Habib had tickled her or something, but Khatoon began giggling. Once, even Habib laughed a little.

Even though Pir Bakhsh had been waiting for some such thing, a joke or some laughter, between the couple, something suddenly gave way within his chest, without his being aware of it. He felt a sudden wave of anger rise within him at the thought of his son abandoning the father to make peace with the wife. But had they actually quarrelled? Did his son consider him worth picking a quarrel with his wife?

Habib and Khatoon were talking and laughing. What could they be talking about and why laughing so much, he wondered. Making his ablutions, he felt the flabbiness of the skin over his hands and arms. Surely, he thought, his son and daughter-in-law were laughing at him, at his age, at the helplessness which comes with age. The goblet slid from his hands, fell down and shattered. Habib and Khatoon jumped down from their beds, looked at Pir Bakhsh sitting next to the broken goblet and quietly went back.

It was good that Khatoon hadn't said anything. But Habib's silence suggested that he had minded the loss of the goblet—not an expensive item, costing just four pice today, even though when Nek Bakht had got it, in the good old days, she had paid just a fistful of millet for it.

Pir Bakhsh still had to wash one of his feet, yet he lacked the courage either to ask for another goblet, or take a cupful of water from the pitcher. He said his prayers anyway, and was astonished to realize that he had no memory of having performed all the different motions of his prayer. He had gone through the whole exercise like a robot.

It was time for Habib to leave for the shop, but he still hadn't said anything to his father about yesterday's incident. Pir Bakhsh sat reciting 'Praise be to God' on his *tasbih*; as he was about to reach the hundredth bead on the string, he realized that instead of 'Praise be to God' he had been repeating 'Habib, Habib.' He put the *tasbih* away and went out of the house. Perhaps Habib hadn't spoken to him because of his wife's presence. As Habib came out, he saw Pir Bakhsh, and said 'Father!'

Pir Bakhsh took a few eager steps towards him, 'Yes, son.'

Habib said, 'Father, you didn't smoke your *hookah* this morning?' In reply Pir Bakhsh thought of saying something reproachful, so that he might get his son's response to his complaint of the previous day. 'How did you ever think of that, son?' he asked. But it was too late, for Habib had already gone back inside, perhaps to dress up the *hookah* for him. Pir Bakhsh followed him in. Habib was already in the kitchen, setting cinders inside the bowl with a pair of tongs. Khatoon sat nearby, her elbows on her knees, her head in her hands, completely indifferent to what her husband was doing.

Pir Bakhsh thought of something. 'Son,' he said, 'my clothes are getting dirty. Bring me a cake of soap when you come home for lunch. I'll go down to the village well and wash them there.'

'No, Father,' Habib said, suddenly startled, 'The clothes can be washed at home.'

Pir Bakhsh felt like smiling. He looked at Khatoon, who still sat in the same posture, staring into the fire. She seemed to him a shy little girl. Perhaps, Habib had already explained things to her.

Pir Bakhsh had perhaps told himself that everything was all right. That was why he now sat smoking his *hookah* calmly. Habib had left for the shop, and Khatoon was in the kitchen getting things ready for lunch. Pir Bakhsh went into his room, took off his clothes, grabbed a sheet from his bed and wrapped it around himself. He came out, walked into the kitchen, and placed his soiled clothes in front of Khatoon.

'What am I to do with these?' she asked him.

'Wash them,' he said, 'Didn't Habib say just now that they could be washed at home. After all, he isn't going to wash them. You'll have to do that.'

'I can't,' Khatoon said, picking up one item of clothing as if it were a dead mouse and dropping it back down. 'I have never washed clothes in my life.'

'Then who is going to do it?' Pir Bakhsh said, making his question sound a little stern.

'You wash them, or Habib, or anybody. I just can't,' Khatoon pushed the clothes towards him and began stirring the ladle in the pot.

Pir Bakhsh was peeved. If Habib had said to him plainly, 'You wash the clothes at home,' it would have been different. But he said they could be washed at home, which could only mean that Khatoon would wash them. He was sure of his son's support in the matter, so he said to her, 'Well, if you can't wash them, neither can I.'

'Nor will I,' she said glowering.

'All right,' Pir Bakhsh threatened, 'I'll go tell Habib.'

Khatoon sprang to her feet. She put her hands on her hips

and rasped: 'Go and tell him. Go right now. I know your son. Don't you utter a word, or I'll have my father beat you, beat both of you, with shoes, in front of the whole village.'

'Beat me with shoes?' Pir Bakhsh repeated those words as though he wasn't sure he had heard them right. Then he said, 'Listen, young lady, I am sixty. All my life, I haven't taken such blather about shoes and beatings from anybody, and I'm not going to now. Your father will come as he comes, but before he does, I'll have my son beat you to within an inch of your life. You stupid girl.'

Khatoon bent down to pick up a clay-pot. She hurled it at Pir Bakhsh who ducked in time. The pot broke and its pieces lay scattered all around. Then Khatoon began wailing loudly and hurling curses at Pir Bakhsh. She lay down on the floor and started stamping her feet and sobbing hysterically.

Pir Bakhsh picked up his dirty clothes, went back into his room, put them back on and rushed out of the house. He was going so fast that he could have trampled anyone who came in his way. When he entered Habib's shop, it was full of customers. He stood in the doorway, panting and watching Habib who was measuring cloth. Then he sat down in a corner.

Gradually, his clenched fists began to ease up, his tightly-clenched jaws relaxed and his hunched up shoulders fell down. When the rush had cleared, and Habib saw him sitting there, he said in surprise, 'Father, you too are here! When did you come? What brought you here? Is anything the matter?'

Pir Bakhsh looked at his son in silence for some time. Then he said, 'No, son, nothing is the matter. I just came to see you, to see how you looked sitting in your shop.'

Habib smiled as though he were blushing. Then he bent down over his ledger and started making some entries.

A WILD WOMAN

'It's here,' someone said, and the crowd moved a couple of steps forward, as though they would have fallen through a cave if they hadn't.

'Which number is it?' asked an old woman from the back of the crowd.

'Five,' said the panwari who stood behind her.

In panic, the old woman pushed through the crowd to make her way. Instead of craning to watch the bus, everybody turned around to look at her.

'What a churlish creature; just about cracked my jaw,' one person said, rubbing his chin.

'Are you crazy?' another person wailed.

Meanwhile the bus pulled in. The conductor, opening the door with a clang, said, 'Ladies first.'

By now the old woman had already reached the middle of the crowd. Grudgingly it parted to let her pass.

The old woman lifted the shawl covering her head and passed her hand over her hair. Then holding the edge of the shawl in her fist and looking victoriously at the crowd, she said to the conductor, 'Lad, your mother must have given you birth remembering the Lord.'

The conductor blushed and said, 'Oh, come on in, *Masi*.'

As she inched forward towards the bus, she said, 'I would have made my way through the crowd anyway. I was already half way through, but what you said just now was worth a thousand rupees.'

She set her foot on the first step, but crumbled, holding tightly to the second step, as though she had climbed some immense height and was feeling dizzy. The conductor lifted her up and helped her to a seat in front of the door. Thereafter, he let the rest of the people in. In the ensuing rush, he found himself pushed to the very end of the bus.

Raising herself a little from the seat, the old woman pressed the cushion underneath with her fingers a couple of times. Finding it soft, she said, 'How nice!' As the bus began moving, she noticed a fair-skinned lady sitting on her right, next to the window. She wore a milky-white, clean-looking *sari* and a pair of gold-rimmed glasses. She had a white leather purse in her hands, and she was peering out of the window.

The old woman also craned her neck to do the same, but saw everything rushing backwards. She had a reeling sensation, rubbed her eyes and quickly turned to look in front. With her fore-finger she tapped the knee of the fair-skinned lady. Knitting her brows the lady turned to face the old woman, who said, 'Don't look out. Your head will spin.'

The lady smiled and said, 'My head doesn't spin.'

'But mine did,' said the old woman.

'So don't look out. Mine doesn't, so I will,' the lady retorted. The old woman turned upon her, 'Will your head spin if you do not look out?'

The smile suddenly vanished from the lady's face. She turned her head away.

The old woman could see only the head of the woman in the seat ahead. She had tucked a pale flower in her hair. The old woman leant forward to get a closer look. Then she tapped the knee of her neighbour and asked her confidentially, 'This flower, is it real or fake?'

'Looks fake,' she answered.

'If it is fake, then it must be made of gold,' she suggested.

'It's gold-coloured, for sure,' the lady said.

'No, it looks real to me, freshly plucked from a bush,' the old woman said.

'Then, of course, it would be real,' the lady answered and started looking out the window.

A little confused, the old woman stared at the lady for a while and, once again, tapped her knee.

'What is it now?' she knitted her brows again.

'It's odd, but my head spins even though you are the one looking out of the window,' the old woman said.

The lady smiled a little.
'Listen,' the woman said.
'What is it?' the lady asked with some annoyance.
'Are you a lady?' The old woman asked.
'What do you mean?' she said, offended by the inquiry.
'From the hospital. Are you from the hospital?'
'No, I am not,' she replied.
'Then what are you?'
'What?'
'What do you do?'
'Nothing.'
'You must do something,' the old woman said, shaking her head.
'Buy your ticket, *Masi*,' she heard the conductor above her head.
'Yes, give it to me,' she said, letting go of the edge of her shawl.
'Where for?' the conductor asked.
'Home, son,' she said sweetly.
The conductor burst out laughing. Even the fair-skinned lady looked at the woman and laughed.
Then the conductor turned to the passengers in the bus and said, 'Did you hear this? I asked this *Masi* where she was going, and she said "home." '
Everybody joined the conductor in laughter.
The conductor enjoyed it much. Patiently and gently he explained to the old lady that everybody was going home; what he wanted to know was the stop where she was getting off.
'Walton,' she said. 'My home is in a village across from there.'
Smiling, he pulled out a stub, punched it and gave it to her, saying, 'It's five annas and a half.'
'Five annas and a half?' she said, undoing the knot at the edge of her shawl. 'Why so much? Ghaunsa told me the fare would be four annas. All he gave me was this four-anna bit.' She held out the circular *chawanni*, the four-anna coin, in her fore-fingers to the conductor.

He said, 'No, Masi, the fare is not four but five annas and a half.'

'Why is that?' she spoke sharply, 'Everybody in the world pays four annas; why five annas and a half from me? I'm no heavier than a bag of bones? Do I take more space than others in the bus? Here, take these four annas.'

'Oh, what a nuisance!' the conductor said. His earlier equanimity seemed to have vanished. Turning towards the passengers, he held forth, 'I say there should be a law against allowing those people to travel in buses who haven't gone through their elementary education. Take this old woman, for example. She boarded the bus at Mayo Hospital, and she wants to go all the way to Walton. She wants to go there, yet she won't pay the regular fare of five annas and a half because she says someone gave her only four annas.'

With the innocence of a child, the old woman interjected, 'Why someone? It was my own Ghaunsa who gave me the four annas.'

The conductor chuckled and continued, 'Yes, because Ghaunsa gave her only four annas. But somebody should make her understand that the bus belongs to the state, not to Ghaunsa. If it were Ghaunsa's, he would surely have charged four annas.'

'Why should he have charged me anything?' she said. 'He's my nephew and he earns his own keep, carrying milk to town everyday on his own cart. It was with him that I came to town today. Let alone four annas, he didn't even ask for four pice. He wouldn't dare. I have raised him like my own son. His sister-in-law is in the hospital. I thought I would go and find out how she was faring, and I would return with him on his milk-cart. But the girl wasn't doing too well, so Ghaunsa decided to stay on. He gave me this four-anna piece to take the bus home. And here you are, asking me for five annas and a half. Are you charging me so much because this seat has a soft cushion? If that's so, let me sit me on a plain seat, or even on the floor. I am a countrywoman. I can sit anywhere.'

'No, *Masi*,' the conductor said, exasperated by now, 'everyone has the same cushioned seat.'

'Then, what do you want me to do now?' she asked, perplexed.

'Give me another anna and a half,' the conductor said.

'How can I? I am telling you I don't have it,' she answered. 'I came empty-handed from home. It was Ghaunsa who lent me this four-anna piece. I'll pay him back tomorrow.'

The conductor was having a hard time keeping his anger under wraps. He said, 'But I have to have the money today because I have punched out your ticket. Hurry up. The bus has called on so many stops, and so many new passengers have boarded it. I have to punch everybody's ticket. If a ticket-checker happens by, he'll have me by my throat. Good folks, please make this woman understand, for God's sake. She wants to go to Walton but doesn't even have fare enough for Model Town. And then she says she will not pay a pice more than four annas.'

The woman with the flower in her hair turned around and said, 'Such people should be body-searched. They hide a lot of small change in their pockets.'

The old woman stood up and screamed over her head, 'Are you my son's woman to know what I have in my pockets? One doesn't get a head full of sense by sticking a cheap flower in her hair, my queen.'

The woman couldn't do more than grind her teeth.

The fair-skinned lady pulled the old woman back by her hand, and she sat down.

'She is a wild one, isn't she?' someone said.

'Who was that?' the old woman turned around and surveyed everyone behind her in the bus. 'Let him say that again and see if I don't pull his tongue out from his throat and throw it out of this window.'

The fair-skinned woman cringed as though the old woman had indeed done that. She visualized a blood-dripping tongue going over her head and out of the window.

The conductor who had meanwhile started punching stubs for other passengers, came back to her and asked her harshly, '*Masi*, are you going to pay the balance or not?'

'Now you are talking like a *thanedar*, lad,' she said. 'I'm telling you, here is the four-anna piece. The six pice that remain, I'll pay you tomorrow. I'll wait for you at the Walton stop early tomorrow morning, and as soon as you get there, I'll put the money in your hand, and you can then make sure if everything is fine.'

'Listen to this one now!' the conductor wailed to the passengers.

But suddenly the tension evident on his face was relieved as he walked to the back of the bus and bent down to talk to an elderly man.

The old woman tapped the knee of the fair-skinned lady again, and when she looked at her, said, 'You see what's been going on?'

The lady tried to explain to her, '*Masi*, the conductor is not wrong. It does cost five and a half annas to get to Walton. And the bus does belong to the government. The conductor is the government's employee; if he charges anyone less than the fare, he has to make up the difference from his own pocket. If the poor fellow doesn't do that, he can lose his job.'

'Oh, oh, the poor man,' she looked at the conductor with affection. 'I have always earned my living by my own hands; why would I take away someone's means of living? And for six pice? I honestly didn't know. It was Ghaunsa who cheated me. But even that poor fellow is not really to blame. He himself comes to town on his milk-cart. What should I do now?'

'Tell you what,' the lady said opening her purse. 'I can...'

In the meanwhile the conductor returned to the old woman's seat. She said, 'Lad, I swear I didn't know that...'

'Nothing to worry about, *Masi*. Everything is taken care of. I'll get you down at Walton.'

The old woman cheered up. She said, 'Didn't I tell you, lad, that your mother had given you birth remembering the Lord? But tell me, if you were finally going to accept the same four-anna piece, why did you raise such a big fuss about five annas and a half?'

'*Masi*, the matter could be squared only with five annas and a half,' the conductor replied.

'But where am I going to get the six pice from?' the woman asked, becoming sad and worried again.

'Don't worry. I got my six pice,' he told her.

'Where from?' she asked.

'That gentleman over there gave them to me,' the conductor said pointing to the elderly man in the back.

'Why?' the woman asked surprised.

'Out of pity,' the conductor said.

The old woman tried to get up but fell back down in her seat. 'Pity on whom?' she demanded.

'On you. Who else?'

The old lady flared up and screamed, 'Let me have a good look at my benefactor.'

The fair-skinned woman snapped her purse shut and began to stare at the old woman.

Grasping the rod overhead and holding on to the backs of the seats, the old woman lunged towards the elderly gentleman. She asked him, 'Were those six pice burning a hole in your pocket that out of pity you had to throw them at me, as one throws a bone at a dog?'

'See? This is what you get for doing good these days?' someone said

The face of the neatly dressed elderly man turned pale. The old woman yelled, 'A magnanimous man you are, you who have taken pity on me, on someone who has spent sixty, maybe seventy years, sowing seeds in the soil and waiting for the plants to grow and ripen; you have thrown six pice into my hands, into the hands which have overturned so much soil that if it were all piled up, it would make a mountain. And you dare take pity on me. Don't you have a mother or a sister at home to take pity on? Didn't you come across any blind beggar along the way to give charity to? Aren't you ashamed of pitying a peasant woman?'

The she turned to the conductor, 'Give him back the six pice he has spat on me. And let me get down. Right here. I'll go back home on foot. I know how to walk.'

She became quiet after that. Inside the bus, one could hear only the sound of the engine running.

A moment later, when the bus pulled in at the next stop, the old woman rushed to the door. Without worrying about the foothold, she leaned out of the door and fell on the road in a heap. Then she got up, shook the dust off her clothes, and started walking towards Walton, with a swiftness nobody would have believed her capable of.

'She was indeed a wild one, wasn't she?' somebody said inside the bus.

THE REST-HOUSE

The ash-coloured stone building was known to the rich folk as the rest-house and to the common people as '*raees khana*'—the rich house. This was so perhaps because there was already a dak-bungalow for the well-to-do and an inn for the poor, where, sitting around the sunken oven, close by the oven-tender, they ate coarse, thick bread with mounds of lentils piled on it, and wondered among themselves which of the two—Maryan, the wife of the caretaker of the rest-house, and Bahishto, the sister of the gardener of the dak-bungalow—was more beautiful. Now and then they also stole a glance at the oven-tender's wife who, although reputedly the queen of some dominion, was now living in disguise as a cook's wife. Rich folk hardly ever stayed at the rest-house. At most, a party of young hunters looking for deer might stop there for the night once in a while. That day Fazloo, the caretaker, with high hopes, cleared the cobwebs from the ceiling, threw out the piles of dead leaves lying in the corners of the yard and emptied the only vase in the building of its stinking water and old, wilted flowers, replacing them with fresh ones procured from the gardener of the dak-bungalow. And when the party left, Fazloo became convinced that the watchmen of the other buildings, all of them, were absolute crooks. Perfect liars, who told him stories about large tips or gratuities and claimed to have eaten nothing but such fabulous dishes as pilaf, *feerni* and *korma* for the duration of their guests' stay. May boils grow on their tongues if they lie to him, they'd say. When Fazloo related those exaggerated tales to Maryan, she would say that those people weren't lying. Had Fazloo ever looked at the wives and daughters of the other watchmen? They wore such expensive silks, they looked like princesses from Patiala. Fatima, the watchman's wife, had come to the well that very morning to do some washing. Maryan had shamed her for stepping out of the house bare-headed. At first Fatima laughed out loud and then, coming near Maryan, showed her the hundred-rupee *dupatta* she was wearing on her head and told *her* to be ashamed instead. 'When I looked closely, she was wearing a *dupatta* finer even than a gossamer. That mustachioed gentleman who had stayed with them—you know, the one whose wife raised dogs in place of children—well, he had had his wife give it to Fatima. And what kind of guests do we get? One of them made off with the only soap-dish the rest-house boasted of. And those wealthy hunters—well, they left Fazloo a grand tip of a *chawanni*—a measly quarter with a dented edge to boot. Bastards!'

'Pig's progeny,' Fazloo agreed with her.

This rest-house was situated at Sakesar, the highest peak in the mountain range in Kohistan. During winter months, layers of clouds and mist covered the mountain and made it look from a distance like an old man who hadn't had a shower in months. Owls hooted atop the chimneys of bungalows dotting the mountain's crests and valleys and cats fought on their fences. Sunshine was a rare occurrence. But as soon as the first breezes of spring stitched green beads on the dried-up branches of trees, and tender blades of grass sprouted from the cracks in the stones; as soon as the fragrance of the greenery below reached Sakesar, and that on Sakesar crept down into the valley; as soon as the newly risen sun lit up the surface of the lake at the foot of Sakesar, and the crops on its slopes began to bloom, the dusting and cleaning of the bungalows started. The caretakers' wives and children removed the cobwebs and washed windows; the gardeners got rid of the debris of the past autumn and planted a variety of seedlings, and the store-owners from the plains below loaded their wares on donkeys and began carting them up. By evening the windows of the servant-quarters beside the bungalows would come to life, and flurried activity begin everywhere, as on the eve of Eid.

Soon big officials arrived with their large families, cruising along the winding Sakesar roads in their shiny limousines. The minute the children of watchmen and gardeners spotted their rich, fair-skinned counterparts in the car windows, they ran after them and when the car had vanished into a bungalow stood watching, their mouths agape, their bodies glued to the gate. Stepping out of the car if, by chance, one of the rich kids looked towards the gate, some of the undaunted ones among the poor quickly raised their hands to their foreheads in greeting. If the greeting was acknowledged, they would look gloatingly at the bashful and timid among their own, as if taunting them: see, they acepted our greetings; now we shall get bats and balls and used shoes as reward. And you will just sit here and watch. One must bow before the rich, you swine; one earns merit that way.

The big officials would be followed by other guests in the dak-bungalow who came from different walks of life. They stayed for a few days and then, after doling out gratuities to the dak-bungalow's different crews, returned to the plains. Among them, some came to earn the honour of being received by the Deputy Commissioner Sahib, others to offer an 'open-basket gift' of some canisters of *ghee*, quantities of eggs, and cages full of quails in connection with the court cases relating to their land-holdings. The number of people who came just to visit Sakesar was really small. Sometimes a party of hermits looking for various herbs came crawling up the mountain slopes to Sakesar and after staying the night at the inn went down the other side of the mountain in the morning. Or when some young deer-hunters were wandering close by Sakesar, they were lured into coming up by the shiny bright bungalows and the coiling blue smoke from their chimneys. They would spend the night at the rest-house and steal away quietly the next morning before being noticed by the caretaker.

'Pigs' progeny!' Fazloo would express his view of such visitors.

'Bastards!' Maryan would chime in.

Once, just as he slunk away, one such hunter had slipped the soap-dish of the rest-house into his bag. That was why Fazloo smoked his hookah unceasingly and Maryan, sitting close by, wrapped yarn around the bobbin of her sewing machine or squashed lice from Sheroo's hair, calling every louse she picked a 'bastard.'

The valley in the east of Sakesar is known as the Soon. The

belief in the villages around here is that the monsoon is born at the summit of Sakesar and as it comes down, it rains on the pastures in the Soon. So the residents of the Soon look towards Sakesar for rain instead of at the sky. The soldiers on furlough peering into their binoculars across the thick growth of trees would sometimes spot a crawling car, but in reality they would be looking for the little rag in the sky that would expand during the night and turn into a cloud, and after pouring down on Sakesar would move towards the villages along the slopes. From Sakesar, these villages seemed to hang precariously, as if a kick from above could send a whole village hurtling down into the plains.

But this year the monsoon had been born in a village in the Soon rather than at the Sakesar peak. Sakesar folks saw the rain falling in the valley and at the mountain range extending all the way to the horizon; Sakesar itself received only moist breezes. Hot, searing winds swept over Khushab and Mianwali, the flatlands in the south and west; and a coolness crept out of the rain-washed valley of Soon and Pakkhar in the north and east, but only a mysterious breeze—sometimes hot, sometimes cold, and sometimes moist—fluttered the curtains of the bungalows in Sakesar, as the affluent sat looking through their binoculars at the clouds racing below in the valley. The water from the foothills, glistening like sheets of silver, coursed down to the lake, and players at the tennis courts interrupted their game to sit and smoke and yawn. And when a strong gust suddenly tossed up the moist fragrance of the land below, the players stretched themselves and stared at the valley with a feeling of helplessness; if the monsoon's crime were actionable, they would have dragged it into a court of law there and then.

A sahib was staying at the dak-bungalow those days. He was not involved in any court case, nor had he come there to offer a 'gift' to any official. He had come merely to spend the monsoon season here and was dismayed by this mischief of the weather: while the rivulets overflowed in the Soon, springs had all but dried up in Sakesar. Hadn't *Savan* been born every year, for the past so many years, on the tops of Sakesar? This is why he had arrived and settled into the dak-bungalow a few days before the start of the monsoon. Now it was the seventh day of *Savan*, the month of the rains, and while it was raining below in the villages of Nowshehra, Anga and Ochhali, here in Sakesar a light dust still hung on the trees and the desolation of thirst had settled in the eyes of people. All day long, the sahib would sit on the verandah of the dak-bungalow poring over books and smoking; in the evening, he would walk by the tennis courts, supremely indifferent to the players, and go down the road which ran along the side of the rest-house. After some time he would return, and a window and two skylights of the dak-bungalow would remain lit for a long while in the night.

Fazloo came to know through the gardener of the dak-bungalow that this sahib had been there last year as well. Then one day he had found much wrong with the dak-bungalow and said there was no building in Sakesar to match the rest-house. Even the three Deputy Commissioners there hadn't been able to find a spot for their bungalows as pleasant as the rest-house. The gardener had looked at the sahib with amazement because the rest-house was quite a lack-lustre building, indeed it was frighteningly drab. The hill on its back blocked off the entire view to the west, and the drooping branches of the trees at the edge of its small front yard were so thick that even the lake below could be seen through them only as patches of glittering stars. Then the rumour had been circulating for the past two years that the rest-house was haunted. The gardener felt sorry for the sahib's lack of taste.

'And then he left,' the gardener said.

'After the rains or earlier?' Fazloo asked out of curiosity, for it had been a long time since the word rest-house had been mentioned in connection with any visitor.

'I don't remember that now,' the gardener said, 'but it was when you and Maryan had gone to the valley for your mother-in-law's funeral. The day after you left, the sahib left too, in a rented car, leaving me a tip of a hundred rupees.'

'Hundred rupees!' Fazloo was beside himself now. 'But who

is he, anyway?'

'Does it matter?' the gardener said nonchalantly. 'Who cares? I care about my tip, which I did get. Think of it. A hundred rupees. Not a small sum, is it? Hard to say it. Even harder to carry all at once.'

Fazloo's brows narrowed and an arched wrinkle formed on his forehead. 'One hundred? Sure you're in your senses?' he asked.

'Yes, yes, a thousand times yes. A hundred rupees, five-times twenty, four-times twenty-five. And a blanket to boot, so soft and warm that if you touched it, you felt you were touching fresh *halva*. He gave it to Bahishto, and all Bahishto did for him was put flowers in the vase in his room two or three times and wash his towel once. That's all. For sure, the man's some saint.'

It had become a matter of habit for Fazloo to be irritated by others' tales of tips or gratuities, but when the gardener first swore by the Holy Book and then by his widowed sister Bahishto, he swallowed an invisible lump and returned to his hut where he narrated the whole incident to Maryan as though the gardener had given him all the details only for her benefit. As she mixed a pinch of salt in the bowl of *lassi*, Maryan said, 'I ask you, Fazloo, why do we have to be stuck here in Sakesar? To take care of the rest-house for what—peanuts? Why not go back down in the Soon and work as we did before? There are so many landowners there; surely someone will give us work and a place to stay. If I could have saved even a little bit from our earnings, I would have kept it for our medical needs. But right now, if Sheroo has a splinter in his foot, I have to sit for hours in front of the hospital, and only then does that bastard of a compounder give a wee bit of the tincture. It's only because we're so destitute that last year the bastard had dared to wink at me.'

Fazloo was already full of resentment against the world; when Maryan reminded him of the compounder, he couldn't contain himself any longer. Hurriedly he picked up an axe from the corner and roared, 'Last year you stopped me in Sheroo's name, but nothing will stop me today. Such pig's progeny have to be taught to behave. Today it is winking, tomorrow they might dare to make a grab at you. Get out of my way now.'

In response to all of Fazloo's frothing and foaming Maryan merely got up and approached him with a smile. She put her hand on Fazloo's holding the axe, and said, 'Don't worry. I didn't take it lying down. I had told him, "Babu, why don't you try winking at your mother, or feeling your sister? You bastard, how dare you wink at me! I can make mincemeat but of scores of men like you." Well, I kept on shouting at him while he stood with his hands folded, begging me—"Sister, please! Please don't swear so loudly; the doctor will hear you." It made me laugh.'

Fazloo let go of the axe but went on cursing the compounder, the watchmen of all the buildings, the gardener, even Bahishto. When Maryan objected to his swearing at Bahishto, he flung an oath at Maryan as well and came out of the hut fuming. In the yard of the rest-house the sahib who was staying at the dak-bungalow stood smoking.

'Salaam,' Fazloo said, his hand involuntarily going up to his forehead. His tensed features suddenly relaxed. He walked towards the sahib, age-old humility becoming visible on his face, and asked, 'What can I do for you, sir?'

The sahib had a few grey hairs on his temples, but his face was a vibrant pink. There was a moist brilliance in the eyes and a glow behind the forehead, as though youth had installed itself permanently in his bearing and was about to ooze out of his pores like drops of blood. He pushed the butt of his cigarette with his forefinger along his thumb and shot it towards Fazloo's hut with such force that Maryan who had been watching the two of them through the window involuntarily moved away. The sahib asked Fazloo gently, 'You are Fazal Din, aren't you?'

Impressed and awed by the man's resounding voice, Fazloo replied, 'Yes, sir. I am Fazloo, the caretaker.'

'Fazal Din or Fazloo the caretaker?' The man asked smiling.

'Fazloo the caretaker is okay,' Fazloo responded humbly.

'Are you single?' The man asked.

'Single, sir?' Fazloo laughed respectfully, 'Not only am I married, I also have a four-year old son.'

'And a wife?'

'I have a wife too.'
'What about your parents?'
'They are all dead, sir.'
'Sorry.'
Fazloo thought it proper to be quiet.

The sahib stood looking at the rest-house for some time, and then he took out a pair of binoculars from his shoulder-bag and started scanning the Soon valley. Slowly turning the binoculars, as he moved from the trees at the edge of the yard to Fazloo's hut, he seemed to stagger. He put the binoculars back in the bag and said with a smile, 'Heavens, your hut seems to have hit me smack in the face.'

Maryan and Sheroo were framed like a photograph in the window, and the smoke from the cigarette butt the man had tossed away was rising in a blue curl in front of their faces.

'Fazloo?'
'Yes, sir.'
'What if I moved out of the dak-bungalow into your rest-house?' Fazloo was breathless with excitement. He felt as if not just he but the sahib too were standing on his head and the rest-house was spinning before his eyes. Finally, he gained control over his emotions, but not without difficulty, and said, 'I wish I could be that lucky, sir.'

'Come on,' the sahib said, 'What's the big deal about that? Actually I prefer this place to the dak-bungalow. I can move in here by the end of the day. Is the place furnished?'

'Furnished?' Fazloo asked. He did not want to mention the incident of the theft of the soap-dish, lest the sahib become mistrustful of the rest-house.

'Like a bedstead?'
'Yes, sir. There are two.'
'A table?'
'Yes. And chairs too. And a vase and a lantern. There is also a bucket in the washroom and ...'

The sahib smiled, lit a fresh cigarette and said, 'Fine, I shall be back soon.'

For some time Fazloo just stood there, as though his feet

were stuck to the ground. Then he ran to the verandah of the rest-house, but turned back and dashed to his hut. Leaning halfway into the window he shouted, 'Maryan!' Then, moving away from the window, he rushed into the hut. Maryan stood there barring his way, looking very grave. Her lips were tightly shut. 'You can't go in,' she said, emphatically.

'Can't go in?' Fazloo asked surprised and out of breath, 'Why not?'

She answered in her earlier tone: 'First, I must get even with you for cursing me.'

'Get even with me for cursing you?' Fazloo was bubbling inside to tell her the good news about the new guest.

'Yes,' Maryan said, 'why did you swear at me?'

'I did. So what? Anyway I didn't mean it.' Fazloo tried to evade the issue.

'So what?' Maryan got hold of his hand and clutched it. 'You mean you can swear at me and think nothing of it? I have never taken abuse from anyone. Do you hear me?' After a pause she added, 'Do you hear me, you bastard?'

Fazloo was taken aback, but suddenly he burst out laughing and hugged her. He lifted her up and threw her on the cot inside. 'God,' he said, sitting beside her, 'you seem like the offspring of a camel to me. My, my, such malice!'

'You yourself are the offspring of a camel,' Maryan shot back, but not with unpleasantness. Now she was smiling and trying to cover her thigh with the upturned edge of her loincloth. They started to laugh even more loudly. Amid their laughter Fazloo stood up with a start, as if stung by a wasp. 'Maryan, listen,' he said, 'the sahib is coming over to the resthouse.'

Maryan's laughter was interrupted.

'He is coming over to our place, do you hear?'

Maryan was befuddled. After a few moments she asked, 'Really?'

'Yes, yes. I swear to God. He's gone to fetch his things.'

Maryan felt depressed. 'But Fazloo, those bastards, the hunters, took away even our soap-dish. The rooms are practically bare. The place looks so deserted. He will move in today, only to move out tomorrow. I say the place's become haunted. The other night the bucket in the washroom was making all kinds of noises.'

But Fazloo didn't bother to tell Maryan that a few days ago he had pulled a dead mouse out of the bucket. Instead he told her that all the sahib wanted was a bed to sleep in—just a bed. Presently the two of them then went to the rest-house, hauled all the stuff out into the verandah, swept the rooms, put the bed back in, and removed the cobwebs from the clothes' hooks. After they had washed the flower-vase, Maryan hurried over to the dak-bungalow to ask Bahishto, the gardener's sister, for some fresh flowers. On the way she saw the gardener and the watchman from the engineers' bungalow. They were carrying luggage on their heads, the sahib trailing behind them a short distance away, puffing at his cigarette. But he was so engrossed in watching the narrow trail as he walked that he didn't so much as raise his eyes when Maryan passed him by. When she returned with the flowers, she found him sitting on the verandah reading a book and Fazloo sprinkling water in the yard. Maryan went inside the hut, called Fazloo and handed him the flowers. Fazloo went inside the rest-house, stuck the flowers into the vase and brought it out and put it in front of the sahib on the table. The sahib was startled: 'Who brought these flowers?'

'My wife.'

'They're from the dak-bungalow, aren't they?'

'Yes, they are, sir. She's has got them from there.'

'Flowers of the damned dak-bungalow all over again,' he said turning the page of the book. 'It's okay if Maryan has got them from the dak-bungalow today. From tomorrow, don't bother with the flowers. Just put some branches and leaves in the vase, grown here in the rest-house. Okay?'

Fazloo was wondering how on earth had the man come to know his wife's name. He was about to ask when the man volunteered, 'The gardener's sister told me your wife's name just a few minutes ago. It's Maryan, isn't it?'

'Yes, sir, it is Maryan.'

'It must have been Maryam. You folks turned it into Maryan.'
'It was always Maryan, sir.'
The man was quiet for a while. Then he slapped the book shut and said, 'My late wife was also called Maryam.'

The pained expression on Fazloo's face and his silence prompted the sahib to explain, 'She was turning off the electric fan when she touched some live wire. She died on the spot. Thank God electricity still hasn't reached Sakesar.'

Cooking pilaf and chicken every day for the next four days left Maryan nearly half-dead. All day long she would sit glued to the hearth, her sleeves rolled up, face flushed, hair flying all over, with wisps of ash from the hearth sticking to it, her hands moving busily, while Sheroo cried away and Fazloo felt increasingly agitated. But after the day's work when they went to their cots at night, at least their stomachs were full and their hearts at ease. Sheroo was unable to keep down the rich food for the first two days, but now he had got used to it. The sahib had given him a soft woollen scarf which he kept wrapped around his neck even at night. It was only after he was deep in sleep that Fazloo, gently pulling it off his neck, would say, 'Let me feel it too, you swine.' Both Maryan and Fazloo would laugh loudly and recall reverentially even the least of their guest's gestures. Maryan prayed for the rain, for the sahib was unhappy without it, always scanning the skies. When the lightening roared in the valley below, and breezes laden with moisture rushing through the trees hit the rest-house, fluttering the pages of his book, upsetting the arrangement of leaves in the vase, and tossing his hair onto his forehead, he would ask Fazloo painfully: 'Fazloo, dosen't this place have a saint or some kind of holy man around that you may ask him for a charm for rain? Some rainy season! You can hear waters raging night long in the rivers of Soon, while up here Sakesar waits helplessly like a bereaved widower? And the funny thing is that no less than a veritable army of clouds passes through Sakesar first. Last year the drizzle wouldn't let up for a minute. All the same, the rains were hardly enjoyable. You cannot enjoy the monsoon in the dak-bungalow, can you? You hear no pitter-patter of rain on its roof. Curtains as thick as quilts hanging in its windows. No difference living in the dak-bungalow or living cooped up in a cave. Listen Fazloo, you've been living here a long time, you should know: when are the rains going to start?' And he would peer down into the valley through his binoculars.

He had got on such close terms with Fazloo that he had told him all about his family life. His wife's name was Maryam, his own Yusuf. His wife had passed away, killed by an electric shock just a month after their wedding. He was so affected by the incident that he started to set out on frequent long trips, none of which was called for. Maryam had died in the rainy season. Just before she died raindrops were singing their choral song on the roof of their bungalow, and flashes of lightning, coming in through the skylights, dazzled her sleep-laden eyes. The fan had been on for some time, but as the rain had turned the weather a bit chilly, he had asked her to turn it off—a request that ruined his new life just as it had begun. He clung to her lifeless body the whole night. The next day when the relatives came to take her away for burial, he left for Nainital. From there he went to Rangoon; from Rangoon to Madras, Bombay, and then on to Quetta through Karachi. After wandering in the sun-scorched mountains of Quetta for a few days, he returned to his native Punjab—the land of beauty and love—but instead of going back to the hills of Murree, he landed here in Sakesar. Standing in the yard of the dak-bungalow, he had taken just one look at the scenery through his binoculars and had been sold to the place. That was why he was here again this year.

'Sakesar is the heart of Punjab,' Yusuf said.

Fazloo disagreed with him for the first time in those four days: 'No, sir, what are you saying? Lahore is the heart of Punjab, not Sakesar. What has Sakesar got? Rocks and brambles. Sure, there's a lake here, but it stinks to high heaven in summers, like a donkey's carcass lying rotting. And the people here, my God, are so hot-tempered; they're not content with just pulling punches or slapping when they're in an argument with someone; they have to pull out their knives and axes and spears. God save us from them, sir.'

But the sahib insisted that no other place in the Punjab deserved to be called its heart. He got on with his litany of praises the next day as well and said to Fazloo, 'All right, leave aside the pleasant climate at Sakesar and the scene of the valley and tell me, where else in the Punjab can you find women as beautiful as those here? Travel from Pindi or Mianwali or Multan to Delhi and you won't find such killing eyes, such thick, long eyelashes, such height and bodies, even such hue of the skin, or gait. I think when the Greek king Alexander attacked the Punjab, one of his army contingents must have stayed on here permanently. How else would the facial features of ninety-five per cent of the people here resemble those of the Greek gods. I seem to be reading Homer whenever I look at anyone here. Women look like Venuses, men like Apollo. Even Ingrid Bergman doesn't have such sharp features, or Valentino such devastating beauty.'

Fazloo sat with his mouth open, as if it had never been closed and would not shut now. Even the pupils of his eyes stopped moving. He just sat there, like a statue, staring at Yusuf's lips. He stayed in the same posture long after Yusuf had stopped talking. Then when Yusuf called him, he was startled, as though waking up from sleep and said, 'Yes.' A shiver ran through his frame. 'You're right,' he said, 'There's no match for the women's beauty here. Mothers here have produced beautiful daughters. God be praised. If you look at it from that angle, this is the heart of the Punjab.'

Yusuf lit a cigarette. Suddenly there was a flash of lightning, and a crack of thunder so loud that the hills kept ringing like copper plates long after. Yusuf ran out of the room into the yard. Then he lunged back inside. The clouds suddenly burst open. A bit of dust flew about in the yard and settled down. Leaves and twigs caught in the gutters were suddenly evicted and flew out in confusion, and Sakesar became rejuvenated in no time at all. Yusuf hadn't yet fully contained his euphoria when Maryan screamed from the window of her hut.

'Aye Fazloo, come quickly. Everything near the hearth is

drenched.'

Lifting his loin-cloth to his knees, Fazloo was about to run out when Yusuf said, 'It was Maryan, I guess.'

'Yes, sir, it was.'

'I've heard her for the first time. Perhaps she observes purdah,' Yusuf said in hasty confusion.

Fazloo again lifted his loin-cloth to the knees and said, 'No, sir, she doesn't; it's just that ...'

She called again from the window, 'Have dogs made off with your ears?'

Fazloo looked at Yusuf in embarrassment. 'The pig's progeny has started cursing.'

'Run along. Go, go,' Yusuf said laughing, 'Lest she dump it on me.'

Fazloo, who had already reached the yard, stopped. Indifferent to the driving rain, he turned around and said, 'She wouldn't dare, sir. I'll cut her tongue off and throw it on live coals.' Then he dashed into the hut.

A little later when he returned he saw Yusuf sitting in the chair, his legs on the table, a cigarette pointlessly burning in his hand that hung down on the side, and humming a couplet:

> Your thought, friend, in this night of rains,
> Is like a sharp knife that cuts through my heart.

That day the sahib's raincoat came in very handy in carrying food from the hut to the rest-house. Fazloo and Maryan would spread it over their heads, walk slowly holding the tray, and come on the verandah. Maryan stopped there and Fazloo carried the dish inside. When he came out, they would again hold the raincoat over their heads and walk back to the hut to bring the next instalment. Once when Maryan was standing outside, leaning against a column, shaking water off the raincoat, Yusuf asked: 'Who is it outside?'

'It's Maryan, sir,' Fazloo said.

'What is she doing standing outside?' Yusuf said, 'It's getting cold. Tell her either to come in or go back to the hut.'

'She'll go back to the hut,' Fazloo said.

After a while Yusuf said, 'She's a good cook, your wife.'

Fazloo said quickly, 'Oh, she's all right, but, really, it's the *ghee* that gives the food its taste.'

Promptly Maryan shot back from the outside, 'Really? Maybe it's your old man who puts the taste there.' She raised her voice, 'If you had to sit in front of the hearth from dawn till dusk, you'll cry for your dead grandmother, you bastard.' And she stomped back to the hut in the soaking rain.

Yusuf laughed so hard that his eyes began to water and his face became beet-red. Still laughing he asked a stupefied Fazloo, 'How are you feeling?'

Grinding his teeth, he said under his breath, 'Pig's progeny.'

Yusuf once again had a fit of laughing. A little later a smile emerged on Fazloo's lips also and he said, 'Sir, your food is getting cold.'

'Doesn't matter. Let your temper cool down first. As for the food, it will warm up inside the stomach. Why are you so upset? You got a blow for a blow. Hers wasn't worse than yours.'

Perhaps Fazloo hadn't yet cooled down fully. 'It isn't past that pig's progeny really to pick up a stone and throw at someone. All families have squabbles, but, sir, it isn't a good habit of hers to let go of herself like that before your honour.'

'But "your honour" enjoyed it tremendously,' Yusuf said, and Fazloo's regret lessened to a great extent.

The rain started up after a brief pause and then turned into a drizzle. Yusuf opened the windows on both sides of the room and began listening to the hum of the drizzle on the roof, on the leaves of the trees, on the stones and the cliff. Before turning in, Fazloo came in to ask if there was anything else he could do. Yusuf said, 'Yes, there is something you can do for me.' Fazloo stood waiting with his hands folded. Yusuf lit a cigarette, drew on it a few times and said, 'Come closer.'

Fazloo moved a few steps forward.

'Closer. Sit here on the bed,' Yusuf patted on the bed to

indicate the place.

'On the bed, sir?' Fazloo was confused. 'How can I sit on the bed, sir?'

Yusuf pulled him by the hand and made him sit next to him. 'Like this,' he said.

Fazloo felt as if he was sitting on a hot griddle, instead of a soft mattress. 'Sir?' he said, baffled and staring at Yusuf, eyes wide open with surprise.

Yusuf seemed a little lost today. In the light of the lantern only his profile was visible. Fazloo had the suspicion that Yusuf's eyes were moist and perhaps a tear-drop glittered on his cheek. The atmosphere had definitely turned eerie because of the constant hum of the drizzle, which had added chill to the darkness of the night. Skylights of a distant building showed through the open window. The leaves and branches in the vase on the table were in disarray. The lantern's tongue was throwing up smoke with every gust that hit it. Different kinds of moths had invaded its glass, one wasp among them, the buzzing of whose wings could be heard above the flutter of the rest of the insects. Fazloo looked at Yusuf again, a shade apprehensively. The tear-drop shining earlier on his eyelid had travelled down to his cheek and a fresh tear was dangling from the eyelids, ready to fall.

'What are you looking at, Fazloo?' Yusuf asked.

Fazloo raised his hesitant hand and pointing towards his cheek could only say, 'These, sir, these ...' He folded his pointing finger and closed his fist.

'These are tears,' Yusuf put his hand on Fazloo's shoulder. 'It has become my habit to shed tears. That's why I wait for the rainy season. I lost my Maryam during the same season. That's why I spend the rainy nights crying. It's not a sign of cowardice to cry. One has to suffer to shed even one tear, and I cry the whole night. I am miserable, Fazloo. I have money, estate, land, bungalows, yet I'm the poorest of the poor. I'm poor without Maryam.' He picked up a handkerchief and wiped his eyes. He inched closer to Fazloo and said, 'I have been so utterly devastated that I shall never again be able to have a home.'

'Why not, sir, why not?' Fazloo thought it his duty to say

something.

'But how?' Yusuf asked.

Fazloo kept quiet. He just wanted to comfort him; he really had no proposals to help Yusuf out.

'But Fazloo,' Yusuf said confidentially, 'if you help me, this dried-up stump can flower again.'

'Me, sir?' Fazloo was facing more surprises than he could possibly take.

'Yes, you—why do you consider yourself so unimportant. You are not an ordinary man. Nobody in the world is. If you want, you can do everything for me. Will you?'

'Of course, sir? If I can, I will. But there's hardly anything I can.'

'Come on, you are at it again. Listen Fazloo, if I am spending my nights here alone, it's not because loneliness is a blessing, but because I'm forced to do so, and ...'

'So, sir,' Fazloo thought of a plan, 'would you like me to sleep in a corner of this room?'

'No, no,' Yusuf smiled. 'I don't want you to ruin Maryan's nights to keep me company. That wouldn't do. Tell me just... No, let it go. You'll mind it if I asked.'

'Why should I mind it, sir? I am at your service.'

'The thing is that you can help me, but you'll have to be very brave to do that. See, up here in Sakesar, or in the valley below....' He became quiet. He got up, shut one of the windows, lowered the wick in the lantern, came back and sat down near Fazloo, who was all ears.

Yusuf started talking fast: 'Listen, Fazloo, my friend, isn't there any woman in Sakesar who might fill my empty nights, any girl who for a hundred rupees, which I'll gladly pay, will agree to keep me company at night, blossom like a flower on the charred branch of my life, and leave in the morning? Wouldn't it make you happy to help fill the void in an unhappy man's life? Fazloo, why do you seem so agitated? Why this shivering? I'll give you ten rupees for every night. I'm not a free-loader. If I were a sex-fiend, I could easily go back to Lahore and set up camp in the "Diamond Market." But I don't want the feigned interest of women there. That's why I have been looking from Rangoon to Quetta. I need a real woman, a real woman...'

Yusuf paused for a moment. Fazloo was panting hard as though he had climbed a steep cliff. During Yusuf's silence his breath came even faster. His pupils rose high in their sockets. He stood up and said, 'No, sir, I'm poor but I won't sell my soul. I can't do it. I've never done anything like that.'

'Fazloo,' Yusuf got hold of Fazloo's hand. His voice became hoarse like that of a crying child, and strings of tears began streaming down his cheeks. 'No, Fazloo, please do this for me. My heart has been desolate for such a long time. You can fill its void if you want to. You'd be doing a great good. People earn a place in heaven by giving water to a thirsty dog. Think of how much more merit you will earn by helping quench a soul's thirst...'

Fazloo pulled his hand free and moved away. He walked out of the room without stopping. At the door he said, 'No, sir, I am a farmer's son, not a pimp.'

Furious, sizzling with anger, as Fazloo crossed the verandah and the yard and reached the door of his hut, the ghostly light of the clay-lamp reminded him of the tiff he had had with Maryan earlier in the evening. She hadn't spoken to him throughout the meal. And then when he had gone to bid goodnight to the sahib, she had just thrown herself on the cot and pulled a sheet over herself. She hadn't even put out the lamp. At the door, Fazloo suddenly stopped, feeling as though the sahib had stripped him of his clothes. He couldn't even bear to imagine that anyone would ever ask him to pimp for a woman, least of all this sahib.

He went inside. He removed his turban and then without putting out the lamp lay flat on the cot and began looking far away through the dark roof of the hut. The drizzle had subsided. A frog was croaking in some pond nearby. The smoke from the lamp was rising straight up and going through the roof like a lance. Sheroo mumbled in his sleep, 'What? So little pilaf, mother? Give me more. And meat too. That piece...' Fazloo raised his head to look at Sheroo. He lay huddled inside the old wrap; it seemed as if he would have injured his ribs had he tried to squeeze himself together any more. Maryan too looked like a wrapped-up bundle. His own bed was cold as ice. He started feeling the cold. He wrapped himself in the sheet and closed his eyes. Cold was streaking into the hut from somewhere. He remembered that he had filled the cracks around the door-frame with mud before the onset of winter. Perhaps the cold was coming in through the window, then. He got up and walked to the window. One panel was open a crack. He was about to shut it when his eyes fell on the window of the rest-house, which at first looked to him like a deep yellow sheet hanging from the wall. Then he noticed a movement at the bottom margin of the sheet. That must have been the sahib's head. So, he was still sitting there in the same posture! Let him sit, he thought, and dream dreams of women. Noisily he shut the window. Maryan was startled. She popped her head out of the sheet to look and a moment later pulled it back in.

'Are you awake?' Fazloo asked, but she kept quiet. Somewhere inside him, he prayed that she would remain quiet, that everyone would remain quiet, and let him fall asleep as he struggled in the stillness to put out the fire raging inside his brain. He went back to his cot and lay there.

'Put out the lamp,' Maryan called from inside her wrap.

'I will, soon,' he said irritably. 'Are you awake?'

Maryan didn't say anything.

Fazloo wanted to hurl a stinging curse at Maryan but was afraid it would destroy the stillness which he craved at this time as much as air.

For some time he kept feeling ashamed of himself. Once he even wanted to cry. Tears were trapped behind his eyelids. Something felt stuck in his throat. All his blood had rushed into his brain. Suddenly there was a jangle in his boiling blood. Quickly he turned over in bed. There was another jangle, and he turned over again as if stung. The jangles and rattles now began coursing through his veins. His ankles began knocking against each other, and he felt his ear-lobes burning. He sat up, put out the clay lamp, and stayed for a long while smelling the acrid smell coming from the smoke of the just extinguished lamp. He went to the door and opened it. A rain-drenched bird flew inside and fell down near the hearth, then it flew up again and perched on a wall like a toy. Perhaps it had fallen asleep.

The whole world was asleep. Only he and the sahib were awake. The sahib had money in his pocket and tears in his eyes. Fazloo's pockets were empty and his eyes were stinging. Inside the hut Sheroo, disturbed by the cold, was turning over and over again in bed and groaning. Fazloo went back inside, bolted the door and put on the lamp. A quilt lay on top of an empty trunk. He picked it up, unfolded it and covered Sheroo with it. Then he put out the lamp and returned to his cot.

He made repeated efforts to fall asleep. He recited the *Ayatul Kursi* a hundred times instead of just three, twirled a lock of his hair for so long that it began to hurt, scratched a tiny mole on the side of his chin so hard and long that it began to bleed. Finally he sat up, leaning against the wall. When his back began to hurt, he threw himself face down on the cot. When he felt the stabs of discomfort in his ribs, he sat up again. Suddenly something exploded in his brain: ten rupees everyday, i.e., two hundred rupees in twenty days, equal to his ten-months salary. Everybody was asleep. Everybody eventually goes to sleep. He needed money, so did women, so did mothers and fathers. All needed money. Maulvi Halim had molested two girls, was caught and put in the slammer; then he got out, people taunted and reproached him for a while; in the end, the world forgot, and he again became the imam of the mosque. People always forget. They do. They go to sleep. Even the watchmen. It is so dark that let alone a woman, one can't see one's own hands. Bahishto has golden rings in her ears and a sheer *dupatta* on her head. And Maryan's ear lobes are bare and the thick sheet covering her head so coarse that if it rubbed against a steel plate long enough, it would turn it into thin paper.

It's the middle of the night and the sahib is still sitting up and crying. He is crying like a woman even though he is a man. There is pleading in his voice instead of challenge. He is a big man, a rich landlord, yet he is so poor, so poor that he begs a

watchman to find him a woman. And he'll even pay for her.
'Maryan, you're awake?'
'What is it?' she asked angrily.
'Oh, you're are still awake,' he said in embarrassment, as if caught naked.

He lay flat on his back for a long time, breathing soundlessly. He thought of his father who used to carry his plough in one hand and his prayer-beads in the other. It was said that the day he missed his prayers would be the doomsday. But he died in prison because the moneylender, despairing of collecting his loan, had dragged him into the court. He was running high temperature when they whisked him to prison. He died there. A tingling shot through Fazloo's body and reached all the way to his fingertips. If one had money, one had respect, good name and health. If one didn't have money, one was condemned to be a caretaker of a desolate rest-house, to listen to Maryan's swearing and Sheroo's groans. One couldn't even do anything for God without money; one couldn't even send the votive offering of oil for the lamps in the mosque, or a meal to the *maulvi* on Thursday. One walked with one's head lowered. One begged, pleaded, and curbed momentary bouts of jealousy over the prosperity of others. And then the women here weren't houris either; they were only women. They weren't fairies who would turn into parrots no sooner than you touched them. Take Bahishto, for example. There's such lunacy in her eyes that on the slightest sign from you she would jump up and sit in your lap. Women like Maryan who didn't observe purdah were rare in this part of the world, yet she observed such purdah that put anyone who dared look at her to overwhelming shame. And that wife of the inn's oven-tender, the *queen*, so fair-skinned that she seemed fashioned from the whitest cotton-cloth, was so greedy that she would run to you for a half-rupee. And those women travelling in and out of town whom you saw crossing the streets with bundles on their heads, and those spinsters who couldn't be married because of poverty, or all those married women, whose husbands were policemen in Hong Kong and could only visit home for three months every five years, but who had already rewarded the old midwife in the village four times during those years for her help. Good lord! One needn't be so sensitive as to feel humiliated at the mention of the word 'woman.'

He got up from his cot, opened the window and looked out. Light still showed through the rest-house window and he could see the sahib still pacing about in the room. Fazloo left the window open, came to the door and stepped out. He walked briskly across the yard all the way to the verandah, but then his feet locked. He stood stock-still like an iron post, every sign of life disappearing from his body. He would perhaps have stood there until the end of time had Yusuf's voice not startled him.

'Why did you stop, Fazloo?' Yusuf asked.

Fazloo felt as if a coil under his feet had come unsprung and tossed him inside the room.

'Sit down,' Yusuf said, sitting on the bed.

Fazloo looked at the door, then glanced at the roof as if it too had an opening, and then began staring fixedly at the wall in front. Rubbing his hands together he stammered, slowly, 'Sir, I shall do it. Beginning tomorrow.'

He felt as though the invisible spring had tossed him back at the door, but Yusuf reached forward and held his hand. With his other hand Yusuf took out a ten-rupee note from his pocket and rubbing it on Fazloo's fingers said, 'You are such a nice, gentle-hearted and noble man that I was wondering why you were so reluctant. This is your reward, just for agreeing.'

The tingling in Fazloo's fingertips had now turned into pain. He clutched the note between his fingertips and raising the hand holding the bill to his forehead said 'Salaam' and left. When he reached his hut he turned around and looked. The light in the rest-house had been put out and it had, like his own hut, sunk into darkness. Fazloo felt as if he had fed someone who had been starving for days. He came inside and lay down on the cot. For a while his eyes remained wide open. He took the note out of his pocket, put it under the pillow, and calmly went to sleep.

In the morning he slept late. After she had made the tea, Maryan shook him by the shoulder. He woke up in agitation and saw Maryan sitting in front of him. Then he looked at Sheroo, who was sitting outside, past the gently falling drizzle, under the tin awning, blowing into his cup of tea. He looked at the patch of sky visible through the window and stretching himself into a yawn said, 'Even the sun isn't up yet.'

'The sun isn't up yet!' Maryan sneered. Perhaps last night's anger hadn't quite left her. 'The sun is halfway across the sky behind the clouds, and for him it isn't morning yet. What were you up to last night, scrounging around like cats and mice, now tugging at the quilt, now banging the window panels, now opening the door, now strolling about outside? You didn't overeat last night, did you?'

Fazloo's gaze was fixed at the closed window. Slowly he recalled that he had opened the window last night to look at the rest-house and had then gone out of the hut without shutting it. 'Who shut this window?' he asked hesitantly.

'I did,' Maryan said.

He wanted to ask her 'when?' but couldn't. He lowered his eyes and noticed many pot-holes in the spotlessly clean floor. He was beginning to feel afraid of Maryan.

'Maryan,' he said, 'want to know the truth? You were cross with me, which made me very sad. I couldn't sleep all night.'

'Bastard,' she said, but in such a tone that Fazloo didn't think it necessary to respond to it in kind. 'If I was cross, so were you. If you didn't sleep, I didn't either. Just look at me.'

So she had been up all night—and she knew everything.

'Look at me,' Maryan said again.

He looked at her. Her eyes were swollen and red. But instead of regret or anger, they reflected love. 'Let's make up,' she said. 'Give me your right hand.'

Fazloo smiled contentedly and placed his right hand on hers. 'These are ten rupees!' she screamed. 'Where did you get so much money? You got your pay only three days ago.'

'The sahib gave it to me,' he said. 'He's very happy with the way we are looking after him.'

'A tip?' Maryan said as though intoxicated. 'May God give him a long, happy and prosperous life. But Fazloo, you know what? Something dreadful happened this morning. I couldn't get any butter for the sahib. Everyone says it was too cold last night for the milk to curdle. The churning never happened. I'm feeling so embarrassed.'

'No matter. Our sahib is a real dervish. And you, pig's offspring, what kind of making up is this? No kiss for me? Shame on you.'

Maryan laughed. She too didn't think it necessary to respond to Fazloo's abuse. She leaned forward, kissed him on the cheek and proffered her own. Fazloo first slapped it gently and then when she tried to move away from him in a huff clasped her in his embrace and kissed her for so long that Sheroo, sitting outside, forgot all about drinking his tea.

Fazloo walked to the rest-house carrying the tea-tray. A feeling of uneasiness overcame him by the time he reached the verandah. With an effort he steadied himself and sidled inside, as though he had forgotten to wash off last night's humiliation from his face. But Yusuf did not bring up last night's conversation. Instead he talked about the pleasant weather and handing him the pair of binaculars said, 'Here, have a look at the marvellous views of Sakesar and Soon. Looks like the landscape paintings of the entire world are displayed everywhere in this area.'

Fazloo took the binoculars and came into the yard. He peered through it at the trees along the lake in the valley below. Then roving over the villages of Chitta and Kotli Ogali, he moved to Anga where white two-storeyed houses shone brightly despite the grey morning. From the longitudinal spread of Anga he moved down to Shakarkot and Saraal and observed the wells and the meticulously mapped flower-beds surrounded by the thick mulberry trees in the pastures to the south of those villages. He next turned his attention to Nowshehra, the central town in the Soon. More than the city centre, he was interested in the school and hospital buildings. Then he looked at the police station, a dark and ugly building at the edge of the old graveyard. Its foundations perhaps lay on some of the old graves. Then sweeping quickly over the villages of Subhral Kufri and Krodhi, he let his eyes halt on the village of Ochhali that stood on the lake's south-western shore. Here by the wells, under the giant mulberry trees a number of tents had been pitched for the so-called 'affluent' folks from the plains who lacked the means to rent a place in the heights of Sakesar because there a mere egg sold for four *annas* and a rose-flower for eight. (Sometimes Bahishto, when her brother the gardener was not around, had even made several people cough up a whole rupee for a rose.)

Fazloo turned around and trained the lens on the bungalows of Sakesar. Ordinarily, one could see the dak-bungalow clearly from the rest-house's yard, but because of the binoculars, Fazloo didn't care to look at it quite yet. The trees looked washed and fresh. The drizzle had studded pearls on the leaves. The leaves of the trees of the rest-house seemed to him as big as his guest's wallet. Finally, his rambling glasses stopped at the dak-bungalow. Bahishto was plucking flowers in the garden. She seemed so close to him that he felt he could talk to her. Her clothes were loose and baggy, much like the outfit of the other women in the area. Here and there, though, they stuck to her body because of the drizzle, revealing prominently its pitiless domes, its heart-breaking arches. Her lips were moving. Perhaps she was humming a song, and the red-beaked parrots perched in a tree were leaning their heads as if listening to her, if not also watching her.

'You haven't fallen in love with the binoculars, have you?' Yusuf asked from inside.

Fazloo was startled. After returning the tea-tray and hurriedly taking his own tea, he came out in the street. Right about this time he usually went out to buy chickens. He'd feel them for the meat, weigh them on his hands, pay for them, bring them home, and slaughter and skin them. But today he had gone out to buy something else. It may not have been his first experience in life, it certainly was the first practical one. Before his marriage, he had secretly loved every pretty girl in the village, hung out on the street corners, played on his flute, sung Heer, but he had never thrown so much as a pebble at anyone to catch attention, nor sighed as a girl approached and passed him by.

He had only looked at girls, and thirsted for them in the quiet privacy of his heart. Then he had found Maryan, who had made him forget the beauty of the rest of the world, even that of the oil-man's daughter for whose oil-presses he had toiled in his dreams, and for whom he had stolen bags of mustard and linseed from the landlord's and delivered them to her house.

Maryan was different from all other girls. The faint line of kohl on the eyelids of her large eyes hadn't quite disappeared despite having been washed time and again during the past five or six years, nor had her ruddy cheeks grown pallid despite years of poverty. Neither had the natural wave in her hair vanished, no matter how often it was subjected to combing with hard wooden combs. About Maryan he had always said that if she didn't swear as much as she did, not even a *navab* could have a woman to match her. For the past five or six years he hadn't thought beyond Maryan. But today he was going to Bahishto. What if Bahishto told her brother? And her brother some big official? What if somebody told Maryan? So? So what? He wasn't getting Bahishto for himself. He saw Bahishto standing in front of him, and her voice helped him overcome his crumbling resolve.

'Where are you headed for, brother Fazloo? Must be looking for chickens. Your sahib will quit only when the whole race of chickens has been wiped out from Sakesar.' And she laughed loudly. There was the tinkling of bells in her laughter.

It was a laughter that could only be born of youthful, healthy blood.

'Want flowers?' she asked. 'Why are you standing looking so confused? Have I ever before charged you for flowers that I might today? Maryan is my friend.'

Various plans of broaching the subject indirectly got mixed up in his brain. His face blanched, lips became dry, the pupils just about disappeared inside their sockets, and, like a lunatic, he spluttered, 'Bahishto?'

'Yes, what?'

'Would you like to spend the night with our sahib? He'll pay you a hundred rupees.' He felt as if he was sinking in the earth.

He couldn't figure out whether he was standing on the summit of Sakesar or sitting at the bottom of the lake, and whether what was falling from the sky was a drizzle or a shower of gravel.

Bahishto grasped his hand so quickly and so hard that the sharp pain in his fingers suddenly made him aware of his senses. She asked in a whisper, 'At what time?'

What? It couldn't be true!

Fazloo took a jump up from the bottom of the lake and was instantly back in the garden of the dak-bungalow.

'After the *Isha* prayer.'

'Where will you meet me?'

'On the other side of the road, say, under the old *kahu* tree.'

'Sure I'll get a hundred?'

'Absolutely.'

'My brother must never find out.'

'Why would I tell?'

'Keep it down.'

'You too.'

After a pause Bahishto smiled and said, 'The sahib has been with you five or six days already.'

'Yes.'

'How much has Maryan made?'

It was as if the sky had fallen and Sakesar caved in. 'Pig's progeny,' he swore at Bahishto and ran, clenching his fists and pressing his lower lip between the teeth.

'Brother Fazloo,' Bahishto called.

But he kept on running. Passing by the rest-house, he ran even faster, straight into the bank of clouds by the wide turning in the road below. He returned home quite late. A dense rain had started and there was considerable chill in the air. A part of the valley looked golden, but there was no sign of the sun. Shivering and wet, Fazloo stepped into the hut.

After delivering the sahib's meal Fazloo lay down quietly on his cot. Maryan brought him his tea, a little earlier than usual, and remarked, 'You look a little sluggish today. Must be the weather. It's changed so suddenly. Take a wrap with you when you go out. The month of rains in Sakesar is like the month after the rains in the Soon. Come on, get up. Drink your tea.'

Quietly he sipped his tea. He got up and wrapped himself in a sheet, and then went out to bring tea over to the sahib. When he returned, he lay down on the cot again. And again, later, after serving the sahib dinner. He didn't say anything to the sahib, nor did the sahib try to interrupt his grave mood, as if he knew there was something beneath the gravity. After their late-night prayers in the Sakesar mosque, as the faithful passed by on the street talking among themselves, Fazloo became alert, but he pulled the sheet over his face again. Inside, his eyes were open and through the coarse cotton sheet, the light of the clay-lamp seemed frightening. Maryan and Sheroo were sleeping peacefully. Maryan had massaged his head for long and then had left his cot stealthily, convinced that he had fallen asleep. He felt a surge of love for Maryan. He thought of going out straight to the dak-bungalow and hurling such abuse at Bahishto as no one had ever heard or imagined. Wrapped in the sheet, he padded out of the hut.

The window of the rest-house was lit. Avoiding the light, as he shuffled towards the street, something moved near the trunk of the old *kahu* tree and he heard: 'Brother Fazloo?'

He stood stock-still. Explosions began to go off in his mind; curses formed in his brain and lingered on the burning tip of his tongue.

Bahishto came closer to him. 'I'm drenched, Fazloo. I've been sitting and waiting for you for so long. The *Isha* prayer's been over long since.'

He remained standing where he was.

'Fazloo, please forgive me. I was merely joking. Had no idea a little joke would so inflame you, and...'

Fazloo held her by her cold, wet hand and walked noiselessly towards the rest-house. Before stepping into the verandah he turned around to look at the window of his hut. He could see a small crack. He had forgotten to turn out the lamp, and he felt as if that crack was laughing at him. Then the crack turned into a sharp knife, which quickly transformed into a pair of eyes— Maryan's eyes, full of sorrow and anger. And when Fazloo rubbed his eyes, it turned back into a crack. He tried to drag Bahishto in by her hand, but she pulled it away and asked quietly, 'Sure it'll be a hundred?'

'Yes, it'll be a hundred,' Fazloo spoke to her for the first time and took her in.

Yusuf sat with his head on his knees and his arms wrapped around the knees. He sat up as he heard the noise. A smile appeared on his lips and spread throughout his face, including the eyes. He got up quickly, shut the window, took Fazloo out on the verandah, patted him on the back, and said, 'You are a wonderful man. I cannot repay you for your favours as long as I live. Here, take it. This is a hundred-rupee note, for Bahishto, and this, ten rupees, for you. Tomorrow we begin a new tab. I am not a bad man, Fazloo. This world is bad, so is this rainy season. Do you understand? Good-night.'

The same tingling sensation of the morning returned to Fazloo's fingertips. Holding both the notes in his fist, he went back to his hut.

He was awake the whole night. Even though he had put out the lamp, he couldn't fall asleep. The sound of Maryan's breathing bothered him. If there was as much as a creak from Sheroo's bed, he shuddered. His eyes hurt. His tongue was dry to its root. His breath came hard. His hands and feet were cold.

He opened the door very quietly and stepped out. Daybreak was close. He rushed towards the rest-house. Inside, the lantern was lit, and Yusuf was asleep. He went into the adjoining room. There, under the light of a tin oil-lamp, Bahishto sat on the bed, dangling her legs. The minute he came in, she grabbed his hand and flared up, 'This sahib of yours—what kind of a man is he? I tell you, Fazloo, he *is* weird. I have spent the night on a bed of thorns. He left me like I was an amputee on a horseback. He was going to pay a hundred rupees, and all that happened after you left was that he lovingly made this bed for me and told me to sit down. Then he put the lantern over there in front and like lunatics began staring at me. I felt ill at ease and cringed. But he said, 'No, no, keep still. I'll look at you, just look at you. If you feel sleepy, go to sleep. I'll watch you sleeping. If you want to cry, go ahead; I'll look at your wet eyes. I just want to *look* at you.' And, Fazloo, he just kept staring at me. At last, when I was tired and lay down, he was still looking at me. Then I slept for a while. When I opened my eyes, he was still there looking. After that I couldn't go to sleep. I just lay down with my eyes shut. And he just sat and stared. When the first rooster crowed, he picked up the lantern and went into the other room. I haven't been able to go back to sleep because I knew it will be morning soon. Every bone in my body hurts, as if someone has held me under the knee and given me a good drubbing. He didn't even touch me, Fazloo. He did not even touch me.'

Fazloo's surprise knew no end. In his eyes, the sahib had suddenly become one of those saintly men who had reached God through the love of boys and girls. Even Maulvi Halim of his village seemed innocent to him now; maybe he too was looking for a means to reach God. And this sahib...

Fazloo put a hundred-rupee note on Bahishto's thigh.

She leaned forward towards the light of the lamp and turned the note around. 'Is it a hundred?'

'Yes, it is,' Fazloo said. 'Go now, the dawn is about to break.'

'And your share in it?' she asked, prompted perhaps by her previous experiences.

'Go! Go now!' Fazloo said embarrassed.

Bahishto got up and groaned. Then she stretched herself, brought down her raised hands quickly and slapped her thighs. She rubbed her eyes with the backs of her hands and wrapped the *dupatta* around her head as tightly as though she were going to say her midnight voluntary prayers. She said, 'You aren't angry because of what I said yesterday, are you?'

Fazloo thought it enough to shake his head.

'I am at your service. Any time at all,' she said and walked out of the room.

Fazloo emerged from the rest-house, light as a feather. He had committed no sin. The sahib had committed no sin. Even Bahishto had committed no sin. The sahib had only looked at her. Who doesn't look at women? Fazloo himself had looked at Bahishto many times. Hadn't he? Nothing wrong in merely looking. Is there?

Fazloo returned to his hut and fell into a deep sleep. In the morning Maryan woke him up. 'What is this new habit of sleeping late? Watchmen shouldn't be doing that,' she counselled affectionately.

Later, when he brought his guest his tea, he found him sitting reading a book and humming to himself. His face looked lively, despite his tired eyes. Even his tierdness had something lively about it. Fazloo looked at him with respect. Both of them smiled and the sahib said, 'Looks like it will be sunny today. The clouds are racing away.'

'Yes, sir,' Fazloo didn't think it proper to say more. He was choking on his admiration for the man.

After his tea, Fazloo went looking for some other woman and very smoothly settled the matter with the wife of the inn's oven-tender. She wasn't beautiful, but she had a personality that made her stand out even in a crowd of pretty women. And she had full and inviting lips. Fazloo comfortably managed his other affairs during the day. At night she came to the old *kahu* tree. He took her over to the rest-house, came back to his hut and went to sleep. He woke up at the right time and made his way stealthily to the rest-house. The lantern was lit and Yusuf was asleep. In the adjoining room the clay-lamp was lit and the oven-tender's young wife was sitting at the edge of the bed, her legs dangling. As soon as she saw Fazloo she began crying.

'What happened? 'Fazloo thought of comforting her.

'Nothing happened, Fazloo,' she said wiping her tears. 'And that is the sad thing that nothing happened. The whole night the man didn't even touch me. He just sat and looked at me for a very long time. He said he just wanted to look at me. That was why he had called me here. I could sleep if I wanted to; he was only going to look....'

'So what's there to cry about?' Fazloo asked.

She cried even more loudly and said, 'I won't get the money now. Who would pay a hundred rupees just to look at someone?' Fazloo handed over the hundred-rupee note to the woman. At first she stared at it open-mouthed, and then she wiped her tears and went out quietly.

Fazloo kept standing for some time. Finally he put out the lamp and came into Yusuf's room. He was still sleeping. Fazloo began to notice a halo around his head, and a light, like that thrown by a lantern, emitting from his forehead. 'How wonderful is the sahib! How nice! How pious! May God this monsoon season never end! May God this rain never end, and the man never leave here,' he prayed and shuffled out.

He had barely stepped out in the street in search of a new woman when the clouds burst. A woman in the street darted to the old *kahu* tree for cover. Fazloo was about to run back into his hut, but emboldened by the sight of the woman decided to try his luck with her. She was a trim and skinny woman with a face like that of a Chinese doll.

He went close to her. 'Where are you going to, sister?'

'To Mianwali,' she said, hiding her small bundle in her lap. 'My man is in jail there. I'm going for the visit.'

Without thinking Fazloo said, 'Stay here tonight.'

'What?' the woman asked surprised.

'I'm saying, it's a matter of just one night. Stay here with me. There is a guest in the rest-house who pays hundred rupees for the night.'

The woman stood erect. The bundle fell and came undone, revealing coarse village biscuits and other snacks. She turned upon him. She hurled such vicious abuse at him that he bolted in fright. 'Go get your mother... your sister. Go ask your wife...' He could hear her even at a distance. He cut onto the wider gravel path and then onto the narrower one, running all the while, feeling pursued relentlessly by the woman's voice, the clap of thunder and the torrential rain. His clothes were drenched and clung to his body. His teeth started chattering from cold. His hands and feet grew numb. Still he kept running. He was afraid of what might happen if Maryan heard the abuse of the travelling woman, or saw him running.

Just then he spotted the open door of one of the servant-quarters next to a bungalow and dashed towards it. Inside, a young woman sat picking stones from a fistful of lentils in a wicker-trough in front. When she saw Fazloo she said, 'The rain overtook you?'

'Yes,' he said and began wringing water out of his sheet and cloak.

'Sit down,' the woman said.

He looked around for a suitable place to sit.

'There may be some fire in the hearth over there,' she said.

Fazloo went and sat down by the hearth. The rain was falling with the same unforgiving intensity.

The young woman had an ordinary face but the ends of her lips had a particular appeal. Her lips were full and looked like they had been squeezed in her plump cheeks. When she talked two dimples formed in each cheek. She said, 'You're the caretaker of the rest-house, aren't you?'

'Yes,' he said, surprised. Problem—he thought; apparently she knew him.

'What do you do here?' Fazloo asked.

'I'm a maid. I give massages to the ladies at night. They give me ten rupees and a meal. I'm managing.'

'Alone, are you?'

'Yes. None of my relatives is alive. They died one after the other. My mother only last week. A lady paid for her shroud.' Her eyes filled with tears, and instead of sifting the lentils, she started wiping the tears from her face.

Fazloo found this woman different from Bahishto and the oven-tender's wife. He couldn't muster enough courage to ask her for anything. He cursed himself for his priestly scruples, for not even finding out which of the Sakesar women could be bought for money. The insults hurled at him by the traveller were still stuck in his brain like needles. Far a long while he sat there poking the fire with a piece of wood. After the rain subsided, he stood up.

'Leaving?' the woman asked.

As soon as he came out he felt himself to be a dastardly coward. If he went away without asking her, who else would he ask in the whole of Sakesar? Maryan?... Frantically, he pulled hard on a lock of his hair, as if he wanted to pluck it from its roots. So, was he going to go away embracing failure? Wouldn't that make his sahib's nights desolate, rob him of his own ten rupees a day—three hundred rupees a month? He swiveled on his heels and returned to the door.

'Forgot something?' the woman asked.

'Yes.'

'What?'

'To ask you for something.'

'What?'

'Just something.'

'What is it?'

'It's not too big a thing,' he said a little fearfully. 'It's worth a hundred rupees.'

'A hundred rupees?' the woman asked surprised. 'For what?'

'It's a matter of one night,' Fazloo said with great courage.

The woman looked at him for the longest time. She couldn't believe it. Tears welled up in her eyes while he watched. When she blinked, they fell into the trough one by one. It was as if she were picking up tear-drops rather than stones from the lentils. Then she put the trough aside and began to cry uncontrollably.

Fazloo came away from the young woman's quarters feeling terribly embarrassed. The rest of the day he kept making the rounds of the bungalows of Sakesar. He saw many maids, watchwomen, women who hawked vegetables, women who were travelling, but just couldn't bring himself to ask any one of them. He didn't even go to the sahib. It was Sheroo who had to deliver the meal to him. And the poor boy had a hard time of it, as he had to carry one dish at a time. By evening Fazloo's mind was made up: he'd ask just anybody he ran into. After all, there was no excuse for such cowardice.

Just as he stepped into the street, he saw the maid he had seen earlier in the day. She was still crying. Her hands were shaking, her lips were blue, and there was a tremor at the edges of her lips. Without looking at Fazloo, she said hesitatingly, 'I'll do it.'

Fazloo felt like jumping with joy. He whispered, 'Well then, come after the *Isha* prayer, after you're done with giving massages. Come to the *kahu* tree over there. All right?'

'I'll be there.' she said. Tears kept falling from her eyes without let-up.

And she was there, still crying. She was crying even when he left her in the sahib's room and turned around to look.

He woke up before sunrise and went to the rest-house. Yusuf was sleeping with the lantern on. In the other room the lamp was still lit and she was sleeping peacefully. Fazloo smiled. He shook her by her big toe. She woke up, looked all around her, then stretched herself into a comforting yawn and said with a smile, 'I was afraid for nothing. Nothing at all. There was no reason to be afraid. He didn't say anything to me. He just kept looking at me. And what's so scary about being looked at?'

Smiling, she wrapped the sheet around herself. Smiling, she took the hundred-rupee note from Fazloo and, smiling, she walked out of the room. Suddenly Fazloo was hit by the devastating feeling that he had set fire to three hundred rupees. Three hundred rupees—fifteen times twenty. One could build a mud-and-straw house with that money. And if one got another three hundred, one could buy a plough and oxen, or open a provisions store to sell lentils and raw sugar. The sahib didn't do anything to these women. He just looked at them. Just looked for his Maryam in their faces or perhaps admired God's handiwork. But he only looked.

He peeked into the sahib's room and slowly walked back to his hut. When he opened the door, Maryan stood there, risen to her full height and facing him. He staggered and went through a swirl of giddiness. All the blood in his body rushed to his brain.

'Where were you?' Maryan asked. Her voice was bitter.

'With the sahib.' Various excuses created a jumble in his brain.

'At this time—why?' she asked with the same bitterness.

'He had a headache,' he came up with the excuse.

'Does he have a headache at this time everyday?' Maryan asked sharply. 'You've been going for three or four days now.'

Fazloo leaned against the door frame for support, his mind

was in a whirl. With difficulty he gained control over his agitation and said, 'Yes, it's that kind of pain. Always starts at this time.'

'And who was that who went out of the rest-house just now?' Maryan's tone was cutting. 'Don't tell me it was the sahib's headache.'

Fazloo felt as though his heart was going to jump out of his ribcage and his brain shatter the skull and shoot through it. He laughed out, a hollow embarrassed alugh. 'All right,' he said, 'may as well tell you the whole story. There's nothing to hide from you. It's really a very small matter, nothing untoward. But at least let me come in.'

Inside, he sat on his cot. Sheroo was sleeping. The wick in the lamp was high and the window was open just a little bit. When Maryan tried to sit down on her own cot, Fazloo pulled her onto his. 'Sit here with me. You pig's progeny, you haven't even kissed me in the last three days.'

'Bastard, you're swearing at me,' she said. 'Now tell me what's been going on for the past three days. You think I'm asleep, eh? Even today I saw you go out, I thought I should find out what you are up to. And when I was looking, a woman came out of the rest-house and went towards the road. I could have kicked up a row then, but kept quiet becuase it would've made you look bad. Who does the sahib think we are? Some low-life touts? And what's your role in all this?'

'You don't know it,' he said. Inwardly he was worried sick. His nerves were taut, his eyes empty and the veins in his temples visibly throbbing, though he had been able to keep his voice steady with a feigned confidence. He put his arm around Maryan's back and gripped her shoulder, and said, 'You don't know, Maryan; this sahib is simply out of this world—so amazing, so guileless. He is really a saint. Just think: a young woman sits in front of him the whole night. He can do anything he wants with her, but he just sits and looks at her. He doesn't even touch her. Only looks at her. In the morning he sends her away with a hundred rupees. Are you listening? One hundred rupees, five score rupees. Just for looking.'

Fazloo felt that all the blood in Maryan's body was flooding into her face.

'Are you listening?' he asked again.

'And who brings these women to him?' Maryan asked without looking at him.

Fazloo tried to wiggle his way out of this one: 'But what's so bad about it? Now, you've gone to the spring so many times to fetch water. How many people must have looked at you! Should I go and pull their eyes out? What's so bad about just looking, and our sahib only looks at women.' He took thirty rupees out of his pocket and placed them in Maryan's lap.

Brushing the money away in disgust, Maryan asked, 'Yes, who brings these women to him?'

'What does it matter who brings them. What matters is he doesn't say anything to them. All he does is look at them, just look at them, and then pay them a hundred rupees.'

After a short pause he confessed quietly, 'I do. I get them for him.'

Maryan jerked his hand away from her shoulder and suddenly started weeping. Fazloo hugged her and kissed her on the back, neck, hair and talked on, 'I swear by God, Maryan; I swear by the Holy Book; Maryan, I swear by you, I've brought him only three women so far, and all have gone back untouched. One was Bahishto, the other the wife of the inn's oven-tender, and the third a maid from those quarters in the south. They took three hundred rupees from him, and he just looked at them. Are you listening? He didn't as much as even touch them. May I die, may you die, may Sheroo die if I lie to you.'

Maryan wiped her tears and asked, 'Do you know whose son you are?'

Fazloo laughed: 'But who says I'm doing anything good. Then again, who says I'm doing anything wrong.'

'It is wrong,' Maryan said, toning down her earlier harshness.

'How?' He pulled Maryan towards himself and forced her to sit leaning against his chest. 'Listen, he makes the woman sit in front of him and looks at her for some time, and then pays her a hundred rupees and lets her leave and goes to sleep in his room. What's so wrong in that?'

Maryan kept quiet.

'I say if, instead of Bahishto, I had made you go to him the very first night, it wouldn't have been such a bad idea.'

Maryan pulled herself out of his grasp and wildly went over to where Sheroo was sleeping. She pulled the blanket off his face and said, 'You see who he is?'

Sheroo was startled and woke up. Fazloo leapt, made him lie down again, patted him on the back and asked Maryan, 'Do you really think I'm all that rotten at heart? The last six years of my life are before you. Will I gladly hand you over to someone? I'd rather throw myself off a cliff than do that. Pig's progeny, why don't you believe me? If we're getting a hundred rupees a day without doing anything, we'll lose nothing but gain a lot. There are still about ten or twelve days left in the rainy season. We can easily earn a thousand rupees. We can then go down in the valley and live a respectable life. He'll only look at you and you keep looking back at him. That's all.'

But Maryan had gone wild. She sat down on the floor and began crying hysterically. Then she started stamping her feet on the ground. 'Shameless wretch,' she wailed. Daylight had begun to filter in through the cracks in the door; the crows had begun crowing and the sparrows chirping; thunder could be heard somewhere in the distance, and Maryan was crying bitterly and wailing: 'Look at the shameless wretch! How he's started pimping for people! The bastard! He's lost all sense of shame. Look, how he throws dust in my eyes. How he throws fire at my face and pours oil on it and says the fire is going out. Says it's not the fire, it's the moon shining. He's the nerve to ask me—me!—to spend the night with the man,...' She started beating her breast and crying loudly.

Fazloo got up from Sheroo's cot, went over to her and sat down next to her. He tried to hold her against his chest, but she threw herself out of his reach. Fazloo went to her and caressed her hair with affection. Maryan looked at him hopefully.

He said, 'He really doesn't do anything. Honest!'

Maryan started crying again.

Fazloo kept talking, 'Pig's progeny, I have sworn by you and told you that he doesn't even touch them. He only looks at them and pays a hundred rupees. Why don't you believe me?'

Suddenly she stood up straight and said, 'All right, if you have lost all shame, then I have one condition.'

Fazloo also stood up and said, 'What is it?'

'Put your hand on my head and swear that you will stick to it.'

'First tell me the condition,' he asked diffidently.

'I'll go to him tonight; if he touches me, I'll have nothing to do with you after that. I will leave you and go wherever I please,' she said. Her voice was devoid of emotion.

Fazloo put his hand on her head without the least bit of hesitation and said, 'It's a deal. Crazy woman, you think all three women were lying? You think I've become so low?'

'Swear by God,' Maryan said.

'I swear by God,' he said laughing. 'Hey, he only looks at them. And I too have a condition.'

'Go on.'

'If he doesn't even touch you, then as long as he is here, you'll go on seeing him. Promise!'

Maryan put her hand on his head and said, 'Promise.'

Then she went outside to make the tea.

'Think about it, he hasn't ever seen you, Maryan,' he followed her out and said. 'He wouldn't even know who you are.'

She was quiet; she kept quiet the whole day. She spoke for the first time after the evening meal was over and Sheroo had gone to sleep. 'Well then,' she said.

Her voice was thorny. It jarred on Fazloo's ears, but he got up quickly and hurried out of the hut. When they reached the yard, Maryan said, 'Fazloo?'

He stopped and asked, 'What?'

She said, 'You do remember the condition, don't you?'

'I do,' he said. 'Have no fear.'

As he was returning after leaving Maryan in the rest-house

and collecting a hundred and ten rupees, he turned around to look. The door and the window had been closed. Just as they had been every night at this time. He walked back to the hut. Ghosts and goblins lurked in the corners, he felt, and a witch danced away in the lamp's flame. He plopped down on Sheroo's bed and then, a while later, stretched out next to him. Sheroo was not fully asleep yet. He asked, 'Who is it?'

Me,' Fazloo said lovingly. 'Today I am going to sleep with my son.'

Sheroo clung to him in joy. Soon his grip relaxed and he went to sleep. Fazloo lay there stiffly for a long while. When his back began to hurt, he got up and started walking about in the room. He walked up and down for a long time. Then he put out the lamp and tried to go to sleep, but got up in agitation, put on the lamp again, placed it on the post of Maryan's cot and kept staring at it for a long time. Outside, the clouds had perhaps dissipated, for the moonlight was visible through the crack in the door. He opened the door and came out, but dashed back in as soon as he looked at the rest-house. He shut the door and stood firmly against it, as if resolved to keep out any and all powers. He stood in the same posture for a long time until he heard the first rooster crow somewhere far in the distance. His heart was beating so fast he found it hard to keep standing any longer. He plunked down on the cot, and then sat up, only to stand up again and noisily open the door and rush out to the rest-house.

He saw a car pull out of the side of the rest-house. It took a serpentine turn onto the main road and sped downhill towards the valley. Like someone possessed, Fazloo ran to the rest-house. The door was shut. He started beating at it. 'Maryan,' he yelled, and that name, turning into a scream rang out and echoed through the mountain. The car took a turn in the distance and throwing its light on Fazloo's pallid face disappeared from view. He thought of going after it by jumping across the ditches. Slowly the door of the rest-house opened. The light of the lantern illuminated the verandah and spilled into a part of the yard. It was Maryan who had opened the door.

'So, you got here at last?' she said. 'You bastard, you lost the bet.' Her voice became hoarse; she broke down and started crying. 'You low, mean wretch, he ravaged me. He gnawed at me. He clung to me the whole night. He clawed me, licked my cheeks. He ...'

But Fazloo didn't stay there. Instead he shuffled away towards the hut with his head drooping. A stretch of cloud had hid the moon and a light drizzle had started. Maryan came after him, sobbing and crying. 'You said he wouldn't even touch me,' she screamed at him. 'But he bit every part of my body. Even last year he had come here for me. He had seen me through his binoculars the very first day he had arrived here. Even this year he came only for me. Are you listening to me, you bastard? Are you listening? Where are you running off to?'

Fazloo was practically running now. Maryan came after him, shouting, 'You lost the bet. But keep those hundred rupees with you, and if you find anyone selling respect or honor, buy yourself a smidgen, because from this day forward you have become the lowest, the worst bastard in the world—a pimp. And now I'm leaving you. You have destroyed everything I had, you bastard. My pride. My honour. ...'

Like a blind man Fazloo stumbled into the wall of his hut, staggered, and crawled towards the door, feeling the wall with his hands. Inside, Sheroo was bawling. Maryan kept screaming, 'He stayed in Sakesar for two whole months just for this one moment. After saying, 'Maryam, Maryam,' he pounced upon me as a dog pounces upon a bone. He had arranged for the rental car yesterday. And after having had his fill of gnawing me, he's just off to Lahore, and he has left you the gratuity of a hundred rupees and of a Maryan who will never enter this house again. She will go into the valley. She will go down into the plains, and when hunger turns her stomach into a sore, she will take off her clothes and sit by the roadside. People throw stones at naked men, but they offer a bed and food to naked women. Who did you think I was?'

Maryan's screams set off a barking chorus among the dogs of the neighbouring bungalows, and the surrounding mountains echoed all at once the hum of the car driving away towards the lake, the dogs' barking and Maryan's wails.

Then, as it were, Maryan became wild. She lunged at Fazloo

and gave a stinging slap across his face. Fazloo fell headlong. His knees hit the ground first, and he lay there motionless.

Maryan turned around and walking past the *kahu* tree came on to the road. Sheroo's cries followed her. 'Let me have a last look at the other bastard also,' she decided, turned and ran back to the rest-house.

Fazloo was still lying senseless near the door of the hut and, inside, Sheroo had bawled himself hoarse. Maryan tried to open the door but instead, in a flash, came to where Fazloo was lying. For a moment she just stood there, frozen like a statue, then she bent down to lift him and help him sit up. He rolled on to one side. Blood and dirt had made his face look scary, made scarier still by the light of the moon racing through the clouds.

'My Fazloo!' she moaned.

She went inside the hut and grabbed the clay-lamp. Sheroo ran and clung to her legs. When she came out holding the lamp, he did too, holding on to her tunic. She lowered the lamp on Fazloo's face and searched for signs of life in his eyelids.

'My Fazloo, my husband, my master,' her wails echoed everywhere. Suddenly she stopped. Fazloo's eyes opened a little. He moved one of his hands slowly. The fist opened and he placed the hundred-rupee note on the flame. As it burned, he said, 'I won't let you go. You cannot leave me and go away.'

Sheroo was holding his face between his hands and staring at his mother.

'Maryan, my poverty tricked me,' Fazloo said haltingly.

The ashes of the note fell down and scattered towards the rest-house.

'Maryan,' he pleaded.

'You'll not die on me, will you?' Maryan asked through her wracking sobs.

'No,' Fazloo answered with confidence.

'Bastard,' she said and clung to him, weeping piteously.

'Pig's progeny,' he responded and started kissing her hair with his blood-stained lips.

The car went slithering along the shoreline of the lake below.

GLOSSARY

'Alak Niranjan, Alak Niranjan!'	literally *alak* means the light, and *niranjan* is one who is beyond the world and does not receive any coloration from it; transcendent light
Allahu Akbar	God is great—a Muslim cry frequently used to express admiration, surprise, or denial; a war-cry
Allama Iqbal	well-known poet-philosopher of the Indian subcontinent (1873-1938)
Amma	mother
ashrafis	a gold coin, once a legal tender in Indo-Pakistan subcontinent: a guinea
Asr prayer	afternoon prayer
arey	an expression of surprise
Azan	the Muslim prayer-call cried from the minaret of a mosque five times a day just before the commencement of the ritual prayer
babuji	respectful term used to address a social superior usually by the lowly; sir
bismillah	'In the name of God'; a formula uttered frequently by Muslims before commencing any activity
blowing on his chest	one blows on one's own or someone else's chest after reciting some prayer or incantation to pass on its effect
burqa	a two-piece wrap-around used as a veil and cover for the body; used by Muslim women in public

GLOSSARY

chapati	a thin, round, baked bread
chaupal	something like a community centre in a village; public meetings may be held here
chongan	a kind of bitter vegetable
Daata sahib	refers to Ali ibn Usman Hujwiri commonly known as Data Ganj Bakhsh
Daata sahib's shrine	refers to Hujwiri's tomb- sanctuary in Lahore
dajjal	Muslim equivalent of Anti christ
dera	a favourite sitting place, something like a pad; here, a thatched shed on the edge of fields for rest
dharm	roughly 'religion' or 'socio-cosmic law'; also: ordinance, statute, law, order, rule, usage, practice
dharmshala	a public residence place for Hindu and Sikh pilgrims
Divali	Hindu festival of lights at which tiny oil lamps are lighted to honour Lakhshmi, the godess of wealth
Du'a-e Ganju ul-Arsh	a special prayer which is supposed to grant the supplicant all the treasures of heaven
dupatta	a length of cloth often thrown loosely over the head and shoulders, or draped across the chest, by women
Eid	a Muslim festival which occurs twice yearly
Granth sahib/Granthiji	one learned in the sacred scriptures of the Sikhs (short moral poems by Guru Nanak and other gurus)
guru	a spiritual guide or teacher.
Guru Gobind	the tenth guru of the Sikhs (d.1708); he is known to have instituted the custom of baptism by water stirred with a dagger. Those who underwent it were known as the Khalsaóthe pure

GLOSSARY

hakim sahib/hakim	a practitioner of traditional herbal medicine; sahib: a title of respect
halva	a sweetmeat
havaldar	a junior police officer; a head constable
haveli	a large and spacious building, a mansion
hookah	a hubble-bubble, water-cooled pipe
huzoor	literally, presence; a title of respect, used while addressing social superiors; 'Your Eminence'
imam	a Muslim well versed in religious knowledge; also a prayer leader; a distinguished and eminent individual
Isha prayer	Muslim night prayer
Jhallianwala Bagh massacre	a public park in the city of Amritsar (India) which became the scene of one of the worst massacres in the history of British rule in India when, in 1919, General Dyer ordered his soldiers to open fire on a gathering of people, killing 312 and wounding nearly 1200
kabaddi	an indigenous South Asian game
kachhera	shorts, knickers, usually worn by Sikh boys
Kalima	the Muslim profession of faith ('There is no god but Allah; Muhammad is the Prophet of God'); this is the major kalima, but there are a number of others in which a Muslim testifies to his faith and belief in all other Prophets, revealed books, angels, and the Day of Judgment
Kalima-e-Shahadat	Muslim profession of faith: I bear witness that there is no god but Allah and that Muhammad is His slave and His messenger

GLOSSARY

kara — bracelet
Kattak — name of the seventh Hindu month, corresponding to October-November
kes — hair; Sikhs are not permitted by their religion to cut any hair on the body
khalsa — lit., the pure ones; a Sikh
Khuda — Persian word for God
Khushhal Khan Khattak — a seventeenth-century poet of the North-West Frontier (1613-89); wrote in Pashto on patriotic causes and sentiments, tribal values and freedom
kirpan — a dagger, worn by Sikh males as a token of their religion
ma — Mother
maharaj — supreme sovereign; title indicative of extreme respect and reverence
malikji — lit., a sovereign or monarch; mode of address for person of consequence, an aristocrat or propertied man
mantras — a mystical formula of invocation or incantation (in Sanskrit)
masi — an aunt
maulvi — one learned in Islamic religion; a distinguished, respected individual; one who instructs children in Quranic lessons and elementary writing and reading
maulviji — *maulvi*: see above, *ji*: an honorific suffix attached to names or titles
mem sahib — an Englishwoman, usually as addressed or referred to by a domestic
misri — rock-sugar or candy
mirasi — a caste of people who are singers or entertainers by profession; well-known for their skill in repartee

GLOSSARY

Muharram	the first month in the Muslim lunar calendar in which the martyrdom of Husain is commemorated
musalla	distortion of 'Muslim'; indicative of dislike and disgust
musalman	Muslim
muezzin	the person who calls the faithul to prayers
munshiji	a clerk or secetary or language teacher
musla	Pejorative for 'Muslim'
namaz	Muslim ritual prayer, offered five times a day at specified times
nambardar	a village revenue collector
Panchayat	a native village court or council of five or more village elders for arbitration
panwari	one who sells cigarettes and *paan* or betel-leaves coated with various pastes for chewing
paratha	a multi-layered flour pancake fried in clarified butter (*ghee*)
parshad	food offered to gods; remnants of food presented to an idol
pice	one-sixty-fourth of a rupee, now obsolete; for a long time the smallest monetary unit in the Indian subcontinent
pir	a Muslim saint, a spiritual guide
purdah	Muslim tradition which compels women to cover themselves from the gaze of men
pukka	ripe; mature; strong; solid; expert; burnt (for bricks); metalled (for road); fast or lasting (for colour)
'Qul huwa 'l-lahu ahad... kufuwan ahad'	'Say, God is One'; chapter 112 of the Quran comprising only four lines; considered the essence of

GLOSSARY

	monotheism; frequently repeated by Muslims
Qasidah Burdah Sharif	in Arabic *burdah* means mantle. An ode written by the blind poet Imam Busiri in praise of the Prophet (PBUH). The story goes that his sight was miraculously restored after its composition
rakat	one part of the prayer which involves standing, bending and prostration; bending
Ramazan	ninth month of the Islamic calendar, during which all healthy Muslims are required to fast daily from dawn to dusk
rattan stool	foot-stool or seat made from wicker-work
sadhu	a Hindu ascetic or mendicant
sahib	a polite form of address for a social equal or superior; Mr, gentleman; sir
sahibji	a polite way of addressing a social superior
salaam	Muslim greeting, the shortened form of 'as-salamu alaikum' ('Peace be on you')
salaat	same as *namaz*
sehra	a flower wreath worn around the head by bride and bridegroom at the wedding ceremony
seth	a rich banker; a capitalist; a merchant
shakkar	sugar
shehnai	subcontinental musical instrument usually associated with weddings and similar to a bagpipe
sikhra	a derogatory term, a distortion of 'Sikh' conveying one's disparagement, or distaste for them
surah	a chapter of the Qur'an

Surah Ar-Rahman	lit., The Beneficent; the fifty-fifth surah in the Qur'an known for its powerful refrain: 'Which of the favours of your Lord will you deny?'
Surah Baqra	lit., The Cow; the second surah in the Qur'an which emphasizes that rightness of conduct, not mere profession of a creed, is the true religion
Surah Nisa	lit., Women. The fourth surah in the Qur'an, deals largely with women's rights and obligations; this issue was addressed when many women were widowed and many children orphaned in the wars
soyem	the third day of mourning for the dead
tasbih	a rosary
taravih	special prayers offered by Muslims in the month of Ramazan, at night
thanedar	a police inspector in charge of a police station
ullo ki pathi	literally, 'disciple of an owl'; idiot, fool; an owl is considered a foolish and inauspicious bird in South Asia
vahguruji	'the Guru is great', 'salutations to the honourable Guru'; a Sikh expression
ved	one who practices the traditional Hindu system of ayurvedic medicine
veranda	a roofed open gallery or portico attached to the exterior of a building
vetiver	East Indian grass cultivated for its fragrant roots which are used for making mats or screens or perfumes

226   GLOSSARY

yaaro   friend; used informally to address friends; pal
zuhr namaz   the Muslim noon prayer

BIBLIOGRAPHY

AHMAD NADEEM QASIMI'S WORKS:
Primary sources

Short story collections:
Chowpal. Lahore: Darul Isha'at Punjab, 1939. Rpt. Lahore: Asatir, 1995.
Bagoolay. Lahore: Maktaba-e-Urdu, 1941. Rpt. Lahore: Asatir, 1995.
Tulu-o-Gharoob. Lahore: Naya Idara, 1942. Rpt. Lahore: Asatir, 1995.
Girdaab. Hyderabad, Deccan: Idara-e-Isha'at-e-Urdu, 1943.
Sailaab. Hyderabad, Deccan: Idara-e-Isha'at-e-Urdu, 1943. (The last two volumes reprinted together as Sailab-o-Girdaab. Lahore: Asatir, 1995).
Aanchal. 1944. Rpt. Lahore: Asatir, 1995.
Aablay. Lahore: Idara-e-Farogh-e-Urdu, 1946. Rpt. Lahore: Asatir, 1995.
Aas Paas. Lahore: Idara-e-Farogh-e-Urdu, 1948. Rpt. Lahore: Asatir, 1995.
Dar-o-Diwaar. Lahore: Maktaba-e-Urdu, 1949. Rpt. Lahore: Asatir, 1995.
Sannata. Lahore: Naya Idara, 1952. Rpt. Lahore: Asatir, 1995.
Baazaar-e-Hayaat. Lahore: Idara-e-Farogh-e-Urdu, 1952. Rpt. Lahore: Asatir, 1995.
Barg-e-Hina. Lahore: Naashereen, 1959. Rpt. Lahore: Asatir, 1995.
Ghar Se Ghar Tak. Rawalpindi: Rawal Kitab Ghar, 1963. Rpt. Lahore: Asatir, 1995.
Kapaas ka Phhool. Lahore: Maktaba-e-Funoon, 1973. Rpt. Lahore: Asatir, 1995.

Neela Paththar. Lahore: Ghalib Publishers, 1980. Rpt. Lahore: Asatir, 1995.
Koh Paimaa. Lahore: Asatir, 1995.

Poetical Works:

Dharhkanain. Lahore: Urdu Academy, 1942.
Rim Jhim. Lahore: Maktaba-e-Kaarvaan, 1944 (Revised and enlarged edition of Rim Jhim).
Jalaal-o-Jamaal. Lahore: Naya Idara, 1946.
Shola-e-Gul. Lahore: Qaumi Dar-ul-Isha'at, 1953.
Dasht-e-Wafa. Lahore: Kitab Numa, 1963.
Muheet. Lahore: Al Tahrir, 1976.
Dawaam. Lahore: 1980.
Lauh-e-Khaak. Lahore: 1988.
Jamaal. Lahore, 1992.
Baseet. Lahore, 1995.

Miscellaneous Works:

Edited Angraiyan. [Selected stories by contemporary Urdu writers]. Hyderabad, Deccan: Idara-e-Isha'at-e-Urdu, 1944.
Edited Naqoosh-e-Latif. [Selected stories by women writers]. Lahore: Idara-e-Farogh-e-Urdu, 1947.
Edited Manto ke Khatoot. Lahore: Kitab Numa, 1962.
Tehzib-o-Fun. [Essays on literary subjects]. Lahore: Pakistan Foundation, 1975.
Edited Hamid Ahmad Khan ki Nazar. [Essays in honor of Professor Hamid Ahmad Khan]. Lahore: 1980.

The stories included in *The Old Banyan* have been taken from the following short story collections:

'A Wild Woman' ('Vehshi') from Barg-e-Hina; 'The Pond with the Bo Tree' ('Pipal Wala Talaab') from Koh Paimaa; 'Theft' ('Chori') from Bagoolay; 'Praise be to Allah' ('Alhamd-o-Lillah'), 'The Rest-house' ('Raees Khana'),

'Mother' ('Maamta'), and 'A Sample' ('Namoona'), from Sannata; 'Parmeshar Singh' ('Parmeshar Singh'), 'The Burial' ('Kafan Dafan'), and 'Old Man Noor' ('Baba Noor'), from Baazaar-e-Hayaat; 'The Unwanted' ('Faaltoo'), and 'Sultan, the Beggar Boy' ('Sultan'), from Ghar se Ghar Tak; 'The Thal Desert' ('Thal'), 'The Old Banyan' ('Aasaib'), and 'Lawrence of Thalabia' ('Lawrence of Thalabia'), from Kapaas ka Phhool.